P9-CDZ-245

BRUMBACK LIBRARY

3 3045 00105 8474

$24.95

920   Fink, Mitchell
FIN   The last days of
       dead celebrities

6/06

THE BRUMBACK LIBRARY
OF VAN WERT COUNTY
VAN WERT, OHIO

THE LAST DAYS OF
DEAD
CELEBRITIES

MITCHELL FINK

miramax books

HYPERION

NEW YORK

926
FIN

For Lois, Jesse, Brian, Miriam,
Larry, Richard and Joan

Copyright © 2006 Mitchell Fink

All rights reserved. No part of this book may be used or reproduced in
any manner whatsoever without the written permission of the Publisher.
Printed in the United States of America. For information address
Hyperion, 77 West 66th Street, New York, NY 10023–6298

Library of Congress Cataloging-in-Publication Data

Fink, Mitchell.
  The last days of dead celebrities / Mitchell Fink.—1st ed.
      p.   cm.
    ISBN 1-4013-5198-0
      1. Celebrities—United States—Miscellanea.   2. Celebrities—
United States—Death—Miscellanea.   3. Death.   I. Title.

  CT215.F57   2006
  920.73—dc22

                                                            2006042048

                          First Edition
              10   9   8   7   6   5   4   3   2   1

Contents

Introduction

CELEBRITIES ARE OUR CONSTANT COMPANIONS. WE FEEL THEIR PRESENCE everywhere. We watch them on TV, and in darkened movie theaters. We listen to their CDs, read their autobiographies, and cheer them on the playing field. We follow their exploits in gossip columns, and keep count of their marriages and divorces. Sometimes we even vote for them.

But we really don't know celebrities like we think we do, and whether who they are in real life comes anywhere close to matching our own carefully developed perceptions. We often hear a lot, some would say too much, about where celebrities stand on the issues, and periodically they even try telling us where we should stand on the issues. But later, when the microphones are turned off and today's newspaper is in the recycle bin, they will invariably find a way to retreat to that protected, insular world, the one the rest of us know little about, where celebrities mostly find aid and comfort in the company of other celebrities.

The fact that they prefer keeping us at arm's length actually works in our favor. It frees us to create and spin whatever kind of legend suits us. We can praise celebrities if we want, ignore them if we can, even put them down, if we must. They have no say in the matter. They remain only who we think they are.

And the media, for all its presence everywhere, doesn't make it any easier for us to know these celebrities at their core. Media generally lives around the edges, casting its huge net into fame-filled waters in hopes of landing the best soundbites, sidebars, and short Q&A's. Media then surrounds its precious catch with vivid four-color layouts, ironic musical bumpers, Halo-inspired graphics, and a loud *whoosh*, all of which prepares us for the next celebrity story, the next red carpet premiere, the next gossip item, and the next breathless set of questions about designer jewelry on loan, what the stars do to stay trim, and how everyone is looking forward to their holiday vacation in Aspen. In between those vacations, we read about their exploding implants in the tabloids, we watch them cry on Barbara Walters, and we hear on *Oprah* about how they were tormented as children.

Then they die.

And naturally the media is right there to cover the end in much the same way as it did the beginning and the middle. Go ahead, pick virtually any celebrity with worldwide fame, young or old, someone who had been ill and was expected to die imminently, or someone whose demise was sudden and shocking, and the reaction on the airwaves and in newspapers and magazines is almost always the same: This was their life, and these are the circumstances surrounding their death. Here are their career highlights, along with profiles of wives and lovers and posthumous quotes from other famous people. And depending on the age of the deceased, the media will also find a way to either salute the celebrity's longevity, or dwell on the shattered promise that always seems to accompany the legacy of one who leaves us too early.

But in every case, the fade to black on TV will always be slow and respectful before the next commercial break, the surviving family members will always be mentioned in the last paragraph of the newspaper obituary, and an eye-catching photograph will always be chosen for the cover of the magazine.

For three decades I lived around those same edges, writing about celebrities in newspaper and magazine columns, talking about them on TV, and chatting with them whenever possible, on the phone or in person, at parties, awards shows, restaurants, bars, and luxury boxes, even on vacations, theirs and mine. The talks were mostly cordial, sometimes embarrassing, other times illuminating, and usually a lot of fun, at least for me.

In the process, I broke a lot of stories, and made a lot of news. I got the facts I needed to do my job, but not many of the feelings. The shrewd ones tend to keep their feelings private, offering up only what they think the press wants to hear, followed by a photogenic smile, an appropriate handshake or air kiss, then a polite "Nice to see you," and always, always, goodbye.

The celebrities who linger too long in the glare of media's hot white light, the ones who can't seem to live without press coverage, you know, the ones who have already revealed more about themselves than we ever wanted to know, well, they simply become less interesting over time.

And yet, even when they die it's big news.

Celebrity death has become so important in the competitive 24-hour-a-day news cycle that newspaper obits are written and TV stories are produced and banked years before the person in question even dies. And while pre-packaged obits can look gorgeous on TV and elegant in print, they never give you the entire story. TV doesn't have the time, the print media doesn't have the space, and neither delivery system has the inclination or the kind of access needed to develop a comprehensive rendering of a famous person's life. And this is especially true when it comes to someone's last days.

Ernest Hemingway once wrote that all good stories end in death. But if death occurred, say, on a Friday, what was Thursday like for that person? Or Wednesday, Tuesday, and Monday? Were they happy days, filled with positive thoughts of the future? Or were they sad, painful days, filled with remorse and regret, when life at the end of Act III was being viewed more as a prison sentence, needing only to be lived out?

The Last Days of Dead Celebrities is my attempt to examine those days in a way that captures the intimate moments, unravels the murky mysteries, and sets the record straight about who these people were, what they were feeling, and how they were living as death was approaching.

It is not the kind of information one normally finds in clip files, or on the Internet, or even in other books. In order to tell these fifteen stories, it was necessary for me to obtain the cooperation of a subject's family members, close friends, and business associates. I wanted the interviews to be new and exclusive, and I needed people who were there, firsthand witnesses, many of them household names themselves, to share their private, often painstaking accounts of a loved one's physical, emotional, psychological, professional, and spiritual journey to the end of life. And this deeply felt level of sharing practically demanded that they attach their names to their words. For that reason there are no unnamed sources in this book. Everybody with whom I spoke agreed to be on the record, and I am truly grateful that they trusted me enough to be so willing, open, and patient.

I began this project believing I knew a great deal about celebrities. Having completed it, I realize now that I still had a lot to learn. It's the facts about celebrities that separate them from the pack and cause us to prop them up and keep them on a pedestal, or knock them down and push them off. And it's the feelings that bring us much closer together. But while this may just be my feeling, I do suspect that the feelings we exhibit during our last days will turn out to be very much like the ones experienced by the fifteen dead celebrities in this book—frantic and numb, fearful and gallant, dazed and resolute, hopeless, hapless, hopped up, and happy. In other words, terminally unique and completely all over the place.

—Mitchell Fink

John Lennon

October 9, 1940–December 8, 1980

IT TOOK A LONG TIME FOR JOHN LENNON TO FEEL COMFORTABLE IN NEW YORK.

Like so many others before him, Lennon had chosen to settle in the greatest of all American cities after spending a lifetime somewhere else. New York, in any era, has always promised its new residents lives of unparalleled excitement, round-the-clock action, and enough culture and contrasting beliefs to keep them on their toes for centuries.

In public, Lennon seemed to relish the idea of becoming a New Yorker. "I love New York. It's the hottest city going. I haven't been everywhere, but it's the fastest city on earth," was how Beatles chronicler Geoffrey Giuliano quoted the former Beatle in his book *Lennon in America*.

Lennon had even told *Rolling Stone* in 1970 that New York was "the only place I found that could keep up with me. . . . I'm just sort of fascinated by it, like a fucking monster."

The trouble with fucking monsters, of course, is that they can often appear in the guise of an autograph hound, and if the sixties had provided Lennon with anything, it was definitely enough autograph hounds to last a lifetime.

Despite his public pronouncements, Lennon was undoubtedly looking beyond all the noise and fascination of New York on August 13, 1971, when he and his wife, Yoko Ono, moved their belongings into three suites on the seventeenth floor of one of the city's classic Fifth Avenue hotels, the St. Regis.

Lennon wanted something else from New York, something far

more precious and comforting than the speed of the city. Being in New York was a chance, finally, for him to get lost, be anonymous, and walk among thousands of other New Yorkers, free of bodyguards, in a fatigue jacket, sunglasses, floppy hat, and with body language that politely suggested how unnecessary it would be to squeal, scream, cry, or demand an encore.

And for the most part, New York complied because of an unwritten rule that grants all new New Yorkers the benefit of the doubt. The famous and the near famous get it, along with the wannabes and nobodies. You want to be left alone? Fine, New York will leave you alone. You stay on your side of the sidewalk, and I'll stay on mine. Don't brush up against anyone else's body, certainly not without saying, "Excuse me," and life on the street will happily go on. Act like a New Yorker and you become one. Act like a schmuck, and New York will have you for lunch.

From the moment they got to New York, the Lennons kept mostly to themselves and never acted like schmucks. Gone were the lavishly planned bed-ins and the flip comparisons in popularity to Jesus. Sure, they protested the Vietnam War and started hanging out with Abbie Hoffman and Jerry Rubin. But by the early seventies, this was hardly considered radical behavior. As Lennon found out years earlier, when you try to force-feed anything to New York, you do so at your own peril. But ask New Yorkers, rather, to simply "Imagine," and you may get them for all time. John and Yoko asked little of New York beyond that, and in return, to paraphrase a Beatles song, New York let them be.

"He liked it when people came up and said hi," Yoko recalled of those early days in New York. "We had burnt our bridges in London. I don't think that my people, the Japanese, were thrilled with our situation—John and Yoko doing *Two Virgins,* John and Yoko doing bed-ins. And we didn't have many friends. A lot of them turned their backs on us. They didn't like our union. They didn't like the fact that we were so political. A lot of them still blamed me for the breakup of the Beatles. We were different, and we were hoping that New York wouldn't be put off by that."

There is no evidence anywhere remotely suggesting that New York was put off in any way by the Lennons. They were just New York's newest superstars in a town that had seen many. It's not unreasonable, therefore, to assume that Lennon might have been caught off guard by New York's "so what?" attitude toward his fame. Lennon certainly did say at the time that he needed time to get used to the city, mainly because it wasn't his idea to move there. New York had been Yoko's decision, and he went along with it. He was quoted in Giuliano's book as saying, "It was Yoko who sold me on New York. She'd been poor here and knew every inch. She made me walk around the streets, parks, squares, and examine every nook and cranny. In fact, you could say I fell in love with New York on a street corner. . . . Not only was Yoko educated here, but she spent fifteen years living in New York, so, as far as I was concerned, it was just like returning to your wife's hometown."

Nevertheless, if behavior counts for anything, New York had yet to become Lennon's hometown by October 10, 1971. It was one day after his thirty-first birthday, two days after the release of his landmark solo album, *Imagine,* and nearly two months since their move into the St. Regis. John and Yoko were getting dressed in one of their suites, preparing to go out. At that moment, and most likely unbeknownst to them, a Jewish wedding was in full swing in the hotel's main ballroom. It was in between courses, or that time during most Jewish weddings when the bandleader picks up the tempo and coaxes guests onto the dance floor.

The bride, who was nearing thirty, had one sibling, a twenty-seven-year-old brother, and he was in no mood to dance, or even feel merry. He just sat at a table looking at his watch, hoping the time would pass quickly, counting down to the end of his sister's big day. But he knew there were still hours to go and very few choices to make. Leaving the St. Regis and going home was not an option. His mother would have killed him.

But maybe there was a way out: marijuana, the ultimate and least offensive sixties panacea to everything. You want to put on earphones and tune into a coded message on *The White Album,* or something obscure on a Richie Havens record? Smoke a joint. On the other hand, if you want to tune out your sister's wedding and feel like you're a million miles away, even while you're asking a relative to pass the butter, well, that very same joint will likely get you there. And that's precisely what was needed here.

The bride's brother had been tipped off during the ceremony that another wedding guest was holding some good shit. The brother thought, if he could talk his sister into giving him the key to the bridal suite, he and this other guest could go upstairs, get high, and then return to the festivities and hide in plain sight in a decidedly more tolerant state. No one would even know they had been gone.

Of course, it never occurred to either man that John and Yoko were even at the St. Regis, much less readying themselves to go out. At that moment, the only mission facing the two wedding guests was to get into the bridal suite, smoke their pot, and alter their consciousnesses to the point where perhaps even the dance floor might not seem to be such a terrible idea.

But an extraordinary thing happened as the bride's brother put the key in the door to his sister's room: The door to the suite directly across the hall opened and John and Yoko stepped out. The boys would later bemoan the fact that they never had a chance to say hello, much less invite the Lennons inside for a couple of tokes, a perfectly reasonable thought that came up only in retrospect. As soon as John saw these two strangers, he yanked Yoko back inside and slammed his door shut. It was obvious, even to these two disgruntled, pot-smoking wedding guests, that Lennon appeared threatened by the close proximity of other New Yorkers.

There is an old saying from the sixties that goes something like this: "Just because you're paranoid doesn't mean they're not trying to get you." Lennon had nothing to fear from the two men who were trying to enter another suite across the hall. As the two men remembered it, they had their backs to the couple when Lennon opened the door. Certainly no remotely threatening gestures were made. And yet Lennon's first inclination was to retreat and close the door as quickly as possible. Was he paranoid, or simply startled? Did he sense danger in New York in 1971, or was he just being careful? Whatever the case, it was clear that he had not yet made peace with his new surroundings.

Then again, maybe it was just the coldness and formality of extended hotel life that was getting to him. During the more chaotic years, when he was a Beatle, a hotel had performed essentially the same function as a prostitute. In, out, and on to the next town. As opulent as the St. Regis was, two months there was proving to be more than enough. The Lennons needed something a little homier, and on November 1 they left the St. Regis for a Greenwich Village apartment on Bank Street that was both smaller and homier than their hotel suite. The basement apartment had only two rooms, a kitchenette, and a spiral staircase up to a skylight. But the simplicity of it, along with its tranquil setting in a classic downtown neighborhood, proved more in keeping with Lennon's desire to blend into New York.

Photographer Bob Gruen was living in the Village then, in an apartment not far from Lennon's small pad. "I heard about it as soon as they moved into the neighborhood," recalled Gruen. "There was this buzz, like 'Hey, guess who just moved in.' But this being New York, nobody bothered them."

On November 6, just five days after their downtown move, the Lennons ventured uptown, to the famed Apollo Theater in Harlem, and gave a surprise performance to benefit the casualties of the recent Attica prison riots. "I went to the Apollo that night," said Gruen, "because Aretha Franklin was supposed to be there and I was going to photograph her. As I walked into the theater, I heard the announcer onstage say, 'Ladies and gentlemen, John Lennon and Yoko Ono.' It was incredibly exciting. I couldn't believe I was actually going to see John Lennon. They did a couple of funky songs. Backstage afterward, they were standing around waiting for their car, and people were taking pictures of them. So I took a couple of pictures of them standing there. At one point, John said, 'You know, people are always taking pictures of us and we never get to see these pictures. What happens to all the pictures?'

"I said, 'Well, I live around the corner from you. I'll show you my pictures.'

"And he said, 'You live around the corner? Slip them under the door.'

"I said I would, and I made up a couple of prints," said Gruen. "A few days later, I went by their apartment and didn't quite slip them under the door. I rang the bell instead, and Jerry Rubin answered the door. I said, 'I have something for John and Yoko.'

"And Jerry Rubin said, 'Are they expecting you?' When I said no, he said he would take the pictures and give them to them."

Gruen heard nothing from the Lennons until their names came up a few months later when he was asked to shoot pictures of the couple for a story that a writer friend was doing on the hard-driving rock group Elephant's Memory. Jerry Rubin had introduced Lennon to the group, and he was planning to record a few tracks with them for their album.

"The writer asked me if I would like to take pictures of John and Yoko while he interviewed them," said Gruen. "I said I would definitely do it, and that's how I actually ended up meeting them.

"I didn't say anything immediately about me being the guy who was supposed to slip those other pictures under the door because I like to stay rather quiet when I'm taking pictures," said Gruen. "So I just took pictures while they were talking. And because the story was about

Elephant's Memory, I wanted to take a picture of John and Yoko together with the band. They said they were going to the Record Plant that night to record with the band. So I asked if I could come along. They said they'd be working, but if I wanted to wait around until the end of the night, I could take a picture of them with the band. And that's what I did. After I took the pictures at the Record Plant later that night, I went home, printed the pictures, and sent them to the magazine that was going to publish the story.

"I figured that my job was done, and no one else would need my pictures," said Gruen. "But then, I ran into one of the members of Elephant's Memory, and he said they'd been trying to contact me because I had the only pictures of them together with John and Yoko in the studio, and they wanted to see them. He brought me over to [the Lennons'] Bank Street apartment and that was the first time we really got to talk. I spent the afternoon there, talking and showing them my other pictures. And we just formed a relationship. At the end of that meeting, Yoko told me to start coming to the studio so I could take pictures of them. She said she wanted me to be involved with them. And so that's what I did."

The Lennons obviously liked Gruen's work but, more important, he had earned their trust. He said he would drop off the pictures from the Apollo, and he did. He never chased after the Lennons in an attempt to get more work, and he never tried to contact them after the Elephant's Memory shoot. He had proved himself without really trying. He was in.

Elliot Mintz's relationship with John and Yoko began in a similar fashion. A veteran West Coast public relations executive, Mintz had a side job in the early seventies hosting a nighttime radio show on KLOS-FM, the ABC affiliate station in Los Angeles. In 1971, he interviewed Yoko by phone, and then sent her the tape. "John apparently heard it and liked it," recalled Mintz. "Yoko then suggested that he, too, should do a phone interview with me, and he did it. A few days later, he called me to say that he was pleased with the way the interview went. He just liked the texture of it. Thus we began a telephonic friendship, John, Yoko, and myself, and we'd all speak virtually every day or every night for months. I'm an insomniac. I don't sleep. I'm up until 4 A.M., Pacific Time. That was their wake-up time in New York. So we would talk all the time."

By the spring of 1972, one of the subjects that monopolized these late-night talks was Lennon's desire to see America. And in this regard, he was really on even footing with his wife. Yoko might have thought of herself as a New Yorker by virtue of her fifteen years there, but when it came to the rest of the country, she was as much of a tourist as her husband.

"John had seen the United States only from an airplane, as a Beatle," said Mintz. "And Yoko had never seen the United States, outside of New York. So they got into this old white Nash Rambler, with a driver, and they drove from New York to Los Angeles, stopping off along the way to sleep, to go to all-night diners and twenty-four-hour coffee shops. Imagine yourself in 1972 sitting in an all-night coffee shop in Nevada and John and Yoko walk in. Well, as they got closer to Los Angeles, they took a wrong turn on the freeway and wound up in a field near Santa Barbara. And they called me and said they would like to meet me. Of course, I knew what they looked like. But they had never seen me. I drove up to Santa Barbara, found the white Rambler, got into the car, and we hugged. That's how we met."

Mintz's long phone calls with the Lennons continued unabated after the couple returned to New York. He talked them through their move from Bank Street to the Dakota, the landmark apartment complex on the corner of West Seventy-second Street and Central Park West. And he came to New York often to be with them for most special occasions, including the birth of their son, Sean, in 1975, and most of the traditional holidays. In the process, Mintz, like Gruen, proved to be someone the Lennons could trust.

"From the time that I met them to the time that he ran out of time, I spent most of my Thanksgivings, Christmases, and New Year's Eves with them," said Mintz. "I live alone in Los Angeles. I've never been married and I have no children. They were my extended family. But I want to make one thing clear: I never worked for John. There's probably been a misconception about that over the years. But no dollars ever traded hands."

The Lennons used some of the money they never gave Mintz to eventually purchase five apartments in the Dakota, two for actual living and three smaller spaces for employees and storage. The highlights of their eight years together at the Dakota have been well-documented: In the fall of 1973, John and Yoko separated. He went to Los Angeles with their secretary, May Pang, while Yoko remained in New York by herself. John said at the time that Yoko kicked him out. She said the separation was inevitable, and added that it might actually do him some good.

Fifteen months later, in January 1975, John returned to New York, reunited with Yoko, and got her pregnant, in that order. The couple's only child together, Sean Taro Ono Lennon, was born at New York Hospital on October 9, the very same day that his father turned thirty-five.

By the time Sean was one, John Lennon was experiencing a new kind of freedom. For the first time since becoming a Beatle, he had no recording contract, having been dropped by his label, EMI-Capitol. Also during that year, he was finally awarded a green card and the promise of possible U.S. citizenship. And, most important, he had this one-year-old baby whom he desperately wanted to be with night and day.

With no professional commitments hanging over his head, and money issues nonexistent, Lennon retired from show business, beginning what Mintz described as "John's cocooning period."

"Between '75 and '80, he was with Sean every day," said Mintz. "And all those stories you've read about Yoko taking care of business downstairs and John being the house husband, in spite of anything anyone's ever said to the contrary, those stories were all true."

Many writers over the years have attempted to debunk the image of Lennon at home doing the chores, most notably Albert Goldman in his book *The Lives of John Lennon*. Goldman always asserted that Lennon made up this "big lie" about his housebound lifestyle to reinforce the validity of his wife's business skills in hopes that the public would take her more seriously.

For his part, Lennon remained totally consistent about the quieter life he was leading after Sean's birth. "I've been baking bread and looking after the baby" was how Lennon began his now-historic 1980 *Playboy* interview with writer David Sheff. Stunned by Lennon's characterization of himself during the preceding few years, Sheff asked whether it was possible that Yoko had been controlling him. The question was enough to send Lennon into a rage.

"If you think I'm being controlled like a dog on a leash because I do things with her," Lennon said, "then screw you! Because—fuck you brother and sister, you don't know what's happening!"

Lennon went on to say that his wife was the teacher "and I'm the pupil. . . . She's taught me everything I fucking know. . . . She was there . . . when I was the 'Nowhere Man.'"

According to Mintz, Lennon's version of how he and Yoko led their lives in the late 1970s "is 100 percent accurate."

"That's what he did," said Mintz. "He cocooned. I don't think that reading *Rolling Stone* was so important during those years, and I don't think he paid that much attention to trends in music.

"But all during this so-called silent period, John remained incredibly interested in current events and politics," said Mintz. "He read the papers every day, and he used to call me to watch the evening news, which he saw in New York three hours ahead of me. He would tell me things to look for. He watched a lot of television, nonfiction television, primarily the news. He would have had a field day with all the cable talk shows today. He wouldn't have slept. He would have been glued to Fox and CNN. That's all he would be doing, that and sending e-mails, which hadn't been invented yet.

"But he was very up on the politics of the time, and, of course, John's political persuasions are extremely well known, so you can imagine his overall feelings about the emerging Reagan administration and the conservatism in the country," said Mintz. "And it has also been well documented that John continued to be under constant FBI surveillance, which he always viewed as a force with which to be reckoned. John and Yoko never told anybody how to vote. And John never voted because he wasn't a citizen. So he had no political party affiliation. He basically felt that both parties were about the same. Having said that, I do think that the coming emergence of Reaganism did send a chill up his spine. Not because of Ronald Reagan himself, but because John perceived that the country was moving in a direction that was the antithesis of the things he embraced in his life, like 'Give Peace a Chance' and the point of view expressed in 'Imagine.' If Ronald Reagan had read the lyrics to 'Imagine,' he probably would have recoiled in horror."

It was one of the few times in Lennon's life, according to Yoko, that he didn't purposely go out and make waves. "You must understand," she said, "we had a very difficult time with immigration. But when John finally got his green card, he thought, well, he has a son, he has his green card. Maybe this is not the time to be too dangerous."

Then came the summer of 1980. Against the political backdrop of fifty-two Americans still being held hostage in Iran, which greatly diminished the chances of Jimmy Carter's reelection bid and made Reagan look more and more like the next president of the United States,

Lennon traveled with a five-man crew to Bermuda on his yacht, *Isis*. His intention was to rent a house on the island and simply while away his time swimming and sailing. But something else happened on Bermuda, and it turned out to be a burst of creative energy that saw him writing more than a dozen songs in three weeks.

He knew Yoko also had been writing songs in New York, and they would spend days on the phone singing their latest compositions to each other. It was clear to both of them that they would start recording a new album as soon he got back.

"He was so excited on the phone," recalled Yoko. "He said, 'I wrote two songs.'

"And I said, 'I have two songs. Let's make an EP.'

"And then the next day, he said, 'Now I have two more.'

"And I said, 'Well, maybe now it should be an album.' That's how it started. We decided to work on a theme, and he was very excited about that. He just kept thanking me and thanking me."

On Tuesday, August 5, John and Yoko entered the Hit Factory, on West Fifty-fourth Street in New York, to begin recording the album, *Double Fantasy*. Producer Jack Douglas was at the controls, and photographer Bob Gruen was given almost free reign to document the sessions with candid pictures.

"I visited the studio on and off from late summer through the end of the backing track sessions," said Gruen. "I was there a number of times while they recorded. We really had no set appointments. I just did things as the situation came up. John was extremely positive about the music he was making, and excited to be back in the studio. He was coming from a position of real strength in his life. He had spent five years out of the limelight, and he had taken time to raise his son and learn about parenting and about living.

"The album was to be about the relationship between a man and a woman," said Gruen. "And in that regard it was very much a John and Yoko project, not just John Lennon. A track of his would follow a track of hers, and then they'd stop to talk about their feelings and deal with the relationship. To me, he appeared so grounded."

"I had been in a hundred recording studios with different artists, and I'd been with John in various studios, as well," said Mintz. "The recording of *Double Fantasy* was unique because in many ways it was a metaphor for the way John's life was coming to completion. All these recording studios—the Hit Factory, where John and Yoko recorded the album, or the Record Plant, where it was mixed—have closed-circuit cameras at the front door. They have this so an engineer can see who is ringing the buzzer. A lot of sessions sometimes go on into the middle of the night. The studio may not be in the best neighborhood. So they need these cameras for security reasons. One of the things I remember about the *Double Fantasy* sessions was John and Yoko pinning a large photograph of Sean to the face of the TV monitor above the recording console. You couldn't see who was outside, but for John and Yoko it was more important to see Sean staring down at the console.

"Yoko also created this small anteroom just off of the control room, a white room, twenty by fifteen," said Mintz, "that she made to look like a mini version of their living room at the Dakota. The lighting in this room was lowered, and it was filled with candles and incense. A Japanese woman named Toshi served tea. It was a room John and Yoko would go to when there was a lull in the session. I remember going with them into the room. John was wearing slacks and a jacket and a shirt that was open at the collar. In that room, he spoke about the project softly, tentatively, and rhapsodically. It was a quiet room, unlike any room I'd ever seen at a rock and roll recording session. None of the other musicians or technical people ever entered that room. It was mostly a room where John and Yoko could relax."

On Thursday, October 9, a skywriting plane flew over Central Park and spelled out the smoky message "Happy Birthday John & Sean. Love Yoko." Below the message was a dual birthday party that Yoko threw at Warner LeRoy's famed Central Park restaurant, Tavern on the Green.

"Mainly we concentrated on Sean," said Yoko. "He had a great time at the party. It was mostly his friends at the party, kids from school, a few parents, Sean's best friend, Max LeRoy, and his parents, Warner and Kay LeRoy. It was John's birthday and Sean's birthday, but John wanted it to be a day for Sean."

Sean's father kept mostly to himself in the cavernous multiroom restaurant, watching the party as though he were there as an observer and not a celebrant. There was, after all, much to reflect on. He was now forty.

"I don't think he felt forty was necessarily a milestone age for him," said Yoko, looking back at the day. "I mean, he wrote the song, 'Life Begins at Forty,' which was a serious song when he first wrote it. Then he listened to his own lyrics, and he said, 'I can't do this. I have to make it funny.' So he wound up creating a comic song about turning forty. That's how he wanted to look at it, especially that day. I think he wanted to play down his age and focus on Sean."

Mintz made one other trip to New York in early November, specifically to hear John and Yoko's new album. "The engineer would prepare cassettes for John, and he would take them back to the Dakota and play them on the little stereo in his bedroom," said Mintz. "He had none of the fancy equipment at home. He always believed music should be listened to the way it comes out on a car radio."

Mintz went back to the Dakota with John and Yoko that night, into what was called the "old bedroom," facing West Seventy-second Street. John's primitive hi-fi system was on one side of the bed. At the foot of the bed was a television, a large-screen TV that John had purchased a few years before in Tokyo. Mintz was with him in Japan when he bought the TV.

"He was one of the first people to import a large-screen TV from Japan," said Mintz. "But he really needed a large screen, because without his eyeglasses on he couldn't see more than four or five feet in front of him."

John and Yoko's bed was nothing more than a mattress on top of a piece of plywood, supported on each side by two church pews that the couple had gotten from an old church in the South. Behind the bed was a brick wall, and in front of it, up against the foot, was the large-screen TV. On either side of the television were these two large old-fashioned dental cabinets, the kind that you might see in a Norman Rockwell painting from the 1930s, with twenty or thirty sliding drawers, basically for clothing and John's ties.

"The whole look was simple, and it just worked," said Mintz. "And the room, of course, was either lit by candles or so dimly lit that you could hardly see a thing. And that's how I first heard *Double Fantasy*, in that setting. John put the cassette on and he kicked back in bed. He was in his pajamas, Yoko was in her nightgown, and I sat in a white wicker rocking chair on Yoko's side of the bed. The music just wafted throughout the open room. And the two of them were very stiff and quiet. The TV was on, with the sound off. John didn't have his glasses on, so to him everything was completely out of focus. He referred to the TV as his electronic fireplace."

When the music was over, Mintz and Lennon talked into the night. Yoko fell asleep. "She usually went to sleep when John and I spoke," said Mintz. "Yoko does not sleep the way most people sleep. She takes a series of catnaps during every twenty-four-hour period. She'll go down for two or three hours, come up, do what she has to do, and when she gets tired she goes to sleep again. She can sleep at the drop of a dime. She had heard thousands of hours of the John and Elliot dialogue. And with my kind of late-night FM voice, and John mostly talking about things Yoko already knew about, I would expect her to fall asleep. And that night she did.

"John was enthusiastic about everything that night, not only about the record coming out, but also about what the record symbolized, and where he was with his family," said Mintz. "A few weeks prior to this he had prepared his first loaf of bread that he baked in his oven. He sent me a Polaroid picture of the loaf of bread, which to him was a symbol of pride that he could do such a thing as create a loaf of bread. I still have the Polaroid of the loaf of bread. I know there's the impression that his life was very frenetic, very busy, but in fact it was Yoko who was generating a lot of the business stuff and taking the phone calls. John just seemed content with where he was, and completely at peace in terms of his relationship with Sean. Each night before he slept, he would put Sean to sleep by cradling him in his arms and whispering into his ears the various things that the two of them did that day.

"I asked him about going out on the road and performing live, assuming the record was a success, and he was affirmative about all of it," said Mintz. "He basically said, 'Whatever Mother thinks we should do.' In fact, Yoko had already laid the groundwork for a mini-tour, not something that would take them around the world on a jet plane, like Mick Jagger does with the Rolling Stones. It was just going to be some key locations in key cities."

There came a point in the middle of the night when Lennon was finally through talking. He wasn't bashful about kicking Mintz out. He just simply said, "Okay, I think I'm going to close my eyes now."

"He said, 'Let me walk you to the door.'

"And I said, 'John, I know my way to the door.' But he was insistent," said Mintz. "So he got up, in his pajamas, and he led me to the door. There was a chain of bells hanging on the doorknob, on the inside of their front door. They were Tibetan or Buddhist bells, on a small chain not much thicker than a woman's large necklace. They rang with a high-pitched tone, not loud, not like gongs. And as we got to the door, he turned the knob and opened it, and the bells started ringing.

And for no particular reason that I could discern, he smiled at me, and said, 'It's our alarm system.'"

Thanksgiving at the Lennon apartment, just a week after the release of *Double Fantasy,* turned out to be a simple celebration, with only three people in attendance that night: John, Yoko, and Sean.

"It seemed like we were the only family we had then," said Yoko. "Thanksgiving is about collecting your family, and mine was in Japan, and John's was in England. John was an only child, his parents were both gone, and Thanksgiving is not an English holiday. So who were we going to invite? I mean, I could have called Japan, and said, 'Come to Thanksgiving at our house.' And they would have said, 'What?'"

"I didn't cook," said Yoko. "We had turkey brought in. But we were very into the idea of Thanksgiving. This whole idea of a pilgrimage, and the white people learning from the Indians, that was an important concept for Sean to learn. He was born an American, and Thanksgiving is an American thing. And we were feeling very American at that time, especially since John had just gotten his green card. We felt like we were starting over as an American family."

It is no coincidence that the song "(Just Like) Starting Over" became the album's first single. "It was not written until very late in the process," said Yoko. "It was like it suddenly came from left field. But we were starting over in a big way. We had the child we never thought we'd have. We tried so many times, and I was always having a miscarriage or something. So this was a big, important thing to us."

And it became a big disappointment when the single did not do as well in England as the Lennons had expected. "When the single hit Britain, we thought it would go to number one. When it got stuck at eight, I felt very responsible," said Yoko. "I felt I had to make sure that this whole project was good for John. And now the record stopped in England. I went to John, and I said, 'Look, I'm sorry. It's eight.'

"He knew exactly what I meant," she said. "It was eight, and it was not going to go up any further. He just looked at me, and he said, 'Hey, you know, I still have my family.' But he also knew that a lot of what we did over the years was not popular. He had pride in what he was doing, and he was doing something he believed in. He was an avant-garde artist in that way. You do something not because you think it will be popular. You do it because you believe in it."

Back in California, Mintz continued his regular phone dialogue with the Lennons, speaking to Yoko daily, and to John maybe three, four times a week. "With the album still relatively new," said Mintz, "he talked to me about what I thought the public reaction to his reemergence might be, after all that time away. And I recall asking him, 'Do you care? Does it matter?'

"He snickered," said Mintz. "He said for years he was always concerned when he saw any of the pop stars in the magazines because he was never one who enjoyed going to places like Studio 54 and having his picture taken. Because he had been out of the loop for so long, he wondered whether or not he would even be remembered, and whether or not the music would still be relevant or significant. I believe his questions to me on the phone were more rhetorical than anything else. He did say that none of his contemporaries had ever put their women on the same level as he did with Yoko. That's why *Double Fantasy* was so special to him, because it was not a reemergence of Beatle John coming back to say hello again, but a statement of where he was in his life.

"By this time he had also given up any kind of drug use," said Mintz. "He was very clear, very in-tune. He would divide his conversations between what was going on with the music, what was going on at the house, and what was going on in the political world. Whatever occurred on the news he would want me to pay attention. He also told me he didn't feel tired anymore. There was a long period of time that he complained of lethargy and weariness. But in these few conversations he was all upbeat."

On Thursday night, December 4, Bob Gruen met Lennon at the Record Plant, on West Forty-fourth Street, where he was mixing Yoko's single "Walking on Thin Ice." The song had been hastily recorded after *Double Fantasy* was completed.

"They did all their mixing at the Record Plant," said Gruen. "I took a number of pictures of John and Yoko around the studio that night. They posed in front of an eight-foot-tall guitar that John had fabricated for an avant-garde festival. It was too big for them to take home, so they ended up loaning it to the Record Plant for a while. I knew he had made it, so I wanted them posing in front of it.

"Then he told me about this coat he had at home, this fancy gold and red braided jacket with Japanese writing on it," said Gruen. "He wanted me to shoot pictures of him wearing this coat, so we made another plan for me to come back the next night, and I did."

While Yoko spent most of Friday night, December 5, putting various vocal effects on her single, Gruen sat with Lennon on the floor of the Record Plant and talked.

"For a long time we talked about the future," said Gruen. "He was very excited that he had come back, and very excited about what Yoko had managed to do on the album. He was really amused by the fact that she was getting great reviews and that her music was being called new and interesting, as opposed to his music, which some critics called a bit tamer and middle of the road. He was very excited about that because he really liked Yoko's influence. He also talked about taking a couple of weeks off for the holidays, and then he wanted to start rehearsing with a band and record some videos by the end of January. He estimated that they'd probably be performing live by March. He even talked about the possibility of doing concerts in Japan. We both had a common interest in Japan. We were talking about places where we were going to go shopping, and restaurants where we were going to eat."

It was dawn on Saturday, December 6, by the time Yoko finished her work in the studio. All during the night Lennon never put on the braided jacket, and now he was carrying it over his arm as he walked outside with Yoko and Gruen.

"It must have been six or seven in the morning when we got outside," said Gruen. "I asked John if we could take the pictures right then, and Yoko said, 'Oh, I feel tired. Let's do it another time.'

"And John said to her, 'Look, you've kept him up all night. Let's take some pictures.' So he put on the jacket and I took about half a roll of pictures out on the sidewalk. A car was waiting for them. John said to me, 'See you later,' and they left."

That afternoon, Lennon went by himself to his favorite West Side haunt, Cafe La Fortuna, a small Italian coffee shop on West Seventy-first Street, just around the corner from the Dakota. John and Yoko were regulars at Cafe La Fortuna, right from the time it opened in 1976. They would often go in together, with or without Sean, and there were many more times that Lennon could be found there by himself, drinking cappuccino, nibbling on Italian-made chocolates, reading the newspapers, and talking with the restaurant's owner, Vincent Urwand.

Lennon viewed La Fortuna as a safe haven, and over time he established the kind of relationship with Urwand that allowed for much teasing and playful banter. Urwand even teased him that day about *Double Fantasy.*

"Look, you've had all those years of wildness and success in the Beatles," Urwand was quoting as saying in Ray Coleman's exhaustively researched John Lennon biography, *Lennon*.

"You don't need the money," argued Urwand. "What are you doing all this for? You're enjoying being a husband and father!"

According to Coleman's book, Lennon responded first by laughing, and then saying to Urwand, "I swore I'd look after that boy until he was five, and he's five and I feel like getting back to my music. The urge is there. It's been a long time since I wrote a song, but they're coming thick and fast now."

Back at the Dakota that night, Lennon phoned his aunt Mimi, his mother's sister and the woman most responsible for his upbringing, and gushed about the new album. Coleman documented the exchange, quoting Lennon's aunt as saying to him from her home in England, "John, you're an idealist looking for a lost horizon. You would make a saint cry!"

To which Lennon responded, "Oh, Mimi, don't be like that. . . . I'll *see you soon* and we'll bring Sean. Goodnight, God bless, Mimi."

John and Yoko also talked that night about their planned trip to San Francisco. They discussed leaving New York on Wednesday, December 10, which would give them a few days to do nothing prior to their weekend appearance at a rally to help Asian workers gain the same kind of equal rights and equal pay as their Caucasian colleagues.

"It was about Asians, and we have an Asian kid," said Yoko. "John really was looking forward to that benefit. When he said, 'Okay, let's do it,' it meant another kind of beginning for us, one where we could once again take a political stance in public."

On Sunday night, December 7, Lennon sat down with the cassette to Yoko's single "Walking on Thin Ice" and proceeded to listen to it over and over again. "He listened to it like crazy, all weekend long," said Yoko. "It almost drove me crazy. There's this room in the apartment, overlooking the park, and he was lying down on the couch, or half sitting, with his legs on the floor. And that Sunday night, he just kept listening to the song, and listening to the song. I went to sleep. And when I came back into the room early Monday morning, he was still listening. He said it was the best song I ever wrote, but there was something else going on. The song is really a very strange song. But at the same time there was something in the air that was starting to accelerate. I felt an incredible vibe around us. Not an actual noise, but a strong vibe circling us. I started talking to him over that vibration. I said, 'John, good morning.' And he was still listening to the song."

Later that morning, Lennon had his hair cut at a nearby salon and then returned home to do a photo shoot with Yoko for photographer Annie Leibovitz. At 1 P.M., Lennon did a phone interview with a disc jockey from the RKO Radio Network. John and Yoko spent the remainder of the afternoon making phone calls and playing with Sean. The only real plan they had was to return to the Record Plant so they could continue tinkering with Yoko's song.

"It was getting late," recalled Yoko, "and we both said, 'Oh, we better go now.' We were getting to be like this old couple who really knew each other so well, and knew each other's moves so well. I went out that weekend and I bought some chocolates because John loved chocolate. I had gone out to get something, I don't remember what, and I thought, 'Oh, I better get some chocolate for him.' And I did.

"Then I came upstairs, and before I could open the door, he opened it from the inside, and he said, 'I knew you were coming back.'

"I said, 'How did you know that?'

"He said, 'I just knew.'

"I said, 'I thought of your chocolate, and I got you some.'"

Lennon graciously took the chocolate from his wife and set it down on a table, but he never took a bite.

At approximately 5 P.M. on Monday, December 8, John and Yoko came downstairs and were met outside by two fans, Paul Goresh, a photographer from New Jersey, and Mark David Chapman, a twenty-five-year-old former hospital security guard from Decatur, Georgia. Goresh had stationed himself outside the Dakota on several occasions, and as a result his face was recognizable to the Lennons. Chapman, however, was a new face, and when he thrust his copy of *Double Fantasy* in front of Lennon in hopes of getting an autograph, John complied. He scribbled "John Lennon 1980" on the album, and then handed it back to its owner.

John and Yoko knew they were not going to pull another all-nighter at the Record Plant. Most of the work on Yoko's song had been done, and producer Jack Douglas promised that he would have a master copy finished by 9 A.M. the following morning. The Lennons were grateful to get out of the studio at a relatively early hour. As Yoko said, "John wanted to get home early enough to say good night to Sean."

Goresh was already gone by the time John and Yoko returned to the

Dakota. But Chapman was still there, waiting. The time was 10:49 P.M. Yoko got out of the limousine first, followed by her husband. Chapman said hello to her as she walked by, and then, as Lennon passed him, Chapman called out, "Mr. Lennon?"

As Lennon turned around, Chapman pulled out a .38 revolver, dropped into a combat stance, and fired five shots at point-blank range. The bullets hit Lennon in the back, shoulder, and arm. He managed to stagger up the few steps to the building's front desk before dropping to the floor and moaning, "I'm shot. I'm shot."

The desk clerk, Jay Hastings, pressed an alarm button that was wired directly to the Twentieth Precinct, and within two minutes police were on the scene. Lennon was taken by a police car to the emergency room at Roosevelt Hospital, on West Fifty-ninth Street. A team of seven doctors worked feverishly to save Lennon's life, but the blood loss was too great, and he died.

"It wasn't possible to resuscitate him by any means," said Dr. Stephen Lynn, the hospital's director of emergency services.

Chapman, who never left the scene outside the Dakota, offered no resistance and was taken into custody.

Some years later, Chapman was recorded on audiotape explaining his actions, portions of which aired on *Dateline NBC* in November 2005. He characterized Lennon as, ". . . a successful man who kind of had the world on a chain, so to speak, and there I was, not even a link on that chain, just a person who had no personality . . . and something in me just broke."

The news of Lennon's death was announced to a stunned world by Howard Cosell during a broadcast of ABC's *Monday Night Football*.

"One of the great figures of the entire world, one of the great artists, was shot to death, horribly, at the Dakota Apartments, 72nd Street and Central Park West, in New York City. John Lennon is dead," Cosell said on the air. "He was the most important member of the Beatles, and the Beatles, led by John Lennon, created music that touched the whole of civilization. Not just people in Liverpool, where the group was born, but the people of the world."

Mintz heard the news, called American Airlines immediately, and flew to New York that night. "I inventoried all of John's possessions after his death," said Mintz. "My responsibility at that point was certainly to Yoko, and she wanted me to inventory his possessions and place them away for safekeeping. It was an operation that took months.

His clothing came home from the hospital in a brown paper bag. In the bag was the cassette of 'Walking on Thin Ice,' which suggests to me that on the final night of his life, in the final moments of his life, that may have been the last song he ever heard. I always thought there was a metaphor in the fact that 'Thin Ice' was in his possession when his life ended at the hands of a man who had obtained his last autograph. Those two things, taken together, must have made for a strange crossing."

Yoko didn't notice the chocolate she had brought in for her husband until days after his murder. It was still sitting on the table where he had left it. "I didn't like chocolate at all," she said. "But after John's passing, I thought, 'Should I throw it away? No, that would be wasteful.' So I said to myself, 'Well, okay, I'm going to eat the chocolate, you know. And I did."

Mintz, who remains a fixture in Yoko's life to this day, said that very little about her Dakota apartment has changed since Lennon's death in 1980. "Everything looks pretty much the same, except she now has a new bedroom," said Mintz. "She doesn't sleep in the old bedroom. For months after John's death she slept in their bed in the old bedroom. For a while, she got solid comfort being in that room. Now she uses it as a guestroom.

"In terms of how Yoko is doing on a day-to-day basis," Mintz added, "if she's not traveling, she's in that apartment, most of the time by herself. There's not much going on. She's devoted her life to his memories, and she just doesn't laugh as much anymore."

Lee Strasberg

November 17, 1901–February 17, 1982

THE GREAT ACTING TEACHER LEE STRASBERG LOVED BEING AROUND PEOPLE SO much that he often chose to take the subway to work rather than ride as a passenger in his own chauffer-driven midnight-blue Volvo station wagon.

It's not that Strasberg didn't appreciate his full-time driver, a large, soft-spoken African American named Willie Dove. In fact, Strasberg relished his time in the car with Dove, especially when they engaged in deep, passionate conversations about politics and jazz. But the boss also liked the idea that on any given day he could leave his Central Park West apartment and walk around the corner, past the landmark Dakota, to his favorite Sabrett hot dog stand on West Seventy-second Street for a quick, steaming hot dog before catching the crowded downtown train at Broadway.

Anna Strasberg said it "drove me wild" that her husband liked to periodically sneak a hot dog on the street, but since she preferred riding in the car with Dove to taking the subway anywhere, she couldn't stop him from eating the hot dogs as often as she would have liked. But even on days when he took the subway and she went by car, they always wound up at exactly the same place, either the Actors Studio on West Forty-fourth Street, where Strasberg had served as artistic director since 1951, or the Lee Strasberg Theatre Institute, which the couple established in 1969 for the purpose of making Strasberg's work available to a wider public.

Anna Strasberg is quite sure that her husband did not take the subway to work on Monday, December 8, 1980. "We rode together in the car that day," she said. "I remember it because of what happened at the Dakota."

The Strasbergs had returned home from the institute late that afternoon when Anna suddenly remembered that she forgot to pick up a cake she had ordered from a bakery on the other side of Columbus Avenue. So she left her apartment building, which sat one block north of the Dakota, and walked around the corner at Seventy-second Street. As she passed the Upper West Side's most famous residence, she noticed a man in a raincoat and a few other people standing around a parked limousine. She presumed the limo belonged to John Lennon and Yoko Ono because the Lennons were the biggest celebrities living in the Dakota, and there were always fans and photographers waiting for them outside the building.

"I thought to myself, 'Don't these people outside ever go home?' I also remember thinking," recalled Anna, "that the limousine didn't have to be outside the gates of the Dakota. There was more than enough room inside the courtyard."

Later that night, as the Strasbergs were preparing for sleep, the doorman rang up to announce that Willie Dove was on his way upstairs. Dove had not been expected until the following morning.

"Willie ran into the apartment," said Anna, "and he told us that John Lennon had just been shot. Lee burst into tears, and he said, 'Now they're killing artists.' That was his reaction."

The Hungarian-born Israel Lee Strasberg, the youngest of four children and just seven years old when he landed with his family on Ellis Island, started reacting viscerally to artists from the moment he joined the Students of Art and Drama, an amateur group at the Chrystie Street Settlement House in Greenwich Village. The year was 1920, and it took Strasberg another four years to make his professional acting debut, playing a soldier in *Processional*, a Theater Guild production at New York's Garrick Theater.

In 1931, Strasberg and two of his friends, directors Harold Clurman and Cheryl Crawford, cofounded the Group Theatre, a New York–based company that set out to produce plays that dealt mostly with the contemporary issues of the time and how those issues affected the common man.

Clurman later called Strasberg "one of the few artists among American theater directors. He is the director of introverted feeling, of strong emotion curbed by ascetic control, sentiment of great intensity muted by delicacy, pride, fear, shame. The effect he produces is a classic hush, tense and tragic, a constant conflict so held in check that a kind of beautiful spareness results. The roots are clearly in the intimate experience of a complex psychology, an acute awareness of human contradiction and suffering."

Strasberg used a probing examination of introverted feelings to develop what came to be known as the Method, a unique process of acting preparation first invented by the Russian acting teacher Constantin Stanislavsky. Strasberg adapted Stanislavsky's teachings to the American theater, and in time the Method became the basis of study at both the Actors Studio and the Lee Strasberg Theatre Institute.

The actors who honed their skills under Strasberg's tutelage are among the greatest this country has ever produced. Just a partial list would include Marlon Brando, James Dean, Marilyn Monroe, Sidney Poitier, Paul Newman, Jane Fonda, Anne Bancroft, Jack Nicholson, Robert De Niro, and Al Pacino. And although he had never met John Lennon, Strasberg, like many others, could cry at Lennon's passing, just for the sake of lost art.

After Lennon's murder, Strasberg slowly retreated from subway travel, as though just walking around the Dakota had become too painful a reminder, and he began depending more and more on Willie Dove's careful hand behind the wheel of the Volvo. Anna Strasberg remembers one night in December 1981, a year after Lennon's death, when her husband was preparing to deliver a lecture at New York University on the history of the theater. It was a cold and rainy night. Dove was double-parked on Central Park West, waiting for the Strasbergs to come downstairs.

"Lee looked tired, and it was horrible outside," she said. "I said to him, 'Do you really need to be doing this? You can always reschedule it for another time. You can do it when we get back from vacation.'

"But he insisted on going. He said, 'I must do it tonight.' So we went," she said. "And he was brilliant, electric. It was as if he knew he needed to be doing this right then."

But his success at NYU that night did not stop her from worrying about him. The South American–born Anna Mizrahi was always concerned about his well-being, almost from the moment she met him in 1967, at the West Coast branch of the Actors Studio in Los Angeles. Strasberg was nearly sixty-six at the time, and she was, in her own words, "much, much younger." He already had two grown children, Susan and John, from a previous marriage, and Anna had never been married. But he proposed to her three months later, and they were wed in January 1968. It was never Strasberg's intention to have more children, especially at his age, but Anna very much wanted to be a mother. The couple went on to produce two sons, Adam Lee Strasberg, who was born in 1969, and his younger brother, David Lee Strasberg, who arrived in 1971.

Their father-to-be had been living in the Central Park West apartment for eight years before Anna moved in as his wife. Just being married was a new experience for her, but being married to Strasberg also meant that she might wake up in the morning to find total strangers slowly walking up and down the apartment's interior hallway looking at the many photographs, theater posters, and framed articles about her husband's early accomplishments that hung on the walls.

"That happened all the time with us," she said. "I was a very private person. I wasn't brought up to be that public about my private life. But we got married on a Sunday and the next day I woke up, and I said, 'Good morning, darling,' and Lee was having a meeting in the living room with a group of Japanese people. They kept bowing, and I kept thinking, 'Where am I?'

"And Lee said, 'Gentlemen, my wife.' After that," she said, "I learned never ever to come out of our bedroom unless I was fully dressed. Once I left the room, I knew I might find almost anyone in the house with us."

For the first few weeks after their wedding, when they were alone, the newlyweds sat at opposite ends of a long dining room table and had their meal served to them by a cook. They were so far apart that they practically had to shout just to hear each other.

"I said to him that I needed a less formal environment, with more laughter. Lee had a wonderful sense of humor," she said, "but I really taught him how to laugh. To say he taught me a lot would be the silliest statement in the world. I was not only young in years, but also in experience. I was naïve and I went from just discovering life to being taken to the top of the mountain. Here I was, with people who had contributed great things to their country. The Group Theatre was like a tree, but its roots went deep and were intertwined. And did they all fight with one another? Oh, yes. I watched them fight a lot. But it wasn't petty fighting. It was fighting for ideas. He fought with director

Elia Kazan. He fought with Harold Clurman, and he loved Harold. Lee said wonderful things about Harold in the press, and when Harold found out what he had said, he called Lee, and he said, 'I heard you said wonderful things about me, and we fight so much.'

"And Lee said, 'Harold, we fight for ideas.'

"Lee taught me so much, about life, about the arts, about people, and about history," said Anna. "But he also learned from me, and we had a trust between us. I took such great care of him. I would wake up, and say, 'Do you want some water? I'll get you water.' We became so intertwined. For years his sensuality went into the work, and now for the first time in a long time someone was treating him as a man. And suddenly the home was no longer a place where people came and sat in awe of him. It was a place where people laughed. We put up a basketball hoop at the end of the hall where children played, our children, and their friends. It was a very happy time."

Following the NYU lecture in December, the Strasbergs left New York for a holiday vacation at the La Quinta Resort and Club, a desert oasis in the hills near San Diego. "It was just us and the boys," said Anna. "It was a time for Lee to be quiet in the mornings, because he was always talking. But at La Quinta he could be quiet and read the paper and have breakfast."

But on the family's first day there, Frank Capra, the legendary director of such American movie classics as *It's a Wonderful Life* and *Mr. Smith Goes to Washington*, bounded into the dining room as if he were on his way to the podium to accept an Oscar.

"He was just the happiest, nicest man," said Anna, "and obviously Lee knew him, and he knew Lee, and naturally he wanted to talk to Lee. Now this wasn't necessarily the case with Capra, but it happened all the time: Someone would spot Lee, and they would want to talk to him. The person would come over and sit down and start talking to him as though I didn't exist. Sometimes they even elbowed me out of the way to get to him."

Anna said she learned how to drive a car just so she could be alone with her husband. On one morning at La Quinta, she hired a young actor she knew to watch the children so she and Lee could get into their rented car and drive through the mountains.

"This happened just before New Year's," she said. "We had left the grounds at La Quinta, and we were driving up and down the hills, and Lee said something to me that surprised me. We had the classical music station on, and we were just listening and driving. The mountains were so beautiful, and he said, 'Anna, promise me something: When you write a book, and you will, promise me that you don't settle scores for me.'

"I said, 'I'm not going to write a book because I'm not going to observe my life. I just want to live my life with you.' I paused for a beat, and then said, 'And why wouldn't I settle scores?'

"He laughed," said Anna, "but then he added, 'I don't want you to settle scores.'

"So I promised him that I wouldn't settle scores," she said, "but then I added, 'Can I at least set the record straight?' And he just threw his head back and laughed some more."

But she remembered it as a "strange conversation."

"He said, 'Don't be fooled' of this. 'Make sure' of that. I just thought he was being overprotective," she said, not thinking at all about her future, or his.

In a way, these gentle warnings to his wife, coming as 1982 was about to begin, are eerily reminiscent of a movie conversation that took place some years earlier between two towering actors, both of whom were disciples of Strasberg's Method in real life. The movie, of course, is *The Godfather*, and the memorable conversation occurs near the end of the film when Brando, as Don Corleone, tells his son Michael, played by Pacino, how to spot a potential traitor.

At the time director Francis Ford Coppola was shooting that scene, no one, and certainly not Strasberg, could have predicted that he would be offered a role in *The Godfather* sequel. In all his years in the theater, Strasberg had never acted in a movie, so when an opportunity presented itself for him to play Hyman Roth in *The Godfather: Part II*, his first inclination was to say no.

"Kazan was offered the part first," remembered Anna. "But he didn't think it was a big enough role, so he said no. Then they came to Lee. They asked him to do a screen test, and he said no. But Al never let up on him. Al had always wanted Lee for the part, and he even asked me to help him. He said, 'Anna, you have to convince him.'

"I said, 'Al, I love the man. I don't want to talk him into doing something he doesn't want to do.'"

But there was no quit in Pacino. Strasberg was in his living room answering questions from a reporter from the BBC one day when Pacino suddenly came into the apartment and handed his mentor the

Godfather II script, right in the middle of Strasberg's interview. Strasberg read the script later that night. After he finished, he asked his wife whether she wanted to look at it.

"I said no," recalled Anna. "I said, 'Darling, if you want to do it, I just want you to have a good time. Close your eyes and we'll do it. Or not. What difference does it make? You don't need anyone, and you don't need anything. You've proven who you are and you have nothing else to prove.'"

The Strasbergs flew to Los Angeles that Christmas and were at the Beverly Hills Hotel, having lunch by the pool, when the captain came over to their table to say that a "scruffy man who says he is Al Pacino has asked to be let in so he could see you."

Strasberg said, "Oh, yes, that must be Al."

It was Pacino, and he wasn't alone. Francis Ford Coppola was with him. "We had just flown in from New York," said Anna. "Lee was very tired, and Francis just sat there staring at him, and then they left. Lee got a call later asking for a meeting, and he said that he didn't have time for a meeting because he was teaching."

The Strasbergs had been invited to the wrap party for *The Godfather*, which was being held in Hollywood on the Paramount lot. Anna wanted to accept the invitation, which surprised her husband. He said, "You never want to go to parties. Why this one?"

"Our friend, Burgess Meredith, was doing *The Day of the Locust* on another lot at Paramount," said Anna, "so I told Lee that we could do both things, go to the party, and visit with Burgess."

They went, she said, "and as soon as we got to the *Godfather* party, Bobby De Niro came over to me, and he said, 'So, is he going to do it?' I told him I didn't know. Then we sat down at a table, and Lee sat next to Francis's father, Carmine Coppola, and Carmine had worked with Arturo Toscanini. Well, Lee wanted to hear everything about the great Toscanini. Lee just lit up listening to Carmine talking about him. Francis walked over and he saw this, and the next day Paramount called Lee and offered him the part of Hyman Roth."

Strasberg didn't immediately say yes, or no. "They weren't offering him much money," said Anna. "In fact, he was making a lot more money teaching. So I said to him, 'If they really want you, you should at least get paid.' They came back with a better offer, and he accepted."

Coppola shot many of the Cuban scenes for *Godfather II* in Santo Domingo, the capital city of the Dominican Republic. Strasberg didn't like the idea that he was far away from home without his wife and two young sons, and so he sent for them.

"We were at the hotel in Santo Domingo," said Anna, "and the boys were playing with Al in the pool. He was the monster, and they were trying to drown him. And I'll never forget, Lee was sitting in a chaise lounge saying to the children, 'Be careful, boys. He's an actor. They need him for the next scene, so be gentle.'

"And then someone from the crew came to the pool, and they said, 'Mr. Pacino, Mr. Strasberg, it's time to go to wardrobe.' Well, they left," said Anna. "And when they returned, Adam and David saw that this monster they were trying to drown suddenly had his hair slicked back and sports clothes on. The boys knew it was no longer playtime. They saw their father and their friend, the monster Al, as characters."

The Strasberg boys never saw *Godfather II* until years later, when they were away at college. Someone once asked Adam why he didn't see the film when he was younger. He said, "My mom didn't want me to see my dad getting shot."

But during the filming, Adam and David were mesmerized watching their father interact with other actors in the movie. Strasberg saw this, yet he knew not to push his sons too early. The *New York Times* ran a short piece on Monday, February 8, 1982, in which Strasberg explained his feelings about starting kids off in acting at a time when they may not be ready.

"Young people," he said, "should not be encouraged to go into the theater." That kind of decision, he added, should be made "'when they are more conscious of the problems.'"

Strasberg gave the interview to the *Times* after it became known that Adam, then twelve, and David, eleven, were being sought by director Ira Cirker to play two immigrant boys in an Actors Studio production of a Victor Wolfson play, *My Prince the King*. Cirker had first approached Anna Strasberg about her sons, and she said no. And her husband agreed completely with her decision.

But the boys had different ideas. Adam didn't like it that his parents were talking for him. "Why don't you let us decide?" he said.

So they did let the boys decide for themselves, and they chose to join the production. As Adam told the *New York Times*, "I wanted to see what acting is like." After rehearsing for a few days he found out. "It's hard," he added.

David was quoted in the same article, and he seemed more upbeat.

"The easy part," he said, "is learning your lines. The hard part is being able to say them and do the main part of acting."

What the boys didn't tell the *Times* was how they had been second-guessing their decision about being in the play, which was scheduled to open Tuesday, February 9, for a two-week run. "Once they started," said Anna, "they didn't want to do it. But they had given their word so they had to do it, and they did."

By Friday, February 12, Adam and David had settled into the production, and while their parents tried to see every performance, Strasberg still needed to go back and forth between the Actors Studio and the Institute on Fifteenth Street. That Friday, he directed a session at the Actors Studio, and watched the young actor Randy Rocca perform *Hamlet*.

"I thought Randy was brilliant," said Anna. "He was all over the stage. Everything came pouring out of him, and I found him fascinating to watch. When I told that to Lee, he held his palm up to me, and he said, 'Darling . . .' And I could see that he was getting angry. And he proceeded to critique Randy. He said, 'Art is in the choice, and the choice is that which conditions art.'

"For some stupid reason," said Anna, "I wrote down those words on a piece of paper. I was sitting next to Lee and I wrote it down. And Lee went on to describe art, talent, skill, and each thing he defined so clearly, like he needed to do this. I had never seen him so wonderful. Rocca died a few years later. He was killed in a motorcycle accident. He wasn't wearing a helmet. But on that night he loved Lee's criticism because he understood what Lee was saying.

"Actors often got mad at Lee because they knew they couldn't fool him," said Anna. "Actors have this thing. It's like, 'If I want to seduce you, you'll be mine forever.' That kind of thing. And Lee's eyes were just these big beautiful blue eyes, and he looked at you and nothing else existed. Nobody existed except you. It's a very seductive thing. He didn't move. He was just so focused, so concentrated on what you were doing. And it's every actor's thing: 'Oh, I can fool the master.' And sometimes they did. But just because he didn't call them on it didn't mean he bought it. It was just an extraordinary thing to see."

The Strasbergs exchanged Valentine's Day cards on Sunday, February 14, and then spent the better part of the afternoon preparing for a very big night on the town. Strasberg had been asked to participate in producer Alexander Cohen's made-for-television spectacle *Night of 100 Stars*, which ABC was taping at Radio City Music Hall.

The amount of superstar talent that Cohen had assembled, due in part to the fact that the evening was planned as an anniversary benefit for the one-hundred-year-old Actors' Fund of America, was nevertheless extraordinary. The incredible turnout of stars included George Burns, Orson Welles, Robin Williams, Gene Kelly, Elizabeth Taylor, James Stewart, Myrna Loy, Gregory Peck, Ginger Rogers, Paul Newman, Bette Davis, James Cagney, Lena Horne, Jack Lemmon, Liza Minnelli, David Letterman, Pearl Bailey, Celeste Holm, Carol Channing, Ethel Merman, Mary Martin, Mickey Rooney, Ann Miller, and Warren Beatty, who appeared arm-in-arm with Diane Keaton, his costar in the movie *Reds*, and his new girlfriend in real life.

Cohen had also hired Michael Bennett, director of the Broadway smash *A Chorus Line*, to stage another kind of chorus line, one that teamed Radio City's forty famed Rockettes with forty male stars. This was a group that included Pacino, De Niro, Strasberg, Rocky Graziano, Peter Allen, Burt Lancaster, James Mason, Roger Moore, Milton Berle, Anthony Quinn, William Shatner, and Christopher Reeve.

"During the night," said Anna, "so many great actors came over to Lee and practically kneeled at his feet just to talk to him. It was a long event, and when it was over, I said to him, 'Lee, would you mind, darling? I don't want to go to the after-party. I just want to go home with you.' And he said okay. We gave our party tickets to the Al-and-Bobby group so they could take in another two of their friends.

"I loved going home," she said. "I mean, I spent my life dreaming of someone with whom I could spend my time, you know, and here I had this man whom I adored. To say I loved him is like saying that I breathe. And when we got home, he sat on the edge of the bed, and he said, 'Isn't it wonderful, Anna. Look at what actors do for one another. Look at the love actors have.' He was just so moved, and I thought about how happy I was that he was asked to be one of the one hundred stars, because it made him so happy."

On Monday, February 15, Strasberg saw his two sons again in *My Prince the King*. He couldn't stay for the entire performance because he had one more class to teach at the Institute. Anna waited for the boys to finish, and when they came out of the Actors Studio, on West Forty-fourth Street, Willie Dove was waiting to take them all downtown to meet Lee. There are many ways to drive from East Fifteenth Street in

Manhattan to Central Park West. Decisions are usually made depending on the traffic, which in New York can turn from light to gridlock in the blink of a red light. Anna Strasberg does not recall traffic conditions that night, but she did remember that on the return ride home Willie Dove chose to get to the West Side from the East Side by using the Central Park transverse at Sixty-sixth Street.

"We were driving across the park," said Anna, "and Lee was talking to the boys about the month of February, and the fact that it has only twenty-eight days, except in leap years when it has twenty-nine. And as he talked, I started thinking about February, and why I had never liked February, because it's always so cold and dismal.

"And then one of the boys—I don't remember which one, I think it was David—said, 'Dad, when you are talking to actors, you seem to be completely in their world.'

"And Adam said, 'Better he should be in that world than in the ordinary world.' Or something like that," said Anna. "But they were bantering with him. And then one of the kids said, 'Dad, do you have any notes for us on our performance?'

"And he just told them not to act," she said. "He said to them, 'See what you're doing now? That's what you do. The only difference is the playwright gives you the circumstances.'"

On Tuesday, February 16, public relations executive John Springer, a longtime friend of the Strasbergs, called to inform Lee that the American Theatre Critics Association had elected him to the Theater Hall of Fame, a Broadway-sponsored organization that was established in 1971 for the purpose of honoring lifetime achievement in the American theater.

"Lee said the strangest thing to me after John Springer called him with the news," said Anna. "He said, 'Anna, you will accept the award for me because I won't be there.'

She thought, Won't be there? "I knew we were planning to go out to L.A.," she said, "but I also knew that we would be back in New York when the award was given out on March 29.

"He even told me what to say when I accepted the award for him," she said. "He said, 'Tell them I want to thank the theater for giving me an identity, and I want to thank America for giving me a home.' I thought that was beautiful, but I didn't think too much more about it at the time."

Later that day, Strasberg taught two classes at the Institute and afterward Willie Dove drove him home. Anna asked her husband if he was hungry, and he said no. He had eaten earlier, he said, and he was fine. She then left the apartment with Dove, and they picked up her sons on West Forty-fourth Street. When she returned, Lee was sitting quietly and reading. "I don't know what he was reading," she said, "but he loved reading Shakespeare, and he loved reading Keats, especially all the letters that Keats used to write to his brother."

Adam and David took their baths and went to sleep because they had school the next morning. Then, as their parents went to bed, "I asked something about one of the exercises Lee was teaching," said Anna. "I've forgotten what he said, but I remember saying to him, 'Oh, come on now, Lee,' and then I gave him my version of the exercise, and he just started to laugh, and he questioned me about it, saying, 'You mean, you think that's what I was doing?' And so on. It was just husband-and-wife nonsense, first about the acting exercise, then about his relaxation techniques. He just thought I was being funny. Finally, I said, 'Oh, Strasberg,' and we got into bed and we hugged and slept close, like we always did."

It was still dark out, early on Wednesday, February 17, when Anna heard her husband get up and go to the bathroom. "I thought, 'Why is he getting up so early?' He was standing over the sink breathing heavy and gasping," she said. "I heard a deep intake of breath. I sat up and called out, 'Lee?'

"He said, 'It's okay,' and he came back and got into bed. But as soon as he was in the bed," she said, "he was breathing heavy again. I knew he was in trouble, and in the dark I called 911, and I said, 'Could you please send an ambulance right away to the address on Central Park West. Please hurry.' As they were asking my name, I could see that Lee was really in big trouble."

Anna then called out to Adam, her oldest son, and shouted for him to wake David. "I think your father needs us now," she said.

The two boys came running into their parents' bedroom and they both climbed into the bed. "Adam was holding his father on one side," said Anna, "and David was on the other side, and I was saying, 'Lee, stay with me, darling. Stay. Stay. We're getting help right away.'"

When the ambulance arrived, Anna called her answering service, Bell's, one of the most elite Manhattan answering services at the time, and she asked the operator to call Lee's doctor, Susan Strasberg, Al Pacino, and John Springer and apprise them of the situation. Anna didn't have to give the Bell's operator anyone's home phone number because all four used the same service.

Anna wanted Lee to be taken to Mount Sinai Medial Center, which was on the other side of Central Park, on Fifth Avenue. But the ambulance driver said they couldn't do that. Because it was a city ambulance, he had to be taken to the nearest hospital, which in this case was Roosevelt, the same hospital John Lennon had been taken to a little more than two years earlier. Anna called Bell's again to make sure the service had the right hospital.

The attendants had no trouble getting Strasberg onto the gurney, but the stacks of books in the foyer made it difficult to maneuver him out through the front door. "The boys and I started moving the books," said Anna, "and all I could think about was that Lee was upset about how we were treating his books. Then one of the attendants said to me, 'Mrs. Strasberg, do you know what is happening? Your husband is experiencing a heart attack.'"

She nodded that she knew. In fact, she knew it was a heart attack even before she called 911. What she didn't know was whether he would pull through.

But with the books finally out of the way the attendants were able to push Strasberg's gurney into the elevator. Anna wanted to ride in the ambulance, but she didn't want to leave her sons behind. So the three of them got into a police car and followed the ambulance to the hospital. On the way to Roosevelt the ambulance came to a complete and unannounced stop in front of Lincoln Center, the world's largest performing arts center and home to such New York cultural icons as the New York Philharmonic, Metropolitan Opera, New York City Ballet, and the Juilliard School.

The famous fountain, which had served as a romantic meeting place ever since Lincoln Center opened in 1962, was quiet and dry. The streets were practically empty. It was still too early for anyone to be rushing off to work. New Yorkers always move slower in February, the month Lee had talked about with his boys in the car, the month Anna didn't like, the month nobody ever seems to like.

Anna couldn't understand why the ambulance had stopped. She wanted to get out of the police car, but an officer stopped her. He said to her, "You don't want to see this." Anna didn't know until much later that her husband had gone into cardiac arrest in the ambulance, which had stopped so the attendants could work on him.

By the time the ambulance and the police car arrived at the hospital, the emergency room was already crowded with people. Pacino, John Springer, Susan Strasberg, her brother John, and actress Ellen Burstyn were there. Even Ethel Merman showed up. "A lot of people were screaming," said Anna. "It was a mob scene. I don't know how they all knew. I guess Bell's called everybody."

Doctors pulled a curtain around Strasberg and began feverishly working on him. Anna was on the other side of the curtain, and she stopped one of the doctors, a woman, and she said, "Would you tell him that I'm here. I'm his wife."

The doctor disappeared behind the curtain, but Anna heard her say, "Your wife is here, Mr. Strasberg."

He responded, "Thank you," and those were the last words Anna heard him say.

Doctors pronounced him dead at 7:56 A.M. "He said, 'Thank you,' and then he died," said Anna. "I thought he was going to be all right. As soon as the doctors told us, Al fell to his knees and cried. I kept saying, 'It's not true, Al. Don't listen to them. It's not true.' I told my boys it wasn't true."

A doctor tried to give Anna a sedative, but she wouldn't take it. "I wanted to feel everything," she said. "I said, 'I don't want anyone to touch him.'

"They said, 'Mrs. Strasberg, we have to clean him.'

She said, "We will do that. My boys and I will do that. We will clean him. We will wrap him, and we will take care of him. Can we have him? He's ours.

"They thought I was crazy," said Anna. "But they left us alone with him, and we cleaned him, me and the boys. He had the most beautiful, angelic smile on his face. I cut a lock from his white hair, which I still have. Then I called Johnny Strasberg in, and I said, 'Do you want to be alone with your father for a minute and talk to him privately? I think he can still hear us.'

"We had to figure out what to say to the press," said Anna, "and I can remember Ellen Burstyn arguing with John Springer about what to say. Everyone was still screaming, and I became frightened for the boys. Willie Dove had gotten there, and I asked him to watch Adam and David while I went downstairs to look at a coffin. Then Willie took us home. Al came with us. It was very cold outside."

Various New York synagogues were considered for the funeral, along with St. Patrick's Cathedral, on Fifth Avenue. As Anna was trying to make up her mind where to hold the service, someone from the Shubert family called offering the Shubert Theater on West Forty-fourth Street. Anna chose the Shubert. And why not? Her husband had devoted his life to the theater, and the Shubert was unquestionably the most famous of all the Broadway houses.

"It just felt right to do it there," she said.

The funeral was scheduled for 11 A.M., on Thursday, February 18. By 9 A.M., the Strasberg apartment on Central Park West was filled with family and friends, among them Marlo Thomas, who was so concerned that there weren't enough limousines that she got on the phone and ordered more. And still, there weren't enough cars for everyone.

"By the time I went downstairs with Al and the two boys," said Anna, "all the limos were gone. But Willie was still there, just in case, so he drove the four of us to the Shubert in the Volvo station wagon."

An eclectic group of mourners, among them Robert De Niro, Dustin Hoffman, Jon Voight, Ruth Gordon, Lee Grant, José Ferrer, Jill Clayburgh, Ben Gazzara, Marie Osmond, Celeste Holm, and Cher, were already in their seats when Anna walked in with Pacino and her two sons. Paul Newman and Anthony Quinn stood in the back of the orchestra section.

"We were actually the last people to arrive at the Shubert, and incredibly," said Anna, "all the seats were filled. The ushers had to make people move, so we could squeeze in."

The *New York Times* reported that fifteen bouquets of spring flowers surrounded Strasberg's plain wooden coffin. A picture book, *Saint Francis of Assisi*, sat on top of the coffin. Rabbi Bernard Mandelbaum, executive director of the Synagogue Council of America, recited Hebrew prayers, and Ellen Burstyn read the Twenty-third Psalm.

Other speakers, according to the *New York Times* account, included Strasberg's son, John, actors Shelley Winters and Geraldine Fitzgerald, and Pulitzer Prize–winning playwright Sidney Kingsley, who said, "A man is a dream or he is nothing. Lee's dreams were larger than his talents for teaching acting. In the last few days, he encouraged new plans for rejuvenating the American theater. He told us to 'get on with it—you only have ten seconds before you become a whisper in the night.'"

Later, as Strasberg's coffin was being lowered into the ground during the burial service at Westchester Hills Cemetery, in Hastings-on-Hudson, New York, Adam Strasberg picked up some of the floral arrangements and tossed them down on top of the coffin. Some of the people standing nearby tried to restrain him, but he waved them off. "It's all right," he said. "My father will make those flowers grow."

The entire day was "a blur" to her, said Anna, but she did remember one man who came up to her at the end of the day. "I'm certain he was in the Mafia," she said, "but I have no idea who he was. He handed me his card and whispered in my ear. He said, 'If anyone makes you cry, you call me.'"

Anna never made that call, but she has cried often since her husband's death. "I think Lee had a deep instinctual feeling that his end was coming," she said. "You could tell by the way he dealt with me, and others. I think in his own way he was gracious about it. He didn't want to hang on. He could have fought to live, perhaps, but I know he would not have wanted to be dependent on anyone. The things he laid forth toward the end, and the clarity with which he delivered his messages to us, definitely left us with something."

And in retrospect, Anna is convinced she made the right decision calling for her sons to climb into bed with their father as he was dying. "I asked them about that later," she said, "and they were both grateful they weren't shut out. He was their dad. They feel, as I do, that we comforted him and he didn't die alone."

Since his death, Anna has made it a practice to visit her husband's grave every Sunday that she's in New York. "I brought a large rock back from California, and that has become his headstone," she said. "It used to be right outside our house in Los Angeles, right near the room where Lee played music and read. I had the rock flown back to New York and taken up to Westchester Hills. But it's a California rock, and it's starting to disintegrate after so many years in the cold weather. I think I'm going to have to get a proper headstone soon, before this one falls apart."

John Belushi
January 24, 1949–March 5, 1982

IN THE 1980 MOVIE *THE BLUES BROTHERS*, DAN AYKROYD'S CHARACTER, Elwood Blues, said repeatedly that he and his brother, Jake, played by John Belushi, were on "a mission from God." The mission, if you remember the plot line, was to save their childhood orphanage by reuniting their old band members and staging a benefit concert.

By the summer of 1981, Aykroyd was on a slightly different mission from God, one with life-or-death implications that the actor designed to play out as an elaborate scheme in a beach community far from the movie world in Hollywood: Dan Aykroyd's mission was to save John Belushi from himself.

The plan, as Aykroyd explained it, was to keep his best friend and business partner away from cocaine. Aykroyd knew this would not be especially easy given Belushi's longtime romance with the drug and the fact that cocaine just seemed to follow him around. It also didn't help that there was more cocaine in the United States at that time than at any other time in history.

"An extremely powerful grade of cocaine had been coming into the country starting from the late seventies," Aykroyd recalled. "The drug kept getting more powerful and more powerful. It was plentiful, and uncut, and it was flooding the country. There were emergency-room deaths all the time."

Aykroyd, of course, was hardly a wallflower when it came to cocaine, but he hadn't been in Belushi's league for years. As an original member of the *Saturday Night Live* ensemble group known as the Not

Ready for Prime Time Players, Aykroyd was in a position, he said, "to try all of it.

"And I did," he said. "I had done it all in college. It was a time of experimentation, and I did my part. In the sixties, there was a sort of license among us to do almost anything. But I had left it all behind, all the chemicals, the powders, the pills."

Belushi, clearly, had not, and Aykroyd knew that by the summer of 1981 he needed to do something drastic to help him. "We were on Martha's Vineyard for most of June, July, and August," Aykroyd recalled. "There was no cocaine around because I conspired with John's wife, Judy, and our friend on the Vineyard, Larry Bilzerian, to keep it away from our part of the island."

Using a network of friends, family, security guards, and even the local police, Aykroyd formed a protective ring around Belushi, without his knowledge, that effectively separated him from both the drug dealers and anyone else who may have been suspected of carrying cocaine. "We had these lobster fests on the beach," Aykroyd said, "incredible parties we used to throw where you'd boil up lobster, chicken, seaweed, sausages, and beer-battered shrimp in a clean garbage can newly bought from the hardware store. We dug these holes in the sand, and we put the can in, with heated coals underneath, and we'd pour all the contents out on a surfboard and people would eat with their hands and drink beer and red wine. Police would be on the beach to make sure no one bothered us. It was a really incredible time and we felt very special."

And the best part, Aykroyd said, was that Belushi could party freely and have the best time of his life, without having to do any of it on cocaine. "We were really sharp about it," said Aykroyd. "We bounced people out of Martha's Vineyard if we thought they were trying to get the drugs to him. Basically, we escorted them right to the ferry. We had set up a beautiful guard, and it worked."

At the time, Aykroyd was living in a Japanese-style house on a hill in Chilmark, and Belushi lived on a cliff overlooking the ocean in a house he had bought from Robert S. McNamara, the former secretary of defense. "We called the place Skull Beach," Aykroyd said, "and we had a truck and Jeeps and we'd hold demolition derbies. We were coming off the success of the *Blues Brothers* records and movie. The movie had made $72 million, and both records sold platinum. It was a summer of abundance and fun, and no cocaine.

"I would hear John's Jeep pull up, and there he was, driving himself, and he was a terrible driver," said Aykroyd. "And he would come up to the house and he'd have a pack of Camels, and he'd come in with his shades on and his army pants and his black pullover sweater. And even though he was heavy, he really had charisma and he was beautiful looking—what a beautiful-looking man. He looked like some kind of kingpin. The sun brought out that swarthy tone in his skin and his hair was long and he always had a smile on his face. And he would grab my friend John Daveikis, a buddy of mine from college, and he'd give him a hug, and he'd say, 'What do you have cooking?' And we'd have some soup on, and later when I'd come back from the beach, John would be asleep on the couch—snoring, peaceful, at rest."

Judy Belushi said the image of her husband fast asleep on the couch has been reinforced over the years by the sheer number of photos she has of him in that blissful state.

"He could be a good couch potato," she said. "He was a big reader on the couch, nonfiction books mostly, and *Catcher in the Rye*, which he would reread. Newspapers too. But he was never one to just settle on the couch to watch TV. He was the type of person that a couch molded around. I have photos of him lying in the courtyard in New York City, dozing off or with a book. He napped a lot on Martha's Vineyard. That was such a peaceful time, on Martha's Vineyard. There was such peace.

"I hate to say this, because it's going to be taken the wrong way, but John was a little like Pigpen in the cartoon *Peanuts*. After he would get up from his couch, there were always ashtrays and ashes and little note pads and crumpled papers around. And pens and pencils and cigarettes. And the food he'd been eating. You know, that Bluto side of him," she said, referring to his character in the movie *Animal House*.

"But I also have to say that he was not a slob," she said. "You've probably read that he would go for days without bathing. Perhaps that was true on rare occasions, when he was doing drugs and had been up all night. But he was a person who bathed, goddamn it. In fact, he could take several showers a day. He had good hygiene."

Judy Belushi now goes by the name Judy Belushi Pisano. Her husband of sixteen years, Victor Pisano, is a writer-director. They have four children: one son together, who is fourteen, and his three daughters from a previous marriage, who are twenty-eight, twenty-five, and twenty-two. The Pisanos live on Martha's Vineyard, and they own property in Georgia. Her life today is structured mostly around her family, but the Belushi she keeps as a middle name is obviously there for a reason.

"John and I had a really good relationship," she said. "It was very easygoing. Energy-wise, we were very similar. We could both be quiet or very energetic. But my energy was much steadier. I think I'm energetic on an even keel. He was more of a person who had bursts of energy. But there were lots of real quiet times, and Martha's Vineyard in the summer of '81 was one of those times."

"That summer was probably one of the greatest times we ever spent together," said Aykroyd. "But then the work season started, and the leaves left the trees, and the cool of the autumn came, and with that cool came all kinds of business decisions that had to be made. We were back in Manhattan, and John started to fall in with these young businessmen from New Jersey. They were owners of various companies, pretty much legit businesses, restaurants and the like. They were rich kids from suburbs who had it passed down from mama and dada, and they started sending cars for John, saying to him, 'Come hang out with us. We'll take care of you. We'll have fun.'"

Belushi had promised his wife that he would not do cocaine for a year. He even made a bet with her that he could stay away from the drug for that length of time. The bet was a new motorcycle, something he had wanted and something she was forever trying to talk him out of getting. He asked her to agree to let him get the bike if he managed to stay off the coke, and she said yes. Belushi's new friends from New Jersey, of course, had other plans. He was their way into show business, and they had the goods to ensure he would cross the Hudson River to see them. At stake was his willpower, and it never had a chance.

"I never knew who those guys were," said Aykroyd. "John told me about them. He'd say a few things like, 'You know, this one owns this, and this guy has a cool pizza place. This guy likes wine, and you like wine. And this one has a bulldozer in his backyard.' He was sharing his new friendships, but it was only because they were enabling him. They had this really, really powerful cocaine and he started in with them. All through the fall he was hanging out with these people, and Judy and I were finding these wax envelopes, and counting them and stacking them up like playing cards. We flushed a lot of stuff down the toilet, and we were confiscating vials. At a certain point, he stopped getting mad at us. Classic addiction behavior. He knew that we were just a joke, and he could just laugh at us because he would just get it somewhere else. So he stopped getting mad, and just started going around us. This was his obsession."

By December, it was obvious to everyone that Belushi's end of the bet with his wife had gone down the toilet, along with all that coke.

"We started to stitch together the first inklings of an intervention, which wasn't really a known technique back then," said Aykroyd. "Judy and I talked to our friends Mitch Glazer and Tim White about all of us stepping in to do something professionally, and maybe get him to a rehab."

"I went to a psychiatrist that December," Judy said. "I didn't think John was bingeing yet, because I had seem him often enough when it was bad. But along with finding help for him, I felt like I needed to look for ways to deal with how I felt."

Judy Belushi, like Aykroyd, was no stranger to coke. But also like Aykroyd, she was no match for her husband. "I had my phase," she said, "probably around the middle *Saturday Night Live* years. I never thought that stopping cocaine would be a problem for me because I never thought of coke as a big deal. I never bought cocaine, but it was always there. A lot of times I'd say to myself, 'I'm not going to do it,' but then I would end up doing it. By '81, I decided that I really didn't like cocaine. It was too expensive, it was bad for us, and it was hurting our relationship. Those seemed like good reasons. Then I'd say, 'Why am I doing it? I'm going to stop.' A month would go by and I still hadn't stopped. Then one day I was on my way to see the psychiatrist. I had hurt my back, and we didn't have a car. So I called a limousine. And because of my back, I couldn't sit up straight in the car. I had to lie down. So I'm lying in the back of a limousine, looking out the window and watching the skyline of New York go by. I thought to myself, 'I'm going to go see a psychiatrist to talk about how I want to quit doing cocaine. What am I doing? Just stop doing it.' And I did. I know that kind of thinking doesn't work for a lot of people, but that's what happened to me. I just stopped."

Needless to say, Judy Belushi also knew that getting her husband to stop would require a lot more than having him depend only on his willpower, which failed every time he tried to depend on it. "He had seen a psychiatrist briefly," she said. "And there were various doctors who tried to be helpful, a throat doctor in L.A., for example, who understood what was going on and gave suggestions. At one point, I talked to a doctor about putting John into an institution. I figured John would pass out at some point, and that would be the time to get him into drug rehab. I actually had three doctors sign something to make that happen. I had the three doctors ready. And when he finally came home and did pass out, I just, you know, I just couldn't do it. On one hand, I wish I had had another chance. But I don't know that it would have changed anything. At the time, it seemed wrong to have someone just fall asleep, and then have people come in and take him away. It just seemed so mean. Now, of course, I wish I could have at least tried."

It didn't help her resolve that Belushi would come home filled with remorse, and say to her, "I don't want to do this anymore. I have to stop."

"He would say that before he went to sleep, and automatically I would feel that I couldn't go through with it," she said. "So we didn't do the doctor thing. And by the way, the doctors weren't encouraging me to do it either. They said they were *willing* to do it, and all that did was make me feel more alone, trying to come to this difficult decision by myself."

Belushi, naturally, didn't make things easier. Like a lot of cunning addicts, he would forget all about his remorse from the night before to concentrate on convincing his wife the following morning that his drug problem maybe wasn't as bad as she made it out to be. He told her many times that he was fine, despite all evidence to the contrary.

"He looked at me the way he could look at me," she said, "and he said, 'I've only done it one time. Can't we just overlook that?'

"I said, 'Nope.'

"He said, 'No motorcycle?'

"And I said, 'Right. No motorcycle.'"

And because she had stopped doing cocaine, it gave her more time in the shrink's office to pound away at her husband's drug habits. "I would sit there and give the psychiatrist the whole thing: 'My husband does this. My husband does that. I'm so worried. I don't know what to do.'

"And the psychiatrist said, 'Well, the first thing you need to do is think about yourself. You're like an overworked mother. There's only so much you can do for him. You're not thinking of yourself. You need to stop and take some time for yourself.'"

Belushi didn't like that his wife was seeing a shrink. According to Bob Woodward's book *Wired*, Belushi was angry that any doctor might "have the power to intrude on his relationship with Judy."

Woodward even recounted Belushi's saying to Aykroyd, "Ah, shit, you know her shrink is telling her yarns about me, telling her stories, telling her that I'm no good for her, telling her that I have a repetitious bent on partying and getting high and stuff."

According to Judy, there was ultimately only one issue in the psychiatrist's office that mattered. "The psychiatrist asked me, 'What's the one thing that worries you most about John right now?'

"And I said, 'I'm afraid that he's going to die.'"

The Belushis traveled to Los Angeles together in January 1982. John needed to be on the West Coast because of *Noble Rot*, a movie script he had been working on with Don Novello, his friend from *Saturday Night Live* who had created the character of Father Guido Sarducci. And Judy wanted to be with her husband so they could celebrate her birthday together on January 7. She also felt she should be there to somehow watch over him and keep him out of trouble. There was a time, she said, when she was very good at keeping her husband away from the hangers-on she deemed undesirable.

"I used to be pretty good at getting rid of people," she said. "I'm not very big, but I seem to frighten people. I remember one time we were backstage with the comedian Sam Kinison, and somebody kept bothering him. I took the person by the hand, and I said, 'Okay, I think you've had enough time with Sam, and now you should leave the dressing room.' I just sort of walked the person to the door and he left. And Sam said, 'Wow, am I glad you did that.'"

If Belushi was glad to have his wife act as a buffer in Los Angeles, he sure didn't show it. In fact, she said, he barely stayed in one place long enough for her to push others out of the way.

"It was obvious that he was doing a lot of drugs," she said. "He knew I wasn't happy. There was tension between us, and he would just up and sort of run from me. He would just go out and be gone. And because I was no longer getting high, I started to see how pissed off he was that I had stopped. It was not a good time. We weren't getting along.

"But at the same time," she said, "he'd give me that whole routine of 'I'm sorry. I know I've been a jerk. I know why you're worried. I know what's going on. I don't want you to worry. I'm going to be okay. I just have to finish the script.'

"There was definitely the combination of having a lot of pressure from work, wanting to get it done, and taking the drugs to do it," she said. "And then he'd be afraid to stop because then maybe he wouldn't finish."

The merry-go-round in his head led to the inevitable self-doubt that sooner or later creeps into the minds of all drug addicts. "When John did drugs," said Judy, "he would eventually question whether he had any talent without the drugs. The first time he said that I couldn't believe he would think that way. I would tell him, 'It's a drug. It doesn't give you anything.'"

Except maybe the desire for more drugs.

On their next trip to Los Angeles together, in February, Belushi casually mentioned the word *heroin* to his wife. She said the subject seemed to come out of left field.

"He said, 'I know what you're worried about. You think I'm doing heroin.'

"This surprised me," she said, "because I didn't think he was doing heroin. I was shocked he would say that. It startled me. I said, 'Why would you say that?'

"He said, 'Because I think you've been so worried.'

"I said, 'Okay, so are you?'

"And he said no. Then he told me about a time, many years before, when he tried heroin. He didn't like needles. He didn't like to have shots. He never wanted to give blood," she said. "But he started talking about the time in the late seventies when he had an accident and hurt his knee. He was in the hospital and they had given him morphine and Demerol. Those kinds of drugs made him nasty and really angry and volatile. So he told me that when he got out of the hospital, he snorted some heroin. He said he had only done a little, but he didn't like it and hadn't done it since. And he promised me, right then in Los Angeles, that he would never think of doing heroin again. He said, 'You don't have to worry about it.'

"I returned to New York," she said, "and I left him in Los Angeles with his promise."

Judy Belushi never knew whether her husband was keeping his promise in L.A. In a way, it was probably easier on her that she didn't know. Just thinking about it made her nervous. "Of course, I was nervous," she said. "If he called me regularly, that would be an indication that things with him were normal. Or what I called normal, which would mean a non-drug issue, like the problems he was having getting *Noble Rot* off the ground. If they were those kinds of problems, he would call me several times a day, and every night. But when he was out doing a lot of drugs, I might not hear from him for a day, or even days."

Novello hadn't heard from Belushi in a few days, and they were in Los Angeles together, supposedly trying to finish *Noble Rot*. By the time Belushi finally met up with his co-writer, on Monday, February 22, at the famous Sunset Boulevard breakfast hangout Schwab's Drug Store, he was already desperate on a number of levels. He desperately wanted the important businesspeople in his life—his manager, Bernie Brillstein; his agent, Michael Ovitz; and the then head of Paramount Pictures, Michael Eisner—to all sign off on how wonderfully funny *Noble Rot* would be as a movie.

And he desperately wanted more drugs.

If there were businessmen from New Jersey and a handful of dealers in New York who could all combine to keep Belushi happy, there was easily double the number in L.A., where the Hollywood night owls and sycophants could all smell him coming from three thousand miles away. Unlike the boys in Jersey, these people were already in Hollywood, and of Hollywood. Even if they had no careers, they had phone books filled with the names of those who did. The coke whores of the early eighties were an industry unto themselves in Hollywood, and whenever Belushi blew into town, he was like their Uncle Sugar from New York. He came loaded with a cash per diem that the studio or his manager gave him, and they were there, breathlessly waiting to take it all from him. They loved him, and he loved their coke. It was the perfect relationship.

"It was the roaring eighties," said Aykroyd. "Sunset Strip was reborn again. You could go into the Rainbow Room and there were dealers and coke everywhere. And there's a beautiful woman sitting next to you, and you think, 'Wow, there might be a chance that she will have sex with me, if I get drugs for her.' A lot of people used to think that way. You wouldn't be getting it for yourself. You'd be getting it for her! In fact, cocaine is the worst thing for sex. It's a total anti-aphrodisiac. So is Ecstasy. It doesn't free women or men up for sex. It just makes everyone talk more."

Unfortunately, the words Belushi needed to hear and the approval he desperately wanted from the other important L.A. people in his life was proving a lot harder to come by. Belushi returned to New York on Tuesday, February 23, and all he received over the next two days was bad news and more bad news. Brillstein didn't like the script. Ovitz didn't like the script. Eisner didn't like the script. In fact, nobody seemed to like *Noble Rot*. Most people who read it actually came away hating it, even if they didn't want to come right out and say so to Belushi. They loved him, too, just like the coke whores. And because he loved their money, and the access they gave him to continue being famous, it was important for all sides that the relationships remain intact.

And that might have happened, had it not been for the drugs.

"He didn't look good. He was tired. And he was still doing drugs" was how Judy Belushi described her husband after he got back from L.A. According to Woodward's book, she was so suspicious of his drug use in California that she took the clothes he brought back from his trip and burned all of them in the fireplace.

By Friday, February 26, Belushi was fairly out of his mind over the negative reaction to his work. He argued with Brillstein. He fired and rehired Ovitz. And he tried to get Eisner to agree to meet him the following Monday in Los Angeles, at the Pico-Burnside Baths, or the *schvitz*, as the old-timers called it, that place where men go to sit in steam rooms and sweat off at least some of their unsightly weight gain.

Aykroyd thought it was a very bad idea for Belushi to be going back to L.A. for any reason, especially to discuss a script, which was just as easy to do on the phone. And he told Belushi as much, late that Friday night at a downtown New York bar. In *Wired*, Bob Woodward quotes Aykroyd saying to his friend, "It's only one script. . . . Take two weeks off. That's what I do as a writer."

Aykroyd even offered to help Belushi with a rewrite of *Noble Rot*. He reminded Belushi that writers suffer rejection all the time. It goes with the turf. Writing is rewriting, and the best writers have to do it just like the rookies. And Belushi, after all, was a rookie writer. That's why Aykroyd felt his friend would be better off going to Martha's Vineyard for a couple of weeks to cool out. Then, with a little time under his belt, he could attack the script again, with or without his *Blues Brothers* partner.

Trying to talk Belushi out of going to Los Angeles was something Aykroyd had done more than once. "Dan and I had lots of conversations over the years where we'd say to each other, 'He's doing it again. What are we going to do?'" recalled Judy. "One time they took a big cross-country drive. They were in the car together for a few days. Totally clean. And John would say, 'Wow, am I glad not to be doing that anymore.'"

Belushi felt no such gratitude that Friday night as Aykroyd talked to him at the bar. For one thing, he was too stoned to hear much of anything. And it was still only the middle of the night. There were still a couple of hours to go before sunup.

The Belushi merry-go-round cranked up again the next night, Saturday, February 27, when he and his wife met Michael and Carol Klenfner for a quick, post–*Saturday Night Live* dinner at Sabor, a Cuban restaurant on Cornelia Street. The Klenfners were music industry fixtures in New York. She was a well-known publicist, and he was an industry veteran who knew everyone in the business and had close ties to virtually every important record executive in the world. Klenfner had successfully promoted the *Blues Brothers* album and Belushi was the godfather of the Klenfners' four-year-old daughter, Kate.

After dinner, the two couples piled into Klenfner's 1980 Buick Century and headed uptown to the Ziegfeld Theater to see the last showing of the new movie *Quest for Fire*. It was obvious to Judy Belushi that her husband was more interested in finding cocaine than he was in watching a movie about prehistoric cavemen.

"In the middle of the movie," she said, "he jumped up and said, 'I'm going to go to the bathroom.' And he didn't come back. I started thinking, 'He's been gone too long. He's probably looking for drugs.' I thought about going home, and I thought about looking for him. And then I realized that New York is a big place."

She did get up from her seat to go looking for him in the theater, and found him outside, sitting alone in the Ziegfeld courtyard on West Fifty-fourth Street. "He was so on edge," she said. "He was into his drug thing, and he was talking about having to go back to Los Angeles to finish the project. He said, 'I have to go back. I need to do more writing.'

"I said, 'Why can't Don Novello come here?'

"And he said, 'No, I have to go there.' I don't remember anything else he said out there in the courtyard. I just remember watching him, realizing that he had a much better support system in New York than he did in Los Angeles."

After the movie, the Belushis and the Klenfners went back downtown to the Odeon, a hip Tribeca restaurant on West Broadway. They downed a quick second dinner, and as Michael Klenfner recalled it, "John started peeing outside on the street. Somebody yelled to him from a car. I don't remember the exact comment, but it was very sad, something to the effect of, 'It's really a shame that John Belushi has to pee outside.'

"He was uncontrollable that night," said Klenfner. "When Belushi was good, he was oh so good. A warm, loving, sweet, nice brother. But then when he became bad, he was miserable to be around. Instead of the four of us going out as two couples, I felt like the three of us were put into roles we didn't want to be in. Suddenly, we were like his security chief, his doctor, and his shrink. We had eaten the same dinner, and now he had to be watched outside while he peed on the wall of the Odeon. In a strange way, peeing outside for him at that point was a better alternative than walking back inside to use the bathroom. I pictured him getting to the bar and thirty people would be grabbing him for a pop of cocaine, and another drink. It was like a catch-22. Keith and Brian McNally, the two brothers who owned the Odeon, were probably just as happy that he didn't come back inside to pee."

From the Odeon, the Klenfners and the Belushis went to another SoHo hangout, the Green Street Restaurant, where a few *Saturday Night Live* cast members were winding down at a post-show party.

"The Green Street Restaurant is not one of the most comfortable places for a party," said Klenfner. "It's not wide. It's fine if you're sitting for dinner, but it's terrible for a party because it's long and narrow, and crowded when people are forced to stand. And as I recall, there was no place to stand that night. Remember, this was our Saturday night, too. I'm with my wife, and John is with Judy, not some girl he just picked up in the street. I had hoped to end the evening on an up tick, where maybe we have a last cappuccino somewhere, and we all smile and hug and kiss and say good night."

That is not exactly what happened. Carol Klenfner had had enough, and she went home. Belushi sent his wife home in a taxi.

"It was close to four in the morning, and I wanted him to come home with me," said Judy. "I said, 'Why don't you come home?'

"And he said, 'No, I don't want to go home.'

"I said, 'Well, I'm going home.' I kissed him good-bye, and I got into the cab. I was really pissed off. And as I turned around in the cab, I saw him leaning up against the building. He was looking at me, and he gave me a little wave."

Belushi kept his friend Klenfner out until dawn. All Belushi cared about was finding more drugs.

"In retrospect," said Klenfner, "he was always looking for drugs. Drugs used to find him, like a magnet. I'm not copping out about my own behavior that night, but I wasn't getting really high because I was driving my car. I'm fanatical about my car. I was more inclined to say, 'Get your fucking fingerprints off the dashboard,' than ask for another hit of blow. We drove around plenty that night, and the thing I thought about most was getting my car washed."

By sunrise, they were on East Tenth Street, and Belushi was banging on the door of the Tenth Street Russian & Turkish Baths, New York's oldest and most famous *schvitz*. Klenfner was a regular at the *schvitz*, and Belushi had accompanied him there on numerous occasions.

According to Klenfner, Belushi always tried to be on his best behavior at the *schvitz*. "He never wanted to look like a schmuck at the *schvitz*," was how Klenfner put it. "Wiseguys used to hang out there, and I would tell John, 'You can fuck around, but don't fuck around too much because these are guys you don't want to have to start apologizing to.'"

But there were no wiseguys at the *schvitz* that morning. Only Jake, the custodian, was there, and he hadn't awakened yet. Belushi's banging got him up. "Jake was a concentration camp survivor with a number on his arm," said Klenfner. "Jake liked John. Jake liked that he was a celebrity. Jake used to love to talk to John. So he opened the place for us. I got undressed. Belushi got undressed. And we went into the steam room. I think I threw an extra bucket of water or two into the oven to make it very hot. I was hoping that John would just fall asleep, and he did. He left the steam room, covered himself with a towel, sat down in a chair, and the next thing I heard was his snoring. Jake and I then got him down on a bed, threw a few blankets on him, said good night, and I went home. I left him at the *schvitz*, fast asleep. He must have stayed there for hours."

Even after he woke up, on Sunday, February 28, Belushi still didn't feel like going home. He had an afternoon flight booked to L.A., and he didn't want to hear his wife telling him again not to go. He didn't want to hear it again from Aykroyd either, so he chose not to call him. What he did do, according to Woodward's book, was borrow money at the *schvitz* so he could buy more cocaine. Looking good at the *schvitz* was obviously no longer the point. Getting high was all that mattered.

"He had asked me to pack for him," Judy Belushi said. "And I put, like, three things in his suitcase. I mean, I just gave him a little more than a change of clothes. I didn't want him to go, but if he was going to go, I wanted him back quickly. So I packed light, even though I knew he could obviously buy more clothes in Los Angeles."

She had a real bad feeling about her husband's trip. He had been back and forth many times, but she was especially fearful this time. "For whatever reason," she said, "he always seemed to have more problems with drugs in L.A. Maybe because we lived in New York we had more time. We had a home in New York, a home base, and with it a structure and a commitment. He was committed to our marriage, but drugs certainly made it difficult. We had some bad times, and somehow we got through them. But I felt something different about this trip. I mean, I don't know. Maybe it was a premonition."

Belushi called his wife later that day. He said he was sending someone to the apartment to pick up his bag. They both knew he couldn't face her. But that didn't stop her from making one last attempt on the phone to get him to change his mind. "I said, 'Why are you going back?'

"He said, 'I have to go back. I'll only be a few days.'"

On Monday, March 1, Michael Eisner drove west from his office at Paramount to meet Belushi at his hotel, the Chateau Marmont, just off Sunset, where he was encamped in his favorite bungalow, number three. The meeting had been changed to the Chateau after Belushi found out that the Pico-Burnside Baths were closed on Mondays. Woodward's book points out that Eisner was very relieved that he wouldn't have to conduct a business meeting draped in a towel.

This time Eisner pulled no punches with Belushi and told him the script to *Noble Rot* was terrible. But the studio executive did come with an alternate plan. Paramount already owned another property, something called *National Lampoon's The Joy of Sex, a Dirty Love Story.* The story was about a person's sexual initiation at various stages of life, from a baby in a diaper to an old man. Eisner felt Belushi would be perfect. He could play all the characters. Penny Marshall would direct. She was a big television star, and this would mark her debut as a film director. All Belushi had to do was forget about *Noble Rot* for now, and make *Joy of Sex* instead.

Belushi said he'd think about it. But in fact he had other ideas that day, and they had nothing to do with the movies.

It was after his meeting with Eisner that Belushi visited April Milstead, one of his Hollywood drug friends. According to Woodward he had but one request: heroin. Milstead didn't have any in her possession, but she knew someone who did. That person was Cathy Evelyn Smith. Neither Aykroyd nor Judy Belushi nor even Klenfner had ever heard of Ms. Smith, this thirty-five-year-old Canadian-born woman who had, in no special order, lived with Gordon Lightfoot, driven a tour bus for Hoyt Axton, slept with no less than three members of The Band—Levon Helm, Rick Danko, and Richard Manuel—and hung out with the Rolling Stones. She was also a heroin addict who dealt drugs as a way to feed her habit.

Belushi had met Smith back in the early days of *Saturday Night Live*, during her Gordon Lightfoot years. But he had not seen her again until the night of Monday, March 1, when she arrived at Milstead's apartment on Martel Street, in Hollywood. Belushi was already there, waiting for her. And she did not come empty-handed. After all the obligatory greetings, Cathy Evelyn Smith proceeded to shoot up Belushi with his first ever "speedball," a mixture of cocaine and heroin.

Later that night, when the party moved back to Belushi's bungalow, Smith gave Belushi a second shot, this time just straight cocaine, followed by a third shot, also cocaine. Belushi's last run had begun in dead earnest.

But even he knew he had to keep up appearances where his wife was concerned. During one of their phone conversations that week, he told her that he was sleeping a lot in L.A., and feeling much better for it. He even apologized for his behavior in New York. But she could see right through his remorse, all the way to the drugs, to the elephant that sat in whatever room Belushi was in. She even told him he was out of control, and like always he told her not to worry.

"Then he called me again," she recalled, "and he said, 'You're not going to believe what they want me to do. They want me to wear a diaper in a movie I don't even want to do.' He sounded really hurt by it. He said, 'I don't want to wear a diaper.' Then he said, 'I love you.' Then he hung up."

For obvious reasons, he never mentioned Cathy Smith. Aykroyd has a name for Smith. He calls her "the dark angel from the reaper."

"John called me on the phone that week, and he told me he was hanging out with this Canadian girl. He said he liked her. He thought she was cool. He said I'd like her," said Aykroyd. "I wish I had met her and seen what she was doing. I know I would've said, 'You can't do this to the guy. He's overweight. He smokes cigarettes. The lungs aren't strong.' I mean, you shouldn't ever be hitting anyone with a speedball. And playing with needles? I mean, if I had seen that, she would've gotten the same treatment as everyone else. I would have told her, 'If you want to be friends with this man, you can't bring this around.' That was our standard talk to everyone."

But Aykroyd wasn't there to tell anybody anything. The protective ring he had formed around Belushi on Martha's Vineyard was useless in Los Angeles. His mission from God to protect his friend from himself had stalled, leaving God to go it alone against Belushi, who was no longer afraid of needles; Smith, his new supplier; Milstead, who had introduced the two and took her finder's fee in drugs; or Milstead's live-in boyfriend, Charlie Pearson.

On Tuesday morning, March 2, this seemingly unlikely foursome, Belushi's cartel of choice, all had breakfast together at Duke's, a West Hollywood hangout on Santa Monica Boulevard. Exactly what they talked about at the table is not known. It is probably safe to assume, however, that the subject of God never came up.

Later that day, Belushi shot more cocaine with Smith, and then wound up holding court that night at On the Rox, the private club above the Roxy nightclub on Sunset. Michael Eisner came to see Belushi at On the Rox. He brought along his wife, Jane, and his closest studio colleague, Jeffrey Katzenberg. They were on a mission, too, and it involved neither God nor drugs. All they wanted to do was seal the deal on the *Joy of Sex* movie. What they got in return was an unnerving interaction with Belushi and a feeling that he had become a pathetic caricature of himself. In *Wired*, Woodward quoted Jane Eisner as saying, "I feel as though I've just seen *Sunset Boulevard*," a reference that compared Belushi to the famous pathetic lead character played by Gloria Swanson.

On Wednesday, March 3, Belushi went into hiding. For a while, he cooped himself up with Milstead, Pearson, and Smith at Milstead's apartment on Martel. Then he gave them the slip and went to Westwood. Bernie Brillstein tried to reach him and couldn't. Belushi's trainer and friend Bill Wallace looked all over town for him that day, but couldn't find him. Wallace instructed everyone he spoke with that day not to give Belushi any money, regardless of his reasons for wanting it. Wallace had been working out with Belushi, running him through drills that included kickboxing and martial arts. But Wallace knew his client well enough to know that he hadn't pulled a disappearing act so he could continue exercising in private. Wallace knew that Belushi was in big trouble.

Klenfner knew it, too, all the way back in New York. "I had a friend named Dino Barbis," said Klenfner. "Dino's wife, Sue, worked at the Chateau Marmont, in reservations. She had very good knowledge of the comings and goings of everybody there, and she knew that Belushi was my friend. She was calling me that week and saying there were people coming in and out of John's bungalow that she had never seen before. I couldn't say, 'All right, throw them out.' How could I? I had no idea who they were. One of them was Cathy Smith. Sue didn't know her name then, but she described her as 'not very attractive.' But that was all she said."

Klenfner did talk to Aykroyd and Judy Belushi about the possibility of at least one of them going out to Los Angeles to bring Belushi home. Aykroyd was deemed the most likely candidate. He wanted to go, but he was up to his eyeballs in New York trying to write *Ghostbusters,* a movie about three unemployed parapsychology professors who set up shop as a unique ghost removal service. Columbia Pictures was developing the project as a starring vehicle for Aykroyd, Belushi, and Eddie Murphy.

"I got a very slurred phone call from him on the answering machine," said Aykroyd. "He sounded really fucked up. I was in the middle of writing. I thought, 'Okay, I'm going to finish writing this quarter of the *Ghostbusters* script.' I was on a run, which for a writer is an important thing, and I figured that if I could just get to this certain page in the script, then I'd go out there to get him.'"

But that plan was scrapped on Thursday, March 4, when Belushi left a message with his wife saying he would be on the red-eye that night. "In my mind," she said, "I was waiting for him to come home. I thought he'd be home the next morning."

Instead of preparing to leave Los Angeles, Belushi spent part of his day badgering Brillstein to give him $1,500. According to Woodward's book, Belushi had his eye on a certain guitar and said he needed the money to buy it. Brillstein didn't believe him, and yet he gave him the money anyway. Belushi took the cash to Milstead's. Then he went to the Beverly Hills home of his writer friend Nelson Lyon, where he proceeded to shoot more cocaine. Needless to say, Belushi never got on the plane. Nevertheless, his wife sat up in New York and thought about their future.

"One of the issues I was dealing with at that very time was children. I was thinking that kids would be a good thing for us," she said. "We were never in the same place at the same time around that issue. Either I didn't want to have a baby when he wanted one, or I wanted one and he didn't. We were living a fast life. I don't mean regarding drugs. But life was on a fast track. His career was the big thing. He needed it, and I was happy to be a supporter.

"We used to joke that if we ever had a baby, it would have a big belly and skinny legs," she said. "We talked about names. We walked around the issue periodically, but we never really got down to it. He once said something very telling. He said, 'I like being the only child.' He was childlike, and he took a lot of care. But he would have been a great father. He would have been a terrible father if he were off doing drugs. But he was great with kids."

She even did the math. "I thought, 'I'm thirty-one. He's thirty-three. Maybe it's time.' Kids are not something you can think about forever. So, I was kind of throwing that around, literally thinking through what I wanted to talk to him about when he came home, that maybe children should be in our future. I remember lying on the couch watching television and thinking about what I wanted to talk to him about. I wasn't 100 percent sure that I wanted a child, but I wanted to talk about it. I probably did want one, and I wanted that to become a dialogue. I wanted us to think about it and talk about it. I'm not saying I was ready to just lay it all on him when he came home, but I wanted it out in the open, at least get him to start thinking about it."

But the only thing on Belushi's mind in Los Angeles was keeping the party going. He hung out for a while that night at On the Rox with actors Robert De Niro, Harry Dean Stanton, and the club's owner, music producer Lou Adler. De Niro was also staying at the Chateau Marmont, and Belushi talked to him about the two meeting later at his bungalow.

Belushi snorted more cocaine at On the Rox, then left with Smith and Nelson Lyon. On their way back to the Chateau, Belushi threw up. Woodward quoted Belushi as blaming his nausea on some bad food he might have eaten at the Rainbow, another hangout across the alley from On the Rox. Belushi vomited again in his bathroom at the bungalow, and then left Lyon to hold down the fort while he and Smith went out again, presumably to score more drugs.

Comedian Robin Williams stopped by Belushi's bungalow, and

waited with Lyon for Belushi to return. Woodward reported that Williams didn't like the vibe in the bungalow and felt especially uncomfortable around Smith and Lyon, so he left. De Niro eventually got there, but he didn't stay long either. Then, finally, Lyon left.

Now Smith and Belushi were alone. He asked her for one more speedball, and she was only too happy to oblige. She also gave herself a shot. Then they showered together, but did not have sex. According to Woodward's book, Smith wanted sex, but Belushi had no desire whatsoever. The speedball had seen to that. Belushi said he was chilly, and she helped him get under the covers. Then he seemed to be having trouble breathing, and she gave him water. She asked if he was hungry, and he mumbled he wasn't. She ordered room service for herself and signed his name. Then, at 10:15 in the morning, on Friday, March 5, she left the Chateau to go to one of her favorite bars on Santa Monica Boulevard. The last thing she remembered hearing was the sound of Belushi snoring.

Bill Wallace got to the bungalow a little before noon and found Belushi lying motionless on his side. He tried waking him. There was no response. Then he tried CPR. Nothing. Although Wallace didn't want to believe it, he knew Belushi was dead. Wallace later told Woodward that he pounded Belushi's barrel chest, and wailed, "You dumb son of a bitch! You dumb son of a bitch! You dumb son of a bitch!"

Klenfner was sitting in Jimmy Ienner's office at Millennium Records, on West Fifty-seventh Street, when he received an urgent message to call Sue Barbis at the Chateau Marmont.

"She said, 'Michael, five minutes ago the manager of the hotel called the LAPD because John is not moving. I think he's dead.'

"I said, 'What?'

"She said, 'There was no movement when the manager went in, and I was right behind him. I didn't walk completely into the room, but he didn't look good to me.'"

Klenfner's motorcycle was parked on the street. He quickly got on it and raced downtown to Belushi's apartment on Morton Street. In that moment, all he could think about was Judy.

Aykroyd had just written a line of dialogue for Belushi's character in *Ghostbusters* when his phone rang. It was Bernie Brillstein calling from L.A. "He said, 'He's gone, pal. He's gone. He's gone.' He was crying," Aykroyd said. "He said, 'I guess it was the drugs.' How? How? We all wanted to know how? You don't think that will ever happen. The people doing it don't think it will ever happen. Friends think, 'Oh, he's fucked up. We'll get him into rehab. He'll clean up. It's just a matter of time, but I have my own life, and I've got to do this and that. You don't think that death is coming.

"I got up from my typewriter right away—how about that? I was working on a Royal typewriter back then. That's how old we are now. So I got up and I walked out of the office. I was alone. I don't think our secretary was in. I bolted down to the street. It was a beautiful day in New York. It was clear. The sky was a severe clear sky, blue forever. Just like a spring day. And the headline was already on the street. 'Belushi Dead at 33.' I think it was the *New York Post*. I mean, right there, minutes after Bernie called me. And already they were selling papers. I thought, 'How quickly did all this happen?'"

Aykroyd also wanted to get to Judy, and he did so on foot, all the way from his office at Twenty-third Street and Fifth Avenue to Belushi's apartment on Morton Street. Klenfner was already there when Aykroyd arrived. "You could see the look of resignation on Judy's face right away," said Aykroyd.

"The story of John's last few weeks don't make him appear very loving," said Judy. "But he was a very loving person. He just doesn't come off that way. His behavior was not very likable then, but I loved him through all of it."

"We lost a great genius," said Aykroyd, "and he goes on to immortality and will be remembered like all of these beautiful young people who die when they're young and vibrant and at their peak. We had lots of plans, John and I. I was twenty-nine. He was thirty-three. We were selling millions of records, the movies were successful enough for us to get other jobs. We were building a couple of companies together, but the powders and pills got to him. John was the classic alpha male Albanian American. You couldn't tell someone like him what to do and where to go. He knew we were concerned about him. He knew he was doing wrong. He knew he had to stop. That's what the summer of '81 was all about. When we had him on Martha's Vineyard, we really had him. Once he got back into Manhattan, and then started going to L.A. again, we lost him. He got sucked into that flow.

"What people have to remember," said Aykroyd, "is that we lost a man who was literate, funny and knew all about literature, science, and philosophy. His friends were people like Lauren Bacall and Jim Garrison. He dealt with the highest levels in Hollywood. Usually when I have to talk to a studio, I'll have my agent call the business affairs guy. John was a powerful man. He talked to the studio heads directly. Everyone loved him. They loved receiving calls from him. Everybody who hung out with him had a great time. He was one of these guys who walked into a room and all eyes were on him. He was someone you'd want to run away with. He really was wonderful. He was a lot of fun, but when the drugs and the dark angel entered the picture, the reaper took his life."

Belushi was buried on Tuesday, March 9, at Abel's Hill Cemetery on Martha's Vineyard. Aykroyd dressed for the occasion in a black leather jacket and black jeans. He also led the funeral procession on his motorcycle. Two days later, a memorial service was held for Belushi in New York at the Cathedral Church of Saint John the Divine, on Amsterdam Avenue. There were one thousand people inside the church, mostly friends, family, and invited guests. And yet Judy Belushi was never more touched than when she exited the building following the service and found that some of her neighbors from Morton Street had come uptown to pay their respects by standing outside on the street.

"As I got into the limo," she said, "I saw these three ladies who were always on our block walking their dogs. And I remember looking over, and they were crying."

Dan Aykroyd doesn't cry over what might have been, but he remains haunted, even to this day, that he didn't just drop everything and go to Los Angeles to bring his friend home. "I'll always feel guilty that I didn't get a hold of him, that I didn't get out there fast enough," he said. "It's bothered me all these years. Really, really bothered me."

But Aykroyd also knows that drug addicts like Belushi won't accept help from anyone until they themselves are entirely ready and willing to receive it.

"Alex Taylor [singer James Taylor's older brother] was a wonderful friend of mine, and a cocaine addict," said Aykroyd. "I gave him shit about it a week or two before he died of a cocaine-alcohol mix. I really gave it to him.

"I also gave the talk to River Phoenix," said Aykroyd. "He came to my farm the summer before he died in 1993. He brought his girlfriend, Samantha Mathis, and we had a wonderful time. No drugs. We just drank red wine and ate steaks and chicken. He was a vegetarian, and I was eating a lot of steak. And he used to get on me about it. He was a great teaser. He really would put you in your place. He was a brilliant guy. I tried to warn him, but the drugs got him, too. I'll never forget how small he looked in his little coffin, diminished, like a mouse in a matchbox.

"I even gave Chris Farley the talk," said Aykroyd. "I said, 'You don't want to emulate John. You don't want to die at thirty-three.' But he didn't listen either. People are captains of their own ships. But I'll still give the talk today when I think that someone I love is in danger."

Having survived those years, Aykroyd feels well beyond any danger regarding himself. But he's also smart enough to know that there are no free passes in this life.

"That's why I ride my bike a little slower now," he said.

Orson Welles

May 6, 1915–October 10, 1985

THERE WAS ALWAYS SOMETHING DIFFERENT ABOUT THE PROSTITUTES IN FRONT of the Bank of America branch at Ogden and Sunset. If you didn't know any better, you might think they were bank customers, or tellers on a cigarette break. There were tall ones, squat ones, muscular ones, and some that were painfully thin. They were black, white, and Asian, a few strikingly beautiful, and others who were worn, weathered, and close to middle age. But they all had their own individual styles and a collective fashion sense that set them far apart from their hiked-up, hot pants–wearing counterparts, those stereotypical Hugh Grant–beckoning sidestreet hookers who patrolled other areas of Hollywood in the 1980s.

The B-of-A hookers seemed to have class. They wore two-piece jogging suits, and gray business suits, and skirts below their knees. They had ponytails and pageboy cuts, and leather pocketbooks with shoulder straps. And when they walked, which wasn't often, on account of the sheer volume of men in their BMWs and Chevy Camaros who sensed they'd found heaven on earth on Ogden, they walked east on Sunset. But never more than a few blocks. They might get past Genesee and then Spaulding, to the next block, Stanley, but that was it. For these gals, the outermost boundary was the old Screen Actors Guild building at the corner of Stanley and Sunset. Stanley was the dividing line. Venture east of Stanley and you're at the 7-Eleven and the beginning of a much seedier Hollywood.

Perhaps no one in the area was more aware of the neighborhood's unspoken sociological landmarks than Orson Welles. He lived on Stanley, just north of Sunset, in an elegantly faded three-story Tara-like mini-mansion owned by his longtime Croatian companion, Oja (pronounced Oya) Kordar. Welles even had a name for the area. He called it "the suburbs of the cinema."

"I loved that line," remembered Welles's cameraman and close friend Gary Graver. "We'd be sitting in front of the fireplace, which we had going all the time, even when it was hot outside, and he'd say, 'Gary, here we are, you and I, two very talented men, living in the heart of Hollywood but working in the suburbs of the cinema.' Orson was always coming out with lines like that."

Graver's relationship with Welles dates back to the late sixties. The young cameraman had just returned to Los Angeles after serving a tour of duty with the navy in Vietnam, and he was having breakfast at Schwab's Drug Store on Sunset. Schwab's was within easy walking distance from Stanley in a town where no one walked except the hookers.

"I had been making horror movies and motorcycle pictures, which passed for trendy stuff at the time," said Graver. "But down deep I was a snob. I preferred foreign films, and better directors. So I'm sitting at Schwab's and someone says that Orson Welles is in town. I figured he would be staying at the Beverly Hills Hotel, so I went to the pay phone in the back of Schwab's and I called the hotel. Not only was he there, but he answered his own phone. I told him who I was, and said that I wanted to work with him. I offered my services as a cameraman.

"He said, 'I can't talk to you now. I'm going to New York.' I figured he was just brushing me off, so I went home," said Graver. "When I walked in the door, my phone was ringing. It was Orson. He said, 'Gary, get over here right away. I've got to talk to you.'"

Graver immediately left his San Fernando Valley house and drove back over the hill to the Beverly Hills Hotel. Welles was encamped in one of the hotel's famed bungalows. "We talked for about thirty minutes or so," said Graver, "and he suddenly said, 'You know, I've been looking for an American cameraman, and you're the second cameraman in my life who ever called me up and said they wanted to work with me.' He said the first one was Gregg Toland, who shot *Citizen Kane*. 'And now you,' he said."

According to Graver, Welles then looked out his window and appeared startled by something he saw. "He quickly grabbed me by the back of my shirt and pushed me to the floor of the bungalow," recalled Graver. "He put his big hand on me and kept me on the floor. I thought, 'God, this is weird. Here's this huge guy, and he's holding me down on the floor.'

"Finally, we got up and he was looking out the window. I said, 'What's wrong?'

"And he said, 'God, it's Ruth Gordon, the actress. If I let her in, she'll talk forever.'"

Only when Gordon, who was small for most women and easily one fourth the size of Welles, was safely past the bungalow did he release his grip on Graver. But Welles never released his hold. "He became like a father to me," said Graver. "I saw him practically every day for the next fifteen years."

And those were mostly good days for Welles, according to Graver, who insisted that the great director, once hailed as a film genius and later shunned by the Hollywood studio system, did not go into his advancing years a bitter man. "Quite the contrary," said Graver. "He was happy professionally, and romantically."

Welles had been married three times, and then spent the last twenty years of his life living with Kordar on Stanley. He never married her because his third wife, Paola Mori, a Catholic, refused to grant him a divorce. Paola was Mrs. Orson Welles until the day he died, living in a house in Las Vegas that was paid for with his money and owned outright by him during the entire time she resided there.

Welles never minded that he was living rent-free in Kordar's house. He owned the one house in Vegas, and he figured owning one house was enough. On the face of it, it seemed like a screwy arrangement all the way around, but Graver said it worked just fine for Welles. He used his own money to build a heated pool there, which he swam in practically every day. He had a kitchen filled with vitamins and he was religious about his daily regimen. He wrote nearly every day in that house. Graver constantly shot film of him in that house. And Welles edited their work in the garage. And he did it all with money in his pocket and a continuing stream of money coming in.

"There was always money," said Graver. "He used to show me a stack of credit cards. He had a SAG pension. He had the greatest voice and was always in demand for voice-overs and radio stuff. He performed classic storytelling on Japanese radio and for European countries. He could always make a good living because of his voice. And he was getting five hundred thousand a year plus residuals for doing

Gallo wine commercials. He never stopped working. He was doing good and, more important, he was feeling good."

And when he wasn't working on one side of the camera or the other, he was sitting at a table in that house on Stanley performing magic tricks. Welles, who toiled for years on a script he called *The Magic Show*, was the kind of magician who would do tricks for anyone in the house who agreed to sit still long enough to want to be fooled. And that group of willing participants mostly included Graver, Welles's driver Fred Gillette, Kordar, her nephew Sasha, who lived upstairs on the third floor, and Allessandro Tosca, an Italian prince who lived a few blocks away and made a mediocre living working as Welles's production manager.

"Orson did illusions and a lot of mental tricks," said Graver, "and we shot footage periodically over the years for *The Magic Show*. If he was appearing on *The Merv Griffin Show*, or *The Tonight Show Starring Johnny Carson*, he'd want to show off his skills as a magician. I would sometimes appear in the audience as a stooge. Or else I'd be backstage as his assistant. We'd have something gimmicked up and planned. He'd plant something in my pocket and then he'd fish it out in front of the audience. Naturally, they would be surprised, along with either Merv or Johnny, and Orson would be hailed as a great magician. I did everything with him. I was more than just his cameraman. We were like best friends. I traveled with them a lot, with Orson and Oja. We lived in hotels all throughout Europe—Spain, France, Belgium, and England. I drove the car around Europe. I made the coffee. I assisted him with everything."

Welles's routine by the early fall of 1985 was comfortable and fairly simple: swimming, magic tricks, and working on his movies during the day, followed by dinner at Ma Maison almost every night.

Ma Maison at one time was the hottest restaurant in Los Angeles. What the world knows today as "California cuisine" was in fact born in the kitchen at Ma Maison in the late 1970s. Wolfgang Puck, who was largely credited with inventing this new style of cooking, was the head chef at Ma Maison until he left to open Spago in 1982. Most celebrities followed him to Spago, but not Welles. He often had two meals a day at Ma Maison, mostly out of loyalty to the restaurant's owner, Patrick Terrail.

Terrail never fully recovered from the loss of Puck, who went on to become a superstar in the food world. And still it never stopped

Welles from his Ma Maison routine. Terrail was so grateful for the support that he purposely never told Welles that a new office building would soon replace Ma Maison on Melrose Avenue. Terrail did eventually move his restaurant into a nearby hotel, but even he knew that this was a temporary and embarrassing final stop before the inevitable oblivion.

In Welles's case, there was no inkling by him or anyone around him that his own end was near. He had been dieting, but he was still overweight and often short of breath. But for weeks he had been swimming regularly, dieting, trying to stay fit, and acting in and directing the many projects he was moving along in the long and arduous process of making movies without the financial backing of the big Hollywood studios.

One such project was called *The Dreamers*. It was one of the last things Graver did with him. "I went to his house and shot a twenty-minute black-and-white segment of him playing Marcus, an old Jewish man in a top hat," said Graver. "It was a beautiful performance. I shot it against the window in the living room with just two lights. Orson always wanted me to bring all my lights every time. I never knew what he might have wanted next. But he always knew. The script was always ready when I arrived, and Orson was always ready to direct his scenes."

Welles never wanted to be a director for hire, and that deal-breaker remained in place right up to the end. Graver said that the last picture Welles was offered to direct was *Popeye*. Graver said that when Welles passed on the project, he told him, "It just wasn't the material for an Orson Welles movie. I never want to do anything I haven't written. For the rest of my life I'm the author."

But after the writing, acting, directing, and editing, there was always the unenviable and prickly task of raising money. The top hat Welles wore to play Marcus ultimately had to be replaced with another hat, that of the producer.

"He wanted to do *King Lear* as a movie, and he was looking for money to finish *The Dreamers*," said Graver. "About the only thing that disappointed him was when it looked like he'd raised the money for a particular project, and suddenly the money would disappear. The French, for example, looked like they were going to give him the money to do *King Lear* in Europe, and it fell through. So that kind of thing disappointed him. And he was also crushed and hurt if he got a bad write-up or review. He didn't like it if people mocked him. It made him depressed. But otherwise he was in good spirits that week. He may have played old men in the movies, but he really never behaved like one. He was always bouncing around and full of life."

And he was still writing other scripts. One in particular delved into the assassination of Robert F. Kennedy. It was to be called *The Assasin*.

"Orson was fascinated with the Bobby Kennedy assassination," said Graver. "He was not a friend of Kennedy's, but he thought it was an extraordinary story. Orson always believed that Sirhan Sirhan knew a lot more than he was letting on. He would say, 'The guy's a prisoner. He goes before the parole board and he says he doesn't remember anything. It's amazing that the authorities can't get to him so they can find out what really happened.' I believe the *The Assasin* script is still around."

October 7, 1985, was a Monday. Kordar, who had parents in Croatia and was often traveling back and forth to help care for them, was back in Croatia on another of her trips. Only Welles and Kordar's nephew Sasha were staying in the house on Stanley. The plan that day was for Graver to meet Welles at UCLA. The university had given Welles permission to film on an auditorium stage, and he wanted to scout the location. The film was to be a video version of *Julius Caesar*, with Welles playing every role that William Shakespeare had written for his play.

"I came in my car," recalled Graver. "Freddie used his car to drive Orson. Freddie had the funniest looking Buick, with weird windows that were shaped almost like the heart from a deck of cards. I think the car was twenty years old. Orson didn't have a car. He stopped driving in the 1940s. Apparently, he was at this party and some drunk woman asked him for a ride home. He crossed over the railroad tracks in Beverly Hills and hit a bump and the woman fell out. She got up and immediately threatened to sue him. He just parked the car, walked away, and never drove again. In the movie *The Long, Hot Summer*, he drove a Jeep all over the place. What most people didn't know was that someone was always around to push the Jeep. He hated driving, even in character."

And by the end he also hated walking. Swimming he could handle. Walking he could not. Officials at UCLA knew this so they provided a wheelchair for him, and he sat in the chair on the auditorium stage talking to the school stagehands and telling them how he wanted the lights positioned for the shoot, which was scheduled to begin later that week.

"I stood behind him with my back to the edge of the stage so he couldn't slip back and fall into the orchestra pit," said Graver. "I was very protective of him. I didn't want him to hurt himself."

Welles and Graver spent the better part of the next hour scribbling notes and making plans for the upcoming shoot. Freddie then drove Welles back to Hollywood, and Graver returned to his home in the valley.

The next day Welles called Graver and said he was postponing the UCLA shoot. "He said he wanted to tweak the script," said Graver. "He thought he could make it better."

That same day Welles had lunch at Ma Maison with actor Burt Reynolds. Frank Brady wrote in *Citizen Welles* that the two men spent most of their time at the restaurant talking about Welles's long labor of love, *The Magic Show.* Some years before, Welles had filmed an interview with Reynolds for the film, and in the intervening time Reynolds had lost a lot of weight. According to Brady, Welles wondered whether Reynolds wouldn't mind sitting in front of the camera again for a quick interview.

"Reynolds was doubtful; he was, however, eager to work with Orson, and they discussed other possibilities," wrote Brady. "Reynolds told him that he would be happy to act in virtually any vehicle that Orson might direct and that Orson could use Burt's name in trying to gain backing for films.

"Orson picked at his food," wrote Brady. "Reynolds noted that he looked quite drawn and tired. Orson acknowledged that he wasn't looking well. He had just seen the series of photographs taken of him by Michael O'Neill for a story that *People* magazine was doing on him, and he was appalled by his appearance." Brady quoted Welles telling Reynolds, "I look like I'm about to be laid out in a coffin."

According to Merv Griffin, the image of Welles picking at his food at Ma Maison was often an act on the great actor's part, performed as a way of throwing off a luncheon companion.

"I went to Ma Maison with him once, and the two of us sat in a little dark area and not out under the main tent," said Griffin. "He had a little piece of fish. I thought, 'He doesn't eat anything. How could he be this heavy?' And sure enough, on the way home I was coming back from my theater on Vine Street and I saw his car. I said to my driver, 'Hey, just for fun let's follow him to see where he goes.' And he went to Pink's hot dog stand on La Brea. His driver went in and then came out with a box filled with hot dogs. Orson would stuff them down in the back of the car after picking at a piece of fish at Ma Maison."

By his own count, Griffin has forty hours of tape on Welles, representing the many hour-long and ninety-minute appearances Welles made on Griffin's TV talk show. And like Graver before him, Griffin first met Welles at his Beverly Hills Hotel bungalow. "It was right outside his bungalow," recalled Griffin. "I introduced myself, and he said, 'I know who you are, and I want to come on your show.'

"I said, 'We've been waiting a number of years trying to get you.'

"He said, 'I'm ready now.'

"So I said, 'Great. We'll get a date set and we'll do it.'"

For Griffin, getting Welles to commit to his show was a big deal. *The Tonight Show* with Johnny Carson was usually where the truly big stars in Hollywood went first when they wanted to promote something on TV. Griffin was understandably excited about his coup.

"A fellow on my staff named Paul Solomon was assigned to pre-interview Orson, and he was very nervous about it," said Griffin. "We had put together an entire ninety-minute show saluting Orson Welles. We had clips from *Citizen Kane* and *The Lady from Shanghai*, all of his great films. Two days before he was scheduled to be on Paul called him. He taped the call and he still has the tape. He said, 'Mr. Welles, we're very happy. We put together a great salute to you.' There was dead silence on the other end of the line. And Paul said, 'We have clips from all your films, and we'll talk about Rita Hayworth, Marlene Dietrich, William Randolph Hearst, everything.'

"When Paul finished his speech, all you hear on the tape is, 'Fuck you, fuck you, fuck you, fuck you.' That's what Orson thought of the idea. The next thing he said was, 'I do not take walks down memory lane. I talk about today and the future.'

"As a talk show host, I thought, 'Oh, my God, I'm dead.'"

Griffin, of course, turned out to be overreacting. His interviews over the years with Welles are classics, if for no other reason than for the forum Griffin gave him to be an exaggerated version of himself. But there were always those rules: No walks down memory lane. No probing questions into his past. It was therefore quite a surprise to Griffin when Welles changed the rules on Wednesday, October 9, 1985.

Welles was the scheduled guest that day. Griffin was in his dressing room just prior to the afternoon taping when one of his bookers knocked on his door. The booker said to Griffin, "Mr. Welles wants to see you. He's backstage waiting for you."

"I hated hearing that," remembered Griffin. "I never liked seeing a guest before a show. I always felt it might compromise the spontaneity."

But it was Welles who wanted to see him, so he went. "I came downstairs and he was standing there," said Griffin. "I said, 'Hi, Orson.'

"And he said, 'Merv, you know all those little questions that you've been wanting to ask me all these years, the little gossipy things you always wanted to know, and I wouldn't let you ask me, the things about Rita and Marlene, Hearst, and all that?'

"I said, 'Yes.'

"He said, 'I feel very expansive tonight. Ask me.'

"I was stunned, and delighted," said Griffin. "After almost forty hours together on the air over a period of many years this was a complete reversal on his part."

With tape rolling, Griffin came out on stage, did a bit of a monologue about all the pasta he had consumed in Italy recently, and then got right down to business. "Well," he said, "my first guest is an eloquent and frequent visitor to this show. He's obviously going to do something amazing when he comes out here with these cards. He captures our attention with every word he speaks. Would you welcome the one and only Orson Welles."

Welles walked onstage with the help of a cane, and the two men embraced. Then Welles made a joke about the twenty pounds Griffin had lost, calling it the same twenty pounds "that you lost last year."

Griffin then complimented Welles about his own weight loss, which Welles sloughed off with the self-deprecating line: "Losing a lot with me is so little."

Griffin began the magic portion of the show by announcing that he had two decks of cards "untouched by human hands."

"Seals provided to us by the property department," said Welles, who directed Griffin, "Give me one of them, either one. And now I would like you to check on a monitor because I want you to be sure that the audience out there is getting the picture what's going to happen."

"You don't want me here next to you?" asked Griffin

"I'll call on you at the moment of the climax," said Welles, and everyone laughed at the obvious double entendre.

Welles then motioned to a member of the audience, and said, "All right. Would you hold this, please? That's right. Do me a favor and unseal it. Thank you.

"We're going to do a little card cheating," he said to the entire audience. "You know that there isn't as much card cheating as there used to be, on as grand a scale, because we don't travel nowadays on liners. When you used to go back and forth across the ocean in five days, that was just the right turnaround to set up the mark, make the killing, go back in the other direction. And there were great men. People like Titanic Thompson.

"I'll tell you what I'd like you to do," he said, shifting his attention back to the audience member. "Would you shuffle the pack very well, please? Two, three times, I don't care how many times.

"And Titanic Thompson, as a matter of fact, had a niece," Welles continued to his rapt audience, "who is alive and well, and you all know her because she became a famous movie actress. And she used to work with him on the boats when she was a young girl. That's why I can't tell her name. But she's told me a lot about how they used to work. And of course the real cheating is minuscule. It's dealing a second or a third or a bottom card, or a little work with a shiner. Cold decking. Hold out. All that kind of thing was used once or twice in a game if it was necessary. But sometimes the game and its outcome depended on the whammer, because whamming is a very interesting aspect of card cheating. You know the psychologists have tried to study why people are gamblers. Well, the answer is easy: we want to make some easy money. But the parapsychologists have discovered what the professional gamblers have always believed in, which was whamming: the ability of some people to influence the outcome without touching the cards. Now of course you don't believe that. But maybe we can prove it.

"Have you shuffled the cards well?" Welles asked his assistant from the audience, who was not Gary Graver, by the way, because he was not with Welles at the *Griffin* show that day.

The audience member had indeed been shuffling the cards. "Have you taken all of the jokers out?" asked Welles.

"I shuffled them in," answered the audience member. "Is that okay?"

Welles acted like he couldn't believe what his assistant had gone ahead and done. "You shuffled them in?" he asked incredulously. "Look, look, take out the jokers, would you, because it must be a legitimate pack."

Welles then motioned for a woman in the audience to stand up. "Stand up, miss. Thank you. Would you throw the case of cards anywhere in the audience, please. Would you pass the case to any gentleman who has a pocket.

"You have a pocket?" he asked of another man. "Good. We're going to use it later. Good. Good."

Then, turning back to his original assistant, Welles said, "You have completed your operation?"

"I'm looking for one more joker," came the answer.

"All right, now. Now, whamming!" Welles said, speaking once again to everyone in the studio.

Griffin asked, "Orson, do you need me yet?" There was no reply. Welles was on too much of a roll.

"Whamming," he said again. "Whamming is an art which everyone has to some degree."

The four jokers were all handed to Welles, but he clearly didn't care about them any longer. "And there are whammers in this audience," he bellowed. "I bet a lot of you are and don't know it. In other words, there is an ability to influence objects which we are not physically controlling. And all of us can do it to just a little extent. Now talking to some dice isn't going to help us at all. That's useless. But if all of us will work together for the sake of this lady who's going to watch this show, who's giving you a lot of pleasure as movie goers, I want you to wham as she used to wham.

"And in order to do that," he said to one audience member, "I'm going to ask you to cut your deck into two parts and bring them up here, or rather put them up on the stage, right like that in two parts. Thank you. Thank you very much. Now whoever has that deck, will you, sir, toss it or hand it to a gentleman who also has a pocket. Would both of you come forward here and stand here. That's very nice of you. Thank you. I want to make it very clear to you, ladies and gentlemen, at no time do I touch these cards. Nor does my old friend Merv Griffin, who seems to have left us.

"Hello, what's your name?" he asked of another audience member. "How are you? And you're? Hi."

Welles now had two people onstage with him, and he directed them as only he could. "Now, what I'd like you to do is you come over here and represent this group of cards. And you represent this group of cards. I want you to pick up that deck, please. With your hand. Will you please count the cards down, face down, on the stage floor. Now you can stop anytime you want. I'm not going to try to influence you, but you stop when you feel like it. Did I influence you? But someone in the audience did. Probably a lot of you, because you don't know the card he should stop at. But if you were whamming properly, it all worked. Now would you take the rest of those cards and put them face up on the stage, spread them out. Now we could have stopped at any of those cards, right? Okay.

"You, sir, the same thing," he said to the other person. "Pick up your deck. Again count down. Now you can stop when you feel any influence at all. On your own initiative, you stop. You won't change your mind? Would you like to take the card from the bottom or the middle or the other cards? You stick with that, absolutely? Will you take the rest of the cards and smear them out. The cards could have been any one of those, right? Will you put those cards in your pocket?

"And you put these cards in yours," he said to the first person.

And then to the entire audience, he said, "We are left with two piles of cards which have been randomly placed in their position. They are in the condition they are because of very secret whammers in this gathering.

"All right, now. Here's what you do, sir. Please pick up that group of cards and deal me. You're a dealer," he said to the first audience member. "Deal me two hands face down. One, two. One, two. That's right.

"Will you do the same thing?" he asked of the second person. "You're the second dealer. Now you're dealing to somebody that we're wishing very well to, a lady that we hope we have served by the cumulative effects of our whamming. Will you turn over the top card there? The ace of spades. Will you turn over the top card of that? The ace of hearts. Will you turn over that card? The ace of clubs. Now it would be impossible if that should turn out to be the ace of diamonds. But just on the chance that a genius of a whammer is in this audience, would you turn it over?"

Indeed, it was the ace of diamonds. "By God, we did it," Welles said, feigning amazement. "Thank you."

Griffin never asked Welles to reveal the name of the actress and daughter of Titanic Thompson, and Welles never gave her up on his own. But after a commercial break Griffin did allude to Welles's seventieth birthday, which had occurred five months earlier in May. "I mean,

I would have planned a major birthday cake," Griffin said. "You celebrated a big birthday, didn't you?"

"I didn't celebrate it, I just had it," Welles responded. "At my age, nobody celebrates a birthday. . . . In my hot youth, yes. I used to pretend it was my birthday when I took a girl out to dinner. And then I'd have the waiter bring a cake in and sing 'Happy Birthday.' And I'd use that as an excuse to extend the evening. One night a friend of mine, Ty Power, God rest him, whose birthday happened to be the same day as mine, May 6, came in in February and saw a waiter singing 'Happy Birthday' to me while I sat next to a pretty girl. And I got the dirtiest look I ever had in my life.

"I'll tell you what happened to me that made me happy about being seventy years old," he said to the applause of an audience showing the polite appreciation that he had managed to get even that far. "I thought I was seventy last year. So I went through all the misery of being seventy a year ago. So this one is free. . . . I hate birthdays, you know. Really. Because you always think, 'Wouldn't it be nice if it was a lot less candles on the cake?' As it is now, when they bring out a cake with my right number of candles, it looks like the Chicago fire."

Griffin asked Welles how he was feeling for a man of seventy, and he just rolled his eyes, as though disgusted. "All these old people that walk around saying they feel just the way they did when they were kids. Liars," Welles said, "every one of them."

The focus of the show then shifted to *Orson Welles: A Biography*, or as Welles put it, "the unauthorized biography," which had just come out. The author, Barbara Leaming, was waiting in the wings and was due to join Welles and Griffin in a later segment. Welles proudly declared the book a best seller, but said he did not cooperate with Leaming during her research and writing.

"I'm speaking to her," he said. "We became friendly, really, after she finished writing the book. I refused even to see her for two years. She was four years doing research. And everything she has in the book is from another source. And she has researched. In other words, she doesn't give opinions. Or, if she says something that I say, somebody has told her that. I didn't cooperate at all."

Griffin asked Welles whether he had read the book, and he said no. "I haven't read it," he said, "because I became very fond of her after she finished, and I'd like to remain that way. I don't know what she's got in that book. People seem to think that she treats me in a kindly way, and I'd like to believe it's true. But no actor was ever happy with a good notice."

Griffin asked whether Welles felt any joy in his life. "Oh, yes," he said, "there are certain parts of almost every day that are joyous. I'm not essentially a happy person, but I have all kinds of joy. There's a difference, you know, because joy is a great big electrical experience. And just happiness is, oh, I don't know, a warthog could be happy, and I don't want to knock warthogs. Why did I think about them?"

"What about painful times?" asked Griffin.

"Enough of those to do," said Welles. "I'm saving those for my book. . . . All kinds of pain. Bad conscience pain too, you know. That's the worst. The regrets. The things you didn't do. The times you didn't behave as well as you ought to have. That's the real pain."

"The women in your life are . . . ?" asked Griffin.

"Women in my life," he said. "If you think that I'm going to write a succession of boasts or lies about conquest in that nature, you're mistaken. I think there's much too much talk and not enough action in the world."

"But one of your wives," said Griffin. "Oh, I have envied you so many years for Rita Hayworth."

"That's one of the dearest and sweetest women that ever lived," said Welles.

Griffin mentioned the fact that Hayworth, Welles's second wife, had suffered with Alzheimer's disease, which was a relatively new medical diagnosis. People who had never heard of Alzheimer's had mistakenly believed that Hayworth was walking around most of the time in a drunken stupor.

"Well, I never believed that she was a drunkard," said Welles. "I didn't know about Alzheimer's disease, but I believed that something like that was wrong with her, when that began to happen. I wasn't seeing her, but I was hearing these stories. And it was so foreign to her nature. It was so unlike her."

Welles recalled the moment when he first laid eyes on Hayworth. He saw her, he said, "In a full page in *Life* magazine. I was in South America, and I saw that picture and vowed that I was going to see that girl. It was awfully hard to get her on the phone."

"Did you also vow that you would marry her?" asked Griffin.

"Yeah, and we were a long time together," said Welles. "I think I was lucky enough to be with her longer than any of the other men in her life. She is a dear person, and she was a wonderful wife, an extraordinary girl in every way. And I've never heard of anybody that sounds like an enemy of hers . . . she's half gypsy, you know. And she never got mad at me once. But she used to throw the stuff around the house a little bit when she'd think about Harry Cohn [the powerful studio mogul who headed Columbia Pictures during Hollywood's Golden Age].

"We must remember that he got the biggest funeral that anybody ever had in Hollywood, the biggest turnout," Welles said of Cohn's farewell in 1958. "And somebody said to the wonderful Billy Wilder, 'Why are there so many people here at Harry Cohn's funeral?' And he said, 'Well, give the people what they want.'"

Griffin then asked Welles about the enigmatic Marlene Dietrich, who reportedly once said of Welles, "People should cross themselves when they say his name."

"We know really very little about her except her performances," Griffin said of Dietrich. "What kind of woman is she?"

"Well, she's the most loyal friend that anybody could ever ask for," said Welles. "Her loyalty is ferocious. Her professionalism is impeccable. She has a marvelous sense of humor. She was one of the all-time glamour people. And we did our magic show together, you know, for a long time. And so we had not only a long friendship, but also a long professional association."

Griffin then shifted the conversation to the popular genre of TV shows in 1985, the nighttime soap operas, the one-hour prime-time dramas like *Dynasty*, *Dallas*, and *Falcon Crest*.

Welles called these shows "a perfectly legitimate form. I acted in soap operas in the day to make my living," he said. "I did a lot of those. I remember I played a cad in one of them. I was trying to seduce a girl. It took us about thirteen weeks in one rumble seat to get anywhere. It was the same plot as we see on TV now."

Griffin asked Welles how old he was when stardom came to him. "I was young," said Welles.

"All that success at that age," said Griffin. "Hard to handle or easy to handle?"

"Anybody who has trouble being successful," said Welles, "doesn't have any sympathy from me."

"Right," said Griffin. "But at twenty-two, Orson, you were the child genius of Broadway."

"I was a success at sixteen," said Welles. "I was a star in Dublin. So I was an old-timer by [the time I was twenty-two]. I was just awful busy, you know, and awful lucky. I had a tremendous streak of luck and I was very grateful for that. I'm not being falsely modest talking about luck. I do really think it has everything to do with anybody's life."

Welles and Griffin were joined by Barbara Leaming in the next segment, and she said she had chased Welles for two years, to no avail. "While Orson was hiding," she said, "I decided that the life was just so great I was going to find out no matter what he did. And so I read all of his private letters, everything that everybody else had saved and he had thrown away. . . . My whole house is filled with Orson's old letters. He once said to me, 'It must be like the Grotto of Lourdes in there.' But it was such a great subject. I mean, no matter how hard he hid, I kept running. And finally, he was just so very nice. At the end of two years he wrote me a lovely letter. And he said, 'I'm so sorry, but I'm not going to cooperate with you.' He hadn't even answered a letter for two years."

"I never asked her to show me what she was writing," said Welles. "I never asked to check even a fact."

Griffin asked Leaming what had surprised her the most to learn about Welles. "Oh," she said, "I think without any question how funny he was. But in terms of his life, I think it was the ups and the downs in childhood. . . . When Orson was saying before that he was in Dublin at sixteen and an enormous success, what he isn't telling you is that at seventeen he was a huge failure in New York."

"Why should I blabber about these little, uh, doubts?" shrugged Welles.

"Most of these actors don't tell you about the failures," said Griffin.

"I'm sure you don't remember this," Leaming said to Welles, "but it's one of my favorite stories. When Orson came back from Dublin with great notices saying this is just such a discovery, he rushed right into the Shubert office in New York, with his *New York Times* review, saying, 'Ah, he's wonderful.' And they said to him, 'Yes, kiddie, can we help you?'

"You don't remember that," she said, turning back to Welles, "but Roger told me that."

"It's an invention," said Welles.

"It isn't an invention, Orson."

"It's an invention of Roger Hill's," Welles said, making sure to mention the culprit's entire name.

"Roger is Orson's oldest friend and his former schoolteacher," said Leaming. "And what Orson doesn't remember or won't admit, Roger will tell you very willingly."

"He's in his nineties," said Welles, "and we talk on the phone every two or three days."

"He's the most wonderful person," added Leaming. "You know, Orson said something to me very early on. He said, 'You know, you're never going to understand me unless you know the people that were around me.' And that was one of the reasons I spent a lot of time talking to other people, even after I had chased Orson and had gotten him."

Griffin asked about areas of Welles's life that the book uncovered for the first time. Leaming mentioned his political career. It was widely known for years that Welles had strong ties to Franklin Roosevelt.

"But I also had a political column, and I also was the editor of a magazine. I was very busy in that area for a while," said Welles. "So long ago, I almost forgot."

Welles even admitted that he had considered running for office. Roosevelt, in fact, had encouraged him to do it. "The thing that fascinated me," Leaming said to Welles, "was that there was a strong possibility that you were going to run in Wisconsin. When [Joseph] McCarthy was the other candidate."

"And I decided not to," said Welles. "And it's always been on my conscience. Everybody told me that . . . I couldn't win, and the war hero would. So I quit. I didn't even start, not quit. And supposing I had won. There never would have been a McCarthy era."

"But you did have some kind of official function with Roosevelt?" Griffin wondered.

"I didn't have an official function," said Welles. "Most of us who were around him were unofficial. There were only a few people with titles on the door, you know."

"But did you ever rehearse him for his fireside chats?" asked Griffin.

"Oh, he didn't need rehearsal," said Welles. "He was a superb actor."

"Did Eleanor like you?"

"No."

"Tell him why not, Orson," said Leaming.

"No."

"Come on, Orson," implored Leaming, "tell him the truth."

"Why did Eleanor Roosevelt hate you?" asked Griffin.

"You probably have some lie," Welles said to his biographer.

"No," she said, "you told me this. What about the cooking? Tell him about the cooking, what you said."

"Oh," said Welles, "I made some remark about the cuisine at the White House."

"And she didn't like it?" said Griffin.

"No, I don't think that's why she didn't like me," Welles said. "She didn't trust me. I had a tendency when I visited to keep the president up too late. And I came out of that having a bad influence. I adored and admired her, but it was one of the many cases of unrequited friendship in my life.

"He liked talk," Welles said of FDR. "He liked sitting up, and they didn't like him to do it."

"Somebody said that Mrs. Roosevelt once called Orson 'a pubescent backroom boy,'" said Leaming.

"Never heard that," said Welles.

"You were awfully young, though, even then," said Leaming. "You were young for a long time."

"Roosevelt had something against me, which is that I did *A Christmas Carol* every year on the radio," said Welles. "Until I started doing that it had been a great family institution for all the children and grandchildren to gather around, and for Mr. Roosevelt to read it aloud. And once they had it on the radio, they said, 'We want to hear it on the radio.'"

"We want to hear Orson," said Griffin.

"He didn't like that," said Welles.

"What did you find out about the women in his life?" Griffin asked Leaming.

"There he goes again," barked Welles.

"And his appreciation of them," Griffin added respectfully.

"I found out a lot," said Leaming. "First of all, that was a very difficult area to cover. Because every time, it seemed, when I was in New York, I would go out to dinner and I would find another lady who wanted to tell me her stories of her romances with Orson. And then I would call Orson on the phone and I would say, 'So-and-so told me a great story about a big romance with you.' And Orson would say, 'It's not true. It's absolutely not true. What gentleman would ever tell you if it was true?' So then I would have to go back to these women and say, 'Mr. Welles denies that you ever had anything going on.' Put me in a very difficult position."

"Your mistake was in going back to them," said Welles.

"Approximately how many where there?" asked Griffin.

"Thousands," said Leaming.

"Look at the two of them," said Welles. "Can you see? Have you ever seen a more gossipy couple?"

"Be quiet, Orson. Just don't talk," said Leaming. "Okay, when Orson was out here in the forties, he . . ."

"Name names," Griffin chirped excitedly. "Everything."

"Oh, no," said Leaming. "Are you kidding? We'll be in court. He had a hunchback dwarf who was his driver. Shorty."

"Yes," said Welles.

"He took notes," said Leaming. "And he loved Orson. He called Orson the Boss. And what Shorty would do was to report everything to anyone who would listen. And I think he would also make up things half of the time, too. Because he'd say, 'Oh, you know all those women, they loved the Boss, they just loved the Boss.' So I had people forty years later who were remembering these stories, these absolutely outrageous stories, which I still don't know if they are true or not. And I'd say, 'How'd you find that out?' And they'd say, 'Oh, Shorty told us.'"

"So you see," said Welles, "it's all a tissue of lies from a lot of people safely gone to their reward.

"He was a great character," Welles said of his former driver. "He'd been a burglar, a second-story man. . . . Joe Cotten and I used to have him working for us in New York. When we went to Hollywood, we tossed to see who would lose and the one who lost got Shorty. But he was devoted and wonderful. And once when I was broke or very close to it, one of the many times when that has happened, and Shorty heard about it, he was living in retirement here in California. And I was in Paris. And he arrived suddenly in Paris with his entire earnings, which he wanted to give me. And I said, 'Of course not. You go back with them and God love you.' And I took him to the airport. Only he took a plane for Vegas."

In the show's final segment, Griffin ran clips from a number of Welles's best-known works, including *The Third Man*, with the aforementioned Joseph Cotten; *The Stranger,* with Loretta Young and Edward G. Robinson; and of course the 1941 classic, *Citizen Kane.*

Griffin asked whether *Kane* was "a great boon to your career, or a detriment?"

"Well, it was a great piece of luck because people liked it," said Welles. "If they hadn't liked it, it would have been bad. It's as simple as that."

Then, watching another clip, Griffin said, "And this next, your favorite film isn't it?"

"Yes," said Welles. "There I am as Falstaff. And that's Keith Baxter who gave a wonderful performance as Prince Hal in a combination of Shakespearean plays called *Chimes at Midnight.* It was hardly seen in America. It was a huge hit in Europe. The man who bought it didn't have the financial resources to sell it."

Griffin asked whether Welles thought *Chimes at Midnight,* released in 1966 when Welles was fifty-one, represented his best work ever. "Ask her," Welles said, pointing to Leaming. "She's a professor of movies. She knows more about things like that than I do."

So Griffin asked Leaming. "I think, unquestionably," she said. "I mean, I think that's one of the things for me that I hope people will do, is look at the other half of Orson's career. *Chimes at Midnight* seems to me to be so much of everything that I had ever hoped Orson would do. It's *Citizen Kane* forty times over."

And speaking of *Kane,* it was hardly ever a Hollywood secret that Welles based the film's lead character, newspaper tycoon Charles Foster Kane, almost entirely on the real-life newspaper tycoon William Randolph Hearst. Hearst was so incensed after Welles's movie came out that he vowed to use his enormous power to see that the filmmaker was denied work in America. Griffin asked Welles whether Hearst had managed to hurt his career.

"Yes, sure," said Welles. "But I didn't do him any good either."

Griffin concluded the interviews by congratulating Leaming on the book and praising her for getting Welles to talk about his past.

"She knows more than I do," said Welles.

The taping ended with Griffin's on-air goodbyes. "I went right to my dressing room, took off my makeup, got into the car, and went home," recalled Griffin. "I never saw any of my guests after a show, and I didn't see him."

Welles and Leaming also left Griffin's theater on Vine, but instead of going their separate ways, they followed each other to Ma Maison and had a quiet supper. Welles stayed on after Leaming left, and Patrick Terrail joined him at his table.

"He was happy about everything that night," said Terrail. "He was happy about the *Griffin* show because he thought it went well. He was happy because he was in the middle of a renegotiation and close to a new contract with Gallo. And that meant a lot of money. Everything was going his way, and he was in a good mood. He was just in good spirits all the way around."

Welles finished his dinner, went home, and died.

Early the next morning, his driver, Fred Gillette, discovered his boss's body lying in a single bed on the second floor at the house on Stanley. A portable typewriter sat balanced and still on the dead man's stomach. It was determined that Welles had suffered a fatal heart attack while typing a script during the early morning hours of October 10.

"He always liked to type lying down," said Terrail.

That same morning, actor Paul Stewart was at the Directors Guild of America building on Sunset when someone ran in saying they had just heard the news on the radio that Welles had suffered a heart attack and was presumed dead. Stewart surely knew Welles and he also knew that Welles lived in Kordar's house on Stanley. And with the DGA building situated only a few blocks west of the well-dressed hookers on Ogden, Stewart didn't have far to go to get to the house. It took only minutes for him to pass the Bank of America, and then Genesee and Spaulding, until, finally, the traffic light at Stanley.

When Stewart made his left off Sunset, he saw other lights, the flashing lights of the paramedics and police in front of Kordar's house. Welles's body was still in the house with the authorities. And because Stewart knew the house and the driver, Gillette, he had little difficulty gaining access through the front gates.

An eerily reminiscent feeling overcame Stewart as he approached Welles's body. More than four decades earlier Stewart had been in *Citizen Kane* with Welles. But more than that, it was Stewart's character, Raymond the butler, who discovers the dead body of Welles's character, Charles Foster Kane. In the movie, the butler describes the death scene to a reporter.

"And if that isn't an incredible example of life imitating art," said
Gary Graver, "then there is no such thing."

The Merv Griffin Show, taped with Welles on the last day of his
life, was broadcast in its entirety on October 14, four days after his
death.

Lucille Ball

August 6, 1911–April 26, 1989

IT WAS EARLY MORNING ON MARCH 29, 1989, ACADEMY AWARDS DAY IN LOS Angeles, and already dozens of fans had secured key positions behind the blue wooden horses on Horn Avenue in West Hollywood. The fans knew the wait wouldn't be too long by superstar-gazing celebrity standards, maybe nine hours at most. A few brought along folding chairs to set up on the pavement, but most were content to lean against the police barricades and fiddle with their cameras and autograph books. And maybe, if they were lucky, they could develop some kind of relationship with the unending stream of security personnel, party planners, and food handlers who were scurrying in and out of the restaurant across the street known as Spago.

And if they worked it right, who knows, maybe these forged alliances would pay off later in the night, when it counted.

No demographic study had ever been done on the subject, but the fans who trudged up the little hill on Horn Avenue to stand in front of Spago on Oscar night were always much shrewder than their battle-tested compatriots who camped out on bleacher benches in downtown Los Angeles. While it is true that the bleacher bums claimed a unique vantage point from which to view arriving celebrities on the red carpet, most of these fans always saw their night end at precisely 5 P.M., Pacific time, in precisely the same way. Once the stars were comfortably inside the Shrine Auditorium, site of the sixty-first Academy Awards telecast that night in 1989, the fans outside could do little more than call it a night and go home.

That was not the case on Horn Avenue, a narrow side street that snakes north off Sunset Boulevard, above Tower Records, to a residential neighborhood in the Hollywood Hills. During the 1980s, the most important piece of commercial real estate on Horn was Wolfgang Puck's restaurant Spago, a celebrity mecca that reigned supreme for years as the number one eatery in Los Angeles. And while autograph seekers and members of the paparazzi could be found outside Spago on almost any night, their numbers paled in comparison to the massive crowd that turned out each year to see the designer-clad household names being dropped off and picked up at the most famous of all Academy Awards parties, the one hosted by legendary superagent Irving "Swifty" Lazar at Spago.

A bald, diminutive man in black horn-rimmed glasses, Lazar created an event that was really two lavish dinner parties in one. The early portion of the evening, which included dinner and the viewing of the Academy Awards telecast on big-screen TVs, was reserved mostly for friends of Lazar and his wife, Mary, people like billionaire oilman Marvin Davis, comedians Don Rickles and Bob Newhart, artists David Hockney and Robert Rauschenberg, music executives Berry Gordy and Suzanne de Passe, actresses Suzanne Pleshette and Shirley MacLaine, producer George Schlatter, author Jackie Collins, and soon-to-be California Governor Pete Wilson.

But the real fun always began later in the evening, after the live broadcast, when the stars attending the awards show left the downtown area in their stretch limousines and directed their drivers to Spago. There were always a lot of parties on Oscar night, but in the end all roads led to Spago, where the pesky Lazar divided his time between keeping his celebrity guests happy and making sure that his journalist guests never hovered around the celebrities for too long.

Contemplating the long night ahead one year, former *Los Angeles Daily News* columnist Frank Swertlow stood in the Spago parking lot, rolled up his pants leg, and placed his own black horn-rimmed glasses on his knee. Then, in a high-pitched rasp, he said something mean to no one in particular, and finished by asking the question, "Who am I?"

The answer, of course, was Swifty, and he was in rare form in 1989, patrolling the front door at Spago, watching for gate-crashers and heading off the media people he hated so much and needed so badly.

As soon as *Rain Man* was announced as Best Picture of the year, the stars made their obligatory stop at the annual Governor's Ball, also at the Shrine Auditorium, followed by the predictable celebrity pilgrimage to Lazar's party at Spago. Just a partial list of those who were desperate for Puck's designer pizza that night reads today like a veritable Hall of Fame of broken superstar relationships: Jack Nicholson and Anjelica Huston, Tom Cruise and Mimi Rogers, Don Johnson and Melanie Griffith, Jeff Goldblum and Geena Davis, Bruce Willis and Demi Moore.

They were all there that night, trading their Oscar stories, schmoozing about their kids and their upcoming projects, planning dinner dates they would never keep, and acknowledging Lazar because they had to.

But there was one star who rose above all the others that night, and when she walked into Spago she was in no mood for small talk, or food, or the Lazars. That star was Lucille Ball, and all she really wanted to do was turn right around and go home.

She had been at the Academy Awards as a copresenter with Bob Hope. "He talked her into going," said Lee Tannen, a writer-director and longtime confidante of Lucy's and the author of a glowing book about her, *I Loved Lucy.*

Allan Carr, the Los Angeles showman who produced the Oscars that year and was so roundly criticized for his efforts that he was never asked to do it a second time, wanted these two Hollywood giants—Hope and Ball—to introduce a "Young Hollywood" production number featuring such Hollywood newcomers as Savion Glover, Joely Fisher, Corey Feldman, Chad Lowe, Blair Underwood, Matt Lattanzi, Christian Slater, and Ricki Lake. Hope quickly agreed to do the show, and he told Carr he would personally convince Lucy to do the segment with him.

"Hope called her for days," said Tannen, "and she kept saying, 'No, no, no, no.' And he kept saying, 'Please, please, please, please,' and finally she gave in. But she hated the very idea of it."

Tannen, who was "loosely related," as he described it, to Lucy's second and last husband, one-time comedian Gary Morton, had a lot of access to the great TV star during that entire month of March. On the night of the Oscars, Tannen was staying in the guest quarters behind Lucy's white colonial house, the one with dark green shutters that sat on the corner of North Roxbury Drive and Lexington Road, across the street from James Stewart's garden and his large Tudor house. That particular corner was always an automatic stop for tour buses. Getting Lucille Ball and Jimmy Stewart with just a turn of the head was like hitting the Hollywood jackpot—two icons for the price of one.

Lucy's daughter, Lucie Arnaz, used to tell a story about some of the more brazen tourists who actually knocked on the front door in hopes that her mother might come out to greet them. In fact, one of Lucie's earliest memories of growing up on Roxbury was the sound of the door's metal clacker, and the Asian valet who had to answer the knock and repeatedly tell people, "Lucy not home! Lucy not home!" Many years later, when bulldozers leveled that home so the property's new owner could build one of those disgusting-looking Mediterranean-style villas, Lucie Arnaz went to the demolition site and retrieved the original front door clacker from one of the construction workers.

"They didn't just knock on the clacker," said Tannen. "People also used to come by and drop off scripts. They'd just leave them by the front door, with Lucy's name on them. Somebody even climbed the wall once and slept overnight in the guesthouse. Lucy told me the story. But she never pressed charges because the guy said he saw her do the same thing with Richard Widmark in an episode of *I Love Lucy*. She thought that was humorous."

But Lucy was finding nothing humorous as the Oscars drew closer. Tannen recalled that she came close to canceling her appearance with Hope at the last minute. She examined the wig she had picked out for the Oscars, and the thought of putting it on revolted her.

"That goddamn wig with all that goddamn netting gives me a goddamn headache" was how Tannen quoted her in his book. And she also wasn't too thrilled with the script she received from Carr's Academy Awards office. "Now take a look at this goddamn script they've sent me," she told Tannen, as she flung it across the backgammon table in her living room.

The fact that she had committed to the Oscars only made her angrier with Hope. "Goddamn Hope," she said to Tannen. "Nobody cares what the hell he looks like, but everybody cares what I look like—God, I'm so tired of myself."

Lucy had been tiring of herself for quite some time. She had suffered a mild stroke the previous May, and it had left her with a slightly crooked mouth and a tiny speech impediment that was recognizable only to her. "She hated the way she looked," said Tannen. "She thought she looked and sounded terrible. She didn't, but she thought she did."

After the stroke, Lucy started looking morbidly at her life, as though it were a portent of things to come. "She even expressed that she really didn't want to live that much longer," said Tannen. "Whenever there was an ailment, any little thing, she would say, 'Oh, that's another nail in my coffin.'

"There was a shoulder problem once, nothing serious. It wasn't life-threatening in the least," said Tannen. "But to her everything became serious. She was a bit of a hypochondriac and had a real fear of death. In that awful 2003 TV movie, *Lucy! TV's Comedy Queen*, the only interesting thing the writers hit upon was her obsession with talking about death. She was always thinking that the other shoe was about to drop. She was very superstitious. Death by that time became something that was right around the corner."

The downward spiral of Lucy's negative thinking and low self-image can probably be traced back to November 7, 1986, eighteen months before the stroke, when ABC abruptly announced the cancellation of her Saturday-night sitcom, *Life with Lucy*.

"The sitcom was horrible, and I think everyone knew it but her," said Tannen. "I never thought she should have done it in the first place. But she did it, and when ABC dropped the show it was a huge blow to her."

A few weeks later, on December 2, her first husband, Desi Arnaz, died. "Even though they hadn't been together in years, Desi's death destroyed her," said Tannen. "I'll always believe she never stopped loving him."

The reverse was probably true, as well. Even after their breakup, Arnaz continued to send flowers to his ex-wife on their wedding anniversary. He did it each year until the day he died.

These two events, so close to each other, left Lucy an emotional cripple. In fact, Lucy was feeling so unworthy at the time that she couldn't even get excited about a Kennedy Center honor she was receiving in Washington. The black-tie affair, which was taped five days after Arnaz's death, for airing on December 26, featured Valerie Harper, Bea Arthur, and Pam Dawber performing a medley of songs from Lucy's old movies. President Ronald Reagan and Walter Matthau both pointed out that more people watched her little Ricky being born on *I Love Lucy* than watched the inauguration of President Eisenhower. Reagan called Ball "the finest comedienne of our time."

But these accolades seemed to mean very little. Lucy didn't believe she deserved to be getting such a high honor alone, without Arnaz. "In her mind, the honor should have read 'Lucy and Desi,' especially since he had just died," said Tannen. "Hume Cronyn and his wife, Jessica Tandy, were both honored that same night, along with Lucy, and I remember Lucy saying to me, 'It should be Desi and me, like those two.' And it should have been because he was so much a part of her success."

But the honor that night went just to Lucille Ball, whose heart was broken, and along with it her spirit to be the Lucy everyone loved in public.

By Academy Awards night three years later, Lucy had become a near recluse. Tannen's plan that night was to give her a proper send-off, tell her how beautiful she looked, and then watch the broadcast alone in Lucy's house. Tannen was in the living room when she came down the stairs wearing the same wig she had been bitching about earlier.

She also wore a beaded and sequined black sheath that was designed for her by Ret Turner. The dress had a slit up the left side that allowed for the exposure of Lucy's legs. This was clearly not an accident on Turner's part. Lucy may have been seventy-seven, but her legs, coddled and cared for years before during her showgirl days, looked like they belonged to someone half her age.

The trouble was, it was her heart that wasn't in it. As she got into the limo with Morton, she called out to Tannen and asked him to wait up for her. "I'll be home right after I make a fool of myself," she said.

"The last thing she wanted to do that night was have to stand in front of a billion people at the Oscars and read off a teleprompter, and risk getting the names wrong," said Tannen. "She knew none of these so-called newcomers, and we actually rehearsed the names together before she got dressed. Against her better judgment she went. She did it only because of Bob Hope, and she definitely wasn't happy about it."

And even though she and Hope received a standing ovation when they walked out on stage at the Shrine, Lucy was still in that unhappy mood when she arrived at Spago with Morton.

Lazar, of course, had no idea how Lucy had been feeling, and so he did what he always did when one of Hollywood's truly A-list stars walked into one of his parties. He cleared the area of intrusive journalists and he made sure the Mortons were led to a prime table. Then he stood back and watched as the other stars in the room lined up to pay homage to Lucy. She accepted everyone's best wishes graciously, and she drank. Tannen said that Lucy always preferred bourbon, but she could never drink a lot. "Two drinks for Lucy, and she'd be lit up," said Tannen. "She used to drink a lot more during the Desi days. But in the years I knew her, which was after Desi, she'd have one or two 'slushies,' as we called them, or bourbon. That's what I think she had that night at Spago."

Whatever it was, it seemed to agree with her, at least in terms of the alcohol's ability to change her sour mood into something a little more upbeat. But as giddy as she was becoming, it did not change Lucy's mind about leaving. She wanted to call it a night, and after fifteen minutes of handshakes and air kisses she asked Morton to summon their limo.

The traffic on Sunset by this time was unbearable, monopolized mostly by the limousines that were picking up and dropping off passengers on Horn. But with limo drivers being forced to make tight u-turns in the hills above Spago, cars were not necessarily in front of the restaurant when their precious cargo inside wanted to leave. On most nights at Spago, the timing for quick getaways was impeccable. A celebrity would say something to a waiter, who motioned to the security at the door, who in turn radioed the parking lot attendant, who knew where everyone's limo was at all times.

Oscar nights were not nearly as organized. There were simply too many stars and too many cars, too many TV satellite trucks and too many people on the street.

Hundreds now stood in the narrow passageway between the blue wooden horses on Horn and the thick green underbrush that served almost like a retaining wall that kept fans in the rear from falling into the Tower Records parking lot below. With each star sighting, they surged forward like a giant ocean wave, expecting everything from their celluloid heroes and heroines, and getting very little in return.

When the Mortons emerged on Spago's front patio, they naturally expected to be pointed in the direction of their car. But the car wasn't there yet. A security guard told Morton that the vehicle was no more than a few minutes away.

Lucy turned to her right and walked down the front steps. As soon as the fans across the street saw that red wig, the one she had complained bitterly about, they started shrieking out her name: "Lucy, Lucy, Lucy."

Her wave to the crowd only excited them more. They applauded wildly and yelled out her name again. Her car was still not there. In-credibly, there were no cars in the street at that moment. From the blue wooden horses to the sidewalk in front of Spago the street was empty. Nothing was coming up the hill on Horn. Nothing was going down.

Lucy walked the few steps to the middle of the street, and for a moment she just stood there alone, her body erect, staring at these adoring, cheering fans.

This was not like the standing ovation she had received earlier at the Shrine, when the orchestra played the "I Love Lucy" theme song and she giggled nervously next to Hope. The Shrine audience, typi-cally a high-ticket, high-achieving Hollywood crowd, always stood for those stars who managed to survive and get old. Certainly Lucy and Hope qualified in both categories. But in Hollywood, they also know to stand for the TV cameras, and perhaps subconsciously, for their own success. In Hollywood, you stand up for someone in hopes that someday they'll stand up for you.

The people in front of Spago made no such bargain with one another. They were simply the real people, Lucy's real fans, the smart ones who had chosen this spot over the Academy Awards free-for-all downtown.

"What would she do?" they must have been thinking during that brief moment when Lucy stood in the street and seemed to be doing nothing.

The answer came quickly. Breaking her gaze, Lucy reached down with both hands, hiked up her Ret Turner dress to above her knees, and danced.

At first, she moved from side to side, in time to nothing but the music she must have been hearing in her head. Then came a kick with one leg, then the other. Neither was relatively high by showgirl stan-dards, but the moves were genuine. The dance lasted no more than thirty seconds, but it was obvious that Lucy loved it almost as much as her fans on the street.

Then the car came. She slid into the backseat with her husband, and soon they were motoring down the hill on Horn Avenue. They made a right on Sunset and headed west to her home on Roxbury.

In the process of leaving Spago, a place she did not want to be, on an evening when she would have preferred staying home, all she man-aged to do was give the fans on Horn the best damn show they had seen all night.

Lee Tannen was at Lucy's house, waiting for her to get home, when the limo pulled into the driveway. In his book, Tannen writes that Lucy walked into the house and said, "Jesus, what a bore." Tannen knew nothing about Lucy's little dance on Horn Avenue, but he sensed that her claim of boredom was manufactured. He said she used to talk like that whenever she returned from a Hollywood party.

Figuring the night to be over, Tannen retreated to the guesthouse and prepared for sleep. He hadn't even gotten into bed yet when the intercom buzzed. It was Lucy calling from the main house. She wasn't nearly as tired as she thought. She was on her way to the guesthouse. She wanted to play backgammon.

Morton was never much of a backgammon partner for his wife. In their later years together, he would spend his days playing golf at the nearby Hillcrest Country Club on Pico Boulevard or, in the words of Tannen, "at his office in Beverly Hills making bad business decisions for Lucy."

Even today, Tannen still blames Morton for the *Life with Lucy* debacle. "Lucy didn't need any more money in her life," he said. "She could have lived another fifty years and not spent nearly the money she had. It was never about money for Lucy. But for Gary, it was all about money. He wanted her to do *Life with Lucy* because of the money. That was a really bad decision, a really fatal decision."

"Maybe she loved Gary in her own way," said Tannen, "but I don't think she was ever 'in love' with Gary. It's through Gary that I came to know Lucy, and I'm still critical of him. Gary's real last name was Goldaper. His sister, Helen Maurer, was married to my second cousin, Bob Maurer. Through Helen I met Gary, and through Gary I met Lucy. She married Gary when she was fifty and he was thirty-five. I think she wanted to marry someone as far removed from Desi as possible. And in Gary, she did. He wasn't particularly talented. He wasn't particularly bright. He wasn't particularly handsome. He wasn't particularly rich. In fact, he was poor. She could have married any guy in Hollywood, and she chose to marry this thirty-five-year-old, third-rate comic."

But Morton made her laugh, and according to Tannen, the Mortons always slept in the same room and had an active sex life. "They often spent long stretches away from each other," said Tannen. "But when they were home, they definitely were in the same bedroom."

But late on Oscar night, Lucy left her husband sleeping in that bedroom and soon appeared at the guesthouse door carrying her backgammon board and a small white pocketbook filled with backgammon dollars. The black Ret Turner dress she had worn to the event had been replaced by a white embroidered bathrobe and worn-out pink bunny slippers. Her hair was in rollers. Most of the makeup was gone, but not all of it. Tannen thought she probably decided to play backgammon while taking off her makeup, and having made the decision, she simply left the chore undone to meet him.

"It was very surreal," he said. "I used to say to her, 'Why do you bother with all the makeup and wigs in the first place? Why don't you just go out with your hair the way it looks when you do it yourself? Put on some makeup. Wear the big glasses, if you want to, but be more like you are.' But she wouldn't hear of it. The netting on her wig pulled at her skin and gave her terrible headaches. She looked so ca-daverish. But she wouldn't go on camera any other way. If Lucy said that's what she was going to do, that was it."

She was just as resolute about backgammon. Lucy hosted regular backgammon tournaments in her home, with a regular cast of backgammon players. They included Tannen; his longtime lover, Tom Wells; Thelma Orloff, one of Hollywood's earliest "glamazons" and a friend of Lucy's since the 1930s; Pat and Charles Stone, who were in the jewelry business; actress Ruta Lee; and Helen Maurer, Tannen's cousin by marriage.

"Backgammon was everything to Lucy from the late 1970s on," said Tannen. "As I said in my book, 'If you didn't play, you didn't stay in Lucy's house for too long.'"

Lucy loved to gamble on backgammon, and her games were usu-ally played for the relatively moderate sum of a dollar a point. "We would barbecue hamburgers and frankfurters and have a great time," said Tannen. "I mean, she loved being home. Lucy always loved being home, even going back to the days of Desi. That was one of the big problems in their marriage. She loved being home, and he loved be-ing out. She was always complimentary to Desi in terms of his busi-ness acumen and how he made their careers. Of course, she was a lot less complimentary about his drinking and womanizing and his de-sire to be out all the time."

Lucy's late-night backgammon game with Tannen lasted for about an hour. "Lucy was very unfocused," Tannen recalled in his book. "God only knows what she was thinking. In the middle of a move she just stopped playing, said good night and went upstairs to bed."

When Lucy awakened on the morning of March 30, one of the first things she did was get rid of the Ret Turner dress. "It was taken to a local consignment shop that buys and sells dresses previously worn by famous people," said Tannen. "It's probably hanging in someone's closet right now, or being offered up on eBay."

That same morning, as Tannen was about to leave for a breakfast date with Thelma Orloff at the Beverly Hills Hotel, he noticed a dozen of Lucy's leather scrapbooks, all spread across the living room floor. Lucy had been hard at work since the beginning of the year reorganizing her many clippings and personal mementos. The material dated back to 1933, and Lucy's name was on the cover of each book.

According to Tannen's own book, he tiptoed around the scrapbooks, careful not to open anything without Lucy's permission, when she suddenly appeared in the living room behind him.

"That's my life down there, baby, and nobody really cares" was how Tannen quoted Lucy in his book. "That's all of it, kid, and do you think anybody will ever look at it?"

Tannen had no answer. He knew it was pointless to engage her in a conversation about her self-worth, which was now clearly at an all-time low, despite the wonderful reception she had received at the Oscars, and later that night on Horn Avenue. So Tannen said nothing. Lucy was fully dressed. Her hair was done and her face was made up. She had her own breakfast date somewhere else, and was soon out the door. Tannen cancelled his date with Orloff and spent the rest of the morning pouring over the scrapbooks and marveling at the mint condition of Lucy's memorabilia.

As Tannen recalled in *I Loved Lucy*, "There were movie reviews and press clippings from all the B movies she made in the thirties and forties. There were programs from stage shows she did on the road. There was original art from the Broadway production of *Wildcat*. There were matchbook covers from Ciro's. There were menus from the Brown Derby. There was a napkin from the Mocambo with a forty-year-old Lucy lipstick print.

"But the best part," wrote Tannen, "was all the stuff about Lucy and Desi. There were apology notes from Desi while they were dating, begging Lucy for her forgiveness for seeing other women. There were letters from Lucy forgiving him and saying how lonely and lost she was whenever he wasn't around. There was a telegram from Desi to Lucy's mother, DeDe, on the day they eloped in Connecticut, telling her how much he loved her daughter, and how he would love her until the day he died. There was the invitation to the Catholic Church wedding they had nine years after the civil ceremony, just to please Desi's mom. There were tons of transcripts from Lucy interviews and hundreds of pictures of the Arnaz's at home and on trips around the world.

"I don't know what became of all that stuff." Tannen said, "I imagine Lucie Arnaz has it."

On Thursday, March 30, Gary Morton left for a long out-of-town weekend of golf, and Tannen made plans to return to New York on the Sunday night red-eye. He told Lucy he would not leave for the airport until the conclusion of one of her favorite TV shows, *60 Minutes.* Lucy loved everything about *60 Minutes,* especially one of the magazine show's leading correspondents at the time, Diane Sawyer.

"What a dame," Lucy said of Sawyer in Tannen's book. "I have to meet her some day."

Tannen spent his remaining days with Lucy playing backgammon and feasting on Wolfgang Puck's smoked salmon pizza from Spago. Puck never ran a takeout service for anyone, but that week he made an exception for Lucy, who had called ahead to arrange a reservation for Tannen and a friend. When Tannen finished his dinner, he was handed the boxed pizza by Puck himself, who said that for Lucy it was on the house.

On Saturday, April 1, Tannen and Lucy were alone in the house, playing backgammon, when Lucy suddenly brought up the subject of AIDS. Tannen was gay, it was still the eighties, and she was worried. In his book, Tannen wrote that Lucy couldn't come right out and say "AIDS" out loud. Instead, she danced around the subject by asking him whether he had contracted, in her words, "that thing that's going around."

Tannen said he did not have AIDS, for which Lucy was grateful. Nonetheless, she warned him that when he got back to New York it might be better if he didn't go to the home of Swen Swenson, a singer and dancer who had appeared with Lucy in *Wildcat.* Lucy knew that Swenson was suffering from AIDS, and she feared Tannen could catch the disease if he were in the same house.

Tannen found it "more than a bit frightening," as he wrote, that someone with Lucy's worldliness and sophistication could possibly be so in the dark about AIDS in April 1989. But instead of criticizing her, he just assured her that AIDS could not be passed around in a manner as casual as using silverware owned by someone with the disease. Still, it didn't stop Lucy from breaking down and crying and making Tannen promise to stay away from Swenson's house. He gave his word that he wouldn't go there, and they went back to playing backgammon. (Swenson would die of AIDS a few years later.)

Later that night, during another round of backgammon, this time in the guesthouse, Lucy suddenly got the idea to spy on a party that was already in full progress at the house next to hers on Roxbury. This house, situated on Lucy's north side, was at one time owned by Jack and Mary Benny. The present owners had given Lucy a heads-up that there might be a big commotion on the night of the party on account of the valet parking and traffic on the street. They hoped she wouldn't mind. She didn't.

Lucy led Tannen out a side entrance to the alleyway that separated her house from the party house next door. As luck would have it, there were actually some milk crates in the alley that Lucy and Tannen were able to stand on so they could see over the wall into the neighbor's backyard. Tannen wrote that standing there with Lucy "peeping through the trellis and palm fronds" made him feel like he was in an episode of *I Love Lucy.*

"She called me baby, but she might as well have called me 'Ethel,'" he wrote, referring of course to Lucy's precious sitcom sidekick, Ethel Mertz, played by Vivian Vance. "That's how much I felt like her second banana."

According to Tannen's version of the incident, "Lucy was fascinated by the goings-on, commenting on everything, and eyeing everybody who ironically would have given their eyeteeth to meet the crazy redhead on the other side of the wall."

A half-hour's worth of spying was about all Lucy could manage before the inevitable boredom set in. Soon they were back inside playing even more backgammon. Tannen said he was still involved in a mini-backgammon tournament with Lucy long after valet parking next door dispatched the last car of the night.

After the game broke up, Lucy went upstairs to bed and Tannen made a late-night call to his boyfriend, Tom Wells, in New York. As Tannen played back his day for Wells, his intercom buzzed. It was Lucy. She wanted him to come upstairs to her bedroom. Feeling a little like William Holden being summoned to Gloria Swanson's boudoir in *Sunset Boulevard,* Tannen asked Lucy whether she was feeling all right. She said she was fine. It was her TV set that was giving her problems.

As he wrote in *I Loved Lucy*, Tannen was sweating as he knocked on Lucy's bedroom door. The last time he had been in her bedroom was the previous May, just after her stroke, and he was understandably nervous.

Lucy's appearance quickly put him at ease. According to the book, she was "propped up in her bed surrounded by umpteen pink and lavender pillows, with her toy poodle, Tinker, sound asleep at her side. A babushka was tied around Lucy's head and she had mounds of cold cream on her face. A reading light, which was on next to her bed, was the room's only illumination. She was staring at a television with no picture or sound."

Lucy thought, in her words, that she had "screwed up" the remote channel changer, and she was hoping that Tannen could fix it. He did. He fiddled with one button after the next, and finally the picture and sound came back on. Lucy thanked him and asked that he buzz her on the intercom when he got back to the guesthouse, just to let her know that he had arrived there safely.

Tannen never made that call. He didn't have to. Lucy was buzzing him back before he had a chance to buzz her. "What took you so long?" she asked, her sense of comic timing still impeccable, even in the middle of the night.

April 2 was Tannen's last day with Lucy and it was spent much like the rest of his time on Roxbury: a dip in the pool, followed by some breakfast, and eventually a little backgammon with the lady of the house. Tannen packed to go home, and they played for most of the afternoon in the guesthouse. Lucy dressed for the occasion, wearing a blue-and-white striped, man-tailored shirt, with white slacks and white sandals. There was makeup on her face, and her thinning hair was freshly combed. Tannen described Lucy's appearance that day as "almost angelic."

"She looks like she's in heaven already," he wrote.

At 5 P.M., Lucy finally ended the long backgammon session by telling Tannen that she wanted to show him a video. The video was *Carol + Two*, Carol Burnett's first television special from the 1960s. The show's "plus two" were Zero Mostel and Lucy. Tannen had already seen the video, and Lucy was not about to make him watch the entire show again. But she did want him to see one particular sketch that featured

Burnett and Lucy as sisters. In real life, the two women adored each other. Lucy was a major influence on Burnett's career, and Burnett has acknowledged that fact many times over the years. Lucy was also a tremendous fan of Burnett's and always put her on a pedestal as a comedic equal. In fact, Lucy liked Burnett so much that she sent flowers to the younger star every year on her birthday. And since her fifty-sixth birthday was a little more than three weeks away, on April 26, Lucy made a note not to forget Burnett's flowers.

The sketch Lucy was so crazy about involved Lucy's character trying to say goodbye to her sister and her sister's baby before heading off on a planned vacation. Burnett's character tells her sister that if she says, "Goodbye, baby," the baby will say goodbye to her. Lucy tries saying it, but gets no response. She says it again and again, and each time there is no response from the baby. Clearly frustrated, Lucy begins yelling, "Goodbye, baby!" into the baby's carriage, again to no avail. Finally, she bribes the baby with $500 in cash, and it works. The baby says goodbye. Lucy made Tannen watch the sketch three times, and each time she laughed harder than the time before.

Lucy then prepared a dinner of frankfurters and baked beans for herself and Tannen. She even set up snack tables in the living room so they could both watch Diane Sawyer on *60 Minutes*. But Sawyer didn't have a story on that night, and in fact had already announced that she would be leaving the show at the end of the TV season in May. Lucy may have been disappointed that there was no Sawyer that night, but not enough to change channels. She and Tannen managed to muddle through the Sawyer-less broadcast, watching three investigative pieces by Mike Wallace, Harry Reasoner, and Ed Bradley.

After the show, Lucy managed to convince Tannen to play just a few more games of backgammon before his limo arrived to take him to the airport. When that time finally came, Lucy broke down and cried. Tannen had been a great companion for her, and now he was leaving. He tried to stop her from crying. According to his book, he said, "No tears and no goodbyes, that's what we always said to each other whenever we left one another."

Lucy snapped back, "What do you mean, no goodbyes. Goodbye, baby." Like she had done in the Carol Burnett sketch from the 1960s, Lucy practically followed Tannen to the car and continued repeating, "Goodbye, baby!" at the top of her lungs. The limo driver didn't know what to think. But Tannen knew. He was as choked up as Lucy. But she was the comedian in the group, and sad though she was, she couldn't resist an opportunity to go for a joke.

Tannen called Lucy every day from New York until the morning of April 17, when she started experiencing shooting pains in her chest. According to Warren Harris's book, *Lucy & Desi*, Lucy had just finished breakfast when the pains came on. Gary Morton called his wife's doctor, who said that Lucy needed to get to Cedars-Sinai Medical Center immediately. But Lucy didn't want to go. Harris wrote that Morton was so panicked by Lucy's refusal to seek medical attention that he reached out to Lucy's daughter, Lucie, hoping she could convince her mother that the short trip to the hospital's emergency room in West Hollywood was her only option. Lucie lived nearby, and within minutes she arrived at the Roxbury house and pleaded with her mother to reconsider. Lucy finally agreed, but only on the condition that she could first apply some makeup and get herself dressed.

By 12:45 P.M., Lucille Ball was in an operating room at Cedars-Sinai undergoing open-heart surgery. Her aorta had ruptured, and in a procedure that took seven hours, doctors managed to save her life by replacing a portion of the damaged aorta with tissue from a heart donor.

By 9:45 the next morning, Lucy was lucid enough to ask her husband how her little poodle, Tinker, was getting along at home without her. Doctors were ecstatic. Even though the hospital's spokesman, Ron Wise, had been releasing cautious statements concerning the severity of Lucy's condition, doctors behind the scenes couldn't have been more pleased with the initial progress the patient was making.

One of the operating surgeons, Dr. Robert Kass, told the *Chicago Tribune* that he was optimistic that Lucy could make a full recovery. "The major risk is in the operating room," he said. "The fact that she came through that well makes us all optimistic."

Kass described the surgery as a "high-risk procedure with a fairly substantial mortality rate." Nevertheless, he said it was his belief that Lucy could recover and even perform again one day.

That was indeed good news to the thousands of Lucy fans that had flooded the hospital with calls and get-well cards. Hundreds of floral arrangements came into the hospital for Lucy. At her request, the packages were rerouted to children's hospitals and senior centers throughout the greater Los Angeles area. Fans put up a mammoth WE LOVE LUCY banner on a rooftop across the street from the hospital in hopes that Lucy would see it from her room.

Lee Tannen chose to remain in New York, but he was getting regular hospital reports from his friend Fritz Friedman, a Sony Studios executive whose boyfriend, Dr. Jeffrey Krebs, was one of Lucy's attending physicians and was on duty the day she was brought in.

No phone calls were allowed into or out of Lucy's room, but when she got wind that Dr. Krebs knew Tannen, she started relaying messages to her friend in New York, telling him not to worry and assuring him that she would be fine.

And indeed, it did appear to everyone—her husband, the doctors, Lucie, Tannen, and other close friends—that Lucy was out of the woods and doing better than expected. She even started taking calls, not as Lucille Ball but rather as Diane Belmont, a name she had used in the early days when she worked as a model in New York. Tannen said she had loved the name Diane from the time she was a kid, her appreciation for Diane Sawyer notwithstanding. And Lucy chose Belmont, Tannen said, on a day many years ago when she and some of her friends were driving past Belmont Park on Long Island. So, for a few days at least, she became Diane Belmont again at Cedars-Sinai.

On Wednesday, April 19, Gary Morton told reporters that his wife's "Irish eyes are smiling."

On Tuesday, April 25, Dr. Krebs got word to Tannen that Lucy was well enough to be moved into a private room. Morton even called Tannen to repeat the good news, telling him that Lucy would be expecting his phone call the next day.

But Tannen received another call that day from his friend Fritz Friedman, and the information he passed along was troubling. Apparently, someone had gone into Lucy's room to tell her that as part of her long-term care she would have to live on the ground floor of her house on Roxbury. They did not want her climbing steps, not for a long time, if at all. Tannen was never sure whether it was Morton or one of the doctors who delivered this news to Lucy, but he was sure that she was devastated by the very idea of it.

"There were no bedrooms on the ground floor of Lucy's house," said Tannen, "which meant creating a makeshift bedroom out of the living room, or putting her up in the guest house, where I stayed, or moving to another house altogether, none of which she would ever want to do. Lucy had a great deal of vanity and pride. She would not want to live as an invalid, and I think each of those logistical choices made her feel like one. Whoever told her about this planned scenario of her return home shouldn't have said anything. I'm sure the news destroyed her."

At 5 A.M. the next morning, April 26, Lucy's surgically repaired aorta ruptured again and she went into full cardiac arrest. According to Cedars-Sinai spokesman Ron Wise, "Doctors immediately began working on her, using state-of-the-art techniques. For an hour they struggled feverishly to get her heart started again, but it was to no avail. She was declared dead at 6:04 A.M."

"She really disintegrated so quickly," said Tannen. "Her tombstone should read, 'From Desi's death on December 2, 1986, to her own death on April 26, 1989,' because that was the life of her death. On the death certificate it says 'ruptured aorta,' but I believe Lucy died because she didn't want to live anymore."

Meanwhile, just a few miles away in nearby Century City, Carol Burnett awakened on her fifty-sixth birthday, turned on one of the morning TV shows, and heard the awful news that Lucy had died. Later that afternoon, Burnett received the birthday flowers that Lucy had arranged, along with a handwritten note that read, "Happy Birthday, Kid. Love, Lucy." It may not have been in Lucy's own handwriting, but the words and sentiments were indeed hers, and Burnett knew that immediately. Nevertheless, when reporters called Burnett that day for a quote about Lucy, she didn't bring up the flowers, and neither did they.

"I don't think any public figure—politician or movie star—has ever affected people like this" was what Burnett did say, trying to put her friend and idol into perspective.

"It's like having someone in the family die," she added. "Anybody who ever watched TV felt that Lucy was part of the family. I don't know if that was or ever will be duplicated."

Lyle Alzado

April 3, 1949–May 14, 1992

IT READS TODAY LIKE A WARNING FROM THE GRAVE.

"I think there are a lot of athletes in danger," wrote All-Pro defensive lineman Lyle Alzado in the July 8, 1991, issue of *Sports Illustrated*. "So many of them have taken this same human growth hormone, and so many of them are on steroids. Almost everyone I know. They are so intent on being successful that they're not concerned with anything else. No matter what an athlete tells you, I don't care who, don't believe them if they tell you these substances aren't widely used."

Four months before Alzado wrote those words, the fifteen-year veteran of the National Football League found out that he had brain cancer. It took his illness for Alzado to admit that he had been abusing steroids for most of his adult life.

"Lyle and I were inseparable, from high school on," said Marc Lyons, who was Alzado's teammate at Lawrence High School, on the south shore of Long Island. "I was the quarterback, and Lyle played offensive tackle and defensive end. Obviously, he was the star football player and star athlete at the school. He was also the most misunderstood person I knew. When we were in high school, Lyle drank milk. I could have a six-pack of beer, and all the guys would be drinking beer and liquor. But Lyle was so dedicated that all he did was drink milk. He would never do anything to hurt himself. He was an incredibly dedicated athlete. He also had a wonderful personality, with outstanding social skills. But he didn't do it through the use of alcohol and drugs or anything. And that was during the late 1960s, when there were a lot of drugs around."

Lyons compared his friend's initial interest in steroids to the widely held perception of what might have sparked a similar interest by the great home-run hitter, Mark McGwire. "In all likelihood," said Lyons, "McGwire walked into a health food store and bought andro [the nutritional supplement androstenedione] over the counter. In 1970, Lyle came upon a similar product, Dianabol. I was taking brewer's yeast and wheat germ and lifting weights, trying to make myself bigger and stronger and faster. And so was Lyle. Then he started buying Dianabol. He was just a guy, like thousands of other athletes, who wanted to become bigger and stronger and faster."

Alzado told *Sports Illustrated* that he started on Dianabol, "about 50 milligrams a day," he said [while attending Yankton College], a small school in South Dakota. "The Dianabol was very easy to get, even in those days," Alzado said. "Most athletes go to a gym for their steroids, and I think that's what I did. I remember a couple of weeks later someone mentioned how my biceps seemed to look bigger. I was so proud."

"He was such a great football player to begin with," said Lyons, "and because he was getting bigger the lure of the fame and the fortune and the money was right there in front of him. It's almost like making a deal with the devil. If you can gain another twenty pounds of muscle, or run a little faster and jump a little higher, you make the deal with the devil. You sign on the dotted line, and here comes fame and fortune and everything on the back end that you think you want. But you may not know what it's doing to your body, or how it can destroy you. I watched it destroy Lyle Alzado."

Of course, Alzado didn't know it at the time. "I went up to about 300 pounds from the steroids," Alzado said in that 1991 *Sports Illustrated* article. "People say that steroids can make you mean and moody, and my mood swings were incredible. That's what made me a football player, my mood swings on the field.

"As I progressed," Alzado said, "I changed steroids whenever I felt my body building a tolerance to what I was taking. It's hard to remember all the names now. I studied them a little. And I mixed combinations like a chemist. You had to take them both orally and inject them, mostly into your butt so no one would see the marks. I always gave myself injections at home in my bedroom. I got pretty good at it. I kept the steroids in my dresser."

By the time Alzado got to the Denver Broncos in 1971, "I was like a maniac," he told *Sports Illustrated.* "I outran, outhit, outanythinged everybody. . . . All along I was taking steroids, and I saw that they made me play better and better. I kept on because I knew I had to keep getting more size. I became very violent on the field. Off it, too."

"Lyle was always volatile," said Lyons. "He was always positive, too, but along with that he was hot-tempered and volatile. He could never really stop and smell the roses. He was like a cat on a hot tin roof, and he was never able to sit back and say, 'Wow, look at what I'm accomplishing. I should smell the roses and enjoy my life.' He could never do that, not in his professional life, nor in his personal life."

Alzado's older brother, Peter Alzado, believes the steroids served as a catalyst and then ultimately as a crutch that forced his brother to confront his own inner demons. "My dad was a horrible, violent alcoholic who abused everybody in the family," Peter Alzado said. "Lyle and I used to get up at night when my father would come home, and when we heard the door we'd wait on the top of the steps to see what his attitude was going to be like. If he started abusing my mother, we'd run down the steps to try to divert his attention to us. We were doing this from the time we were three, four, and five years old, and it continued on for eighteen years."

And as Alzado's steroid use increased, so too did his own violent behavior. "I think it terrified Lyle that his behavior was similar to that of my father," Peter Alzado said. "At a certain point Lyle started to recognize his violence off the football field. I don't want to say that he was necessarily abusive to others, but he recognized a lot of my father's behavior in himself and it terrified him."

And yet, he kept right on taking steroids. "You know the pattern," said Peter. "You know it's bad for you. You can even say out loud that it's bad for you. But that doesn't mean you stop."

Lyons said that Alzado's physical appearance started changing dramatically in 1979, when he joined the Cleveland Browns after eight seasons with the Denver Broncos.

"His body was becoming leaner and more muscular," Lyons said, "as opposed to just big and bulky like he was in college, and later on the Broncos. Suddenly, he became much more cut and ripped."

Alzado never actually lived in Cleveland during his three seasons there, and instead made a new home for himself in Los Angeles. According to Peter Alzado, it was in L.A. that his brother's steroid use went out of control. "He started working out in places like Gold's Gym, where there were always plenty of steroids around," he said. "And that's where Lyle began using steroids intensely."

By the time he joined the Los Angeles Raiders in 1982, "he had this big bulge on his side where he was injecting the steroids," Lyons remembered. "By then, anyone who knew him like I knew him knew he was taking a lot of steroids."

With his steroid use seeming to make him a better player on the field, Alzado was voted the NFL's Comeback Player of the Year after the '82 season. In Super Bowl XVIII the following year, the Washington Redskins managed only nine points against the Alzado-led Raider defense, and the Raiders won a lopsided victory, 38–9. With his one Super Bowl ring now on his finger, Alzado retired from the NFL after the '85 season, and promptly went Hollywood, appearing in commercials, shows on TV, and as an actor in a string of mostly terrible movies with titles like *Oceans of Fire, Tapeheads,* and *Zapped Again!*

In the spring of 1990, the forty-one-year-old Alzado attempted a comeback with the Raiders, telling reporters at the time, "I've decided to come out and help the team back to dominance. I have to go to training camp and prove myself. I can still kick ass. I haven't just laid around getting fat. I've worked out every day."

Of course, he said nothing about the steroids, a constant companion during those workouts. In fact, he was 270 pounds at the time of his comeback, and all muscle. "I was a violent player and I miss that," he told reporters then, crediting his appearance to the work of three personal trainers and a new training regimen, plyometrics, which he said enhanced his speed. Alzado even said that after his heavy lifting at Gold's Gym every day he would run on Venice Beach on his hands.

"It's like my body has been taken back in time," he said, leaving out the obvious information, which would have exposed the fact that he was stretching the truth. "I feel stronger, quicker, and I have more endurance."

Only he didn't, and in his one and only preseason game that August, against the Chicago Bears, he recorded no tackles and was never a real factor on defense. It quickly became apparent to Alzado and Raiders management that he was probably better off quitting again.

On Tuesday, August 28, Alzado told a reporter from the *Los Angeles Times* that he reached the decision to retire again following a closed-door meeting with Raiders owner Al Davis. "I just hope I didn't let anybody down," Alzado said of his attempt to play again. "I didn't want to disappoint anybody. I just wanted to perform well. The people who were skeptical about it, I wanted them to at least see that I was capable of it."

Other Raiders players and coaches all rallied around Alzado, saying only laudatory things about him in the press. No one dared mention his steroid use, even though they all knew about it.

"He didn't stop taking steroids during his first retirement," said his brother Peter, "and he had no intention of stopping after his aborted comeback with the Raiders. During his playing days, he would say to me, 'Pete, I'm going to do what I need to do to play the game the way I want to play it, and that's all.' But he continued to do it after he stopped playing. He was addicted to it. It filled an emotional need, an emotional hole."

That emotional hole, which no amount of steroids could fill, was most apparent in Alzado's checkered history with women. Alzado was married four times and had one child, a son, Justin (born in 1982), with his second wife and former high school friend, Cindy Iorio, to whom he was married for three years. She knew about his steroid use, and she tried unsuccessfully to get him to stop.

"He was taking steroids all the time," she told *Newsday*. "I begged him to stop."

But Alzado couldn't hear her, or for that matter any of the other women in his life. "He had four marriages and many other women in between and during those marriages," said Lyons. "He used to say to me, 'How do you stay married to one woman?' That was always part of his frustration."

"He was unable to live in any way without a woman being there," said Peter Alzado. "He would fly a woman to a football game so he could play the game just for her. That really references our whole emotional sustenance, which came from my mother. My mother came from a good, stable, orthodox Jewish family, and that's where our emotional sustenance came from. Lyle needed to have a woman around, someone whom he cared for and who cared for him, a woman he was somehow protecting. He would actually give a little gun to each of his girlfriends and each of his wives. If you were with Lyle, you got a little gun. It had to do with protection and protecting. In turn, he got an emotional connection. That's how he got his sustenance, like we did as children from my mother. We survived my father. But if it weren't for my mom, we probably would've died."

Death was surely the last thing on Lyle Alzado's mind when he met fashion model Kathy Davis, who would become his fourth and last wife. The two were married in March 1991 in Portland, Oregon. Marc Lyons was there. "Another one of Lyle's old friends, Artie Fisher, and I were co-best men," said Lyons. "I went out to Portland with another of our lifelong friends, Ira Gordon, who played center on our Lawrence High School team. We had our tuxedos on, having a good time, when I suddenly noticed that Lyle wasn't dancing at his own wedding. He always danced. He always partied. He always knew how to have a good time."

But he wasn't having a good time and Lyons noticed. "He said he had an ear infection," said Lyons, "and I left it at that. He just seemed very mellow sitting there."

Later that night, Lyons staged an elaborate practical joke on the newlyweds that he said was payback for a practical joke Alzado had pulled on him in 1976.

"On the night of my wedding," said Lyons, "my wife and I were in bed in a hotel room near JFK airport, when suddenly there was a knock at the door. The party was over, and we weren't expecting anyone. I said, 'Who's there?'

"A voice came back, 'It's room service.'

"I said, 'We didn't order anything.'

"And the voice said, 'Oh, yes you did.'"

Lyons opened the door, and there in the hallway was Alzado and a dozen of their Long Island friends. "Lyle had a ukulele," said Lyons. "They had pots and pans, and their wives were with them. And they all came parading into the room. My wife pulled the covers over her head, and I laughed like crazy. They stayed for about ten minutes and then they left."

Lyons knew that one day he would get back at Alzado, and his wedding in Portland gave him the opportunity. "A bunch of us chipped in and we got a belly dancer," said Lyons. "Then we got some pots and pans from the kitchen where Lyle was staying. I got a little guitar. We knocked on Lyle's door, and he said, 'Who is it?'

"I said, 'It's room service.'

"He said, 'We didn't order anything.'

"I said, 'Oh, yes you did.'"

Alzado opened the door, and they all stormed in, just like Alzado had done fifteen years earlier. "We banged on the pots and pans, and the belly dancer got right on their bed and started belly dancing," said Lyons. "We got Lyle back very good."

Lyons returned to the East Coast the following day, and heard the news three weeks later that his famous friend had been diagnosed with inoperable brain cancer. "What he thought was an ear infection," said Lyons, "was obviously much worse."

As a player, Alzado always made himself available to the press. And now that he had become sick, he saw no reason to change his personality and hide. He talked openly to *Sports Illustrated* in the July 8, 1991, issue about the onset of his illness.

"Kathy was getting on me pretty good about the steroids," he said, "and I promised her I wouldn't take anything more after our wedding. I started tapering down even before the wedding. I think I was so excited about marrying Kathy that I didn't allow myself to notice that I was starting to get sicker. When I watch the video of the wedding, I see that, when I'm walking back down the aisle with her, I'm almost limping, listing to the right.

"Two days later," he continued, "in the apartment in Marina del Rey where we were living at the time, I started feeling dizzy. I couldn't talk. And I was seeing double. They put me in the hospital and took all kinds of tests and they told me I had some sort of virus. I went home and got worse and worse. I didn't eat for four days.

"Finally," he said, "Kathy insisted to the doctors that I go back in, and they did a brain biopsy. I woke up the morning after, and they told me I had cancer."

Alzado vowed to beat his illness, and even allowed his new wife to talk to the press on his behalf. "My husband is a fighter and he is going to beat this," she told the *Los Angeles Times.* "He is strong. The only way I can look at it is that he's going to get better, and we are going to have a baby. I have to try and reinforce a positive attitude."

Alzado's illness gave him the perfect opportunity to come clean about the steroids, especially since he believed absolutely that his cancer was a direct result of his steroid use. Former Raiders team doctor, internist Robert Huizenga, agreed.

"I think there's no question," Huizenga said in the same *Sports Illustrated* issue. "We know anabolic steroids have cancer-forming ability. We know that growth hormones have cancer-growing ability."

Dr. Forest Tennant, a former drug advisor to the NFL, gave numerous interviews at the time, backing up the assertions made by Alzado and Huizenga. "Anabolic steroids depress the immune system and lymphocytes," Tennant told the *New York Times*. "[Alzado] has lymphoma. You don't have to be a rocket scientist to figure out the connection."

But there were also many dissenters in the medical community, among them Dr. Gary Wadler, a steroid expert at Cornell University Medical Center and North Shore University Hospital, in Manhasset, New York. He told the *Chicago Tribune* that no connection could be proved in Alzado's case.

"We were unable to really substantiate any cause-and-effect relationship beyond mere speculation and Lyle Alzado's own contention that this somehow was related," he said.

But the issue, ultimately, was that Alzado was a very sick man, and his new wife responded by circling the wagons around him. She became, according to Peter Alzado, the gatekeeper to her husband's life, a conscious move on her part that effectively separated him from his family and friends.

Peter Alzado had endured other periods of estrangement from his kid brother, but this new one was especially difficult to take, considering how sick Lyle was getting. "We had been off and on for years," Peter said. "There were times when we were very much in touch and there were times when we weren't. Everyone in the family always felt the responsibility to take care of everyone else in the family. But there were many times that Lyle was unresponsive to those needs. I'm not necessarily talking about financial needs. My mother suffered a nervous breakdown in the early seventies, and while Lyle was responsive some of the time, he was never consistent. I am certain that his steroid use contributed to his inability to respond emotionally. But I don't blame him for any of that. Very often when people grow up in the kind of atmosphere we grew up in, they distance themselves from it. I've experienced that in my life, and Lyle did, too. The memories were too painful, and since he was living a different life anyway, he didn't want to go back to those feelings."

Peter Alzado found out about his brother's illness on the radio, in a news report. He immediately drove down to Los Angeles from his home in Ashland, Oregon, to see his stricken sibling. "I realized that for all the difficulties and all of the resentments and anger that developed over a period of time, when someone you love is ill, all those things disappear," he said. "They just mean nothing, and the only thing that matters is that you love this person and they are ill. So it really made me realize that love is love and that's all there is when push comes to shove. So I went down there, and I drove down every week to see him.

"We talked about our growing up," he said. "There was a bond that developed with Lyle and me that started when we were sitting at the top of the steps waiting for my father to come home. So it was just family. It was just Lyle and me, just like it had been when we were growing up."

But the weekly visits didn't last long. "Most everybody from his prior life was not able to speak with him after a certain point. Kathy shut everybody out."

Lyons initially regarded Kathy as "a nice girl, a pleasant enough girl. Lyle was happy with her," he said, "and that was good enough for me."

But in a way, it was not entirely good enough for Lyle Alzado. Peter Alzado didn't come right out and say that his brother cheated on Kathy like he had cheated on all the other women throughout his life. But Peter did say that Lyle attempted to reconcile with his third wife, Kris Tavaglione, after he married Kathy.

"He wanted to get back with Kris," said Peter. "He was married to Kathy and he was out of the hospital and in remission, and he wanted very much to get back with Kris. So he set up a meeting with Kris to see if she would take him back, and she wouldn't. Although I know that she still loved him, they had their difficulties. I was at the meeting. Kris was there, of course, and Lyle, and my brother Billy, and I believe that a friend of Kris's was there, as well. And Kris declined to take him back. I know that she loved Lyle deeply, but in that relationship as in all the others Lyle began exhibiting more and more of my father's behavior. I know it horrified him and it ruined his marriages."

The period of remission turned out to be just a few months, and as Alzado's health worsened, so too did his contact with his family. "I started receiving phone calls late at night," Peter recalled. "I knew it was Lyle on the phone, but he had lost his voice and wasn't able to talk. It was just silence on the phone. So I would talk. I would tell him that I loved him and I hoped he wasn't in pain. I also told him that I knew he was separating himself from us, and that it was okay.

"There was a pattern Lyle developed for himself when it came to the women in his life," he said. "It played out over a long period of time, and it always involved his establishing strong emotional connections with women. He would protect them and in return they would protect him from whatever evils there were in the world. And once the pattern was established, he would find a way to destroy the relationship. And I remember telling him on the phone that I understood what he was going through. I don't think I actually said, 'Lyle, you can break the pattern.' But I did say that I understood what he needed to do. I said it was okay with me that he allowed Kathy to separate him from everyone he knew. I said it was okay that he felt he had to do that. This may sound really fucked up, but I'm certain that Kathy established the idea with Lyle that he was bad and was no good. Lyle was already full of guilt. He fucked every woman he could. He behaved badly during his life, and to him that made him just like my father. So here comes Kathy, the next woman, and she's going to protect him. But in order to do that she had to keep him away from everybody else who loved him because they represented the past and the bad behavior. And Lyle went along with it.

"And I told him that it was okay," said Peter. "He had to do what he had to do. He had to play the pattern out. He had to play the game out because he didn't know how else to do it. He didn't know how else to live. That's how he lived. He was probably scared and terrified, so he just stayed in the emotional patterns that he had established during his life. He was never able to break through those patterns in the past, and he wasn't doing it now."

Lyons was one Alzado friend who managed to retain some access. In early January 1992, Lyons and Ira Gordon both flew out to Los Angeles to attend a major black-tie fundraiser that was being planned in Alzado's honor. The gala event was scheduled to be held Saturday night, January 11, in the grand ballroom at the Beverly Hilton Hotel in Beverly Hills. According to the *Los Angeles Times*, the lineup of stars included Dionne Warwick, who would sing the national anthem, George Foreman, who would narrate a film of a fight that Alzado had once staged with Muhammad Ali, and rocker Jerry Lee Lewis, who had agreed to sing one of his classic showstoppers, "Great Balls of Fire."

But on Friday, January 10, Alzado's longtime manager and event organizer, Greg Campbell, suffered a mild heart attack. Campbell abruptly cancelled the event the following day, but not because of his health. The reason for the cancellation, he said, was a lack of funds to properly put on the event. *USA Today* reported that Campbell's break-even amount for the event was $400,000, and all he had received by that day was $75,000 from the Raiders and another $25,000 from Occidental Petroleum.

The Alzados were in their matching Giorgio Armani tuxedos and on their way to the hotel when they heard about the cancellation. Other celebrities, such as Maria Shriver, were called and uninvited. Lyons described the scene in the Beverly Hilton lobby that day as a fiasco.

"I've done fundraising events for twenty-five years," said Lyons, "and it was clear there was something wrong with the planning for this one. Ira and I were mortified that it had to be cancelled."

Some of Alzado's other friends tried to save the evening by quickly organizing a smaller dinner at a local restaurant. "One of Lyle's movie-star friends said, 'Don't worry, don't worry. We'll all meet at so-and-so. It'll be great,'" said Lyons, recounting the evening. "About two hundred people showed up. Friends, family, we all sat at tables eating and drinking. The evening went on, and everybody left except Lyle's real friends. And then the bill came. It could have been $4,000, but I don't remember the exact amount. Lyle was sick and sitting in a corner. The Hollywood people had all gone, and now his closest friends had to deal with the check. It's just typical of how people used to get over on Lyle. Even sick he was getting ripped off. And here we were, just regular working people, and we had to chip in and use our credit cards to pay the bill. It was a scam, a Los Angeles scam. We flew out wanting to help with this big dinner, and all of Lyle's friends got stuck with the tab. It was terrible. And Lyle was so very weak at that point. His spirits were down. He knew it was over."

In March, Kathy Alzado moved her husband to Portland so he could undergo a chemotherapy program at the Oregon Health and Science University. The *Boston Globe* reported that the radical therapy, developed by Dr. Edward A. Neuwelt, involved injecting concentrated sugars into Alzado's blood vessels in the hope they would open up enough to allow the cancer-fighting drugs to reach the source of his disease.

Peter Alzado had no idea his brother had moved to Oregon. And while he couldn't recall precisely who told him, he said the news definitely didn't come from his new sister-in-law, or any other member of her family. "We weren't notified of anything through the Davis family," he said. "These are people who knew Lyle for only months, not years. The whole thing was fucking nuts."

Lyons did manage to get through to Kathy Alzado in Portland. "Initially, I thought it was a good thing that they took him up there," said Lyons. "But as it turned out, I think Kathy's family manipulated him and took advantage of the situation. I don't know if it was Kathy directly, or whether she was led by her family."

Money, which Alzado had very little of at that point, having already declared bankruptcy, was the furthest thing from his mind during the next few weeks in Oregon. The chemo wasn't working. The weight was melting off. And chances for survival seemed remote. Peter Alzado believes his brother had become resigned to his fate.

"Lyle was ruled by guilt," he said. "He was very guilty about the steroids, and I think he felt that the cancer was his payback. I have a few theories about this. No one really knows about the human growth hormone he took, and where the hell it came from. I guess it came from a cadaver. This may have contributed to his brain cancer, or maybe it didn't. But Lyle felt somehow that when football was over for him, life was over for him. And however that manifested itself in combination with the steroids, it may have had something to do with Lyle's being vulnerable to the disease.

"In his mind," Peter Alzado continued, "he justified it because he felt he deserved it. He deserved to get sick. People think we're crazy for saying that, but that was Lyle's psychological makeup. I'm not saying that he wanted to die, because he didn't. He didn't want to get sick either. But I think he felt he got his due."

Alzado only got sicker and sicker that spring, and on Thursday, May 14, he finally let go and passed away. He was in bed at home when he died. Kathy Alzado was at his side. Marc Lyons heard the news on the radio.

"No one called me," he said. "I jumped on a plane with Ira Gordon and we went out there. Kathy's family had shut everyone out. But we flew out there and they were cordial to us. We went to their house. We were there for the wedding, so we knew where to go. We called her, and we said, 'We're going to be there.' She didn't stop us. She was nice to us."

Lyons said that eighteen people, including himself, Gordon, and Raiders owner Al Davis, spoke during the outdoor funeral. "As Al Davis was delivering his eulogy," said Lyons, "a white dove flew out of a tree and landed on Lyle's casket. We were all blown away. It was the most amazing thing I've ever seen. Where did the dove even come from? Nobody knew."

No one from Alzado's nuclear family attended his funeral, Peter Alzado said, because no one in Portland thought to call them. "I think I found out that my brother had died," he said, "when I got a call from our other brother, Billy. I know we weren't notified through Kathy Davis's family."

Peter Alzado, who today serves as artistic director of Oregon Stage Works, a theater group in Ashland, Oregon, hastily organized a memorial service for his brother in Ashland. "My mother came," he said, "along with my brother Billy. My wife, Isabelle, was there, with our children. We had a rabbi come to the house to conduct a service."

During the service, Peter Alzado read a poem he had just written for Lyle. He feels now, as he did then, that his poem captures the pain and struggle and reality of his brother's life. Titled simply, "Brother," the poem begins, "On Arlington Road," which is where the Alzado family lived in Cedarhurst, Long Island,

> brothers and sisters, stained yellow and red, upstairs against the closet wall making promises. Flashing circling sirens pin their arms encircled against a carousel of squeaky leather and "Daddy Don't!"
>
> Soft in the cold leathery night you murmur, "Mommy . . . hold me Mommy, Mommy hold me." Later, cuddled in her arms, dirty little clothes torn at the knee, your heart pounds against the thought, and pounds against the terror of being HIM!
>
> But what . . . is there? And so, you pound, you hold fast and pound and pound and pound against and pound against and pound more and pound into the glory!
>
> And still it's there—with glitter—covered. And only, please, only in the arms of strangers.
>
> And pound with all your might, and still . . . still . . . And should a stranger be a friend, and see beneath the shine, pound, pound! And streaming tears run away, run fast. And it's still there insinuating, undaunted, stronger for the years of pounding and stronger still for running.

The emptiness—it's bigger, it cracks and grows and munches a piece of your brain.

Oh, give me strangers and let them cradle me now, and make me a silver cup and let's drink to heroism. And make it shine to catch my breath and blind them from what I fear— on a winter's night in a carousel of patches and screams.

And throw away the beveled glass and give me soft pink light, and statues to pounding.

And give me needles to fill the hole, and please, oh please, surround me with strangers.

And cradle me, mommy. Cradle me, and give me clean white monsters to suck me dry and make me suffer for being . . . for be- ing . . . HIM!

And Mommy . . . cradle me, Mommy, Mommy cradle me, and hold me warm and close, and finally I will still my voice and close my eyes against the terror of being HIM!

"At the bottom of his heart, he meant well," Peter Alzado said of his poem's lead character. "He was very generous and a sweet guy who looked at himself as a hero. That was how he played out his life. The public reaction to Lyle, and to his celebrity, enabled him to avoid looking at the things that caused him pain and sorrow and eventually his death.

"If Lyle did something bad to somebody," Peter explained, "and that person complained about it, Lyle would say, 'Well, fuck you.' He'd walk down the street and meet somebody new, a total stranger, and they would say, 'Oh, my God, it's Lyle Alzado.'

"And Lyle would say, 'Do you know what so-and-so over there did?'

"And the stranger would say, 'Oh, Lyle, they are so fucked up. They don't realize how great you are.'"

Peter insisted this was how his brother made new friends. "Usu- ally," he said, "if Lyle had a choice between doing business with an up- standing, substantial person and a scumbag, he'd go with the scumbag. I'm not saying this happened in every case, with everyone around him, but there was a deep, very self-destructive aspect to my brother that he was never able to get under control. And he didn't have to get it under control because he was Lyle Alzado."

He was surely never able to control the financial side of his life. When he died, he was for all practical purposes broke. Money did come in later, thanks to the thinking of Raiders owner Al Davis and the mother of another childhood friend, Larry Sheeps. According to Lyons, Sheeps's mother sold Alzado a $1 million life insurance policy a couple of years before he became ill. "And Al Davis knew that Lyle was not a good businessman, and that he was hanging around with rogues," said Lyons. "So he deferred $1 million of Lyle's football salary, which came through a few years after he died."

Lyons said that the net proceeds from those two deals, "roughly $1.6 million," were divided equally between Kathy Alzado and Lyle's son, Justin. "But there was also tons of memorabilia," said Lyons. "Justin got his father's Super Bowl ring, and Kathy got everything else."

Then there is the matter of proper recognition, which Lyons feels has eluded his friend, even posthumously. "ESPN did a big story on Lyle after he died," said Lyons, who appeared on the broadcast. "But they didn't go after the real story because, let's face it, ESPN is in bed with the NFL. Until recently the steroid problem in baseball was being swept under the mat, and the problem in baseball is nothing compared to what it is in football. Think about it: Lyle is probably the only athlete in all of sports to come out and say that steroids are posing a health problem in the future, and the powers that be say there is no conclusive proof. That's ridiculous.

"They're turning their backs on the problem and in the process they have made out my friend to be the villain," said Lyons. "He's been blackballed from the Hall of Fame because of that, no question about it. Nobody is going to lobby for him to be in the Hall of Fame. And he should be there. He was the NFL Player of the Year and a perennial All-Pro. He was a phenomenal athlete and a wonderful guy, but he made a deal with the devil. He had to stay big and strong. He wanted to make a comeback, and it killed him.

"Unfortunately, poor Lyle has been made out to be the whipping boy in the entire steroids story," said Lyons. "If he had known that steroids would do what they did to him, he certainly wouldn't have taken them. But in those days there was no education. And there's still no education. Steroids continue to be rampant in pro sports."

Alzado's son, Justin, believes there is still time for others to learn from his father's mistakes. "I understand the goal of some of these guys; that athletes are ambitious people," he told the *Los Angeles Times* ten years after his father's death. "At the same time I'm disappointed my dad's words are going unheard. He made a strong effort to warn others of the risks of steroids and, hopefully, they'll see the big picture in the end."

If only Lyle Alzado could have lived long enough to realize a plan he had for his own big picture. "His life lasted forty-three years instead of seventy-three or eighty-three," said Lyons. "We always joked about going to Miami Beach when we were old and walking on the beach. But Lyle made that deal with the devil, and the devil came back and said, 'Okay, I gave you what you wanted. Now I want what I want.' And because of that, Ira Gordon and I will get to walk the beaches of Miami one day, and Lyle won't."

Arthur Ashe

July 10, 1943–February 6, 1993

DONALD DELL HAD KNOWN ARTHUR ASHE SINCE THE LATE 1960S. AS HIS lawyer and most trusted business advisor, Dell was there with Ashe during his extraordinary ride to the top of the tennis world, from the U.S. Open, Australian Open, and his numerous wins as a member of the U.S. Davis Cup team to what is perhaps his greatest triumph in the sport—his 1975 upset of number-one seed Jimmy Connors to win the men's singles title at Wimbledon. Following the stunning victory, the first ever by a black man at Wimbledon, Richard Evans, who covered the event for *World Tennis,* wrote that Ashe's win "spread happiness and satisfaction throughout the sporting world because it had turned a good man and a fine sportsman into a great champion."

But it was the good man and not necessarily the great champion that Dell responded to most in Ashe. Dell always considered himself Ashe's closest friend, and Ashe never once exhibited actions to suggest otherwise. The two men had been traveling companions before Ashe met his wife, Jeanne-Marie Moutoussamy, in 1976, and they continued right on traveling as two couples afterward.

The vacation that Carolyn and Donald Dell took with Jeanne and Arthur Ashe in late August 1988 started out as just one of those trips. That it happened to be in the Adirondacks matters little to the story. In retrospect, Ashe could have fainted anywhere. But this is where it happened, and Dell didn't think much about it when it did. Ashe simply got dizzy. Then he rested, and that was the end of it.

"We had planned to go out the next day to play golf," recalled Dell, a former captain of the U.S. Davis Cup team who represented athletes under the banner of his company ProServ, which he later sold to the entertainment giant SFX.

"Arthur was going to give me a golf lesson," continued Dell. "I had never played golf before, and Arthur loved golf. I had never even hit a golf ball. There we were on the first tee and Arthur was starting to show me the swing, and suddenly he got dizzy again and he fell over. We went to a hospital in New York a day or two later thinking that he might have had some sort of brain tumor, or something in his head."

Doctors performed brain surgery on Ashe and found no brain tumor. Dell remembered how he and Carolyn breathed a sigh of relief. "We were on an elevator in the hospital, going up to see Arthur," he said, "and I said to Carolyn, 'God, this is great news. He's okay. He doesn't have a brain tumor.' One of the nurses from Arthur's floor was on the elevator. We knew the hospital well and everyone there knew Arthur because he had been in and out of there a number of times with a lot of medical things, including two open-heart surgeries.

"The nurse on the elevator turned to us," said Dell, "and we said, 'Isn't this great? He doesn't have a brain tumor.' But she didn't react very strongly, so we got off the elevator and I turned to my wife, and I said, 'There's something phony going on here because that nurse who works on Arthur's floor didn't react at all.' The nurses loved him. He was extremely popular there and extremely well known. But this was a very weird reaction. We got to Arthur's room and the doctor was there with Jeanne and a few others, very select close friends, maybe six people in all including Jeanne. The doctor announced that Arthur did not have a brain tumor and everybody cheered. Everybody was happy.

"Arthur was sitting up," recalled Dell. "You could see the staples around his head. His head was stapled back together by metal staples. It was the damnedest thing I ever saw. We stayed for an hour or two and I noticed that Jeanne did not look happy. You could just tell that something was wrong. But nobody said anything. Two days later, Jeanne called me on the phone, and she said, 'Donald, Arthur has something he wants to tell you.' Arthur got on the phone, and I said, 'Arthur, how are you feeling?'

"I'll never forget how he said it," recalled Dell, "He said, 'The doctors tell me I have AIDS, but I don't really believe it.'

"It seems that during the brain operation," said Dell, "blood came out of his head. The blood was tested and it indicated, without a doubt, that he had AIDS. Understand, he was not HIV-positive like Magic Johnson (who revealed his condition at a press conference in November 1991, more than three years after Ashe received his diagnosis). Arthur was already in the fourth stage of AIDS when we found out. Magic Johnson has been HIV-positive for more than a decade. He never moved into that last stage, the final stage of AIDS. There's a hell of a big difference between HIV and full-blown AIDS, and Arthur was being told he had full-blown AIDS."

Dell did the math: Ashe had undergone a second heart surgery in 1983, a double bypass. Following the operation, he felt rundown, and in his own words, "unbelievably low." Doctors thought a blood transfusion might help restore his energy, and Ashe went for it. And why not? It seemed to him like a perfect quick fix. After all, plenty of blood was available in blood banks throughout the nation. Of course, none of it was being screened for AIDS because, as Dell said, "In the early eighties, no one had a clue what AIDS was, and so the blood was never protected."

Ashe ultimately came to the logical conclusion that the blood he received in 1983 was tainted. But, in 1988, with the public still believing that AIDS was the disease that happened to homosexuals and drug addicts, Ashe, who was neither homosexual nor a drug addict, insisted that his diagnosis be kept secret.

"Arthur told only a few people the truth about his condition," said Dell, "and he asked us to absolutely deny it if anyone asked. I told bold-faced lies for two years to some of my very, very best friends. They would come up and say, 'Arthur really looks sick. He looks pale. Are the rumors true?'

"And I would say, 'What rumors? What are you talking about?'

"They'd say, 'I heard he has AIDS.'

"I said, 'No, no.'

"And they'd say, 'Donald, you know him better than anybody. Can I rest on that?'

"And I'd say, 'Absolutely.'

"So I was fiercely protective," said Dell. "I didn't mind that I was doing it. I wasn't worried or concerned ethically about lying, except maybe to one or two very close friends. But I didn't feel badly because that's what he wanted. Arthur was worried about his daughter, Camera, and what she might have to face in school. He was worried that she'd be made fun of. He was worried that people might think he was bisexual. Remember, not too many people really understood what the hell AIDS was about. People feel differently about it today. We know so much more medically. But back then, no.

"I remember one day," said Dell. "Joe Cullman, a great friend of mine, a chairman of Philip Morris, loved Arthur. Arthur was on the Philip Morris sportsmanship and sports advisory group. Joe was the chair and he put Arthur on as a good will gesture. I mean, Arthur didn't smoke. He didn't believe in smoking. But he had accepted Joe's invitation to join the group. Joe knew everybody, and one day he came up to me at the U.S. Open, and he said, 'God, Donald, I've heard this terrible rumor and you're the only one who's going to tell me the truth. Does he have AIDS?'

"I said, 'Of course not, Joe. Don't be absurd. And goddamnit, go back and tell all those people that the rumor is false.'"

Dell wasn't the only one who lied in Ashe's behalf. Ashe lied, too. "Sometimes, indirectly, I had to lie about AIDS," Ashe wrote in his memoir, *Days of Grace*, which was co-authored with Arnold Rampersad.

"Now and then," Ashe continued, "I had to lie about it directly. In November 1991, when I wanted to go to South Africa, I lied on the application for my visa and said that I did not have an infectious disease. But I never lied without a sharp twinge of conscience, even in lying to the government of South Africa."

But Ashe could not bring himself to lie to Gene Policinski, *USA Today*'s managing editor for sports, when the two men spoke by phone on Tuesday, April 7, 1992. Earlier in the day, the paper's lead tennis reporter, Doug Smith, a longtime Ashe friend, asked Ashe for a response to the rumor that he had AIDS. Like Joe Cullman, Policinski and Smith had been hearing the rumor, but their positions at the newspaper demanded some sort of confirmation from Ashe before going ahead and printing the story as fact.

Ashe gave no answer to Smith, and instead picked up the phone to call his boss. Policinski was not immediately available, but Ashe was told he'd call him right back, which he promptly did. Ashe softened his stance slightly with Policinski. "Could be," Ashe wrote in his book, recounting his reply to the same question.

"I could not lie to him," Ashe recalled in his book. "'Look,' I said with some force, 'the public has no right to know in this case.'

"As I saw this situation," Ashe wrote, "the public's right to know really meant the newspaper's right to print. . . . The law was on the side of the newspaper, but ethically its demand was wrong, as well as unnecessary."

Policinski, of course, saw it differently. "I couldn't just assume from his responses that the story was accurate, but the fact that he was spending a lot of time on it and not simply denying it certainly perked my reporter's instincts," said Policinski, who today serves as executive director of the First Amendment Center, a nonprofit, non-partisan educational group in Nashville, Tennessee.

"*USA Today* had a very, very firm policy, which I agreed with, not to use unnamed sources in a story," recalled Policinski. "I told Arthur also that we had no intention of backing into the story by saying 'Arthur Ashe denies he has AIDS.' Basically, it was a polite and informative conversation. It was a very serious conversation, obviously. I always hesitate to say 'cordial,' because we were talking about serious subjects, but it was very polite and informative. Neither of us had ever spoken to each other before, but I had great respect for him, and I felt that he respected my position, as well."

The two men went back and forth on the issue, and it soon became clear to Ashe that Policinski would never view the situation as a non-story. Nevertheless, Ashe still tried to buy time with the newspaperman. "He did ask me if we could give him some time," Policinski said. "It was an odd amount of hours, thirty-six or thirty-eight hours, to make a decision about disclosing his health. What I said next led to the conclusion of the conversation. I said, 'I really can't help you plan any of this. I don't think it would be appropriate. I understand that you neither confirm nor deny the story.' And then I laid out our approach again, saying that we didn't use unnamed sources, and that because of the gravity of this I would require two first-person named sources in the story, which was not unusual for a major story. I told him again that we wouldn't back into the story. He offered another gentle request for more time, and I just stopped the conversation at that point."

Dell was on a plane to San Francisco, and the moment he disembarked there was a message from Ashe to stop whatever he was doing, from wherever he was, and call him immediately. The message was marked urgent.

"So I called him," Dell said, "and I said, 'What's the matter?'"

"He said, 'They found out. They know about the AIDS, and the story is coming out tomorrow in *USA Today.*'"

"I said, 'Are you sure about that?' And he recounted his conversation with Gene Policinski. I got right back on a redeye," said Dell, "and flew back to New York."

Ashe decided to hold a press conference the next day, and he called sportswriter and friend Frank Deford and asked for his help in crafting a public statement about his physical condition. Ashe recounted in his book that he barely slept that Tuesday night, thinking he would wake up on Wednesday, April 8, and see the story in *USA Today.* He did race out to buy the paper that next morning. He ran through it quickly at the newsstand and was relieved to find that the story about him was not there. But he also knew that the game was over, that it was only a matter of time before the story somehow got out. As he later wrote in *Days of Grace,* "Match point had come, and I had lost it."

Later that afternoon, from the HBO corporate offices in New York, Ashe stood at a podium and told the world that he had AIDS. He said that the questions asked of him by *USA Today* "put me in the unenviable position of having to lie if I wanted to protect our privacy.

"No one should have to make that choice," he insisted. "I am sorry that I have been forced to make this revelation now. After all, I am not running for some office of public trust, nor do I have stockholders to account to. It is only that I fall under the dubious umbrella of, quote, public figure, end quote."

"There were five hundred people in that room," Dell remembered. "We thought there would be fifty, and it was just an absolute mob scene. As Arthur was probably two-thirds of the way through, he started to talk about his daughter, Camera, and how, because of her, he had asked us to deny the rumor and lie for him. But as he brought up Camera's name, he completely lost it and his voice stopped and he started to cry. I moved forward to encourage him, but before I could get there Jeanne was right there next to him and she immediately picked up Arthur's statement right where he left off, which was quite lovely. And then I guess after two or three sentences, Arthur regained his composure and kept talking."

For weeks afterward press pundits debated the issues surrounding what Ashe had referred to as his "outing." Pulitzer Prize–winning columnist Anna Quindlen erred on the side of keeping Ashe's illness a secret.

"This story makes me queasy," Quindlen wrote in the *New York Times.* "Perhaps it is the disparity between the value of the information conveyed and the magnitude of pain inflicted."

Jonathan Yardley went even further in the *Washington Post.* "We tell ourselves that we are serving the public," he wrote, "but the blood-thirstiness and competitiveness with which we pursue our quarries are evidence enough that we are in search of nothing more noble than headlines."

Policinski disagrees. "I feel now as I did then," he said, "that the health and illness of a public figure is news. We said at the time that we had no special zone for AIDS, for or against, positive or negative. We have to remember that AIDS as an illness in 1992 was essentially believed to be fatal. There was no helpful drug cocktail, as there is to-day. Just the fact that there was little chance of survival made it news. And in this case, a great public figure of the twentieth century, Arthur Ashe, was dying of a disease. That's news. I felt at the time, as I do now, that it was right to at least ask him about the story."

"I don't buy that at all, and I never have," countered Dell. "I think it's totally different when it comes to revealing very personal issues about someone's life. That can be so detrimental to the person and equally detrimental to his wife and family. Yes, Arthur Ashe was a public figure, but he was not a politician. He was not seeking any-body's vote. He was a role model by definition because he was a well-known athlete. But as that kind of public figure, I think he had every right to keep personal things personal. The public's right to know and all that publicity is a lot of hogwash. I think the press plays that card all the time. They say the public needs to know. Well, the public didn't know for three and a half years and it didn't change anyone's life but Arthur's."

The Ashes tried vainly to come up with someone who might have tipped off the press, but the source was never identified and certainly never came forward. "I knew it was only a matter of time before the news came out anyway," said Dell. "Arthur was getting thinner and thinner, and in front of your very eyes he was literally wasting away and nobody could understand why. We thought probably that some-one called Doug Smith, who was Arthur's friend but also a reporter, and said something like, 'You really ought to check into this because Arthur is really sick.' Or, 'You ought to call Arthur.' I've never pursued it, but I think Jeanne felt it was somebody around the family, an exte-rior force. I mean, Doug Smith was in the family, Arthur's tennis fam-ily. Arthur really liked him and trusted him. But he never would have approached Arthur with that kind of question if somebody hadn't placed a call or said something to his editor. Of course, it could've been anybody. It could've been somebody down the street who thought, 'Gee, he looks sickly.'"

And since there was no magic pill, there wasn't much Ashe's doctors could do to slow down the deterioration. "It was a death sentence," said Dell, "and the only issue was, 'How many months does he have? How many weeks? How many days? Nobody knew.'"

Ashe was front-page news now, and people reacted by coming at him from all sides. "I've managed and represented athletes throughout my professional life," said Dell, "and people have no idea what it's like when someone walks up to a famous athlete on the street, or at a party. They say, 'Can I just have two minutes of your time?' And you're signing autographs and listening to their life stories or their problems, and two minutes turns into five minutes, and five minutes becomes ten minutes, and you could give up half your day if you're that kind of well-known celebrity."

Ashe had been dealing with those little interruptions for years. But after he made his announcement the demands on his time by the outside world suddenly took on a darker tone. And autographs were the least of it. "We were besieged by calls and requests from all different types of groups, which we routinely got throughout his career. But these calls were so desperate. These calls came from people who were worried about dying, or worried about friends dying, and we couldn't just say to them, 'Well, look, I'll come to that event next year.' Or 'I'll call you and do a film or something for you next month.' I represented Michael Jordan for nine years and we had a million requests. But no one said to me, 'Listen, we have to see him next week or my brother-in-law might die.' Or 'There are six guys in Philadelphia. They're only going to be alive for two more weeks. Could you come down to visit with them?' Those are the kinds of requests we were getting for Arthur."

Ashe expected to be criticized by gay rights activists for not announcing his disease sooner, and he was. "I'm sure they thought he could have helped people more and raised more money and awareness," said Dell, "but at the time he wanted peace and privacy with his family, which was a normal human reaction."

Still, had it been up to just Arthur Ashe, he probably would have said yes to everything. And while he did agree to many of those requests, his own condition was no less desperate than that of the callers. Dell, who had lived for years in the Washington, D.C., area, started spending most of his time in New York, so he could be with his friend. "Arthur went into the hospital a couple of times during that period," said Dell. "The hospital even had what they jokingly called 'Arthur Ashe's room,' because he always got the room with the best view."

One hospital stay in particular came right after the New Year began in 1993. Ashe had been in Miami to teach a tennis clinic at the Doral Resort and Country Club. His wife and daughter were with him. Everything seemed fine until he started having difficulty breathing on New Year's Day. Then came a high fever. Ashe was advised by his New York doctors to see doctors in Miami, which he did. By this time, Ashe had medical people he could call in virtually any city. But in this case he felt more comfortable returning to Manhattan and his hospital of choice, New York Hospital, on the Upper East Side. What Dell referred to as "Arthur Ashe's room" was in fact a room on the sixteenth floor that had been named after the Greek shipping magnate Stavros Niarchos. Ashe himself described the room in *Days of Grace.*

"I didn't ask for the room; it was assigned to me," he said. "Undoubtedly it was the most luxurious hospital room I had ever had, and I have had quite a few. Apart from an intravenous feeding stand parked discreetly in a corner, my iron bed, mechanized and grimly practical, was perhaps the sole reminder that I was in a hospital. The elegant wood floors are stained dark; the ceilings are high; the furniture, which includes a sofa upholstered in leather, would hardly disgrace the living room of a fine house."

The room, as Dell said, did have a great view. To the south, Ashe had a clear sight line to the Chrysler Building and the Empire State Building. When he looked east, he saw Roosevelt Island and Queens. A doctor told him that the room had been made famous years before when a young Massachusetts senator named John F. Kennedy had to be hospitalized and stayed there. Ashe had known more than a few world leaders, including someone who was about to become one—William Jefferson Clinton. Ashe had supported Clinton in the 1992 presidential election, and was rewarded with an invitation to Clinton's inauguration on Wednesday, January 20. The event was only a couple of weeks away. The invitation sat on the table near Ashe's hospital bed. But it was nothing more than a keepsake now. He knew he was too sick to attend.

Ashe didn't want a lot of people knowing that he was back in the hospital. Other than Jeanne and Camera, his visitors included only those from his inner circle of friends: Dell; Frank Deford; physicians

Eddie Mandeville and Doug Stein, who was also Camera's godfather; Dr. Paul Smith, pastor of the First Presbyterian Church of Brooklyn Heights; and Andrew Young, the former mayor of Atlanta who had officiated at Ashe's wedding ceremony.

"These are some of my friends," wrote Ashe, "but only a few of my friends, most of whom had no idea I was in the hospital. Jeanne and I kept my illness out of the news, where my name seemed to have been everywhere lately, at year's end. The honors and awards had come thick and fast. They pleased me, but they were not nearly as consoling as the visits of these friends, and the knowledge that people I have known for a lifetime were thinking about me and wishing me well. Whatever happens, I know that I am not going to be alone at the end. That is not to be my fate. Of course, in a sense, we are always alone at the end."

Ashe was released from the hospital on Monday, January 18, two days before Clinton's inauguration. It was also Martin Luther King Day, which gave the Ashe family something more to celebrate beyond just being able to get him home. Ashe would still have to watch the inauguration on TV, but at least he was home and that meant a great deal to everyone around him. In fact, while the actual event was being broadcast live on television, Ashe wrote a letter to his daughter, the entire content of which became the final chapter of his book, *Days of Grace.* In the chapter titled "My Dear Camera," Ashe told his daughter how much Maya Angelou's poem, which Angelou read at Clinton's inauguration, had meant to him.

"When I was a boy not much older than you," he wrote to Camera, "one of the most haunting spirituals I heard on many a Sunday morning in church spoke movingly of a 'rest beyond the river.' These words and music meant that no matter how harsh and unrelenting life on earth may have been for us as slaves or in what passed for our freedom, once we have crossed the river—that is, death—we will find on the other side God's promise of eternal peace. The river is death and yet it is also life. Rivers flow forever and are ever-changing. At no two moments in time is a river the same. The water in the river is always changing. Life is like that, Maya Angelou wisely reminded us today at the inauguration."

It was clear to Donald Dell, only in retrospect, that Ashe was readying himself for the inevitable.

"To be honest," said Dell, "I think that those around him denied what was happening to him more than he did. I think we kept dreaming that they would find some sort of miracle cure. Jeanne and I even talked about it. We didn't discuss it at any length, or with any depth, because we really didn't believe it. But we were just sort of hoping. Arthur, on the other hand, was in his own mind getting everything in shape and ready. We re-did a will for him and he paid off certain things. At his request, we gave things to certain people that he wanted them to have. I mean, he wasn't sitting there thinking he was going to die on such-and-such a date. It wasn't like that. But he was clearly getting weaker, and as he became weaker, he started losing the ability to fight off even a cold. And he couldn't fight off the cold because he had no immune system. That's the tragedy of full-blown AIDS."

In his writing, though, Ashe tried to remain upbeat. "Thus far, I have been steadfast," he wrote in *Days of Grace*, almost as though he were counting down the days. "At night, I get into bed and I go straight to sleep. Is this bravery, or only denial? My wife, Jeanne, thinks that I practice denial a fair amount of the time. Wisely, she makes a distinction between good denial and bad denial. The latter is when I walked around with a pain in my chest but brushed off the hurt and declined to go to my doctor. Good denial is my refusal to dwell on the idea of death, or even to accept as a fact the notion that I will die soon from heart disease or from an illness related to AIDS—to me, this is not denial, but a simple acknowledgment of the facts of my case.

"I am a fortunate, blessed man," he continued. "Aside from AIDS and heart disease, I have no problems. My stepmother, about whom I care deeply both for my sake and for my dead father's, is in fine health; my wife is in fine health; my daughter radiates vitality. I have loving friends in abundance. I have the support of skilled doctors and nurses. I need nothing that money can buy. So why should I complain? And beyond them, I have God to help me."

On Sunday, January 31, Eddie Mandeville and Doug Stein came over to Ashe's apartment to watch the Dallas Cowboys destroy the Buffalo Bills, 52–17, in Super Bowl XXVII. Ashe had been scheduled to speak at an AIDS fund-raiser on Saturday, February 6, in Hartford, Connecticut. He was hoping to keep his commitment, but his wife stepped in and had him cancel the appearance.

"It was brutally cold that week in New York," Dell remembered. "Very windy, too. Temperatures in the twenties. Jeanne just put her foot down and said, 'You're not going to Hartford. I don't care how important it is.' The event organizers sent a crew over to Arthur's house and he did ten or fifteen minutes on tape for them."

By Wednesday, February 3, "Arthur was getting a little wacko in the apartment," said Dell, who estimated that at approximately 6 P.M., "Arthur just got up and walked three or four blocks to buy a newspaper. Then he walked back. When he got back inside, he was cold and shivering. It was obvious that he needed to go right back into the hospital."

On Thursday, February 4, Dell visited Ashe again at New York Hospital. "I had to go down to Atlanta on business," he said, "and I wanted to see Arthur before I left," said Dell. "We had our visit, and he said, 'I would like to walk down to the elevator with you.'

"I said, 'Arthur, it's too far down the hall.'

"He said, 'No, it's fine. We'll just walk and talk as we walk.'

"We walked all the way down the hall," said Dell. "He shook my hand at the elevator, and looking back, I believe he knew he didn't have much time left. I didn't know that. But maybe it was just his way of saying good-bye. I don't know, it's just a guess, but on all my other visits, and I visited Arthur in the hospital many, many times, he never got out of bed to walk me all the way to the elevator. But this time he did. Maybe he just wanted the exercise, but we talked a lot. Then he shook my hand, hugged me, and said goodbye, and I got on the elevator."

On Saturday, February 6, Dell called Jeanne from Atlanta to check on her husband's condition. "I remember it clearly," said Dell. "It was about eight thirty in the morning, and she said, 'God, he's doing much better. The doctors say he's made a mild recovery. There's no need for you to fly back. Things are looking a lot better, and he's going to be coming out in a day or two. You'll come up and see him when you're back.'

"I remember it so well because I was so happy," said Dell. "I was having breakfast with Robert Muller, the president of Reebok at the time, and he knew Arthur really well. And I said, 'Roberto, we got lucky. He's going to be out of the hospital by tomorrow or the next day. He's feeling better.'"

Dell and Jerry Solomon, the president and number-two executive under Dell at ProServ, flew back to Washington together on an early afternoon flight. Dell's wife was waiting for him at the gate when he arrived. "She pulled me aside, and said, 'We need to talk alone.' I waved Jerry on, and Carolyn said, 'We have to go up to New York right now because Arthur died.'

"I almost fainted," said Dell. "I said, 'What are you talking about? I just talked to Jeanne this morning. She said he was doing fine.'

"And Carolyn said, 'He died about an hour ago.' Then she told me that Jeanne had given instructions to the doctors not to move Arthur's body until Carolyn and I arrived. Jeanne knew we would want to see him. Carolyn said, 'We have to go right away because they can't just leave him there.' So I told Jerry what had happened, and we got right on a shuttle flight."

Dell cried as he recalled walking into Ashe's hospital room. "It was lovely to see him, don't misunderstand me," he said. "But it's horrible to remember. Jeanne had already left. She had been there for a couple of hours after Arthur died, and then she went home. It was just Carolyn and me in the room. Arthur was just lying there in bed, dead. He looked okay, but he was dead. And we just sort of talked to him in general about what had gone on in his life. You know, the nice things. In a funny way, it was a very thoughtful thing for Jeanne to do because the hospital never does anything like that. But she made sure they left him there so we could see him. It would've just been awful to never see him again. I mean, there was nothing I could do. He was dead. But at least I could see him."

Back at Ashe's East Side apartment, his widow was agonizing over how to break the news to Camera, who was only six years old. Moutoussamy-Ashe later described the moment to *Ebony* writer Laura Randolph: "She was very calm and controlled and immediately wanted to watch a video. It was interesting because she digested it bit by bit. When I first told her, her response was all in her eyes. She just looked at me kind of helplessly."

The ensuing months were equally hard on both Camera and her mother. "When Arthur was away," *Ebony* quoted Moutoussamy-Ashe as saying, "he would call Camera every morning while I was getting her dressed to say goodbye to her. If the phone rings at ten after seven in the morning, I still think it's him."

In late June 1993, a little more than four months after Ashe's death, Moutoussamy-Ashe traveled to Wimbledon, the scene of Ashe's greatest triumph on a tennis court, and made a point to go directly to the HBO booth where her husband and Jim Lampley had worked for twelve years as TV coanchors during the tournament.

"I'd ascended those steps for the past twelve years," Moutoussamy-Ashe recounted to Randolph, "but walking into that booth and seeing

Jim Lampley sitting there without Arthur beside him was probably my toughest moment since Arthur died. Even though I knew he wasn't going to be there, I broke down and cried. And so did Jim Lampley. Arthur was so beautiful sitting in that chair with the lights on him and his jacket and his big smile. He used to keep a jelly doughnut sitting on the side of his chair and he'd try to sneak a bite without me catching him. When I walked into that studio, all of those little things just flashed in front of my face and I broke down and cried. But it was nothing I had any control over."

Donald Dell feels the void in his life even today. "Arthur was the best friend I ever had," said Dell. "He always made you feel good when you were around him, and by example he always inspired you to do better, to be a better person. Arthur had a tremendous belief that people were much more good than bad. All people. You could slap him once, or even defraud him once or twice, and he always gave everyone the benefit of the doubt."

Margaux Hemingway
February 16, 1955–July 1, 1996

THE WERE ALWAYS SO BUSY FACT-CHECKING EVERY WORD IN *PEOPLE* MAGAZINE that no one there ever had the time or the inclination to watch daytime television, least of all a syndicated talk show like *Geraldo*.

Not that anyone at *People* in the mid-1990s would ever admit to watching *Geraldo* at any hour, day or night. To the upper management at *People*, Geraldo Rivera was always a few letters down in the alphabet of celebrity hierarchy, and never in the same league with the real stars whose faces sold magazines, like Richard Gere and Princess Di. Geraldo did receive world-wide acclaim hosting *Rivera Live* on cable, where he kept the world up to date on O.J. Simpson, and in the process unleashed a frightening new breed of caustic blond-haired former prosecutors. He even managed to remain relatively calm as a prime-time partisan referee in this faster-paced, free-wheeling format that featured rancorous political discourse and spirited legal debate.

But the daytime Geraldo, the tabloid-blaring, trailer park–courting Geraldo, well, that was another story entirely. That Geraldo, the one who once got punched on the air during a daytime broadcast, was considered by *People* to be relevant only as a guilty pleasure. To the magazine, that Geraldo was an outdated personality who needed to be bound and gagged and left on a pile somewhere, near the rotting celebrity carcasses of Jerry Springer, Richard Bey, and Morton Downey Jr.

These were the kind of TV stars that only aroused serious interest at *People* if they were facing a life-threatening illness, or they committed a crime, or their children were seeking emancipation.

It is therefore very safe to assume that no one at *People,* not the big shots, not even the guys in the mailroom, were tuned in to the April 9, 1996, installment of *Geraldo,* when Margaux Hemingway was the featured guest. All she did that day on TV was talk at length about her bulimia, her alcoholism, and that awful moment in the mid-1970s when she slit her wrists after a long night of partying at Studio 54. She even showed Geraldo her nearly two-decades-old scars.

A celebrity confessional filled with that kind of rich pathos and impending tragedy usually signals a loud alarm at *People.* Photo editors are sent scurrying for pictures of old boyfriends, and correspondents are dispatched to circle their prey and await further instructions.

You might have expected that to be the case with Hemingway, whose mere mention of the word *suicide* on television should have been enough to make a few hearts at *People* beat faster. After all, suicide was a very familiar subject in her family. Her great-grandfather, Clarence Hemingway, committed suicide. His celebrated son, Ernest Hemingway, took his own life, as did his siblings Ursula and Leicester.

But *Geraldo* had aired under *People*'s normally efficient radar, so no forces were marshaled, and no early obits were written. Instead, the magazine went completely in the opposite direction and invited Margaux Hemingway to be its celebrity guest host to a group of *People* advertisers who were being lavishly treated to a few days at a spa in Miami Beach.

Getting celebrities to show their faces at charity functions, political fund-raisers, movie premieres, and even spa getaways was very big business by the mid-1990s. An event was practically guaranteed to be a success if the right celebrity was there to put a face on it. Want to save the rain forest? Convince Robin Williams to do a ten-minute standup. Want to set a record for live charity auction items? Bring in Rosie O'Donnell as the auctioneer. Want to be noticed at the White House Correspondents' Dinner? Make sure Julia Roberts is at your table. A celebrity guarantees media coverage. Media coverage guarantees more media coverage. And more media coverage guarantees that your charity, or your candidate, or your movie, or your magazine is everywhere. Even if it isn't really everywhere, it only has to seem that way to be that way.

It is unclear whether Margaux Hemingway was *People*'s first, second, or last choice to represent the magazine and mingle with advertisers at the Doral Saturnia Spa, right after Mother's Day 1996.

It had been more than twenty years since this six-foot-tall Oregon-born, Idaho-raised beauty blew into New York and scored a $1 million contract with Fabergé. It was a time when $1 million was still $1 million, and the deal provided Hemingway with a launching pad to success. It never hurt her image that she was the granddaughter of the great American novelist, but since he had been dead since 1961, Grandpa Ernest did nothing to help her wind up on the covers of such magazines as *Time* and *Vogue*.

But, despite bold predictions by producer Dino De Laurentiis that he was going to make her a star, the film career Hemingway wanted never amounted to much. And by the late 1980s, she was trying to kick alcohol at the Betty Ford Center in Rancho Mirage, California.

Hemingway attempted to jump-start her career in 1990 by posing nude in *Playboy*, and when that didn't work, there were infomercials for baldness, and later a contract with the Psychic Friends Hotline.

But things were changing for the better, and everyone around Hemingway knew it. By the time she walked into the Doral Saturnia Spa to do her bit for *People*, she could say she was the host of *Wild Guide*, a planned fall television series on nature and the environment that Westinghouse was producing for the Animal Planet Network. Hemingway had also been negotiating with the Home Shopping Network to market a new perfume, Margaux Hemingway's Rainforest Elixir. And there was even some talk of a new clothing and jewelry line.

Her appearance at the spa in Miami Beach, while welcomed by advertisers, was actually a surprise to Louise Lague, *People*'s manager of special projects and the organizer of the Doral event.

"I had no idea that the New York sales staff had arranged for her to be our celebrity guest," said Lague. "I'm sure the clients didn't know either. But they were thrilled to meet an actual celebrity."

Lague described Hemingway as looking very calm. "Not sedated, but sedate," she said. "She seemed very serene and not particularly depressed. I remember that she had her hair pulled back very simply in a rubber band. She was very gracious with people. She answered everyone's questions. She may not have been a hot star at that point, but the clients all knew who she was."

And she received her share of pampering right along with them, getting facials and massages and gift bags filled with creams and lotions and the May 6 "50 Most Beautiful People" issue of *People*. "The spa trip was pegged to the 'Most Beautiful' issue," said Lague, "but it was a very informal environment. Margaux wore a sweatshirt and sweatpants and she showed up for all her beauty appointments. We would all meet for lunch and dinner, and I remember watching her pray silently over her meal before eating. She said in a very soft-spoken way that she was following some sort of Eastern thing. She just kind of bowed her head and had a moment of silence. In a group of eighteen to twenty people, it can look a little unusual watching someone pray over their food at a corporate event. But it's not unheard of, and it wasn't weird. She didn't look particularly happy, and she didn't look particularly unhappy. There was just not a lot of emotion going on, one way or another."

On Friday, June 7, Hemingway gave an interview to the Prodigy Computer Network, in which she seemed to get some of that emotion back. She said, "I believe in rolling with the punches. You have to keep fighting. That's what life is all about, leading with your heart."

Leading with her heart is something Hemingway had been doing for most of her adult life. Her first marriage, to hamburger scion Errol Wetson, lasted for only a year and ended in 1978. By 1979, she was married again, to Venezuelan film director Bernard Foucher. They stayed together for three years, and were finally divorced in 1985. There were many men after Foucher, some of whom Hemingway managed to date at the same time.

Investment banker Stuart Sundlun never fooled himself into thinking that Hemingway was his and his alone. Theirs was a long-time on-again-off-again romance that was complicated by the fact that he lived three thousand miles away from her in New York. But she called him in early June and wondered if he was free to fly down to the Bahamas to meet her. Hemingway had received an offer to film a segment in the Bahamas for a TV fishing show. It was an independent, one-time-only job, unconnected to her work for *Wild Guide*. Sundlun wanted to meet her and agreed to go. They had lived together from 1986 to 1989. He helped her get through her Betty Ford experience, and as he said, "We always remained involved.

"We were always close," said Sundlun. "At times we were boyfriend/girlfriend. At times we weren't. The TV people in the Bahamas wanted her to do some deep-sea fishing. But when we got down there, she realized that she wasn't into the whole macho thing—the drinking beer, the going out and hauling in fish. That was her granddad's kind of deal. The vibe just wasn't great in the Bahamas, so we said, 'Let's get out of here.' We flew back to Miami, and from there I went back to New York, and she went back to L.A. And we made plans to meet over the July Fourth weekend in Newport, Rhode Island."

Sundlun probably never gave it much thought, but another man, Rev. Bill Minson, was waiting for Hemingway back in Los Angeles. Minson is a former Hollywood talent agent who left the business to form Tuday, a ministry in Santa Monica that provides spiritual counseling to urban youth. And like Sundlun, he and Hemingway would be together for a few days, and then not see each other for many more days. But Minson did connect with Hemingway after her return from the Bahamas.

"Margaux and I had been friends for years," said Minson. "I remember taking Margaux to Little Richard's house, and up to Robert Guillaume's house, where I played a lot of tennis. And Guillaume would say to me, 'What are you doing with this woman?'

"And I'd say, 'What do you mean, what am I doing with this woman? She's very interested in me. I'm very interested in her.' John Forsythe was another one who questioned me about Margaux. He would just really goof on me. But Margaux, meanwhile, was always very encouraging about my ministry. She would talk to Forsythe and the others about my ministry, and she'd set up meetings for me to meet other people."

Minson said that he and Hemingway became a serious item in 1995. "We started spending time together again in '95 and '96, and she even went to church with me one Sunday," Minson recalled. "It was the West Angeles Church of God in Christ, in South Central L.A. We went to hear Bishop Charles Blake. My son Rudo, who was just finishing high school at the time, came with us. After the service, my son said to me, 'Daddy, did you hear what Margaux was saying about being ready for a man in her life?' I said yes. And he said, 'Don't you get it?'

"I said, 'No. What do you mean?'

"He said, 'Well, you and Margaux are together all the time.'

"I said, 'Okay, but we're just friends.'

"He said, 'Daddy, you still don't get it.' He said, 'If you weren't my father, I'd tell you that you were stupid.'

"Well, that got my attention and I thought about it," said Minson. "The next time I called her, I left a message saying, 'I was just wondering if you'd like to go out and have dinner, maybe go to a movie.'

"And when I came back," he said, "she had left a message saying, 'You know, I have a date with this producer tonight, but I cancelled it. I'd like to go out with you.'

"To make a long story short," he said, "we went out and we talked for hours, like we never talked before. And we began to fall in love and spend time together. We would take long walks on the beach. We would just look at the ocean and hold hands. Sometimes we'd pray. Or we'd talk. This was a remarkable woman, despite the problems that she had in her life, which she fought to overcome. And she never hid from her problems. When she encountered other people with similar problems, she would encourage them and she would share some of her personal battles about what she had overcome. This was a champion of a woman, with championship qualities."

On Sunday, June 16, Father's Day, Minson and Hemingway visited with Guillaume, and then went hiking in one of her favorite areas of Santa Monica Canyon, up a path that began near the intersection of Pacific Coast Highway and the western tip of Sunset Boulevard.

"It was the most glorious day," Minson remembered. "We would stop and hug and look out over the ocean. She wanted to talk about some of her girlfriends, the women in her life. Her friends had been complaining that she was not spending enough time with them, because she was spending so much time with me."

One of those women, Jennifer Josephs, hiked with Hemingway that same week, also up Santa Monica Canyon. But according to Josephs, the two men Hemingway talked about most that day were not named Bill Minson or Stuart Sundlun. The two men uppermost in her mind, Josephs said, were producer Robert Evans, whom she was also dating at the time, and her ex-husband Bernard Foucher.

"Margaux was a little down that day we hiked," recalled Josephs, a Los Angeles real estate developer who met Hemingway in 1973 while working as a sports photographer for *Powder,* a skiing magazine. "She always said that Bernard was one of the great loves of her life, and she talked about her desire to somehow get back together with him. She had gone to Venezuela to see him a few weeks before, and she came back crushed because he had wanted her to come down to discuss how she might help him promoting one of his projects. And she had wanted something much more. In the old days, Bernard had really taken care of her. Margaux was like the little girl who really wanted someone to take care of her. I mean, she was just so in love with

Bernard. He was fun and dashing and extremely intelligent and charming and an adventurer, all the things that she loved."

Josephs had never heard of Minson, but she described Sundlun as one of Hemingway's "best, best friends."

"He was like her rock," she said, "a person who was really consistent in her life. She really, really trusted Stuart. He is a great guy who was madly in love with her. But Bernard was really the one. Margaux was just someone who wanted to love and be loved, just like everybody else here. She was lonely. It's difficult meeting people when you are as high-voltage as Margaux—beautiful, intelligent, famous, and on top of everything else she was tall. So that really narrows the field. Margaux's ideal guy would be like an Indiana Jones. And that was Bernard."

Of Evans, Josephs said, "He talked a lot about helping her career, but he never actually did anything for her.

"You have to understand how it was with Margaux," said Josephs. "A lot of men wanted a piece of her. A lot of men over the years were pretty infatuated with her."

After their hike, the two women had breakfast together at a coffee shop in Marina del Rey. "I always felt good after a hike with Margaux," said Josephs. "Because of her height she took very, very big steps, and she used to laugh that I could keep up with her. She was a mountain girl at heart, and a little girl inside. She was really a 'Gee whiz, baby cakes' kind of girl. People have to remember, she was the first supermodel, the first million-dollar cover girl. My father used to say, 'When a fire burns too hot, it burns itself out early.' I think it was really difficult that her life and her career had peaked at such a young age. She had such huge success, and she was so young and so vulnerable at that time. It was very difficult trying to get back to that, and back to herself. I always thought Margaux was at her happiest when she was back in Ketchum, Idaho, living in a log cabin and skiing a lot."

Her equally modest living conditions in Los Angeles were dictated by years of issues over money. According to Josephs, "Margaux had terrible tax problems, and she owed a lot of money to the government. She managed to pay it off over years, but there were always problems with money."

Money was one of the reasons she moved from her small apartment in the Marina to an even smaller one, above a garage and behind a house on Fraser Avenue, a block off the beach in Santa Monica. Josephs and Hemingway talked about her new apartment during their hike.

"She hadn't moved in yet," said Josephs, "but she was excited that she'd found another place."

Hemingway asked Minson to help her with the move. "It was a great day," he said, "moving from the Marina to the apartment on Frasier. I mean, all we did was hold hands and hug. The workmen did everything. But she was happy. That's the important thing. She was like a child at the Ringling Brothers circus for the first time. You saw it in her smile, in her glee, in her sound."

Hemingway was flashing a big smile on Wednesday, June 26, when she met Judy Stabile for dinner at Hal's, a hip bar and grill near the beach in Venice. Stabile, the daughter of Jerry Lewis's bandleader and manager, Dick Stabile, had known Hemingway since 1990.

"We met through a mutual friend, a publicist named Yanou Collart, who had been a friend of my family's," said Judy Stabile, who works as an artist out of her studio in Venice. "It was Yanou who took Margaux to the Gallipoli Islands for her famous nude photo session with *Playboy*. Yanou was at my studio one day to see my work, and she asked me if I wanted to meet Margaux Hemingway, who lived near me. At the time, she was living in a beautiful place in Santa Monica. Then she moved to Venice. Then to the Marina, and finally to that little room she had on Frasier. I was never there, and she had just moved in. She said she was very happy there.

"But when I met her, we just seemed to click. We just hit it off," said Stabile. "I adored her, and she adored me. And she had the nicest disposition. Never said a bad word about anybody, ever. But she was always up against the wall because of her emotional problems. She had epilepsy. She suffered from schizophrenia and manic depression. That was a family disease.

"She was just starting to read books by her grandfather," said Stabile. "She hadn't read him when we met, which I always found pretty surprising." It is more than likely that Hemingway was slow to read any of Ernest Hemingway's works because in addition to everything else, she suffered from dyslexia.

But during dinner that night with Stabile, Hemingway couldn't stop raving about the animals she grew to adore while working on *Wild Guide*. "She talked mostly about the manatees, and how much she loved them," said Stabile. "She called her experience with the manatees one of the best times she'd ever had. It was obvious to me that Margaux was trying to center herself emotionally. That was a constant quest for her, centering herself emotionally. She figured if she were well emotionally, the career would follow. She was trying to get her emotional stuff squared away the night we had dinner."

What she didn't tell Stabile was that the Westinghouse producers had already informed her that they were not going forward with the *Wild Guide* series. The show hadn't even begun and it was over. Which meant Hemingway was out of a job, and keeping the news to herself. She did suggest another kind of outdoor activity to Stabile, one that didn't involve manatees, and the idea caught Stabile completely off guard.

"She asked me if I wanted to go skydiving with her," said Stabile. "I told her, 'No, not particularly.'" After dinner, the two women said good night and talked about getting together again in a few days.

But Hemingway's night wasn't over. Since she was already in Venice, she stopped at the home of another friend, Gigi Gaston, who had a relationship with Hemingway dating back to 1982, when they both had the same manager in New York. Gaston, who currently manages singer Sophie B. Hawkins and was shooting *The Cream Will Rise*, a documentary on her client, when Hemingway showed up that night, recalled her first ever meeting with the tall cover girl in New York.

"Our manager, Billy Barnes, suggested that the three of us get together for brunch one day," said Gaston. "As Margaux and I were being introduced, she put her hand out to shake my hand, but she missed and hit my breast. We all laughed and became great friends.

"When she showed up unannounced at my house that Wednesday night," said Gaston, "I was busy unloading equipment. Sophie was there with me, and so was the crew. It was ten o'clock at night. Margaux knew my house well, because she was my roommate there for about a year when she was trying to get things together. The documentary crew was leaving, and Sophie had just returned from the store with coffee. When I looked up and saw Margaux, I thought, 'My God, what is Margaux doing in front of my house?' She always liked to go to bed fairly early, unless she was out working or out at a party. But there she was, sitting in her white Ford Bronco, parked in front of my house.

"And I thought, 'Doesn't she get it? I have to be up at five in the morning.' I was in work mode," said Gaston, "and I didn't want to have to deal with anyone's problems. I had been up for days and on the road for weeks following Sophie around on her tour, and I wasn't being a very sympathetic friend at that moment. But she came in, I said hello, and she sat down on my green couch. I said, 'So what's going on?'

"She said, 'Nothing. I just wanted to come by and see you.'

"We had been like sisters," said Gaston, "so I could say just about anything to her. I said, 'Well, you know, I have to get up very early in the morning. I have a shoot. I have a crew coming here at five o'clock. I can't sit here and talk. I just don't have time to talk.' So I just went about my business and started setting up the equipment for the next day, and Sophie started talking to Margaux. Sophie was really great to her. Sophie also said that Margaux was hardly present that night. Sophie said that Margaux didn't even know I was impatient and not being attentive as a friend."

Only in retrospect did Gaston realize that Margaux appeared "very out of it" that night, and nothing like the relaxed person she seemed to be with Stabile, just hours earlier.

"It wasn't like she was on drugs," said Gaston, "but she did seem tranquilized. I know she took a lot of medication for her epilepsy. And once in a while she would drool and not realize it. I think that night she was probably a step or so before drooling. She had a dazed look in her eyes. She obviously needed some contact with a friend. I should have seen the signs, but I didn't."

Whatever state Hemingway was suddenly in, she still had it together enough to invite Gaston and Hawkins to have dinner with her in her new apartment. "She asked us to come over that Friday night," said Gaston. "She was saying, 'My apartment is so great. You've got to come for dinner. We'll all cook. It will be so much fun. It will be like old times, Gigi.'

"I said, 'Great,' and we made the date," said Gaston. "I then went to sleep and left Sophie and Margaux talking on the couch. They probably talked for a half hour, no more, because Sophie needed to get to sleep, too. She had been staying at my house all that week, and she had to get up early, just like me. But the plan was made to go to Margaux's on Friday night."

On Thursday morning, June 27, Gaston mentioned to Hawkins that Hemingway had seemed in a very strange place the night before. Hawkins recounted her half hour on the couch with Hemingway and realized that their friend was simply looking for a connection. "Sophie said that nothing she was saying seemed to register with Margaux," Gaston said, "until she took her into the guest bedroom. That was Margaux's room during the year she lived with me. Sophie showed her an old picture of Margaux and me in Idaho. I keep the picture in that room. As soon as Margaux saw the photo, Sophie said she was connected again. She was totally happy and very animated."

Sundlun spoke to Hemingway by phone on Thursday and offered to come out to Los Angeles for the weekend to see her. The two had plans to meet the following week in Newport for a long July Fourth weekend, and Sundlun was attempting to move up those plans. But she deferred.

"She said it didn't look like a good weekend," he said, "so I didn't go."

Hemingway had dinner Thursday night at Cicada with Linda Livingston, the director of film and television at BMI, the music licensing agency, and Millie Kaiserman, a blues singer. The restaurant, on Melrose Avenue in West Hollywood, was a haven for celebrities on most nights. But on Thursdays, there was even a greater concentration of well-known people, primarily because of Kaiserman, who performed each week in the restaurant's back room. By 1996, she had built a real cult following, and on any particular Thursday it was not uncommon to see the likes of Diana Ross, David Bowie, and Tom Jones, all getting out of their chairs to sing with her.

"Millie was an unbelievable singer," said Livingston, who managed Kaiserman and was understandably biased. "Everyone wanted to hear Millie, and sing with Millie."

Hemingway qualified on both counts. In fact, she introduced Kaiserman to Livingston in the late seventies, and the three women remained good friends.

During dinner that Thursday night, just prior to Kaiserman's first set, Hemingway said that the owner of her new apartment on Fraiser was already trying to evict her, after just ten days. "Margaux described her landlord as 'some crazy lady' who was really nuts," said Livingston. "Apparently, the landlord didn't like where Margaux kept her bicycle, and she didn't like her trash cans, and she wanted her out. Margaux could see just a little of the beach from this apartment, and I said, 'Okay, now it's time to get a place on the beach, just like you always wanted.'

"She said she was fine about being evicted," said Livingston. "And while she hadn't left this place yet, she said she was uncomfortable with the vibe of the apartment because this woman lived in the front of the building, very close to her second-floor room. So she asked if she could spend the night at my apartment in the Marina, and I said absolutely."

Kaiserman's first set began a little after 9 P.M., and by the time she was scat-singing her way through the blues standard "Rock Me Baby," Hemingway was ready to get up and sing with her. At five feet four inches in height, Kaiserman had to reach up to give her much taller friend the microphone. "But Margaux took it with great style," said Livingston. "Margaux was a very good singer, and she loved to scat. Millie and Margaux had a great time, passing the mike back and forth, scatting at each other."

"She would scat sometimes in a voice message," said Minson. "She once left me a message in which she sang, 'Billy boy, Billy boy, it's that Margaux, Margaux girl. Looking for you, scat, dat, diddley-doo, did-dley-doo.' I came home to that. She loved singing. Really loved singing."

As the back room at Cicada began emptying out after Kaiserman's first set, Hemingway said she was tired. She knew Livingston would want to remain at Cicada for the second set. "Margaux wanted to leave," said Livingston, "so I gave her the key to my apartment. She left, and I stayed until the end of the second set. Millie also lived in the Marina, so I drove her home and then drove back to my place."

When Livingston entered her one-bedroom apartment, she found Hemingway on the living room couch watching David Letterman on TV. "She seemed fine," Livingston recalled. "She said she was going to get up early and try to not wake me up because she wanted to go hiking in Santa Monica Canyon. She loved hiking up there. I said, 'Okay, great. I'll see you over the weekend.'

"My couch pulls out into a bed, and I pulled it out for Margaux, and said good night. When I woke up the next morning, she was gone," said Livingston. "The bed was folded back into a couch, and she had left everything nice and tidy."

Livingston reiterated that Hemingway had seemed okay to her that Thursday night. "If she was depressed, it was because of this woman who owned the house," said Livingston. "But she was feeling good because she knew she was going to start looking for a new place, a better place."

But she was not okay, and by Friday morning, June 28, she was reaching out again, looking for another emotional connection to get through another day, or maybe even just another hour.

Painter and writer and longtime friend Zachary Selig said Hemingway called him in New York that morning. "She was very desperate and anxious and asked me if I would marry her," said Selig, who had no idea he was the fifth man in two weeks that she was considering as possible marriage material.

"I thought she was just reaching out like she normally did, to make a connection and have some sense of security," said Selig. "So here she was, asking me to marry her. I thought, 'Well, sure Margaux.' I mean, she'd said it before. And because she'd said it before, I thought, 'Well, this doesn't mean anything.'

"Then she said, 'Pray for me. There's something big that's going to happen.'

"I thought, 'Okay, she's keeping a secret. She's got some project. She's going to consummate a deal that she's been working on,' all of that. I said, 'Margaux, you know I always pray for you.'

"She said she'd been in the process of moving," said Selig, "and I started thinking about the medications she took. She did not sound hyper. Her voice was not this desperate, hyper voice she used to have prior to being on whatever medication she took for her seizures. She was kind of slowed down a little. But she didn't sound odd. There was nothing odd about it. Usually, I could pick up on something like that with Margaux. She was just Margaux being Margaux.

"It was a normal conversation," he said. "She said, 'Pray for me. There's something big that's going to happen.'

"And I said, 'Oh, what?'

"And she said, 'You'll see. You'll see. Everybody's going to see.'"

Hemingway was obviously at a point where she was reaching out to a lot of people, men and women alike, and in her mind, at least, the assumption has to be that she perceived she was getting nowhere. And a voice message she received that Friday could not possibly have helped her situation. It was Gigi Gaston, calling from her shoot with Sophie B. Hawkins to cancel the dinner plans they had made for that night at Hemingway's apartment.

"We were in Del Mar, and I knew the shoot was going to be much longer than we thought it would be," said Gaston. "So I called to say that there was no chance that we would be able to get back in time for dinner. I never spoke to Margaux. I just left her a message saying we couldn't make it, and why. I never heard back from her."

But Caren Elin did hear from her on Friday, and knew immediately by the sound of Hemingway's voice that she was in serious trouble. A chiropractor by trade and an author of a book on reincarnation, Elin was at a Buddhist temple in Pomona, on the outskirts of Los Angeles, when she received a page from Hemingway.

"I had just gotten out of a hospital, and I was really weak and frail," remembered Elin. "I had guests with me from Pennsylvania, and I was walking through the temple's gardens when Margaux's page came in. I was really surprised that she was paging me. But I excused myself from my company, and I went to a pay phone.

"Margaux picked up her phone, and when I told her that I had left company to call her, she asked me why," said Elin, who never got to answer the question because Hemingway kept right on talking.

"She said, 'Please, please, Caren, I need to know. Does everybody get to see the light? Does everybody go to the light?'

"I was just overcome by the question," said Elin. "I thought about it for a moment, and I said, 'It all depends.' And suddenly I was led to tell her, 'The only place you can resolve problems, Margaux, is here in the body, and here in life. It isn't on the other side.'

"She kept saying, 'other side, other side,'" said Elin. "And I said to her, 'Margaux, if you have problems, let's talk about them. Let's resolve whatever is bothering you now.' And she asked why I thought she had a problem. And I said, 'I can just hear it in your voice.' There was a great sadness to Margaux's voice. She was depressed, and as far as I could tell, really depressed. Even though she had spent that week with many people, people who were practically with her day and night, she was always wanting to be spiritual, always wanting to experience the real inner communication with her higher self. She wanted to see the light. She wanted to be the light."

Elin said she stood at the temple pay phone in Pomona and talked to Hemingway for at least thirty minutes. "I was pleading with her that she could resolve things here," said Elin. "Her voice was slurring. Margaux had that deep voice, so I never knew for sure whether it was the medication, and how much of it she had taken. But I definitely had the feeling she had taken it. I never knew for sure because I didn't speak to Margaux on the phone all that often. I always spoke to her in person, which was probably just three times in my life. She once took me to a tea-leaf reader for my birthday, and the other few times we were with friends. So we weren't deep and close. But we were meaningful friends. I would talk to her about reincarnation and spirituality. And because she had dyslexia, she couldn't read like an avid reader, so I would tell her, 'If you need anything explained, I'll do it.'"

Hemingway did not ask Elin to explain suicide to her, but the chiropractor felt the situation was dire enough for her launch into the subject right then, from Pomona. "I knew from my work about suicide experiences," she said. "I told Margaux that committing suicide is like being stuck in a broken place. I told her that she would leave behind a lot of hurt. I said a lot of people would be hurt. I said that suicide would force her to relive the experience over and over again, like a broken record. I told her, 'Margaux, please, whatever you do, don't take your life.'"

When Elin got back to her house in Los Angeles that night, there was a message from Hemingway on her answering machine. The message was: "God loves me. God loves you. I love you. God bless. Margaux."

Gigi Gaston and Sophie B. Hawkins didn't get back to Venice until very late on Friday. Gaston said they were both so tired from the day's shoot in Del Mar that they went right to sleep, Gaston in her room, and Hawkins on the living room couch.

Early on Saturday morning, June 29, Hawkins was awakened by the sound of someone banging on the gate in front of Gaston's house, shouting out, "Gigi! Gigi!" It was Hemingway, standing outside, calling out Gaston's name. "Sophie came running in to wake me up," said Gaston, "and by the time I got to the front door, she was gone."

A neighbor of Hemingway's, Peter Osterlund, was widely quoted as saying that he also saw her on Saturday, looking haggard and tired. "She seemed rather upset and sad," Osterlund later told the Associated Press, adding that Hemingway's appearance "was obvious enough that it stuck in my mind."

But she was not answering her phone. Judy Stabile tried various times over the weekend to reach Hemingway, but none of her phone messages were returned. "Others were trying to reach her, too," said Stabile. "We were all trying to reach her. She wasn't answering any phone calls over the weekend. So on Monday, July 1, at about one o'clock in the afternoon, I went over to her apartment to see what was up."

Hemingway's white Ford Bronco was parked out in front, but she didn't answer her bell. Stabile found a ladder, climbed it, and looked in a window. A woman she believed to be Hemingway was on her back in bed and lying still. Two construction workers were working nearby, and Stabile asked them to break into the apartment. They did, and when they came back outside, they told Stabile that the woman on the bed was dead.

It was a very hot day in Los Angeles that Monday. It had been hot all weekend. There was no air-conditioning inside the Frasier Avenue apartment, and the body on the bed had already partially decomposed. But Stabile wouldn't need to have dental records checked. She knew it was Hemingway.

Stabile called Gaston, who was in Brentwood, shooting footage of Hawkins on a tennis court. The two women left Brentwood immediately, and they were standing on Frasier Street with Stabile when Hemingway's body was carried out of the apartment.

On Saturday, July 6, Hemingway's ashes were buried in Ketchum, Idaho, not far from a memorial to her famous grandfather. It took more than two months for the Los Angeles County Coroner's office to issue its full report, but on Tuesday, August 20, it was finally confirmed that Hemingway had succumbed due to "acute barbiturate intoxication." The medical examiner had found a large quantity of phenobarbital in Hemingway's system, which the coroner's office said was consistent with an intentional overdose. A prescription for phenobarbital was never found.

Caren Elin didn't need an official report to tell her that Hemingway had taken her own life. "The way she talked to me was all the proof I needed," said Elin. "There is no doubt. She absolutely intended to kill herself, and she succeeded."

Jennifer Josephs agreed with Elin. "I think she took her own life, but that's just my opinion, my feeling," said Josephs. "I think she may have just thought there was a better place than this one. I'm not a doctor, but the idea that she could have taken one hundred phenobarbital by accident seems pretty outrageous. My assumption has to be that she absolutely committed suicide."

Other friends, though, still believe otherwise. "I don't believe she killed herself," said Stabile. "She had emotional problems, but she was trying to deal with them. I think she was just overmedicated. I think that she just had too much medication in her. I think her death was accidental. She would have written a note. She would have said something. She would have said good-bye. She wouldn't have asked me to go skydiving on Wednesday night, and then commit suicide a few days later."

And Stabile was also convinced that alcohol played no part in Hemingway's death. "I know all about her experiences before Betty Ford," said Stabile. "But in the six years I knew her, I never saw her take an alcoholic drink. Not once. Never.

"And the reports that came out after her death suggesting that she was an alcoholic and a drug addict, it just wasn't true," said Stabile. "The only drugs she did were prescribed by doctors. She was paranoid. She suffered from paranoia and that was a family disease. She needed phenobarbital for her epilepsy. She had all kinds of medication because she was dealing with so much stuff. She was having a hard time making a living. But she had a zestful life, this woman. She loved to travel, but she had problems.

"If she wanted to purposely kill herself, she would have left some note, something," said Stabile. "I think it was just stupidity and too much medication. Doctors gave her too much medication. You take a few pills and you're almost asleep, and you take a few more. She was in bed when I found her, looking like she had just gone to sleep."

And it was how she was lying in bed and what she was wearing—and what she was not wearing—that led others to agree with Stabile. "When I asked Sophie, 'Do you think she killed herself?' she reminded me of something the detective said when he talked to us," said Gaston. "He said, 'No woman kills herself without underwear on.' Whenever Margaux stayed with me, she never ran around the house naked. She always had on her PJ's, or sweats, or jeans and a T-shirt. And yet, when her body was found, she had only a T-shirt on. No underwear. I remember what the detective said. He said, 'Women are too modest. If they're going to kill themselves, they're not going to do it with just a T-shirt on and no bottoms.'"

Linda Livingston felt the absence of a suicide note spoke volumes. "I knew Margaux for a long, long time," she said. "If she really wanted to commit suicide, she would have done something to say good-bye to us. A note, something."

"Does it really matter?" Stuart Sundlun asked. "If it makes people feel better that it was an accident and not suicide, fine. It's your own personal interpretation of what you feel about the act of suicide. Who knows whether it was an accident or suicide? I don't know. The coroner said it was suicide. Some other people close to the investigation said it was not. What do I know? I'm not a professional.

"But what I do know," he said, "is that Margaux was a note writer.

People usually leave notes, and Margaux was always writing little things down. I can speculate for hours, and I'll wind up ending in the same spot because I don't know what she did or didn't do. I could argue why suicide in her case makes no sense, and I go the opposite way and argue that it seems out of character for her to have done that. Why would she plan something, and not say anything or leave a note? That doesn't make sense. I mean, most people leave notes. Suicide is an active act, not a passive act. Where's the glory in suicide without leaving a note?"

Caren Elin said that notes were found in Hemingway's apartment after her death, but nothing she had written down suggested suicide. "They were just notes," said Elin, "different notes about her, and about her life."

"There is no conclusion to the argument," said Sundlun. "And, of course, it's much easier to believe that she took her own life because of her family history."

To Judy Stabile, that line of logic is a cop-out. "It's not fair to blame this on her family history," she said. "That made it easy for the coroner. That's why as far as I'm concerned, the coroner's report was useless."

And then again, maybe the cause of Hemingway's death is beside the point. The issue of family history would have been brought up regardless. "It is undoubtedly a mistake to let a final act speak for a whole lifetime, but the death of Ernest Hemingway still unconsciously reverberates, despite the family's avoidance of the subject," Hara Estroff Marano wrote in *Psychology Today*, five months after Margaux Hemingway's death. "Margaux could almost never be engaged in a discussion of her family history, friends said. Above all, the Hemingways are people of action; they do not give themselves over to introspection or emotions.

"What Margaux Hemingway inherited in her genes and what vulnerabilities—styles of coping, unspoken beliefs about the future—she acquired in more subtle ways, perhaps even through a kind of emotional abandonment, will never be known for sure," wrote Marano. "This much can be said: It must have been an awful burden because it overtook a lifetime of personal bravery. In this she was truly, Ernest's granddaughter."

Tupac Shakur

June 16, 1971–September 13, 1996

SOBRIETY DATES ARE A LOT LIKE BIRTHDAYS, BUT WITHOUT THE EXPECTATION OF a new bicycle from Mom and Dad, or that gorgeous bracelet from a spouse. Sobriety celebrants do often receive small tokens of their achievement, like a coin with Roman numerals, or an angel-food cake with candles. But the real gift is supposed to be the sobriety itself, and it is always marked by the day the nightmare ended.

This is why Afeni Shakur can never forget May 13, 1991, and how her life changed on that day. Her son, Tupac Amaru Shakur, the eldest of her two children, had been going out of his way to spend less and less time with his mother. And who could blame him? Tupac was at a most critical point in his young career, busily putting the finishing touches on his debut solo album, *2Pacalypse Now*. Afeni was busy, too, but her focus at the time was all about finding that next hit from her crack pipe. Even though Tupac had once supported himself by dealing drugs on the street, his drugs of choice always tended toward the direction of marijuana and alcohol, substances he considered to be as necessary for human survival as bread and water.

His mother, though, had been on a different high. A former member of the Black Panthers who was jailed in 1971 after being charged with taking part in a Panther plot to bomb public places in New York City, Afeni gave birth to Tupac in Harlem one month after her release. Her subsequent addiction to cocaine led inevitably to crack, and ultimately, by 1991, to a level that was dangerously out of her control. Her increasing dependence on the drug, which was obvious to those around her, had become a real embarrassment to her now-twenty-year-old son, serving only to slow down his newfound career momentum.

"My addiction took me way down," Afeni Shakur said. "I was about fifteen or thirty miles underneath the bottom of the garbage can, if you know what I mean."

Then came May 13, 1991, the day that began her road to recovery, her first real day away from crack. "I am a recovering addict," she said proudly. "God knew that I needed to stop that day. God knew that I didn't have another day with crack in me."

Her son, on the other hand, knew no such thing, and he had little confidence in his mother's ability to stop. In fact, he doubted she could even launch any serious attempt to clean up her act. "He wasn't particularly impressed in the beginning," she said. "He was holding back and waiting to see whether I could put one year together."

Even she was suspicious of the recovery process. "When I first got into recovery," Afeni recalled, "I said to myself that I would sit still long enough to figure it all out. I mean, I met the nicest people in recovery. But they had all these little slogans, 'One day at a time,' and the like, and I thought that somebody needed to change these slogans. They were a little too simplistic for me. So I figured I would sit there long enough to come up with something clever and not so simplistic. Today, thank God, my life is filled with those little sayings. I am a living testimony to the idea that I don't have to do crack one day at a time."

It was after Afeni's first year away from crack that her son finally grew to respect what his mother had achieved. "That boy wrote me a nine-page letter," she said. "I proved that I could change my life, and he was won over. That's where his song, 'Dear Mama,' comes from. That's when Tupac lost his anger, when I had a year clean. He realized I was different. That song is like the last notch on a circle. It's the closing of the circle for him."

By August 1996 Afeni Shakur's daily reprieve from the horrors of her crack use had totaled five-plus years and counting. During those five years, her son had become a rap superstar with a long rap sheet and by extension a target for any disgruntled rival intent on wanting to bring him down. Tupac was a big fish in a new kind of competitive fishbowl, this angry environment patrolled by large bejeweled men who carried automatic weapons and drove in oversized sports utility vehicles with tinted windows and stunning silver rims on the tires.

And at the center of this garish bicoastal battle zone was the twenty-five-year-old Tupac Shakur, an ex-con and a singular creative force in music, and a man who had grown mistrustful of outsiders and more and more in need of a mother's unconditional love. And that's exactly what he started getting from Afeni, who had begun over time to prove that she could remain conscious enough to give it to him.

But it was also time for Tupac to move on, and Afeni knew it. Her son had been publicly linked to many well-known women over the years, among them Arnelle Simpson, the daughter of reviled former football great O.J. Simpson, and actress Jada Pinkett, Tupac's high school friend from Baltimore who later married actor and one-time rapper Will Smith.

Pinkett saw Tupac during that summer of 1996, and recalled that the meeting did not go well. Pinkett did not approve of the so-called "thug life" that Tupac had been leading. She saw that life, filled with its guns and money and constant references to women as "bitches," as a recipe for disaster, and she did not refrain from making her feelings known. Of course, Pinkett may as well have been talking to a wall.

"He did not want to hear anything I had to say," Pinkett later told *USA Today*. "He was a very opinionated man. And I'm a very opinionated woman. So us together was always sparks and fire."

Still, she had great compassion for him even though she feared the road he was on. "Nobody knows the demons he carried on his shoulders," she was quoted as saying in that same *USA Today* article. "He was always fighting the world and always fighting himself. He would say, 'I can't commit suicide, but I can't be here like this.'"

Others worried about him, too. Public Enemy's Chuck D told the *Toronto Sun* that Tupac reminded him of a car "heading toward a brick wall at 120 miles per hour without brakes."

Lela Rochon, who costarred with Tupac and Jim Belushi in the movie *Gang Related*, saw ominous warning signs during filming that year. "There was an eerie feeling on the set," Rochon told the *Virginia Pilot*. "I really didn't think we'd get the movie finished. But that was just my feeling. Tupac was arrogant about it, usually. He said he'd be okay. But he told me, too, that he expected to die young."

Rochon called Tupac "a sweetheart—and so charismatic on camera. But, in my opinion," she told the Virginia reporter, "he expected a youthful death."

But the foreshadowing of his own demise, a theme that appeared

over and over again in his music, did not stop him from finding a sat-
isfying romance that year, with Kidada Jones, the daughter of famed
music producer Quincy Jones. Afeni referred to their relationship as
the real thing.

"He told me that August of his intention to marry Kidada. He had
just ordered an engagement ring to give her," said Afeni. "He was also
busy consolidating his business and trying to have a separate life away
from business. He was trying to refine himself. I always think of him
during this period as someone who was trying to get his head out of
the lion's mouth, which was the business. He was very often in that
lion's mouth. But he was very intelligent so he could see where things
were leading. He was doing the footwork necessary for him to be able
to have a different life, and that life included being married to Kidada.
Theirs was a special kind of relationship, intimate in ways other than
sexual. It was a fragile thing that they were trying to build on in the
midst of all of these business commitments. She was around us a lot,
and he was working a lot, mostly in Los Angeles. Tupac and Kidada
came from completely different backgrounds, and I know that he
thought she could teach us the finer points of life, and we could teach
her about the streets. He saw his relationship with Kidada as a marriage of energies."

His energy that month was all about the work. According to his
mother, Tupac was working nineteen hours a day and sleeping five.
And when he did manage to get to sleep, he slept better knowing his
family was close by. And since he had a lot of extra space at the house
he rented in Malibu, he sent for everyone. Afeni, who had been living
in a house Tupac bought for her in the Stone Mountain area of Atlanta, flew to Los Angeles with a planeload of relatives, including her
sister Gloria; Gloria's daughter Jamala; and Jamala's daughter, Imani;
along with Tupac's sister, Sekywia; and her baby daughter, Nzingha.

"Tupac always needed the babies around when he was intense or
intensely working," said Afeni, "so the babies were in his house, my
grandbaby Nzingha and my grandniece, Imani. They became Tupac's
energy source.

"I remember it as an intense period," Afeni recalled. "I just looked
at him and I cried. I saw him working like a slave, figuratively, but in
reality he was a person who had to get these things done. When I look
back on it now, I see how little the rest of us did. We didn't do anything because we were unprepared to do anything. I mean, we didn't

Fans of John Lennon created a makeshift shrine in Central Park. This photo was taken six days after his death.

© Diego Goldberg/CORBIS

© Bettman/CORBIS

Amateur photographer Paul Goresh (left) is shown November 17, 1980 with John Lennon. Ironically, the photo included Lennon's killer, Mark David Chapman, who can be seen in the background.

Photo by Ken Regan

The Strasberg Family. Taken at the Actor's Studio just one day before Lee's death. (from left) Adam, Lee, David, (below) Anna

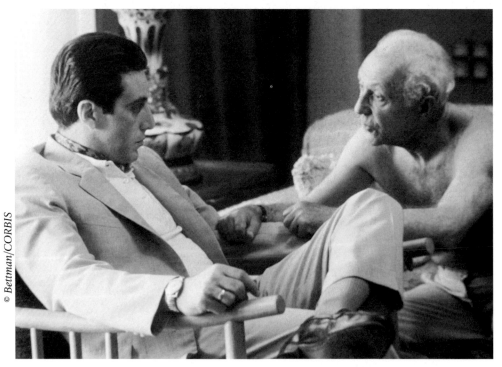

© *Bettman/CORBIS*

Al Pacino and Lee Strasberg in a scene from *The Godfather: Part II*.

Photo by Judy Jacklin

John Belushi, relaxing on a grassy haven at the Martha's Vineyard airport, waiting to board a plane back to New York in 1979.

Photo courtesy of NBC

David Bloom reporting on NBC in the very early days of the Iraq War.

© Reuters/CORBIS

US Army medics, assisted by soldiers, medivac David Bloom out of a camp of the 3rd infantry division, about 20kms outside of Baghdad moments before his death.

John Belushi, relaxing on a grassy haven at the Martha's Vineyard airport, waiting to board a plane back to New York in 1979.

Photo by Judy Jacklin

Photo by Judy Jacklin

John Belushi, holding up the day's catch in a boat off the coast of
Martha's Vineyard, during a 1978 fishing excursion
with singer James Taylor and director John Landis.

© Bettman/CORBIS

Orson Welles (left) gets a ride on a golf cart during a rehearsal for the 1982 "Night of 100 Stars" in New York.

© Richard Melloul/Sygma/CORBIS

Orson Welles in Cannes for the 1983 Cannes Film Festival.

Photo by Lee Tannen

Lucille Ball and her toy poodle, Tinker, in her Beverly Hills backyard in 1982.

© Gregory Pace/CORBIS

Lucille Ball and Gary Morton at a New York City Friars Club Roast
for Red Buttons in 1987.

Lyle Alzado hold-
ing his nephew,
Ciel Alzado,
in August 1985.

Photo by Peter Alzado

Photo by Neal Preston/Corbis

Lyle Alzado
at his Los Angeles
home in July 1991
after he contracted
brain cancer.

© Brooks Kraft/CORBIS

Arthur Ashe, less than six weeks before his death, receiving the first annual AIDS Leadership Award from the Harvard AIDS Institute.

© CORBIS SYGMA

Margaux Hemmingway, one month before her death in California.

© Mojgan B. Azimi/CORBIS OUTLINE

Marion "Suge" Knight on a cellphone, and Tupac Shakur proudly displaying a wad of money two months before his death in Las Vegas.

Photo by Bill Nicholson

John Denver holding a trout he caught at the Shooting
Star Ranch in Montana, two months before his death.

© Bob Millard/ZUMA/CORBIS

Milton Berle celebrates
his 92nd birthday
at the Friar's Club
in Los Angeles.

Milton Berle and his wife Lorna
at The Hollywood Gala Salute
to Milton Berle eight months
before his death.

© Frank Tapper/CORBIS

Ted Williams throwing out the first pitch before the Red Sox game against the New York Mets, June 11, 1999.

© Mike Segar/Reuters/Corbis

© Reuters/CORBIS

Tears flow down the face of 83-year-old baseball legend Ted Williams (center), as daughter Claudia and his son John Henry Williams speak for him at the Ted Williams Museum and Hitters Hall of Fame in Hernando, Florida, less than five months before his death.

Photo courtesy of NBC

David Bloom reporting on NBC in the very early days of the Iraq War.

© *Reuters/CORBIS*

US Army medics, assisted by soldiers, medivac David Bloom out of a camp of the 3rd infantry division, about 20kms outside of Baghdad moments before his death.

Photo by Brigette Barr

Warren Zevon, right, three months after being diagnosed with
terminal cancer, at the Chateau Marmont in Hollywood, with "gonzo"
journalist Hunter S. Thompson, who committed suicide in February, 2005.

© Jim Ruymen/CORBIS

John Ritter with wife
Amy Yasbeck
on April 14, 2003,
at the Project A.L.S.
"Friends Finding a Cure"
gala in Hollywood.

On the day following John
Ritter's death, flowers and
mementos were left at his star
on the Hollywood Walk of
Fame.

© Brendan McDermid/CORBIS

have ourselves a clue. We were living in a total dream world. Our skills were nil or next to nil, and Tupac saw this. He knew that we were of no help. It was like he had to work so the rest of us could survive.

"I feel really bad about that now," she said, "but the truth of the matter is that he was absolutely responsible for all of us. He took it on as his responsibility. He didn't have to, but he did."

The plans that month called for Afeni to return to Atlanta on Saturday, August 31. Gloria, Jamala, Imani, Sekywia, and Nzingha were all scheduled to fly back with her. Whenever Tupac recorded, he always tried to stay in an apartment he kept on Wilshire Boulevard, not far from the offices of his record label, Death Row Records. Just prior to leaving for the airport Afeni drove over to the Wilshire Boulevard apartment building, pulled into the semicircular driveway in front, and asked the doorman to ring up and announce that she was coming upstairs to say goodbye.

"When I got upstairs," she said, "Tupac became very angry with me. I had keys to his apartment. I could have just gone upstairs. But I didn't do that. He said, 'You're my mother. Why would you have to announce yourself?'

"I said, 'I didn't know if you had company. You should have the luxury of asking me to wait downstairs, if that's what you wanted.' He was actually hurt that I was so formal. But we talked for a while upstairs, and we hugged. Then he came downstairs. He was dressed in red," said Afeni. "I can still see him standing there. He came downstairs with me and talked to his sister in the car. He talked to her like a big brother who was proud of his younger sister. I remember thinking, 'We're like a unit, standing here on Wilshire Boulevard.' He was being a good son. I was so proud of him and her and their relationship. I was proud of the growth they had made in their relationship. It was just striking and stunning."

Four days later, on Wednesday, September 4, Tupac was at Radio City Music Hall in New York for a scheduled appearance at the MTV Video Music Awards. That he had come at all was a big deal in his world. Although he was an East Coast native, the fact that he had settled in California branded him forever as a West Coast rapper and the leading representative of his chosen turf. And now here he was in midtown Manhattan, at the virtual center of what some considered enemy rap territory on the East Coast. Obviously, he knew not to come alone, and he arrived surrounded by a small army of West Coast rap royalty, including members of his backup band, the Outlawz; fellow West Coast rapper Snoop Doggy Dogg; and the hulking chairman of Death Row Records, Marion "Suge" Knight.

Tupac began the evening in an affable mood and even explained the origin of a gold medallion he was wearing to a reporter from the *New York Daily News*. The medallion, which the reporter described as "fist-size," hung from a necklace and displayed a woman on her knees, legs outstretched, with a jeweled ribbon covering her private parts. Tupac explained to the reporter that the necklace was a reminder to him of 1989, "because I was broke in 1989.

"Plus, they had me in jail for a year for a crime that I did not commit," Tupac said, referring to his eleven-month incarceration in a New York jail in 1995 for sexually assaulting a female fan.

"So I'm wearing this," he said of the medallion, "to remind me of that."

There was a minor altercation later that night at Radio City when Tupac and his entourage were confronted by six other men. A brief argument ensued, and police were called in to break it up. No arrests were made, and the incident was immediately forgotten.

Young Noble, one of the newest members of Outlawz at the time and a former street drug dealer who credited Tupac and others in the band with helping him turn his life around, was part of Tupac's Radio City posse and he remembered the night clearly.

"When we got to New York," said Young Noble, whose given name is Rufus Cooper III, "we really didn't know what to expect. We didn't know what was going to happen there. You know what I'm saying? We had niggas there who were fresh off to hit him up. There was a lot of East Coast–West Coast media bullshit. Pac knew it would be like that, but he said, 'Fuck it. We're going.'

"Then we got there," Young Noble said, "and, shit, we really had a lot of fun. We went all through New York, hitting up the weed spots, just fucking with the streets. That was one of the happiest times for Pac. He probably felt that New York had something against him, because of how the media covered all the East Coast–West Coast shit. But the streets loved him there, and he was really happy about that. We walked for blocks and blocks that night, through midtown, then up in Harlem. People loved him that night."

And for very good reason: He gave money to total strangers on the street. And it was Young Noble who acted as his bag man. "It happened after the MTV awards, after all the parties," recalled Young Noble. "It started with the bums outside. They were standing outside just trying to get some food or whatever they could. Pac had me carrying around this small briefcase. We had thousands of dollars in cash in that briefcase, maybe twenty thousand in hundred-dollar bills. He just told me to open it up. He said to me, 'Just start passing out hundred-dollar bills to all these people, man.'

"People went fucking crazy," Young Noble said. "It was like he was the damn president, and they were loving him for it. And he did it because he was just a good dude. The East Coast was his original home, and he was happy to be home. And seeing all these people hungry, he said, 'Hey, give them some money. Give them some bills.'"

Only a few members of the Outlawz accompanied Tupac on his New York trip. Another member, E.D.I., whose given name is Malcolm Greenridge, wanted to go, but he was told to remain behind. "It was Tupac's choice that I stayed back in L.A.," said E.D.I., who was given his alias by Tupac as a play on the name of Ugandan president Idi Amin.

"It was nothing personal," said E.D.I. "It was just how we moved, as a group, and how we handled our business. Certain people went to certain events, and certain people stayed back. It didn't matter who we were or which event was being discussed. It had nothing to do with anything. It's just how we rolled."

"It wasn't like we took turns," Young Noble added. "It was just that particular situation. The guys who went with Pac to New York happened to all be from Jersey. I guess Pac figured that if anything bad happened, at least we're all close to home, at least we're not really out of our boundaries. Pac must have figured, 'Okay, we have a whole bunch of homeboys from Jersey and New York.' There must have been sixty of us at the MTV after-party. All these Jersey folks. That's just the way it happened. It probably wasn't even planned."

According to George Pryce, Death Row's public relations head at the time, Tupac was always concerned about his friends' roots. "He called all the Outlawz his 'little homies,'" said Pryce. "He would always talk to me about where so-and-so was from, and what his concerns were about their well-being. He was their teacher as well as their philosopher."

And like the Outlawz, Pryce was around Tupac long enough to know that all plans were fluid and could be changed up to the last minute. As an example, Pryce pointed out the Las Vegas trip he made with Tupac in March of 1996 to see a bout between Tupac's favorite boxer, Mike Tyson, and the reigning WBC heavyweight champ, English-born Frank Bruno. Tupac had always been Tyson's favorite rap artist, and his music was usually playing over the loudspeaker when Tyson entered an arena.

The fight was held at the MGM Grand. Pryce's seat was next to Suge Knight's, but the PR head gave up his ticket so a reporter from the *New York Times Magazine* could spend more time with Knight. Pryce's willingness to leave the arena moments before the fight was about to begin was, after all, the obvious decision considering that the reporter was doing a cover story on Knight's Death Row operation. Pryce was enough of a pro to understand that the more access a reporter gets the more appreciative that reporter becomes, and that appreciation will often come out in the story.

Tupac would be back in Vegas on Saturday, September 7, almost six months after the Tyson-Bruno fight, which Tyson won by TKO in the third round. Pryce arrived in Vegas that morning and checked into the Luxor Hotel. Suge Knight had reserved a number of rooms at the Luxor, and Pryce was given one of them. Tyson was fighting again at the MGM Grand, this time against opponent Bruce Seldon, the reigning WBA heavyweight champ and Jersey Shore native who liked to call himself "the Atlantic City Express." But unlike the fight in March, which marked Bruno's last fight as a professional, Pryce held no ticket to the Tyson-Seldon fight and was content to remain in his hotel room and rest up prior to greeting the swarm of Tyson admirers who would surely be part of Tupac's group when he and Knight and everyone else arrived at Club 662, the Vegas club on East Flamingo Road that Knight was trying to buy.

"Suge always liked to give huge parties after a fight," recalled Pryce. "I had all these blow-up posters of all the Death Row artists, which lined both sides of the long hallway just inside 662. I needed to make sure I was at the club well in advance of their arrival. We were expecting a lot of press."

Young Noble was not in Las Vegas that night. "I didn't go to Vegas," he said, "because I went to New York. So I remained in Los Angeles, and I spent most of that day at Tupac's house in L.A."

E.D.I. did draw the Vegas straw this time, but he did not have a ticket to the fight. "I just remember it being very hot in Vegas that day," he said.

Tupac had been considering blowing off the Vegas trip altogether and instead flying down to Atlanta to see his family. Vegas, however, was a decision motivated strictly by career issues. The media had been told that Tupac would be performing at 662 after the fight. Even Tyson was expected to attend. Knight knew that if Tupac bailed, a lot of people would be disappointed, especially his hand-picked invitees from the media. In the end, Pryce said, Tupac chose Las Vegas "because of his friendship with Mike Tyson.

"He didn't want to let Mike down," said Pryce.

Tupac and Kidada arrived by car in Vegas at 2:30 P.M., and checked into the Luxor. According to a number of postings on Tupac-related Web sites, Kidada had urged Tupac to bring along his bulletproof vest, which he usually wore under his clothing when the situation called for him to be out in public. But on this occasion he didn't take it, all the postings said, because he feared it would make the normally sweltering desert weather feel even hotter.

Tupac also insisted that Kidada remain at the Luxor until after the fight. He said he would be back to pick her up. He figured he would need her later on, at 662, when the most important part of the night began and he took the stage. After all, fans were already lining up outside 662 and it wasn't even dark yet.

At the fight, Tupac and Knight sat ringside, in $1,000 seats. Other well-known celebrities sitting nearby included Roseanne Barr, Charlie Sheen, Louis Gossett Jr., Reggie Jackson, NBA star Gary Payton, rapper M.C. Hammer, members of Run-D.M.C., and the Rev. Jesse Jackson. When Tyson entered the arena, the music playing over the loudspeaker was "Wrote the Glory," a song Tupac wrote as an homage to his favorite fighter.

The music turned out to be longer than the fight. Tupac's favorite fighter ended Bruce Seldon's night in 109 seconds in the first round. Tupac found his way to Tyson's dressing room and hugged him.

At approximately 8:45 P.M., Tupac and his crew were walking through the MGM casino when a man, later identified as Orlando Anderson, a reputed gang member from Lakewood, California, was spotted by one of Tupac's companions. According to many postings on Tupac-related Web sites, Tupac chased Anderson down a hall, caught up with him, and yelled, "You from the South?" A fight broke out, a decidedly one-sided affair with Anderson getting pummeled by Tupac and his friends, one of whom was later identified as Alton McDonald, a Death Row employee, who was seen kicking Anderson. According to police reports, the hotel's video security system captured the entire scuffle on tape. Security guards managed to break up the fight and allowed everyone to leave when Anderson declined to press charges.

Tupac immediately got on his cell phone and called Young Noble in Los Angeles. "He called the house," Young Noble said. "He said he was just letting the niggas know he had gotten into this little scuffle. He wanted us to know about it. I could hear a lot of commotion going on in the background, so he couldn't really talk. I told him, 'Ya'll be safe, man.' I told him, 'Be easy. Calm down about that motherfucker.' Yeah, I think that's the last thing I told him."

When Tupac got back to the Luxor Hotel, he also told Kidada about the fight with Orlando Anderson. "Some nigga started a fight with me for nothin'," one of his Web sites quoted Tupac as saying to his fiancée. But Tupac seemed worried about what just had taken place. He sensed a potential problem, possibly with Anderson, and now he had second thoughts about Kidada's accompanying him to the club. She agreed and said she would stay at the Luxor and wait for him to come back.

Las Vegas Sun reporter Cathy Scott, who later turned her daily coverage into a book, *The Killing of Tupac Shakur*, wrote that before Tupac left the Luxor he changed out of the tan silk shirt and tan slacks combo he wore to the fight and put on a black-and-white basketball tank top over baggy blue jeans. The medallion he wore around his neck when he left the Luxor, according to Scott's book, "was the size of a paperweight—and probably just as heavy—picturing a haloed and winged black man wrestling a serpent with one hand and holding a gun in the other."

The medallion, in fact, turned out to be the closest thing Tupac had on his person that resembled a real weapon. And now he was about to venture out into the Las Vegas night with no bulletproof vest and no gun.

Suge Knight wasn't registered at the Luxor, even though his label was paying for many rooms there. He owned an estate just outside of town, on Monte Rosa Avenue in the Paradise Valley Township, and that's where he was staying. Tupac went directly to Knight's house from the Luxor and relaxed with other guests for about an hour. Then it was time to leave for Club 662.

Tupac wanted to drive in his own vehicle, a Humvee, but Knight was insistent that they ride together, so they could talk business. Knight drove his rented black BMW 750 sedan and Tupac sat in the passenger seat. A caravan of other vehicles, among them a Lexus, BMW station wagon, Miata, and Mercedes, all of which carried friends and body-guards, followed. The time, according to numerous police reports, was shortly after 10 P.M.

On any given Saturday night, the traffic on Las Vegas Boulevard rarely moves much faster than a standstill, with every kind of vehicle, from taxicabs and limos, airport-rented Fords and minivans, to every conceivable make of truck, motorcycle, and RV, all crawling in orderly fashion from one hotel-casino parking lot to the next. The night of September 7, 1996, was no exception.

Forced to move at the same pace as everyone else, Suge Knight's car-avan nevertheless managed to make its presence on the Strip felt by the pounding bass sound of hip-hop music, blaring out of open tinted win-dows and open sun roofs, across the snarling traffic to the pedestrians on the street.

The cars were moving so slowly that people were able to recognize Tupac through his open window. Cathy Scott's book noted that a photo of Tupac, taken by a photographer on the sidewalk, "would later gar-nered between $800 and $5,000 each time it was sold for publication in entertainment and business magazines or aired on TV tabloid and news shows." The time the picture was taken was reported to be 10:55 P.M.

Ten minutes later, Knight was stopped on Las Vegas Boulevard by lo-cal police for playing his music too loudly and not having a license plate properly displayed on the BMW. No tickets were issued, and Knight was free to continue on his way to the club. But they never got there.

The most detailed account of what happened next was painstak-ingly reported by Cathy Scott. Here is how she presented it in her book *The Killing of Tupac Shakur*.

> The convoy was headed east on Flamingo Road when it stopped for a red light at Koval Lane, a busy intersection only a half mile from the Strip across from the Maxim Hotel. One [Death Row] associate pulled up a car-length ahead to the right. Another car stopped directly behind them; in it were rapper Yafeu Fula [also known in the Outlawz as Kadafi, for Libyan leader Moammar Kadafi] and two associates, one a bodyguard and the other a rapper [E.D.I.]. Another car was in front of [Knight's] BMW at the stoplight. The sidewalk and street were heavy with pedestrians.

The BMW was boxed in.

Four young black women, sitting at the same intersection in a Chrysler sedan to the left of the BMW, turned, smiled at Suge and Tupac, and caught their attention.

A moment later, a late-model Cadillac with three to four black men inside pulled up directly to the right of the BMW, and skidded to a stop. A gunman sitting in the back seat on the driver's side stuck a weapon out of the left-rear window of the white Caddy, in full view of [Knight's] entourage. The gunman tracked Tupac from back seat.

Suge and Tupac saw the Caddy, but they had no time to react. Suddenly, the sounds of the night were shattered by the pop pop pop of a killer inside the Cadillac emptying a magazine clip from a high-powered semiautomatic handgun. At least 13 rounds were sprayed (that's how many bullet holes and casings investigators counted) into the passenger side of the BMW. Five bullets pierced the passenger door; some shattered the windows.

Startled and panicky, Tupac tried frantically to scramble into the back seat through the well between the front seats. But he was seat-belted in. In doing so, he exposed his middle and lower torso to the gunfire and took a round in his right hip. Suge grabbed Tupac, pulled him down, and covered him. He yelled, "Get down!" That's when Suge was hit with a fragment in the back of his neck.

Tupac was plugged with bullets at close range. Three rounds pierced his body. One bullet lodged in his chest, entering under his right arm. Another went through his hip, slicing through his lower abdomen, and ended up floating around in his pelvic area. Yet another bullet hit his right hand, shattering the bone of his index finger and knocking off a large chunk of gold from a ring he was wearing on another finger. (Tupac wore three gold-and-diamond rings on his right hand that night.) The gunfire nailed Tupac to the leather bucket seat. Glass and blood were everywhere.

Suge was grazed in the neck from the flying shrapnel and glass fragments. A small fragment lodged in the back of his skull at the base of his neck. Bullets also blew out two of the BMW's tires.

The gunfire ended as quickly as it began. The shooting of Tupac Shakur, executed in cold blood, was over in a matter of seconds.

To this day it remains unclear whether anyone in Knight's caravan ever returned any gunfire at the assailants as they sped off in their late-model Cadillac. Some reports at the time indicated that members of the Tupac-Knight posse did shoot back, but police investigators were never able to substantiate the claims. "There was no evidence" of returned gunfire, Las Vegas Metropolitan Police Sgt. Kevin Manning told Cathy Scott.

Irrefutable, however, is the fact that Knight panicked. Instead of calling 911 for medical help, he made a U-turn on two flat tires and headed back in the direction of the crowded Strip. Scott quoted Knight saying to Tupac, "You need a hospital, Pac. I'm gonna get you to a hospital right now."

Scott also quoted Tupac saying back to Knight, "I need a hospital? You the one shot in the head. Don't you think you need a hospital?"

With some in his caravan following closely behind, Knight drove frantically and erratically, bouncing his rented BMW off the Las Vegas Boulevard median in an attempt to reach the hospital. But the traffic was too heavy, and every move Knight made proved wrong. According to Scott's reporting, Knight ran his last red light at Harmon Avenue, executed another U-turn, and finally came to a stop in the middle of the Strip. In the process, his other two tires, the two remaining good ones, both went flat.

Having no idea what had gone on, police arrived with their guns drawn and ordered Knight and others in his caravan to lie down flat on the street on their stomachs. Paramedics were summoned. Knight was bleeding from the head, but it was soon obvious to the authorities that the person needing more immediate medical attention was not Knight but his passenger.

Tupac was reportedly still conscious when he was loaded into an ambulance for the short trip over to University Medical Center. According to Scott, witnesses on the street heard Tupac say, "I'm dyin', man," just before the ambulance sped off.

George Pryce was at Club 662, waiting for the Death Row contingent to arrive, when he heard the news about the shooting. "I was getting someone a drink when I was called aside and told that Suge and

Pac had been shot and that I better get over to the hospital," said Pryce. "My son David was with me, and we jumped in a cab and went to the hospital. I went to Suge's room first. I couldn't get near Tupac's room because there were so many people in there. But I did see him from just outside the room. He was definitely unconscious.

"I talked with Suge for about twenty minutes and I gave him some water through a straw," said Pryce. "He didn't say much. He did say, 'We're all going to be okay.' He said, 'Don't worry, Papa Hollywood,' which is what he called me. Death Row's lawyer, David Kenner, then instructed me to get on a plane and go back to the office in Los Angeles. He asked if I had my keys to the office, and I said yes. So I was sent back to deal with the press and the barrage of calls that would surely come in."

Young Noble received the news from Tupac assistant Molly Monjauze. "I was alone at Tupac's house," said Young Noble. "Napoleon [another member of the Outlawz, whom Tupac named for Napoleon Bonaparte, but whose real name is Mutah Beale] got a call, too, and he came right over. Molly came and got us, and the three of us went right to Vegas."

According to Cathy Scott's reporting, Yafeu Fula (Kadafi) called his mother to tell her about the shooting, and then instructed her to call Afeni Shakur at her Stone Mountain home outside Atlanta. It was already Sunday, September 8, East Coast time, when Afeni got the call. She gathered her things quickly and made arrangements to fly to Las Vegas with her daughter Sekyiwa.

Tupac, meanwhile, was soon moved into the hospital's trauma center where surgery was performed to remove one of his lungs. The surgery was successful, but his condition was not good. His pulse was weak. His blood pressure was dangerously low. He was placed on life support and breathed with the aid of both a ventilator and respirator.

Hospital spokesman Dale Pugh briefed reporters about the removal of Tupac's lung. "He's back in his room and he remains in critical condition," Scott's reporting quoted Pugh as saying. "He has been conscious. He is under a lot of medication, so he's pretty sedated at this time. He's severely injured. Suffering multiple gunshot wounds is obviously a terrible insult to the human body, so he's requiring intensive care, and he is receiving that right now."

A host of VIP well-wishers were allowed to come by briefly to pay their respects, among them Tupac's fiancée, Kidada Jones; Mike Tyson;

actress Jasmine Guy; M.C. Hammer; Rev. Jesse Jackson; and a local minister, Rev. Willie Davis.

Suge Knight was well enough to receive each visitor, and he chatted with everyone except the police investigators who were anxious to hear his version of the shooting. According to Cathy Scott's reporting at the time, Knight passed word to the investigators that he'd talk to them later in the day, in his hospital room. As for his banged-up BMW, it remained impounded at a local body and towing shop in North Las Vegas. Police had gone over the car several times and found no guns inside, just Knight's cigar case and a Motorola cell phone.

Also on Sunday morning, Jesse Jackson accompanied Rev. Davis and others to the Second Baptist Church in West Las Vegas. Jackson delivered a sermon about Tupac. Scott recorded his comments for her book: "'Before you condemn Tupac for calling women bitches and ho's in his music,' said Jackson, 'you need to understand and know about the background of this man and where he came from. He was raised by a woman who was on crack. He didn't have a real mama. Don't condemn him for talking about his mama and for talking about women.'"

But his "mama," as Jackson referred to her, was a different person by 1996, and she arrived at the hospital that afternoon to find that her son had been put under a drug-induced coma, a common medical procedure with patients who are already unconscious and in extreme physical peril. Still, Afeni had no choice but to think positively and then rely on her faith.

"We thought that he might pull through," she recalled. "But I'll tell what I was feeling after I got there. In that hospital I held on to the principles of my recovery like a crazy person. It's all I had. I knew I was in dangerous territory. I knew it was danger time. So I prayed. I asked God, 'Please, I know I'm powerless in this situation. So God, if you're going to take my child, I want you to just do me one favor. Could you please make him a light on a hill.' And you know what, I believed in that request. And believing in that request, I didn't want his journey from earth to have any weight on it. I wanted his spirit to be released. I didn't want to be pulling it back to the earth. This is how I was. If my baby was leaving, I wanted him to leave on wings. I wanted him to leave free. I wanted him to leave with no encumbrances. And so I would not allow myself to try to pull him back. I said nothing out loud. And every time I thought it, I would say, 'God, please help me release my child. Please.'"

Jesse Jackson returned to the hospital later that day and prayed with Rev. Davis and Afeni at her son's bedside.

The cops came back to talk to Knight only to find that the hospital had released him. Police Sergeant Kevin Manning, acting as both investigator and spokesman to the media, did not hide his frustration over the lack of help he was getting from witnesses. On Monday, September 9, Manning told reporters, "We did not receive a whole lot of cooperation from most of [Tupac's] entourage. It amazes me when they have professional bodyguards that they can't even give us an accurate description of the vehicle."

On Tuesday, September 10, Knight's lawyers arranged to have the Death Row chairman give his witness statement at homicide headquarters on West Charleston Boulevard. A specific time was set for that afternoon, but Knight and his attorneys never showed up.

Afeni Shakur only wanted to sit with her unconscious son and pray. "Let me tell you what I did," she said. "I sat there and read *The Prophet*, by Kahlil Gibran. It says, 'Your children are not your children. They are the sons and daughters of life's longing for itself. They come through you but not from you, and though they are with you, yet they belong not to you.'

"It's a longer poem," she said, "but that's just the essence of it. In a way, it is part of what my recovery has been like. I was so sick inside my heart, and I read this poem over and over and over again. I would meditate over it, and because of my recovery I could put myself in that place. I would act as if I could let my son go until I could let him go. When Tupac discovered what he called 'thug life,' I went back and read *The Prophet*, and that's how I got through it. He came home one day with 'thug life' tattooed across his stomach. Then it was 'thug life' all over his clothes. Understanding *The Prophet* helped give me the ability to allow him the full freedom to express his own self. Suddenly it wasn't so threatening, and it was okay. I used the same principles in the hospital."

Suge Knight finally met with investigators on Wednesday, September 11, but told them nothing. Sergeant Manning issued a press release the next day saying that Knight "was unable to give the investigators any information that would help in determining a motive, nor was he able to help identify possible suspects."

By Friday, September 13, any hope that Tupac might regain consciousness had faded. His heart stopped several times that day, and each time doctors worked feverishly to resuscitate him. Afeni finally made the sober decision not to try again. Tupac was pronounced dead at 4:03 P.M. The cause of death was attributed to respiratory failure and cardiopulmonary arrest.

An autopsy was performed a few hours later, and by 9 P.M., Tupac's body was at a local mortuary, where it was promptly cremated. On Saturday, September 14, Tupac's remains were given to his mother.

Afeni credited the five years of recovery before 1996 with getting her through that heartbreaking week. "Looking back," she said, "I needed that five years of recovery. Had my son left here with me still using and not in my right mind, I just shudder to think of what would have happened to his good name."

What hasn't happened to his good name is the fact that it has yet to be linked to another name, that of the person who killed him. Tupac's death remains an unsolved murder, an open case on the books of the Las Vegas Police Department, and one with very little movement. But consider the chain of events following the death of Tupac Shakur, and it's not surprising that his file is gathering nothing more than dust.

On Wednesday, October 2, just a few weeks after Tupac's death, Orlando Anderson, the man who had been seen by video cameras fighting with Tupac at the MGM Grand, was arrested in the Los Angeles suburb of Compton and booked on suspicion of murdering Tupac, and incredibly, murdering another man, who was killed in Compton six months earlier. But after examining both cases, on Friday, October 4, prosecutors declined to file any charges against Anderson.

On Tuesday, October 22, Suge Knight was put behind bars in Los Angeles County Jail for four alleged parole violations, the most serious of which, according to a *Los Angeles Times* account, was that he was involved in the post–Mike Tyson fight scuffle with Anderson.

On Sunday, November 10, Yafeu Fula, Kadafi in Outlawz-speak, was shot and killed in a housing project hallway in East Orange, New Jersey. Police said his killing was unrelated to Tupac's murder, but it is worth mentioning that Fula was the only man in the Tupac-Knight caravan on September 7 who indicated to Las Vegas police that he might be able to pick out Tupac's killer in a police lineup.

On Monday, November 25, Knight appeared in a Los Angeles courtroom in his jail-issued blue overalls to testify in his own defense about the Orlando Anderson matter. According to the *Los Angeles Times*, Knight said he wound up in the middle of the scuffle because he "was

wearing alligator shoes with wood soles and slipped on the hotel carpet, onto the pile of people."

His attorney, Death Row counsel David Kenner, asked Knight on
the stand whether he had punched anyone during the altercation. "No,
sir," he replied, the *L.A. Times* reported.

Kenner then asked his client whether he had kicked anyone, and
Knight said, "Absolutely not."

After the hotel security videotape of the incident was played in the
courtroom, one of the prosecutors asked Knight whether he was smiling while Anderson was being beaten.

"No," the *Times* reported he said. "I was tired. And upset."

Of course, it is possible that Knight wasn't too upset when news
broke on Sunday, March 9, 1997, that Christopher Wallace, the East
Coast's leading rap star, known as Biggie Smalls and the Notorious
B.I.G., was gunned down in Los Angeles, at the corner of Wilshire
Boulevard and Fairfax Avenue, following a *Vibe* magazine party in Hollywood. Like Tupac, Wallace was a passenger in a vehicle, in his case a
GMC Suburban, which was stopped at a traffic light when an unknown
assailant opened fire from another vehicle, reported at the time to be a
black Jeep.

Naturally, the East Coast–West Coast rap rivalry caused many to
believe that Wallace's murder was carried out as a form of retribution
for the killing of Tupac. But to this day no one from law enforcement
or the media has ever been able to seriously make that case. The Wallace case remains open, unsolved, and completely stalled.

As for Orlando Anderson, his life came to an end on Friday, May
29, 1998, when he was shot and killed in a gun battle that took two
other lives at a car wash in Compton. Again, law enforcement was
never able to prove that Anderson had anything to do with the murder of Tupac, and Knight surely hasn't done anything to help them.

On Friday, August 10, 2001, MTV's Chris Connelly asked Knight
whether he knew who killed Tupac. Knight responded that he did
not know.

"A lot of people think Orlando Anderson killed Tupac," Connelly
said on air.

"Okay, if a lot of you people thought that, that means the authorities knew that. So," he said, holding his arms open wide, "what's the
problem?"

"Do you believe that?" asked Connelly.

"What I believe is not important," said Knight. "I doubt that, but I'll tell you this: Even if I did think that about anybody, it ain't my job to snitch. I would never snitch on nobody. . . . If you're not man enough to believe in an eye for an eye, tooth for a tooth, then you're ratting on them. I would never tell on nobody."

And to this day, he hasn't. Suge Knight has been in and out of jail on a variety of parole offenses since Tupac's murder in 1996, and yet the Death Row chairman remains true to his word: He hasn't snitched on anybody.

E.D.I. hasn't snitched on anyone either. On the night of September 7, 1996, he was in the car with Yafeu Fula, just behind Knight's car, when the person or persons in the late-model Cadillac opened fire on Tupac. Fula told police he might be able to pick out the assailant in a police lineup, and he's dead. E.D.I. never opened his mouth about anything, and he's alive. And he still misses his friend who's not.

"The last few days of Pac's life was like a synopsis of his entire life," said E.D.I. "He was a great man to me. He was a teacher to me. He was a friend and a brother. His music told you that something was going to happen. I can't say it any better than his music. He wasn't any more afraid during those last days than he was during his whole life. Pac was just not the kind of person who feared death. In his mind, death was inevitable."

John Denver

December 31, 1943–October 12, 1997

THERE WAS A TIME IN THE 1970S WHEN JOHN DENVER WAS PROBABLY THE most popular person in Colorado. An avid skier, a concerned environmentalist, and a thrill-seeking adventurer, Denver epitomized the Colorado lifestyle and conveyed a slightly cleaner cut and more mature hippie image, the kind that made it okay for the rest of America to join in. Hey, if John Denver could get high in the Rockies off a combination of thin air, hit songs, and some good shit, well, maybe a few million extra tourists could, too.

His albums in those days sold in the multimillions. He sang about the love he had for his wife, Annie, and he walked the earth with sunshine on his shoulders. He promoted space travel and undersea exploration, and he performed duets with the Muppets. He drove Porsches and flew his own airplanes, and he made us believe in the movies that George Burns really could be God.

In short, everything in John Denver's life was going right until everything in John Denver's life started going wrong.

Pinpointing the moment when that change occurred will always be a matter of conjecture, but this much is definitely true: the phenomenal success Denver enjoyed in the seventies was already beginning to evaporate by the time he and Annie divorced in 1983. At the time, their two adopted children, Zachary and Anna Kate, were nine and six, respectively. They had lived as a family in a mountaintop compound he called Starwood, a sprawling redwood and glass house with a majestic view overlooking, of all things, the Aspen airport. The son of a pilot, Denver would revel in bringing friends out to the pool, in virtually any kind of weather, so they could all watch the endless takeoffs and landings of one small plane after the next. And always he would be struck by the spectacular silence that accompanied each flight. Starwood was situated so high above the airport that planes were already miles away before they ever reached Denver's eye level. In fact, the real beauty of Starwood on most clear days was the ability to see almost everything, and hear almost nothing.

After his breakup with Annie, Denver moved to a rented house in Aspen until the divorce was final. Denver's business manager, Hal Thau, couldn't believe how Denver was living when he first visited his rented house. "It didn't even have proper heat," said Thau. "I said, 'John what are you doing? This place is a hovel. It's ridiculous.' He had plenty of money, and he was doing laundry, doing the cleaning. I said, 'You can get someone to do these things for you,' but that's not who he was. He was never a prima donna. He never needed servants. But in this case I also think he was punishing himself for the fact that his marriage to Annie didn't work out. It was as though he felt like he didn't deserve a good life."

Denver moved back into Starwood after the divorce, and Annie wound up building another house for herself and the kids that was below Starwood but on the same mountain range. Once back at Starwood, Denver made like he was happy, but he was really putting up a good front. He added on new wings to the house, with new guest bedrooms, and he entertained royally. There were other women, of course, and then in 1988 a second wife, Cassandra Delaney, an Australian. The newlyweds lived at Starwood, but life for John Denver in Aspen was never the same. It didn't help that the marriage to Delaney was, according to most of his close friends, a total nightmare.

"Personally, I didn't care for her then, and I still don't care for her," said Denver's longtime road manager and coproducer Kris O'Connor. "I thought she used John. I thought she was bad for John."

O'Connor never changed his opinion of Delaney. But even he was startled to learn, along with others close to Denver, that Delaney had become pregnant shortly after the couple's wedding. For years Denver had been telling friends that he was sterile and could not biologically produce a child. He and Annie had talked about adoption since the seventies. He even had Zachary's name picked out three years before the child was born. So this was not a man who was ever embarrassed by his inability to father his own children. If anything, he embraced the idea that adoption made him no less a parent.

"I knew he couldn't have children," said Thau. "But John said the baby was his, so everyone accepted it as fact. There were never blood tests. He just accepted responsibility for the baby."

The baby turned out to be a girl, Jesse Belle, who was born in 1989. By all accounts, Denver treated her no differently from how he treated Zachary and Anna Kate. "He loved them all equally," said Thau. "He was that kind of guy."

But that kind of guy turned out to be in an awful second marriage, which soon became an acrimonious divorce that played out in court for nearly two years.

"It was a big trial, in an open courtroom in Aspen, with lawyers and accountants on each side," said Thau. "And here's John Denver, probably the least litigious person I have ever known, sitting there throughout this terrible experience, trying to be the stand-up guy he was. I prayed for breaks so I could get a cappuccino or a cup of coffee. The whole thing was just heinous."

And then, on August 21, 1993, it finally appeared to be over. After all the rancor that managed to work its way into the divorce, after more than $1 million in legal fees that Denver paid on both sides, there was one last court proceeding to end it. "John could not have been more thrilled that it had finally come to an end," said O'Connor. "I mean, he was just beside himself."

In fact, he was so beside himself that later that day he was pulled over in Aspen and arrested for drunk driving. He pleaded no contest to a lesser charge and had to play a local anti–drunk driving benefit concert as part of his probation.

Incredibly, on August 21, 1994, exactly one year to the day after his first drunk driving arrest, he was arrested again in Aspen for drunk driv-ing after crashing his Porsche into a tree and sustaining a seven-inch cut on his head. He pleaded innocent, and his lawyers tried to blame the accident on the singer's thyroid condition, which they said caused him to metabolize food and alcohol at half the normal rate. But this time the district attorney in Aspen wanted nothing less than jail time.

"That was probably his low point," said Bill Nicholson, a Vietnam vet who became President Gerald Ford's appointment secretary in 1975 and later an entrepreneur, an environmentalist, and a close friend of

Denver's. "All of a sudden I had calls everywhere. Everybody said, 'John Denver is looking for you. He's got to talk to you right away.'

When the two men finally connected by phone, Denver was seated in his car outside the courthouse. "He was actually waiting to talk to me before he went back in and gave them his decision," recalled Nicholson. "They wanted him to serve some time. They told him he could come in at night, when it was dark, and he could leave at sunup. But they were insistent about him spending X number of nights in the Aspen jail. They said they wouldn't let anybody photograph him. They said they'd keep it quiet when he was serving his time. And he didn't believe them. He felt very betrayed by them after all the things he'd done for Aspen. He was very unhappy and he felt estranged from Aspen, and a lot of the people in it."

Bruce Gordon, an Aspen resident and another Denver friend, agreed. "After that last DUI he felt that the town had closed up on him," said Gordon, the president of an environmental organization called EcoFlight. "He was very upset. He felt ridiculed and judged."

And so he decided to fight the charge and go to trial. After delays on top of more delays, the trial finally ended on July 12, 1997, nearly three years after the arrest, with a hung jury. The district attorney immediately moved to schedule another trial. But a remarkable thing had happened to John Denver in the intervening time: His life started to turn back around, and this time in a positive direction.

Thau traced the start of Denver's healing process to 1996. "It's not a situation where you wake up one morning and say, 'I'm cured,'" said Thau. "But every day he got further and further away from his second divorce and further and further away from the arrests. Every day, every month it got better. There were lessons upon lessons, and pretty soon he felt like he was getting his old life back. He started working more. His dealings with everybody changed for the better. His dealings with me changed for the better. Just the way he sounded, you knew he was getting better. And it wasn't just me. I know a lot of other people felt the same way."

By the spring of 1997, he was touring Europe and doing selected concert dates in the States. "And he was an absolute prince on tour, just amazing," said O'Connor. "We went and did a couple of shows in Maui, then we went in and recorded what we called 'The Train Album.' The actual title was *All Aboard!* and it was a collection of train-related songs like 'I've Been Working on the Railroad,' and a more contempo-rary Vince Gill song called 'Jenny Dreamed of Trains.'"

And Denver was in great voice, according to Milt Okun, his musical mentor and the man who produced all of Denver's hit records. "I went out to see him perform at a concert in the San Fernando Valley," said Okun. "It was four thousand people in an arena. I didn't go out there with him, but afterward he came back to Beverly Hills with me. He was staying at a hotel in Beverly Hills, not far from where I live, and we had a long conversation in the car, just the two of us.

"I remember the conversation so well," recalled Okun. "I said, 'John, you're literally singing better than I've ever heard you sing. The audience was just enraptured.' And it was true. He was singing ab-solutely powerfully, beautifully. The voice was in great shape. But more important, he was delivering the songs.

"And he told me, 'I think I'm singing great too.' He said, 'That's really why I want to do more recording.' And then he said, 'I really owe it to you and to Placido.' He had done this song, 'Perhaps Love,' as a duet with Placido Domingo, some years before. He said, 'You told me something about Placido's singing, and I listen to him all the time now. I listen to his opera recordings even though I don't understand French or Italian.'

"John then referenced 'Perhaps Love,' and he said he noticed that Domingo colors his sound with the meaning of the word. John said that when he heard Domingo sing the line, 'Love to some is like a cloud, to some is strong as steel,' the word *steel* sounded like steel. John said he could even tell that Domingo was doing the same thing in French and Italian. Even though he didn't understand what Domingo was singing, he felt the emotional quality that Domingo was putting over, which is what makes Domingo a genius. I mean, he colors every note, high or low, with the meaning he's trying to get across. And John said, 'I've been trying to do that.'

"And I said, 'Well, you hit a home run. That's why it was so beau-tiful tonight. When you sang the messages of each song; the emotions came through just as clear as ice.'"

Being in Los Angeles also gave Denver a chance to visit with his youngest child, Jesse Belle, who had moved to L.A. with Delaney after the divorce. But the child was eight now, and he knew he needed to be spending more time with her, not less. Denver had enough money, of course, to arrange a second home for himself, but Los Angeles was

never an option because of what Southern California had always represented to him: work, the music business, and a lifestyle that was a bit
faster and a little more desperate than he preferred. He felt there had to
be another way, and after a lot of consideration Denver did what for
him was the next best thing: he rented a house in the Carmel Highlands
area of Monterey, in Northern California. The house was close to the
Monterey Peninsula Airport, close to some of the world's greatest golf
courses, and far enough away from Aspen and the negative publicity
that had followed him all the way through the hung jury trial in July. In
other words, Monterey was perfect. He could see Jesse Belle more often
in L.A., he could fly up and down the California coastline, and just
maybe he could even pick up a few dollars beating his friends on the
golf course at Spyglass Hill. For John Denver, the combination of possibilities was simply too intoxicating to ignore.

"The main reason he took the house in Monterey was to be closer
to Jesse Belle," said Thau. "I did the lease agreement for him. It was a
one-year lease. The house was a simple house, not flashy, nothing special, nothing like the houses in Beverly Hills. Of course, John didn't
care what it was, as long as it was clean. Most of the furniture was
rented. Remember, he didn't know how this was going to work out.
What mattered most was that he could be somewhere other than Aspen for a while. I never even saw the house. We did the entire deal on
the telephone."

With a new round of concert dates scheduled for late September
and early October, Denver used some of his down time in August to
visit his friend Nicholson at his ranch in Montana. "He flew up on his
Learjet, as he always did," said Nicholson, who had his own airstrip
on the property and his own plane, an Aero Commander 1000.

"The ranch was built in 1915," said Nicholson, "and every time
John came up he had his choice of staying in the house or in this cabin,
which is kind of off by itself. And he always chose the cabin. We even
called it John's Cabin. If anybody else was staying in there and John
wanted it, we quietly moved the other people out.

"Anyway," he said, "we have a lot of ponds and lakes on the property, with some very big fish. But there was this one pond that was off-
limits. The rule at the ranch was: No fishing in that pond. There are
cutthroats in there, up to 8 or 9 pounds, and those guys are my pets.
Well, this one morning, probably around 5:45 or 6 A.M., I looked out
the window and there was John, sneaking up on that pond with a fish-

ing rod. I actually snapped a picture of him after he caught an eight-pound cutthroat in that pond. He had this big grin on his face, like he had just been caught doing something he knew he shouldn't be doing, but he couldn't help himself because he loved every minute of it while he was doing it. That kind of look. He was a phenomenal fisherman, and the expression on his face told you how happy he was at that moment in time. People who have tried to make the case that John was depressed and suicidal just didn't know him.

"On another night during that same trip up to the ranch, we were all sitting there watching a movie," said Nicholson. "And Clementine, one of our King Charles spaniels, had climbed up on his lap and had fallen asleep. John reached for his guitar, and started strumming a few chords, which kind of woke her up. And on the spot he made up new words to 'Oh My Darling Clementine,' and he started singing it to this wonderful little dog that he loved. She followed him back to the cabin that night and slept on the bed with him. She obviously loved him, too."

On Saturday, September 6, Denver sent his ex-wife Annie a bouquet of flowers to celebrate her fifty-first birthday. He had been sending her flowers every September 6 since they married in 1967. Even after their breakup he still managed to continue the tradition.

"John and I lived only ten minutes apart in Aspen, and because of the kids we obviously kept a relationship throughout," said Annie. "Sometimes we were friendly. Sometimes we were distant. But always he remembered my birthday."

On Saturday, September 20, Denver was in Baltimore to meet O'Connor and perform a benefit concert for the Cystic Fibrosis Foundation. O'Connor does production for the event each year, and Denver agreed to provide the evening's entertainment at the charity's 1997 renewal.

"We had ten thousand at the arena in Baltimore, and John did thirty songs," said O'Connor. "I think we raised $800,000 for the foundation that night."

O'Connor, who lives in Warrenton, Virginia, got Denver a room at the Ritz-Carlton at Tysons Corner in nearby McLean. "John had five concert dates coming up in Texas, but they were a few days off," said O'Connor. "The choice for him was to go home for a few days, or hang out in Virginia with me and play golf. All he really wanted to do anyway was play golf, so he stayed in Virginia."

O'Connor described Denver as "a pretty good golfer, probably a twelve to fifteen handicap and five or so shots better than me.

"We set up a routine," O'Connor said. "I stayed home with my wife, John stayed at the hotel, and we met every day for golf. We played Lowes Island, which is a real exclusive golf course. We played at River Bend Golf and Country Club, a private place, and we played two days in Warrenton, at a course called South Wales. Every day was great. Every day you knew he was getting stronger, more sure of himself, and confident that he could still have a great career. There was a little popularity coming back. There was new record interest from Sony and RCA. Better deals for him were becoming possible, and he felt great about it.

"Then we went down to Texas and did five shows in five nights," he said. "One-nighters in San Antonio, Fort Worth, Houston, Austin, and Corpus Christi, all thiry-five-hundred-seat theaters, all filled, and all responsive. John had turned a major corner, and he knew it."

On Monday, October 6, Zachary Denver took a short flight from Durango to Denver so he could meet his father at Mile High Stadium for a Denver Broncos football game. Zachary had labored to get through college and took various semesters off through the years. Now twenty-three, he was finally in his senior year at Fort Lewis College in Durango. But this was not to be a night of homework. The Broncos were playing the New England Patriots on ABC's *Monday Night Football*, and while it was still fairly early in the season, both teams were coming into the game undefeated.

"I'm a die-hard Broncos fan," said Zachary. "I had been to a couple of games with my father over the years, and every time it was great."

His father's celebrity got them down on the field at halftime, and it turned out to be a glorious evening with the Broncos winning the game 34–13. Sharing the win with his father on top of a recent summer camping trip with him in the Grand Canyon brought the two men even closer together.

"I talked to my father at least once a week, and the conversations were about the usual things—how I'm doing, how he was doing, sports, flying, the sort of things we both loved," remembered Zachary. "I had flown with him quite a bit, and we'd talk a lot about the specifics of flying when we were up in the air. He loved it up there."

But being "up there," as it were, also meant taking care of his aircraft business down on the ground. And there was some of that business on Denver's plate at the time. Someone had agreed to lease half of Denver's Learjet, and there were papers to sign. But Denver had also owned a second plane, a Christian Eagle biplane, and he needed to sell that one outright because of another purchase he had made on Saturday, September 27. That was the day he bought the Y-shaped high-performance experimental plane known as the Long-EZ, which comes in a kit and is put together much like a model airplane. The Long-EZ Denver bought was built in 1987 and already had between eight hundred and nine hundred hours in the air, according to Van Snow, a veterinarian from Solvang, California, who sold the plane to the singer for an amount reported to be anywhere from $50,000 to $60,000. Snow told *People* magazine that Denver had the plane checked out by two mechanics, who both gave it a thumbs-up. "It's one of the very fastest Long-EZ's in the world, and it's won several competitions," *People* quoted Snow as saying. During the time he owned it, Snow said, "I've had no mechanical problems with it."

The plane had been sanded, primed, and freshly painted, and was in Santa Maria, California, waiting for Denver to pick it up.

But there were still some important things to do before he left Aspen again. One was connecting with his daughter Anna Kate. A twenty-year-old Dartmouth student at the time, Anna Kate was on a break for a few days at home with her mother. On Tuesday, October 7, Denver had Anna Kate over for dinner, and as soon as she left Starwood, Denver called Annie brimming with joy.

"He always had this very exuberant way of talking when he got excited about something," said Annie. "He said to me, 'Oh, Annie, I love our daughter.' You could tell he was just beaming from ear to ear.

"I hadn't talked to him since I got his flowers for my birthday," she said, "so I thanked him again. I said, 'It's so sweet of you to always remember my birthday.'

"And he said, 'Oh, but Annie, I love you.'

"And I said, 'John, I love you, too. Have a wonderful trip to California. I'll speak with you when you get back.'"

Denver also had a barbecue that week in Aspen for some of his closest friends, among them Bruce Gordon. "It was the usual cast of characters, mostly old friends," said Gordon. "We had marinated salmon on the barbecue, and drank a little wine. We played horseshoes. It was like a ritual. We'd done it many times. But this time John seemed excited about this next chapter in his life. He talked about the new plane he was getting. He knew he'd be playing golf in Monterey. He said he really liked his new house up there. He was very optimistic. He was going to be closer to Jesse Belle, and he really liked that. He was even saying that he was on friendlier terms with Jesse Belle's mother, and that was something to be upbeat about, too."

Bill Nicholson reached Denver toward the end of the week and invited him to Alaska. "I had been given a chance to go way out on the Alaskan peninsula, in an area where the last salmon run is and where the big bears come in to feed," said Nicholson. "The natives hadn't opened that area to anyone, and now they were opening it up. My plan was to go in there and camp for a week, watch the big bears and photograph them. The fellow who manages my ranch came, along with a friend of his. I invited John to come along and bring his camera equipment and watch a whole bunch of big bears in a gorgeous setting. He thought about doing it, and then he called me back an hour later and said he couldn't make it. He said he had too much to do. There were some vocal overdubs he had to do in Los Angeles. He was picking up the plane. He had a few golf games planned. Alaska was just not something he could squeeze in."

On Friday, October 10, Denver telephoned Milt Okun in Beverly Hills. "It was actually a very long conversation," said Okun. "He told me about an offer he received from a record label that was associated with BMG. It was a foreign-based label. I'm sure he mentioned the name, but it didn't ring a bell. They had offered him a deal that was different than the kinds of offers he'd been receiving in recent years, which were mostly specialized kinds of albums, like a children's album. There was always interest in an album he wanted to do, which he called *Songs I Wish I Had Written.* And several labels were interested in an album that we were going to do with the Berlin Philharmonic. John was always a big star in Germany. Soon after he became a major star in the States, he had a big success with a double album in Germany called *Henry John Deutschendorf aka John Denver.* If I remember correctly, it sold nine hundred thousand copies, which was enormous for any two-record set, especially from just one foreign country.

"But the potential deal John was talking about on the phone was different," said Okun. "For a long time no one had been willing to let John step up to the plate to let him do new songs. And now someone from this BMG label was saying that he could do an album of all new material. John said it would be a regular recording, the kind we did throughout the seventies.

"Well, you could imagine how excited he was," said Okun. "I said to him, 'John, you've got to hire a lawyer to negotiate this. You can't do it yourself.' He'd made a number of career mistakes handling things by himself. He had Hal Thau, but occasionally John ignored him. And whenever John negotiated a TV deal, or a record deal, inevitably he messed it up. I said to him, 'Since these people want to make a deal, you shouldn't be the one to do it. If you do, you'll do it poorly, and you'll probably lose the deal.

"And he agreed," said Okun. "He asked me who we should use, and I suggested David Braun, a lawyer in Los Angeles. John said yes, and I had my secretary call David Braun later that day to set up an appointment with John for Tuesday, October 14. John said he was going to be in the Bay Area for the weekend, and then he would be coming down to Los Angeles to see Jesse Belle. So he said that Tuesday would be a great day to see David Braun. We made the appointment for Tuesday, October 14, at eleven A.M."

With all their business out of the way, Denver remained on the phone with Okun for another hour, talking mostly about how happy he was. "He mentioned going to the Broncos game with Zack and said he had a marvelous evening," recalled Okun. "He said the same thing about the dinner he had the next night with Anna Kate. He said that both kids were in marvelous shape. He was happy about this new potential record deal, and he was also very excited to be taking possession of this new experimental plane. He said he was getting the plane the next day. He was in a wonderful frame of mind when we hung up."

On that same Friday Denver phoned Roger Nichols, who had been engineering and coproducing some of the singer's most recent projects, including the album *All Aboard!* Nichols had also helped Denver choose the Long-EZ plane he bought from Van Snow.

"He asked me if I wanted to meet him in Santa Maria to pick up the new plane," Nichols wrote on his own Web site. But the engineer/producer couldn't be there on Saturday. "I had to go to Nashville and was going to meet him in Monterey on Sunday," said Nichols.

On Saturday, October 11, Denver flew from Colorado to Santa Maria to pick up his new plane and take one last flying lesson. Records obtained from the National Transportation Safety Board indicated that Denver received a thirty-minute flight and ground checkout in the airplane, which was conducted by another Long-EZ pilot. According to the NTSB, Denver departed Santa Maria for the one-hour flight to Monterey with an estimated twelve and a half gallons of fuel in his plane's right gas tank, and another six and a half gallons in his left gas tank. The pilot who checked Denver out in Santa Maria estimated that a total of nine gallons of fuel would be needed for the Santa Maria to Monterey flight.

Snow told *People* magazine that Denver had appeared ecstatic about his new possession. Snow said that right before Denver left Santa Maria he told people on the ground, "I'm gonna have a great Sunday. I'm gonna play golf, and then I'm gonna fly my new bird."

On Sunday morning, October 12, Bill Twist was standing in the parking lot at the Spyglass Hill Golf Course in Pebble Beach when Denver drove up in his Porsche. Over the years, whenever Denver traveled to San Francisco, he found a way to see Twist, who lived in the Bay Area with his wife, Lynne. By Twist's own estimation, he never saw Denver more than two or three times a year, but they communicated often and had many shared interests.

The two men met in the late seventies as volunteers of the Hunger Project, a San Francisco–based foundation that grew out of the Warner Erhard group, EST. Twist went on to develop business software and head an environmental human rights foundation that does work with indigenous people in the rain forest in South America. According to Twist, Denver never needed coaxing to visit Northern California. "John came up one time just because a mutual friend of ours had a daughter who was in a high school play," said Twist. "John sat there among all the parents who had kids in the play. Our friend was as proud as can be that John Denver had come to see this girl perform in a play. We had played golf a couple of times before, and over dinner that night we talked about finding time to play the course at Spyglass Hill."

Sunday, October 12, and Monday, October 13, were the two dates they had set aside. The plan was to play eighteen holes the first day followed by another eighteen holes on the next day. Twist and his wife had already started a conversation with Denver about maybe getting involved in a project they were doing in the Amazon with indigenous people. "He had always talked about being a spokesman for the environment," said Twist. "He was interested in possibly going down to South America with us, so I thought we might even talk about it that day on the golf course."

But there was clearly something else on Denver's mind when he arrived at Spyglass Hill. "He was a little late getting there," said Twist, "and he made the comment, not necessarily to me, but he made it, sort of like he was thinking out loud. He said he'd had the strangest dream the night before, a wild and upsetting dream. I didn't say anything to him, or ask him about it. He just sort of threw it out there as he was getting out of his car, like this dream was the reason he was late, like he was a little bit disoriented and hadn't slept well. He didn't go into any details. But, you know, when he said it, it seemed a little strange, like he was a little bit off. But I didn't push it."

Denver and Twist were joined by three other men, Michael Flynn, a Spyglass member, Neil Rogin, a writer who had also known Denver from the early days of the Hunger Project, and Jim Linnan, a friend of Twist's from Southern California.

"Spyglass is essentially a public course," said Twist, "but it has a private membership. If you go out with a member, and Michael was a member, not only can you get a preferred tee time but you can also go out as a five-some. And that day we played as a five-some."

By the time the five men took out their drivers on the first tee, whatever had been bothering Denver about his dream seemed to have vanished. He was suddenly much looser and calmer.

"He's very athletic and graceful, with a good swing," said Twist. "He's also very competitive. I don't mean to say he's affected by winning or losing, but he always added a competitive energy and a kind of intensity to the round. He battled, and it didn't matter who he was battling against."

Denver was first to hit that day. "He stepped up to the tee," said Twist, "put his ball down, and he said, 'You know, you guys, when I play at the AT&T at Pebble Beach, the pros hit it right down the middle. Then I get up and I hack it, and I hardly ever get it on the fairway. But they're always so generous to me, and they always make some comment that I won't be hurt by my bad shot, and that everything will turn out okay.'

"He said he hated that the pros had to talk to him like that," said Twist. "Then he boasted to us that this time he was going to put his ball right down the middle, just like the pros. So we were all standing there watching, and he hit this big hook right into the rough. And the four of us said simultaneously, 'Don't worry, John, you won't be hurt by that one.' So that was the beginning of our round. We laughed at John. He laughed at himself. And we were off. The course wasn't crowded. We were playing five, and the weather was sunny and warm. For October, the day couldn't have been more beautiful."

And that kind of beauty certainly wasn't lost on Denver, whose concern for the environment extended even to the golf course itself. "He actually went around the course, and whenever he saw any trash, he picked it up," said Twist. "Even if he was walking down the fairway and he saw something in the rough, he would walk out of his way to pick it up. He never announced he was doing it. Nobody said anything about it when he did do it. But he did it, regularly. And then he'd hold on to the trash until he got to the trash basket at the next tee.

"He also would stop whatever he was doing to help look for someone else's ball," said Twist. "Ask any golfer and they'll have to admit that it can become a real pain looking for someone else's ball. If it's not your ball, most other golfers in the group will inevitably want to call off the search early. But not John. He could spend an eternity looking for someone else's ball. He was the most generous person with his time on the golf course. And it wasn't just with me that day. He didn't know these other guys. He was there that day because of me. But he talked to the others all day. He drew them out. One of the guys, Michael Flynn, the Spyglass member, knows a thousand jokes. John knew a lot of jokes, too, and the two of them ended up trying to one-up each other the whole way around the golf course."

Denver also gambled with his playing partners, and won. Of course, the stakes weren't exactly high—"$2 Nassau," to be precise, which, when translated for the nongolfer, means $2 to the player who scores the lowest on the front nine, $2 to the player who scores the lowest on the back nine, and $2 for the lowest aggregate score. Twist could not recall how Flynn, Rogin, and Linnan all fared that day. But he was very aware of his own intense competition with Denver.

"We may have been playing for a small amount of money," said Twist. "But winning meant the world to him. For example, early in the match there were a lot of 'gimmees,' or short putts that you don't have to actually make because your opponent is willing to concede it to you. John was very liberal with his gimmees on the front nine, which is understandable considering that he was beating me on the front nine.

"But I was gaining on him on the back nine," said Twist. "And suddenly, the same putt that on the front nine was, 'Oh, that's good,' became, 'Oh, that's not bad, but it's not good,' on the back nine. I think I started twitching at fourteen through fifteen. I would have a short putt to make, a putt he wasn't giving me, and just as I was getting ready to putt, he would say, 'Get it close, Bill.' It was good-natured ribbing on his part, but if I remember correctly, he was the only one who said anything out loud while I was standing over a putt."

By the end of the round, Denver had won a grand total of $2. "And he was very pleased with himself about it," said Twist.

"None of us played very well," admitted Twist. "The course was set up almost like the way they had it set up for the AT&T Pebble Beach tournament. It had a thick rough and real fast greens. They may have had some tournament coming up that they were preparing for, and as a result, none of us played very well. None of us scored lower than ninety, maybe even ninety-five. Michael Flynn is a five handicap and Jim Linnan is a ten, and I don't think either one broke ninety. It actually ended up being a kind of blessing in that the course was so tough and we all did so poorly. It sort of bound us all together. We were these warriors. We didn't really take on each other that day as much as we were all out there together taking on the golf course."

Most golf courses in America have what they call "the nineteenth hole," that restaurant, or bar, or grill room where golfers go to relax and eat and quench their thirst and generally start the process of fabricating stories about the round they just completed. Spyglass Hill, of course, has just such a restaurant, which is where Denver, Twist, and the others went after the last $2 changed hands.

"Everyone had a beer except John," said Twist. "He had a combination ice tea and lemonade. He had sort of gotten out of drinking any alcohol at all. He would have a beer every once in a while to quench his thirst. But he didn't want anything that day because his intention was to leave the golf course and go to the airport so he could practice takeoffs and landings in his new plane. In fact, we all had a specific plan. John was going to his plane, and we were going to the Pebble Beach driving range to work on our games so we might be better prepared for the next day's round. The same five of us were playing together on Monday. We tried to talk John into going to the driving range with us. We had all been so horrible out on the course. He could have used the practice just like the rest of us. But he said, 'God, I really want to fly my plane. I haven't flown it all. I just flew it up here and I want to go practice takeoffs and landings.'

"And we said, 'Ah come on, don't do that. You need to work on your game as much as anybody.' We all laughed, but it was clear that he wanted to fly his plane.

"But none of us rushed out," said Twist. "The waiter came over and asked John for his autograph, and he signed the menu. I remember it was a long inscription. John asked the waiter who the autograph was for, and he said his nephew. The waiter said his nephew was eight or nine, and he loved John's music. John wrote a couple of sentences to the nephew and gave the menu back to the waiter. And one of the guys, Jim Linnan, asked John, "God, what is it like when you're out everywhere and people are coming to ask you for your autograph? Don't you ever get annoyed?'

"And I think John's comment was something like, 'Well, you know, sometimes I do get annoyed. But today is such a great day, and I see it as an opportunity to do something for the guy's nephew. You know, it's a gift and a blessing for me to be able to do that.' I thought that was a really nice comment."

There was only one other group of nineteenth-hole golfers in the restaurant when Denver stood up to say his goodbyes. "I don't know if they noticed him immediately," said Twist, "but I was aware that he'd have to pass their table to get out the front door. He shook hands with each one of us and asked where we would be having dinner. We told him about a restaurant in downtown Monterey, and he said, 'Okay, I'll be there.' Then, on second thought, he said, 'God, I'm bushed. I'm really tired. If it ends up that I just want to get some sleep, I may not join you. But I'll either see you there, or see you here tomorrow morning.' Our tee time for Monday was eight-thirty.

"I watched him walk out," said Twist. "I could see he was noticing the other table of men from the corner of his eye, like he was getting ready to respond if one of the men noticed him. And one of the men did look up, and you knew right away that he knew it was John Denver. And John said, 'Good afternoon, gentlemen. Wasn't this a great day?'

"When he walked out," said Twist, "one of the men said, 'That was John Denver.' I remember being struck by the fact that John was conscious of not shunning anybody. If there was an opportunity to say anything, he would always do it."

The four remaining golfers from Denver's group stayed in the restaurant for another forty-five minutes. Flynn, the Spyglass member, then picked up the tab and they all left. But they didn't go to the driving range as originally planned. "Michael had a house in Pebble Beach that he owned with a few other guys, and that's where we were staying," said Twist. "So instead of going to the range we all went back to the house where we changed, cleaned up, and rested a little bit before dinner."

Denver arrived at the Monterey airport shortly before 5 P.M., and went directly to Del Mar Aviation, a private airport terminal where he had been renting a hangar. He left his Porsche parked nearby, with the convertible top down, and his golf bag in the back. Jennifer Cast, a customer service worker at Del Mar, told the *San Francisco Examiner* that she had seen Denver there numerous times in the past.

"He'd come in when he needed to fuel his plane, shoot the breeze," said Cast. "He was friendly. I think everybody in here enjoyed him."

According to records obtained from the NTSB, a maintenance technician assisted Denver in preparation for his practice flight. The technician told NTSB officials that when Denver got himself seated in the airplane, he had difficulty reaching the fuel selector switch.

"The fuel selector switch is in a very difficult location on the Long-EZ," said Denver's friend and fellow pilot Bill Nicholson. "When John bought the plane, it had a pair of vice grip pliers attached to the selector level, which indicated how difficult it was going to be to switch from one fuel tank to the other."

The maintenance technician told NTSB officials that Denver felt he could solve any fuel tank problem by using the in-flight autopilot to hold the airplane level while he turned the fuel selector valve. The technician claimed that he checked Denver's total fuel capacity during preflight and reported to him that his left gas tank indicated less than one-quarter full (about 3.1 gallons), and that his right gas tank indicated less than one-half full (about 3.25 gallons). NTSB records quoted the technician as saying that Denver "declined an offer for additional fuel, saying he would be airborne only about one hour and did not need fuel."

The Monterey Air Traffic Control tower cleared Denver for takeoff at 5:12 P.M. He commenced to perform three touch-and-go landings, "followed by a straight-out departure to the west," NTSB records stated.

At approximately 5:27, the controller asked Denver to recycle his transponder code, a standard procedure for keying in a signal to the control tower for radio identification. NTSB records indicated that

Denver complied with the request. But numerous reports also revealed that his first signal back to the tower wasn't received, so he tried again. And this time he was successful. NTSB investigator George Peterson said that Denver's second attempt at a signal was followed by his question, "Do you have it now?"

The tower tried to radio Denver back, but he never answered.

"I think he simply lost track of time," said Nicholson. "And being a pilot myself, I know that if your plane starts to go on you, there are split-second decisions to make. And the first one is, 'Am I going to try to get out of this plane, or am I going to try to keep it running?' John didn't have an ejection system, so he couldn't eject. But he still had a choice, another split-second decision. He could have attempted to maneuver the plane to a kind of crash landing and in the process destroy the plane. Or, he could focus on trying to get that selector switch turned to the second tank on the theory that whatever fuel was in it would keep the plane going.

"I believe it's just human nature to not want to destroy your airplane," said Nicholson. "So I think he went the fuel selector route, and it was very difficult to operate. The Long-EZ is a very unforgiving plane. When that engine dies, because it's behind you, the plane pitches down drastically. John was a very good pilot, but he was flying a plane he wasn't very familiar with, a plane that hadn't been built to his specifications. He didn't have a chance."

At the Pacific Grove beach area known as Lover's Point, Joan Trust and her elderly mother were seated in a parked car, facing the ocean and admiring the sight. "It was a magnificent day, with a cloudless sky and gorgeous surf," said Trust, whose husband, music publishing executive Sam Trust, had a golf date scheduled with Denver for later in the month. "It was one of those special days, with families on the beach and other people behind us playing golf at Pacific Grove's little municipal course."

Joan Trust had been in the car because her mother no longer had the strength to walk back and forth on the sand. "For her, the easiest way is to just sit in the car with the windows open and look at the ocean, which she loves to do," she said. "I was just at the point of leaving the beach. I put my car in reverse, and just as I did, I heard this loud sound. I wasn't quite sure what it was. And then I realized it was a motor, an engine. I was still facing the ocean, and the sound was behind me. Then it was over me. Then I saw something hit the water."

Trust estimated that the splash she saw in the water was some-where between one hundred and one hundred fifty yards from the shore. "It was just beyond the breaking waves, near some rocks that ex-tend out from the beach," she said. "It happened so quickly. It had come directly over the top of the car and into the water. At first, I thought it might have been something of the navy's or the coast guard, some kind of a drone. I didn't even realize that it might be a plane, with someone in it."

Someone rushed over to Trust's car saying that a small plane had just gone down. The person asked Trust whether she had a phone in her car. She did, and immediately she called 911. "And it was busy, busy, busy," said Trust. "Other people on the beach were obviously calling 911, too."

But it was too late. John Denver was gone.

An investigation by the NTSB concluded that Denver's "diversion of attention from the operation of the airplane and his inadvertent application of right rudder resulted in the loss of airplane control while attempting to manipulate the fuel selector handle."

The board also determined that Denver's "inadequate preflight planning and preparation, specifically his failure to refuel the air-plane, was causal."

The board's report further stated that the decision by the builder of the plane "to locate the unmarked fuel selector handle in a hard-to-access position" was a factor in the accident, along with "unmarked fuel quantity sight gauges, inadequate transition training by the pilot, and his lack of total experience in this type of airplane."

Needless to say, Denver's golfing partners had no reason to think that any of this had occurred just off the shore in nearby Pacific Grove. "We went out to dinner at 7 P.M., and obviously John didn't show up," said Bill Twist. "He had said he might not come, so we thought noth-ing of it. We then went to this local jazz club, but it was Sunday night and nothing was going on. It was dead inside the club, so we left.

"As we went back outside to the car, something strange hap-pened," said Twist. "There was a golf ball sitting in the middle of the street, in downtown Monterey, a brand new shiny white golf ball sit-ting in the middle of the street. Jim Linnan walked over and picked it up and flipped it over to me, and said, 'Here, Twist, here's one of your wild shots from today. I don't think you're going to get in from here.'

"He threw me the ball and I looked at it," said Twist. "All day long

I had been playing a Titleist 3 Professional 100. And the ball he threw me was a Titleist 3 Professional 100. I thought, 'How strange is this? A ball like this is in the middle of the street in Monterey, and there are no golf courses nearby.' So I picked it up and put it in my pocket. Then we went back to Flynn's house and went to bed."

Of the four men, only Jim Linnan stayed up to watch the news. At a little after midnight he saw a report that a small plane had crashed that day in Monterey Bay. The on-air reporter said it was believed to be John Denver's plane, but at that point the TV station hadn't confirmed whether Denver was even in the area that day.

Linnan hurriedly woke up Twist and the others and told them about the report. Flynn called the local police to say that Denver was in town that day, and had been flying his plane. The golfers offered to come down to identify the body, but the police said it wouldn't be necessary. They already knew John Denver was flying that plane, and they already knew he was dead.

The four men all looked at one another with that "What the hell do we do now?" expression on their faces. "We were trying to figure out whether we should go out and play another round of golf in the morning, or simply forget about it and go home," said Twist. "And the decision we made collectively was that, definitely, we should play. That's what John would have wanted us to do."

And so on Monday, October 13, at 8:30 A.M., Twist, Flynn, Rogin, and Linnan went out as a foursome, and took turns hitting a fifth ball in honor of their late golfing companion. "It was a very somber round," said Twist. "But we played. And somewhere on the back nine I found another Titleist 3 Professional 100 that was not my ball. Again, very strange—one Titleist the night before in the middle of the street, and now here's another Titleist, right off the green, in a place where it would have been easily found if anyone had actually been looking for it. I thought, 'Two new Titleist golf balls in twelve hours? It must be a sign from John.'"

The press, of course, saw different signs. In the initial rush to get out their plane crash stories, many reporters went to great lengths trying to link the accident to Denver's past history of drunk driving arrests, as though alcohol might have contributed to the plane's going down. In fact, as subsequent toxicology reports later revealed, there was not a drop of alcohol in Denver's system when he died.

A few weeks after Denver's death, Twist gave the second Titleist he found to Annie Denver. "It was just clear to me that she should have it," he said. "I have the other Titleist at home in a glass container."

A few months later, on Wednesday, February 25, 1998, Denver's name was announced at Radio City Music Hall in New York when *All Aboard!*, the train album he co-produced with Kris O'Connor and Roger Nichols, won the Grammy Award for Best Children's Album, Musical. Accepting the award on Denver's behalf were two of his children, Zachary and Anna Kate.

Milton Berle

July 12, 1908–March 27, 2002

THE BEST JOKES ABOUT MILTON BERLE'S PENIS ALWAYS CAME OUT OF BERLE'S own mouth. The way he figured it, if others in Hollywood were making people laugh by joking about the size of his penis, he should at least have the opportunity to get in on the act. Sometimes all Berle needed to go off on one of his penis riffs was to simply hear that an old crony had sent his regards.

"Oh, sure," Berle would say, responding to the passed-along greeting. "He probably wants me to talk about my cock." And away he went.

"Back in the days when Sammy Davis was dating Kim Novak," Berle would begin, "Sammy and I were in someone's big bathroom in Beverly Hills. I was taking a leak, and Sammy was standing next to me, fixing himself in front of the mirror over the sink. I knew it was only a matter of time before he looked down to steal a peek. They all do. Well, as soon as Sammy saw my cock, he jumped back, and went, 'Whoa!'

"Without missing a beat, I said to him, 'If you had a cock like this, Kim Novak would have to send you back to Hattie McDaniel.'" Of course, if you were too young or unaware to know that Hattie McDaniel played Mammy in *Gone with the Wind,* too bad for you. Berle was not going to alter his rhythm to identify her. He was already on to the next joke, arguably his best one, which he always saved for last.

"You know," he would say, "not everyone in Hollywood believes I have the biggest cock. Some people insist that Forrest Tucker's was bigger." And if you forgot Forrest Tucker, that tall character actor who starred on the TV sitcom *F Troop,* that's okay, too. For the joke to work, all you needed to know was that there might have been someone else in Hollywood with a penis to rival Berle's.

"I don't remember whose house it was," Berle went on, "but Tucker and I were both at this party in Beverly Hills. Someone says, 'Okay, let's settle this once and for all. Why don't you guys go upstairs and measure. Tucker and I agreed. Tucker walked up the stairs first, and as I started to go up my manager patted me on the back, and said, 'Milton, just take out enough to win.'"

"Doing material like that was never an act with Milton. That was his life," recalled his third and last wife, fashion designer Lorna Berle. "It was what he did. He thought funny, and he had a brain full of material. He had something for every occasion. And along the lines of 'take out enough to win,' he would also tell the one about Adam, who said to Eve in the Garden of Eden, 'Stand back. I don't know how big this thing gets.'"

Lorna Berle would not reveal exactly how big her husband got, but she did say, "He was sexy. He was sexual. And he had a sexual vitality that defied his age."

The former Lorna Adams first met Berle on December 13, 1990, at Nicky Blair's, a popular Sunset Strip restaurant in West Hollywood. It was a little over a year after the death of his second wife, former publicist Ruth Cosgrove, to whom he had been married for thirty-six years. In retrospect, Berle had probably been ready to settle down with another woman long before that night in December. In fact, Berle appeared in public just two weeks after Ruth's death in 1989. Billionaire oilman Marvin Davis was opening a Beverly Hills version of New York's famous Carnegie Deli, and Berle wanted to be there, he said at the time, because he was a part owner in the new restaurant.

"Marvin gave me two points in the restaurant," Berle said at the Carnegie's opening night party, "one point for me, and one point for Ruth. But now she's a silent partner."

Great joke, but the Berles probably would have been better off having no points, silent or otherwise, because the restaurant turned out to be a total disaster, and was already out of business by the time Adams and Berle met at Nicky Blair's. "I was having dinner with a friend," she said, "and Milton walked in with his former agent, Danny Welkes. My friend said, 'Isn't that Milton Berle?'

"They sat down a few tables away from us," she recalled, "and we called the waiter over, and I said, 'We'd like to buy Milton Berle a drink.'

"The waiter said, 'Milton Berle doesn't drink.'

"I said, 'Okay, we'll buy them dessert.'

"The waiter said, 'They don't want dessert. But they would like to join you at your table.'

"They came over and sat down at the table," she said. "Milton was eighty-two years old, and so cute. People kept coming over wanting his autograph, and finally he said, 'Let's get out of here, baby,' which is how he talked. We went back to my condo, the four of us, and we had coffee. My girlfriend and Danny then left, and Milton and I stayed up talking until three o'clock in the morning. The next day he called and invited me to dinner. We went out, and from that moment on we went out every single night."

Adams, who was forty-nine when she met Berle, later told *Los Angeles* magazine that he was initially embarrassed by their age difference. "So he would always introduce me to people like, 'Have you met Lorna? She's got three grandchildren.' It used to really piss me off," she told the magazine.

Of course, she wasn't pissed off enough to walk away. Quite the contrary; the two were married on November 26, 1991, and the new Mrs. Berle easily adapted to her husband's showbiz lifestyle, which usually meant going to a lot of restaurants, encountering a lot of people, offering ample opportunity for him to be on.

"Milton was a funny guy," she said, "but more than being funny Milton's addiction was people. He was always up, always in a good mood, happy most of the time, and always ready to tell a joke. Often he would kvetch, but even that made me laugh, because of how he kvetched. It was just his way of being around people. He'd talk with everybody and anybody. He could do a half hour with the busboy, provided of course that he had the busboy's attention. Then he could be funny and be Milton Berle.

"We could go to three, four events a night, easily," she said. "He just never got tired. He was driving up until he was eighty-five or eighty-six, and he stopped only because he got into a very bad accident. He wasn't hurt in the accident, but he totaled the car. After that, Milton sort of reluctantly agreed not to drive. But that was a difficult step for him because he was so vital in every way. This was a man who could go from getting a tooth implant to dinner and a cigar at the Friars Club. Just as long as he could be around people and make them laugh."

Even turning ninety didn't stop Berle from keeping his appointed comedic rounds. He received a standing ovation at a ninetieth birth-day roast, held for him at Westbury Music Fair on Long Island. One after another, comics who were not quite from his generation tried to make him laugh with one one-liner after another.

According to *Entertainment Weekly*, Friars Club regular Dick Capri said that Berle was at an age now "where Angela Lansbury is jailbait."

The magazine also quoted funnyman Jack Carter recalling that Berle grew up in the slums, "only one bathroom on the entire floor. Now he lives in a gorgeous home, ten toilets," Carter said, "and he can't go."

When it was Berle's turn to speak, he fumbled with the micro-phone but recovered quickly enough to turn the mishap into a joke. "There's a switch," Berle said, looking at the mike, "I can't get it down."

The subject of Berle's famous sexual prowess, or comedic lack of it, came up again at another nintieth birthday party for him, this one at the Fifth Avenue penthouse apartment of Denise Rich, the fledgling songwriter and ex-wife of fugitive financier Marc Rich. After all the "Happy Birthday" wishes were sung, Berle got up to acknowledge the crowd, in part to thank everyone, but mostly to use the moment to tell another joke. There he was, he said, ninety years old and married to a woman thirty-three years his junior.

"Having sex is not as easy as it used to be," said the man who sup-posedly had the largest penis in Hollywood. "Lorna and I were sitting at home on the couch, and she suddenly whispered in my ear, 'Milton, let's go upstairs to make love.'

"I said, 'Lorna, one or the other.'"

In truth, by the time the Berles returned to Los Angeles a few days later, life for the ageless comedian really had become "one or the other." And then the sex stopped completely.

"We came back from New York and we went to a party and Milton was very strange at the party," said Lorna. "I mean, he walked into the elevator door. He dozed off in a chair at the party, which is something he never did. Milton was always like the life of everything. I knew some-thing was really wrong, so we went to the doctor the next day and the doctor said that Milton had had a stroke, a stroke at the base of his brain—a brainstem stroke, which really affected his eyes.

"It became very hard for him to eat with a fork after that because the fork couldn't really find the food," she said. "I mean, he'd be off by two inches, not even close. So it was hard for him to eat. But he still wanted to go out to dinner and be around people. I started cutting up his food and putting it on the fork. Or I would order him finger food. Or I'd order a filet and cut it up, and he would eat it with his fingers. It was real hard for him."

But not when it came to getting off a good one-liner. In August 2000, the Berles attended a Democratic Party fund-raiser at a sprawling West Los Angeles estate. The city was hosting the 2000 Democratic National Convention, and the outdoor party was held to celebrate both the two-term presidency of Bill Clinton and the senatorial campaign of his wife, Hillary Rodham Clinton.

At the event, the now ninety-two-year-old Berle was asked whether he was a fan of the Clintons. Without missing a beat, he looked up and said, "Yeah, DeWitt Clinton," a reference to another senator, the New York State senator who helped create the New York public school system in the early 1800s.

"After the stroke his brain was still funny," said Lorna. "Only he could come up with a name like DeWitt Clinton in answer to a question about Bill Clinton. The stroke affected only his eyes. It didn't affect his memory or his speech or his gait or certainly his sense of humor."

Then came a colonoscopy, his first, at age ninety-two. "That's when they found he had colon cancer," said Lorna. "He was having some problems, and the doctor said, 'Okay, let's do this.' They went in and found that he had a tumor. The tumor was up high, under his left rib. The doctor said the tumor was very easy to get to, very operable. But they needed to get a clearance from his heart doctor, and he said it would be too dangerous to operate because of a hardening around Milton's heart. So the decision was made not to operate, due to his advanced age and the fact that they expected the cancer to spread slowly.

"He had never undergone a colonoscopy," she said, "so they couldn't be sure exactly how long he had had the tumor. But they thought it was a fairly new tumor, and they didn't think it would affect his lifespan. The doctor said, 'If it spreads to any other organs, then we'll deal with it when it happens. If it grows larger and there is a blockage that could be life threatening, then we'll go in and do emergency surgery.'

"That was how we left it," she said. "But then Milton got progressively sicker and everything started to go wrong. He would forget he had cancer. I remember, we were at a dinner party one night, and mind you, his mind was perfect. He could recall dates and places and talk about people. But by the end of 2001, someone said something about his cancer, and he turned to me, and he said, 'Do I have cancer?'

"And I said, 'Yes, honey, you have colon cancer.'

"And he said, 'Oh,' and he turned back to the other person and said, 'Yeah, Lorna says I have colon cancer.' It didn't really seem to affect him," she said. "It didn't really register that much. He had this thing about illness. He never, ever got sick in front of anybody, so it was kind of tricky. Those vaudeville players were just so happy to get a job that if they were sick, they couldn't tell anybody so they would act like they weren't sick. Milton could go onstage with a fever, or whatever was wrong, and he would work through the pain, like athletes do. So once he found out he had the cancer, he just totally put it out of his mind."

The Berles had been living in a sixteenth-floor condo on Wilshire Boulevard, and in December 2001, Berle's closest friend in the world, Buddy Arnold, came up to the apartment to say goodbye. Arnold, who along with Berle wrote the theme song to his groundbreaking weekly television show, *Texaco Star Theater*, was a fixture in the comedian's life for half a century. And now, Arnold was moving to Florida and certain that he would never see his best friend again.

"It was very sad when they said goodbye," said Lorna.

Nevertheless, Berle refused to be slowed down by Arnold's departure, or his own frail condition. He spent hours at home taping his act into a cassette recorder, and playing it back to himself. "He would edit it and redo it," said Lorna. "This was what he did his whole life. He kept talking into the machine. He knew he would probably never work again, because of his eyes. He wouldn't be able to see the audience, or cue cards. But that never stopped him from his taping. Often I would hear him late at night talking into his machine and rehearsing his act."

By the beginning of 2002, the ninety-three-year-old Berle remained insistent about keeping up the lifestyle to which he was accustomed. "He still wanted to be out all the time," said Lorna. "I hired a driver because Milton was now in a wheelchair, unable to walk. He had lost a tremendous amount of weight. He was almost skeletal in his appearance, but he still wanted to go out to dinner. One of his favorite places was Mastro's Steakhouse, in Beverly Hills. We would take him up the back elevator at Mastro's, and he'd sit at the table in his wheelchair. I'd cut up his food and he'd eat it with his fingers. But he didn't care because he just loved being around people.

"I remember the night Ben Stiller came over to the table to say hello to him," she said. "Milton was in his wheelchair, but he was very approachable. He wanted to talk to people, even though he couldn't recognize anyone. At this point, he had glaucoma and macular degeneration. Because of the stroke, his eyes were so very bad. He couldn't see a thing. So I would tell him who was coming. I had to explain a lot of things to him. I had to reexplain things. It seemed like everything was breaking down."

"I remember one morning when I walked in and he was holding two teeth in his hand," she said. "He had lost so much weight that his teeth were falling out. I looked at him and he just looked very sad, and he said, 'Does it get any worse?'

"And I said, 'Milton, it's going to be fine. I'm going to call the dentist.' We had something temporary made for him because he still wanted to go out. You can lose a leg and still go out for dinner. Lose a few important teeth and you're not going anywhere. I protected him the best I could. He was going to doctors all the time. We were doing everything to get him to eat. Taking him out to dinner, even when he couldn't eat, sort of helped because it raised his spirits. Maybe he'd eat a little, but he had totally lost his appetite. Everybody was concerned."

Admitting Berle to a hospital was never an issue. Lorna Berle knew her husband wanted to be at home, and she arranged for him to receive in-home care for whatever medical help he needed. "The doctor said that something needed to be done because Milton wasn't getting enough nourishment," she said. "So the decision was made to put a feeding tube in his stomach. That kind of limited his range of motion, but he was pretty much bedridden by then anyway. And of course that had to be changed every four or five hours, so we had round-the-clock nurses."

By February, Berle no longer wanted to see anyone other than Lorna and the medical people caring for him, and so he didn't. But if he believed he was dying, he never let on. "We never talked about it," said Lorna. "He never wanted to talk about it, and so the subject never came up. It was the strangest thing. It was like the elephant in the living room—there, but ignored. I would sit on his bed and talk to him and see how he was feeling, and he never ever once complained about his health—no matter how thin he got, no matter how sick he got. I would say, 'How are you feeling?' And he'd say, 'Pretty good.' He just didn't complain about his health. He'd complain about things like the feeding tube, but that's about it."

Lorna Berle spent nights at her husband's bedside, listening to him speak of the past and watching him stare out at the lights of L.A. "It's a great view," she said, "but it was a blur to Milton because he couldn't see it. For years, he talked about his plans for the future, where he was going to work and what he was going to do. And now he had no plans. So he talked about the past. He talked a lot about his mother and people who were gone, like George Burns. Milton loved George Burns. And he only had nice things to say about his mother, Sarah Berlinger. He talked about what a tough life she had, and how hard she worked, and how much she did for him, and how devoted she was. They were devoted to each other.

"Sometimes," Lorna said, "he talked to people he thought were in the room. He would see visions. And I remember one time he got really mad, and he said, 'Buddy said he'd be right back, and he's not here.' He thought Buddy Arnold had been sitting in a chair talking to him. Then he said something like, 'Fuck him. If he calls me, I'm not going to take his call.' He was hallucinating. He was becoming very confused."

And yet, he was still able to tell a joke. During the first week in March, Berle needed to be taken to the hospital one more time for yet another colonoscopy. Lorna Berle helped the nurses remove Berle's clothes and replace them with a hospital gown. "As they got him on the gurney and started wheeling him away," she said, "he looked up at me, and he said, 'All this for my teeth?'" According to Lorna, that was the last funny line her husband ever uttered.

She knew the end was getting close, but she kept hoping that somehow she would have one last great conversation with him. Sadly, it just wasn't happening. Berle slept during most of March, going in and out of consciousness. On Tuesday, March 26, Lorna sat with him on his bed and asked him how he was feeling. He didn't answer. She asked him if there was anything he wanted, and he didn't answer that either.

"He sipped liquids that day," she said, "and that was pretty much it. He was never unhappy once during those last days, and he was never ever in any pain that I knew about. I never heard him moan or grimace or groan, and he was not taking pain pills. He was very, very quiet. It was like nothing bothered him. He was in his own world."

On Wednesday, March 27, Lorna and her daughter, Susan, were out doing errands when Berle's assistant, Hans, called the boss's wife on her cell phone. "For weeks," said Lorna, "whenever I was out, I'd call home constantly. When you know someone is really ill, and you know they're probably going to die, you never have an idea of when. It could be days, or weeks. You just don't know.

"When Hans called," she said, "he said, 'Something's happened. His breathing has changed.'

"I said, 'I'm coming home right now.' Milton was never ever alone in the house," she said. "Not for one minute. We had round-the-clock people for weeks. And then the last two weeks we had hospice people with us, and they were like angels. Every time I walked into the kitchen someone was there to give me a hug.

"By the time I walked in," she said, "Milton was gone. Susan and I went into the bedroom and I sat on the edge of the bed, and I couldn't stop hugging him and kissing him. I just couldn't let go of him."

Reports of Berle's death all seemed to suggest that he had somehow said goodbye to his wife right before he died. He didn't. Other reports claimed she was with him when he died. And by her own admission, she wasn't. But those are just details. Now in her mid sixties, Lorna Berle still lives in the condo on Wilshire Boulevard. Professionally, she collects art, sculpts, and manages the real estate properties she owns. She has two grown daughters, six grandchildren, and a new man in her life. She didn't want to share any details about him, preferring to keep his identity a secret. After all, Milton Berle is a hard act to follow, most likely because of the size of his life, not to mention the size of one of his body parts.

"That does kind of work against me sometimes," admitted Lorna Berle, who knows she can count on hearing other comedians joke about her late husband's largesse for many years to come. The subject even came up on an episode of Larry David's HBO sitcom, *Curb Your Enthusiasm*. If you recall the scene, David and other cast members are at an afternoon pool party when they spot the host's young son changing his swim trunks. David does a double take, and suddenly they are all marveling at the apparent size of the boy's penis, which we gather from the dialogue is unusually large for someone his age. Later in the episode, when the boy is disrupting a screening, David turns around and yells at the boy's father, "Why don't you get Uncle Miltie out of here, so we could watch this thing?" And like all the great ones, he didn't have to explain the joke either.

Ted Williams

August 30, 1918–July 5, 2002

BY THE TIME TED WILLIAMS HAD PUT AN EXCLAMATION POINT ON HIS CAREER by hitting a home run in his very last time at bat, his legacy had pretty much been established. As they like to say in baseball, "You could look it up."

Williams was a .344 lifetime hitter who had the best career on-base percentage in the history of the game (.483). From his rookie year in 1939 until that last at-bat in 1960, the Boston Red Sox outfielder amassed a total of 521 home runs, 1,839 runs batted in, and a .634 slugging percentage that placed him second only to Babe Ruth's .690. A two-time MVP winner (1946 and 1949), two-time Triple Crown winner (1942 and 1947), and six-time American League batting champ, Williams played in eighteen all-star games, walked more often than any other player in history, and is the last man ever to hit over .400 for an entire season (.406, in 1941).

Incredibly, Williams might have even attained higher numbers had he not served his country in the prime of his career, missing the entire 1943, 1944, and 1945 seasons to be a navy pilot in World War II, and then most of the 1952 and 1953 seasons to serve in Korea.

When he first came up to the big leagues, Williams unashamedly told anyone who would listen that he wanted people to remember him one day by saying, "There goes the greatest hitter who ever lived." Years after his retirement, when he became more of a baseball curmudgeon, Williams altered his epitaph slightly to read, ". . . the best goddamn hitter who ever lived."

By 1999, when Major League Baseball saluted Williams at the all-star game in Boston, and he appeared on the Fenway Park pitcher's mound surrounded by some of the game's best-known contemporary hitters, including Cal Ripken Jr., Tony Gwynn, Ken Griffey Jr., and Mark McGwire, it was impossible to see Williams in any other light than the one he had wanted projected on himself. His health might have been suspect, but it was obvious on the faces of these other great hitters that they were indeed in the company of a man who could out-hit them all.

But in June 2001, a simple coast-to-coast phone call from one Williams family member to another started a bizarre chain reaction that would eventually change the perception of Ted Williams forever. On one end of the line was Williams's only son, John Henry Williams. He was in San Diego, and he was phoning his older half sister, Bobby-Jo Ferrell, in Florida. He said he was calling to ask whether she had ever heard about cryonics, the process of freezing a dead human being in the hopes that the person might one day be thawed out and brought back to life.

"He said he thought it would be 'a great idea to do this to Dad'" was how Bobby-Jo quoted her younger half brother in an open letter that was later posted on a number of Ted Williams–related Web sites.

"I immediately told him that these were not Daddy's wishes and reminded him that Daddy had always wanted to be cremated," wrote Bobby-Jo.

She also brought up the fact that on December 20, 1996, their father signed a last will and testament, instructing that his remains be cremated and his ashes, "sprinkled at sea off the coast of Florida where the water is very deep," according to the language in the document.

But John Henry was not about to engage Bobby-Jo in a legal discussion at that moment. All he wanted to do was get his point across. She described his manner as being very persistent as he tried to get her to see the commercial possibilities that cryonics might offer. "But wouldn't it be neat to sell Dad's DNA?" he asked her. "There are lots of people who would pay big bucks to have little Ted Williamses running around."

This was not something she wanted to hear, but John Henry was not about to back off. On the following night, the two half siblings spoke again, and this time John Henry urged Bobby-Jo to meet him in Scottsdale, Arizona, where the cryonics lab Alcor Life Extension Foundation was located. He thought she might change her mind after witnessing a typical freezing process firsthand.

"Again, I refused," she wrote. "My husband, Mark, then spoke to him, and after getting nowhere with JH, he told him, 'You are not going to do anything like that to your father because those were never his wishes. He is my friend, and you won't do anything like that to my friend.'"

It was like talking to a wall. John Henry would not be moved, and soon his secretary, Eleanor, was sending e-mails to Bobby-Jo and making arrangements for her to meet him in Scottsdale. "They had airline reservations all set up for her," Mark Ferrell said. "Eleanor called and said she had the tickets. And Bobby-Jo kept saying, 'I'm not going out there and visiting any Alcor facility. I know all about cryonics, and I think it's a bunch of bunk. They'll never bring anyone back to life, and this is certainly not what Dad wanted.'"

"From that night forward," recounted Bobby-Jo, "the communication between me and John Henry concerning my Daddy's health slipped away totally. I didn't know it at the time, but JH was beginning to speak to others about this cryonics idea, too."

George Carter had been caring for Ted Williams since the early 1990s. A certified nursing assistant from Pawtucket, Rhode Island, Carter helped rehabilitate Williams after his second stroke in 1994, and was at his side in November 2000 when Williams had a pacemaker installed at Shands Hospital in Gainsville, Florida. Two months later, Carter accompanied Williams to New York, where he underwent open-heart surgery at the Weill Cornell Medical Center. Dr. O. Wayne Isom performed the nine-hour operation, which involved replacing Williams's left mitral valve with pig tissue.

"Isom is the same surgeon who did David Letterman," said Carter. "I met the doctor on the elevator in the hospital soon after he did Ted's operation. John Henry and I were going up to our rooms. The hospital had given us rooms because Ted was an important person, and apparently they do that for all the important people. John Henry and I had gone down to the main floor for a sandwich, and on our way up we met Dr. Isom in the elevator. He was all dressed up in formal clothes. He had been to some kind of testimonial dinner for Larry King, who was another of his heart patients. The doctor said in the elevator, 'You know, Ted's not doing that great now. But he was much worse when he came in. He probably had only five days to live when he got here.'"

Williams survived the operation, and was subsequently transferred to Sharp Memorial Hospital in San Diego for further rehabilitation.

Carter also accompanied Williams to Sharp, and it was there that he first heard about John Henry's idea to freeze his father.

"It was February 23, 2001. I remember the date," Carter said, "because it was my wedding anniversary, and my wife had come to New York so we could celebrate together. John Henry liked my wife, probably because Ted liked her and liked having her around. So anyway, John Henry came to me and said, 'George, I want your wife to go with us. We're leaving tomorrow to go to Donald Sharp Hospital in San Diego. Baseball is bringing in a private plane.' So we got on the plane with Ted and we flew to San Diego. It was my wife and I, John Henry and Frank Brothers, who had only known Ted since he was a ten-year-old kid. Frank's father used to be Ted's fishing guide, and his son Frankie was one of Ted's caretakers, just like me.

"So there we were at Sharp Hospital, and I spent all my time with Ted," said Carter. "He was in ICU for a while, then he got stronger. Frank left for a few days to see his family in Florida, and then he came back. Then Ted started talking a little, and in front of Frankie I asked Ted about the freezing, because we had been hearing all these rumors about it.

"I said, 'Ted, do you still want to be cremated and put with Slugger?' Slugger was his dog, a Dalmatian, who had died and was cremated," said Carter. "It had always been Ted's wish to be cremated, but after Slugger died Ted asked that his ashes and Slugger's ashes be spread over the waters together, in an area where he used to fish.

"So I asked him whether he still wanted to be cremated," said Carter, "and he said, 'Absolutely. That's what I want.'

"I said, 'What about this freezer stuff?'

"And he said, 'No!'"

Carter's wife took ill in San Diego, and he wanted to bring her back east. John Henry arranged for them to fly back with Brothers, and that is when Williams's youngest offspring began his talks with Alcor in earnest.

"Ted was still in intensive care," said Carter, "so he was being taken care of. So the three of us came home together. Then Ted came home, and they started doing rehabilitation at the house. He went on dialysis at Sharp. John Henry rented or bought a dialysis machine and had it put in the house. We had nurses coming in and out. Ted needed other people to give him shots and run the dialysis machine. The house was loaded with medical people, and all kinds of physical therapists. They had him on a bench, stretching his body in an attempt to get him to stand up. He was screaming, 'Let me out of here.'

"The medical people loved it when I walked in," said Carter, "because Ted would always do what I told him. He would eat around me. And he did nothing for these people. So they liked it when I was there. It's my belief that John Henry had all these other medical people around because he wanted his father back to good health as soon as possible. All John Henry ever gave a shit about was Ted's ability to sign his autograph. John Henry was always an asshole about that. Excuse my French, but he was always an asshole."

Brothers's opinion of John Henry was no less harsh. During an appearance on the HBO show *Real Sports,* Brothers told correspondent Bernard Goldberg about Ted Williams's reaction to his son's idea to have him frozen and saved for a later date.

"John Henry called the house," said Brothers, "and said, 'What if we freeze Dad?'

"And we said, 'Are you crazy?'

"John Henry said to his dad, 'Dad, have you ever thought about being frozen?'

"And Ted said, 'Bullshit, you're nuts. I don't want to be frozen. I'm telling you right now, I want to be cremated.'

"'They can [do it],' Brothers quoted John Henry saying, adding, 'You know, Dad, they don't have to freeze your whole body. They can surgically remove just your head.'

According to Brothers, "Ted gritted his teeth, pulled himself back from the table, and said, 'You are absolutely nuts, kid.'"

Well, the "kid" may have been nuts, but he was soon controlling all access to his father. On August 27, 2001, three days before Ted Williams's eighty-third birthday, Bobby-Jo saw her father for the last time. The Williams house, located in Hernando, on Florida's west coast, was in easy walking distance from the home Bobby-Jo shared with her husband, Mark, and yet she would be barred from ever entering her father's property again.

"Before my father's birthday at the end of August, I called his house to make arrangements to bring him his birthday gifts, a cake and balloons. John Henry told me that I wasn't allowed," wrote Bobby-Jo. "I asked, 'Why not?'

"'Because you aren't going to see Dad anymore,' he said in a very dark-toned voice.

"I said, 'You're kidding, right?'

"He said then that I wasn't a 'team player,'" she wrote, "and that I 'was not going to be part of the family anymore.'"

Bobby-Jo was outraged, and she called two of her father's closest friends, Eric Abel and Al Cassidy, to complain. Then she called her half sister and John Henry's younger sibling, Claudia Williams.

"Claudia said she wouldn't help me with John Henry because he had done the same thing to her in the past, that he had made it so that she couldn't see Dad before," Bobby-Jo wrote. "Now that Dad was terribly ill, she refused to 'risk it' with JH because she was afraid she'd be barred, too.

"Shortly after these conversations," she said, "Mr. Abel called my home and spoke to Mark. He said he was glad that Mark had answered the phone because 'this call was not something he wanted to do.' He said that JH had called him to ask him to tell me I was never allowed up to Daddy's house again, and if I did, I would be arrested. JH had power of attorney from my father, and he said there was nothing he could do."

Mark Ferrell went to the local sheriff, "and when I explained to him what was going on, his mouth fell open," said Ferrell. "He said, 'Geez, I don't normally talk about my personal business, but I'm on my second marriage. I'm raising two sons here and I would hate to think that one of them would do such a dastardly deed to me.' Then he said, 'But if you go up to the house and John Henry is living there, I will have to remove you from the property and arrest you.'"

"We went to an attorney and tried to get a copy of the power of attorney," Bobby-Jo said, "and what we got for our five hundred dollars was nothing."

The Ferrells started thinking about how much more they'd have to spend on a lengthy court battle, and the figures scared them enough into naively believing that John Henry might come to his senses and change his mind about their father, and about his half sister's access to him.

"We thought that perhaps this was just another one of his fantasies, that it would go away, because this guy fantasized about everything," said Mark Ferrell. "He saw something in the movie, and it became real life to him. He told *SI.com* that when he was a boy, he cut his mother's one-hundred-acre farm into shapes of baseball diamonds. Well, you know where that came from? The movie *Field of Dreams*. And then John Henry said he wanted to play baseball at the age of thirty-four. That came from the Dennis Quaid movie *The Rookie*. And this cryonics idea probably came from the Mel Gibson movie *Forever Young*. I mean, he lived in a dream world."

Ted Williams might have had the dream career, but there was much tossing and turning in his private life. In 1944, he married Princeton coed Doris Soule. Barbara Joyce, who was called Bobby-Jo from early childhood, was born in 1948, and was six years old when her mother divorced her father. In 1961, nearly a year to the day after his retirement from baseball, Williams married Lee Howard, a socialite model from Chicago. But they separated within months and were finally divorced five years later.

In 1968, Williams married for a third time. His new wife, Dolores Wettach, a former Miss Vermont, gave him two children, John Henry, who was born later that same year, and Claudia, who arrived in 1971.

Mark Ferrell said his father-in-law's third wife was often prone to very strange behavior. "She sent stuffed dolls to the house," said Ferrell. "When anyone would tick her off, she would mail stuffed dolls down to Florida, with needles in the dolls. Pins stuck through the heart. I keep telling the press, 'If you want to know why John Henry was the way he was, go find her.' Well, some reporters did go up to Vermont where she lives, and Dolores chased them off with a shotgun in her jeep."

"There's no doubt that she's a major culprit here," added Carter. "There was a time when I was working on and off for Ted, and one time I quit. And on the day I quit she kicked me in the ass. I mean, literally, right in the ass. Then she went and told her son that I whacked her. If I would have whacked her, I would have killed her."

Meanwhile, it was killing Bobby-Jo that she had no contact with her father. "I wondered day and night what my dad must be thinking, where I had gone, why wasn't I coming to see him," she wrote. "Every time I heard a siren, I got into a panic, wondering if it was going to Daddy's house."

Her only recourse, she felt, was to get on the horn and continue ringing up Ted Williams's long list of friends, so she could tell them about this disturbing fate that awaited her aging father.

If Ted Williams had a best friend, it was undoubtedly Bob Breitbard, the founder of the San Diego Hall of Champions, a sixty-eight-thousand-square-foot sports museum in the Balboa Park area of San Diego. The two men had been close since 1934, when they were both students at Hoover High School in San Diego. Breitbard remembered their graduation day in 1937, when the principal gave them each an award. Williams, of course, played baseball in high school, and Breitbard was a football player. But neither was being cited that day for their individual prowess on the playing field.

"The principal was speaking in front of the whole school," said Breitbard, "and he said the two awards were for each of us being able to type thirty-two words a minute without an error. That was our claim to fame at that time, typing thirty-two words a minute without an error. I always sat in front of Ted in class because he was taller than me, and I didn't want that big tall guy sitting in front of me, blocking my view."

From high school on, if they weren't in the same city at the same time, rarely a week went by that Breitbard didn't at least talk to Williams on the phone. Breitbard said that every conversation with Williams, sometimes four or five a week, always ended the same way, with the two men saying "I love you" to each other.

When Williams was brought out to Sharp Hospital following his open heart surgery in New York, Breitbard was there constantly, hovering over the medical staff and making sure his friend had everything he needed.

It was in San Diego, while Williams was a patient at Sharp, that Breitbard first heard about John Henry's plans to freeze his father. "He mentioned to me that he'd been going over to Arizona on the weekends to see the operation at this place, Alcor," said Breitbard. "I said, 'Jesus, John Henry, that's not what your dad wants. Tell me you're not going to do that.'

"He said, 'I have power of attorney. I can do anything I want.'

"I said, 'Well, that's not what your father wants. He always wanted to be cremated, and then have his ashes scattered with Slugger.'

"And John Henry said to me, 'You don't understand. This is the greatest thing in the world.'

"I said, 'I don't believe that stuff. Don't do it. Please, don't.'

"And he said, 'Well, I think it's great. It would be wonderful to come back a hundred years from now, fifty years from now.'

"I said, 'It's a foolish thing. It's crazy. Don't do it.'

Even though Breitbard could see that John Henry was serious, he made a conscious decision not to broach the subject with his lifelong friend. "I didn't want to bother Ted about it," said Breitbard. "Ted had told me on several occasions about wanting to be cremated. I guess I never thought John Henry would actually do it. And with Ted being sick in the hospital, I didn't think it was the right time to get into a fight or hassle about it, or have Ted get into a hassle with his son. I mean, I thought more of Ted than that. And I would never pit him against his son or anyone. I just knew that what John Henry wanted to do wasn't right. But I didn't think he would ever do it."

Like Breitbard, another of Williams's longtime friends, his business partner Arthur "Buzz" Hamon, didn't think John Henry would ever do it either. At least that's the conclusion he came to initially, when he first heard about the plan from John Henry in San Diego.

"I thought John Henry was going through one of his phases," Hamon told the *Boston Globe*, "like when he wanted to be a race car driver or climb Mount Everest."

But Hamon soon realized that John Henry was serious. When he returned to his home in Greenville, South Carolina, he logged on to Alcor's Web site and found it to be a real and going concern. "I was worried," he confessed to the *Globe*. "I was afraid John Henry had made a deal. Maybe he had." But Hamon, like Breitbard, also chose not to bring his concerns to Williams. He just didn't want to upset his ailing friend.

Elden Auker was pitching for the Boston Red Sox in 1939, when Williams played his rookie year, and the two maintained a close relationship throughout their lives, on and off the field. "I don't know where it all went," said Auker, "but we got to be two old men talking. And I remember Ted saying, 'You know, Elden, I don't know where everybody went. The only people who still call me are you, [other Red Sox teammates] Dominic DiMaggio, Bobby Doerr, and my friend from California, Bob Breitbard. I don't understand why more of them don't call me.'

"Well, I understood," said Auker. "His son, John Henry, cut his phone line off. Ted had a special telephone number, which I had. But it got to be that whenever you called, you would first have to talk to John Henry. He was the gatekeeper. He monitored every call, except the ones that Ted had with Dominic, Bobby, Bob Breitbard, and myself. John Henry was in charge, and he wouldn't let just anyone get to him. John Henry was very possessive of Ted. And that was his business, you know. He made a business earning money off of Ted's reputation. Selling memorabilia, and things like that. And making appearances. But Ted liked all that because John Henry was there with him all the time. He stayed right with him and looked after him. Someone had to do that. And because John Henry was his son, it's only natural that Ted had faith in him, and confidence in him."

Auker knew that battle lines had been drawn between Bobby-Jo Ferrell and her younger half brother. But he saw it as a "family squabble," one he didn't want to get into. "As strongly as I felt about Ted," said Auker, "I just didn't want to be in the middle of his family."

Another friend of Williams's, Joe Camacho, often found himself in the middle of the Williams family, but he didn't necessarily see that as a bad thing. "I never had any problems with John Henry," said Camacho, who was Williams's bench coach from 1969 to 1971 when he managed the old Washington Senators. "It was understood that John Henry showed off for a lot of Ted's friends. But any time my son Jimmy or I called, we always got through. Sometimes John Henry would call us, just because he wanted to talk. And sometimes John Henry would dial our number because Ted wanted him to get us on the line. And several times Claudia would call Jimmy, and she'd say, 'Jimmy, Dad's depressed. Why don't you talk to him?' And Jimmy would get on the phone and talk to him."

Camacho said that John Henry never discussed the plans he was hatching at Alcor. "But I was as dumbfounded as everybody else when I found out," said Camacho. "I'm sure this wasn't Ted's wish. I know that when John Henry talked to Bob Breitbard about it, Bob told him he was crazy."

Most of Camacho's conversations with Williams, especially in his latter years, were about baseball. "[Former Red Sox shortstop] Nomar Garciaparra was always one of Ted's favorite players," said Camacho. "And often I'd be watching a Red Sox game in my house in Fairhaven, Massachusetts, and Ted was watching the same game in Florida, and we'd be on the phone talking about the hitters, especially Garciaparra. Ted loved Garciaparra."

Even with his health failing, Williams could become quite lucid when the subject turned to baseball. John Henry himself acknowledged it. "We test him all the time on who his old buddies were," John Henry told the *Boston Globe*. "Did Bobby Doerr play shortstop? Where did Johnny Pesky play? He gets them right all the time. He even remembers who his high school typing teacher was."

But Williams was miserable, Hamon told the *Globe*, and by early June 2002, he started fearing that his friend would not be able to hold on much longer. "He hated his quality of life," the paper quoted Hamon, who quoted Williams saying, "It's not going to be very long. I don't think I can go on like this."

"I felt bad for Ted," Hamon said on HBO's *Real Sports*. "He'd call my office at my house all the time, and he'd say, 'I feel like I'm isolated. I feel like a prisoner sometimes.' John Henry liked controlling what his father would do and could do."

But according to Hamon, Williams did make one last-ditch effort to regain the control he had lost. As Hamon told *Real Sports*, he was on the phone with Williams in early June, when Williams said to him, "I need a lawyer."

Hamon said he responded, "What do you need a lawyer for?"

"He said, 'I made a mistake at that time.'"

"I heard some noise," Hamon then said, referring to something in the background at Williams's home.

"I don't know what it was," Hamon added, "but the phone went dead, and I never spoke to him again."

Bobby-Jo thought she'd never speak to her father again, but something extraordinary happened on Father's Day, 2002: Ted Williams reached out to her.

"We had been out of town," Mark Ferrell said. "And when we returned, we could see on the caller ID that he had called. He was able to get a nurse, or someone, to make the call. I'm sure he was raising so much hell. I'm sure he wanted to speak to Bobby-Jo, and I'm sure he had someone dial our house.

"Well, on Father's Day we got a call from Claudia," said Ferrell. "She said, 'Mark, is Bobby-Jo there? Dad wants to talk to her.' So I knew he must have been raising hell for Claudia to be calling us.

"So I said, 'Sure,' and I got Bobby-Jo on the phone with him. It was a good conversation, but he was in and out of it. He wanted Bobby-Jo to meet him at the park. And she said, 'What park?'

"And he said, 'You know, the damn park, by the gate.' He was talking about Fenway Park, which is where we always met in the old days."

It was obvious to George Carter that Williams was running out of days. Right after Father's Day, Carter and his wife went to Dartmouth, Massachusetts, to see their son. When they got there, Carter called Claudia. "I said to her, 'I saw your dad before I left, and he didn't look well,'" said Carter. "I told her that I thought the day was coming. We had talked about all this before. I just thought, the quicker the better for Ted. I did not want to see him suffer. She agreed with me. I asked her, 'What have you and John Henry planned if something happens to him? Will you be needing pallbearers?'

"She said, 'John Henry will not talk to me about it. Every time I try to talk to him about it, he won't talk.'"

On Sunday, June 30, Auker phoned Williams's house and managed to get him on the line. "The nurse had to hold the telephone receiver to his ear. He always called my wife 'Mildred, the queen,'" Auker told the *Boston Globe*, adding, "The last thing he said to me was, 'How's the queen? Give her my love.' Then the nurse came on and said he had fallen asleep."

Three days later, on Wednesday, July 3, Breitbard made a similar call, and he, too, got through. "He was coherent," Breitbard said. "He would nod off once in a while, sort of go to sleep on me, but I'll tell you this: I could get him going, because I'd say, 'Ted, hey, goddamn it, talk to me.' And he'd start talking again. And he did pretty well, in his little way."

When it came time to end the conversation, Breitbard once again repeated the same thing he and Williams had been saying to each other for decades. "I said, 'I love you, my dear friend. You're the dearest and best friend I've ever had.' I tried to get that in, hopefully to keep his spirits up. He was the dearest and best friend I ever had. And saying it to each other through the years helped each of us. It was therapy for both of us."

On Friday, July 5, Joe Camacho called Williams's house and the person who answered the phone was not someone Camacho recognized. "I said, 'This is Joe Camacho. I just want to know how Ted is doing.'

"The nurse must have heard my name," said Camacho, "because she grabbed the phone, and said, 'Joe, he died on the way to the hospital.' I couldn't speak for two hours. Then the news started to come on TV, and I called George Carter."

"Joe knew I was in Dartmouth," said Carter, "ten minutes away from his place in Fairhaven. When he called me, I said, 'Oh, God, at least he didn't suffer.' I can only hope he didn't. I then called up Dominic DiMaggio, and he answered the phone. He was also in Massachusetts. I said, 'Dom, this is George Carter. Joe Camacho just called to let me know that Ted just died.'

"Then I called Ted's house, and Al Cassidy answered the phone," said Carter. "I asked to speak to Claudia. Over the years, Claudia and I had a very good relationship. She would talk to me about her problems, like I was a father figure. She was starving for a father. Ted was in his fifties when she was born, so I used to be a good listener for her. I actually took her to an Air Force recruiter one day to get her in the military. I thought it would be the best thing in the world for her. She almost enlisted, and then she changed her mind.

"So I said, 'Al, I just want to give Claudia my condolences.'

"He said, 'Well, she hasn't come out of her room yet, George. She's taking this kind of hard.'

"I said, 'Okay, tell her I'll call her back in a little while.' A couple of hours later, I called her back and Al said that she had left. And since then," said Carter, "she's never talked to me."

Williams's body was taken to a local funeral home, where it was packed in ice. At 8 P.M. that night, the corpse was loaded onto a plane and flown to Arizona, and then driven to the place John Henry Williams decided should be his father's final resting place, the Alcor Life Extension Foundation, in Scottsdale. Eric Abel, acting as the family spokesman, released a simple statement to the media, saying, "Ted Williams was a private person in life, and in death he wished to remain private. He did not wish to have any funeral or funeral services."

But as the Ferrells have maintained all along, Williams did have other wishes, none of which they felt were carried out. Al Cassidy had been named as executor of Williams's estate, and he knew how upset the Ferrells were that the body had even been flown to Alcor in the first place, and so on Wednesday, July 17, twelve days after Williams's death, Cassidy filed a lawsuit in Florida asking the court for some kind of judicial guidance in the matter.

It was six days after that filing, according to the Ferrells' attorney, John Heer, that John Henry Williams produced a handwritten scrap of paper that he claimed was his father's most recent will. The paper, dated November 2, 2000, stated that Ted Williams, John Henry Williams, and Claudia Williams all agree "to be put into bio-stasis after we die.

"This is what we want," the handwritten document said, "to be able to be together in the future, even if it is only a chance."

The piece of paper, partially covered with dirt and oil stains, carried the signatures of John Henry Williams, Claudia Williams, and their father, Ted Williams.

The Ferrells believed the document to be a phony, and they said so. Claudia Williams countered by filing an affidavit to the court attesting to the paper's legitimacy. Cassidy ultimately asked a handwriting expert to examine the piece of paper, and when the expert determined that the signature of Ted Williams was indeed authentic, "Cassidy went to court," said Heer, "and had his own lawsuit dismissed."

Cassidy's move didn't stop George Carter and Frank Brothers from retracing their steps, back to November 2, 2000, when they said they were with Ted Williams at Shands Hospital, in Gainsville. Carter claimed that he and Brothers were caring for Williams twenty-four hours a day, every day, during that period.

"Either Frank or myself slept on a bed beside Ted, and we were with him at all times," recalled Carter. "We had a hotel room across the street, and we were doing twelve-hour shifts. I'd be with Ted for twelve hours and Frankie would be in the hotel, and then we'd switch."

Carter said the decision to even bring Williams to Shands had been made during the early hours of November 1. Carter was at his home in bed when the phone rang. It was Brothers calling from Williams's house. "Frank, who's bigger than me," said Carter, "and younger than me—he's forty-five, I'm sixty-seven—said, 'George, I can't get Ted off the toilet to get him into bed. He won't move.'

"I said, 'Frankie, don't do anything. I'll be up there in a few minutes.' It's about fifteen to twenty minutes from my house to Ted's. So I get up there. Ted would always listen to me, and I got him up. I got him into the wheelchair and we wheeled him into the bedroom, and I got him to bed. I took his vital signs, and I said to Frank, 'Listen, I'm going to call John Henry. Ted's got to go to the hospital.' I always knew when he had to go to the hospital. That's one thing John Henry loved about me. He always gave me credit of saving the old man's life, several times.

"So I called John Henry, and I said, 'Look, don't panic. I don't want you driving over here like a maniac, but your father has got to go into the hospital. I took his vital signs, and I know he's got to go into the hospital.'

"John Henry came over, and we called an ambulance," said Carter. "The guy in the ambulance had never been to Ted's house before, and he was a jerk. Ted said, 'I don't want to go to the hospital.' So the guy wouldn't take him. I told the guy to take off, and said to John Henry that we could put his father in the back seat of the Suburban, and he'd be comfortable.

"And that's what we did," said Carter. "Frank and I drove Ted in the

Suburban, and John Henry followed in his car. We got him checked in. The whole deal took almost all night. But after he was in, and the sun was coming up, John Henry and I walked out onto the patio, where people in the hospital go to smoke, and I told John Henry that I would call Bobby-Jo and Claudia to tell them that their dad was in the hospital.

"And John Henry said, 'No. I'll handle it.'

"Three days later, Claudia called me up and chewed my ass out from one end to other," said Carter. "She said, 'Why didn't you tell me my father was in the hospital? I just found out now.'

"I said, 'Claudia, I told your brother I wanted to call you and Bobby-Jo, and he said no. He said he would handle it. So if you're pissed off at anybody, call up your asshole brother. He's the guy that screwed up here.'

"My question is," said Carter, "how could she have signed that paper, on that day, when she didn't even know until a few days later that her father was in the hospital?

"John Henry had lawyers and secretaries at his fingertips," said Carter. "Why didn't he use them to draw up a new will? He had his father sign a shitty little piece of paper with no witnesses, no nothing. It would have taken him two minutes to change the real will. All he had to do was call in the proper authorities and have his father change the top line to say, 'I want to be frozen instead of cremated.' That's all John Henry had to do, but his intentions were not proper.

"I went to college for a few years," said Carter. "I took business and law. I don't pretend to be a lawyer, but I have been a policeman. Don't insult my intelligence. What does a piece of paper with Ted's signature on it, saying he wants to be frozen, really mean? It means nothing. There's no way he could have signed that paper on the date they all supposedly signed it. Didn't do it. Didn't happen."

But the Ferrells didn't have the money needed to fight the matter in court, said Heer, and in October 2002, Bobby-Jo signed a settlement agreement with her father's estate and received a reported $200,000, her share of an insurance trust that her father had put aside for his three children.

All remained quiet on the Ted Williams front until the summer of 2003, when the issue exploded in the pages of *Sports Illustrated* under the blaring headline "What Really Happened to Ted Williams: A year after the jarring news that the Splendid Splinter was being frozen in a cryonics lab, new details, including a decapitation, suggest that one of America's greatest heroes may never rest in peace."

In his story, *Sports Illustrated* writer Tom Verducci recounted how Alcor chief operating officer Larry Johnson had traveled to Williams's home in the summer of 2001 hoping to meet with him. But the meeting never took place. According to Verducci's story, a "disoriented" Williams was heard "hollering from a back room" while John Henry met with Johnson and Todd Soard, another Alcor rep.

Sports Illustrated even obtained a copy of Williams's seven-page Consent for Cryonic Suspension form, only to find that the signature line had been left blank.

In the days that followed Williams's death, there had been numerous press reports suggesting that his body was resting upside down in a liquid-nitrogen tank at Alcor. But it was Verducci, in *Sports Illustrated*, who later found out that Williams in fact had been beheaded, and that his head was being "stored in a liquid-nitrogen-filled steel can that resembles a lobster pot.

"The silver neuro-can, as it's known at Alcor, is marked in black with Williams's patient ID number, A-1949," the story said.

Verducci wrote that Williams's head "has been shaved, drilled with holes, accidentally cracked as many as ten times and moved among three receptacles."

As to the Hall of Famer's body, that is in the same room, near the head, "resting upright in one of nine liquid-nitrogen-filled, nine-foot-tall cylindrical steel tanks that Alcor staffers refer to as Dewars," which Verducci characterized as "a wink at scotch-making barrels.

"Williams," according to Verducci, "is in tank number 6."

Breitbard couldn't believe what had happened to his lifelong best friend. "I'm terribly outraged," he said after reading Verducci's story. "It's ludicrous what they've done to an icon, someone so tremendously popular in this world."

Johnson was so embarrassed by the situation at Alcor that he resigned and offered an apology on the now-defunct Ted Williams Web site www.freeted.com.

"There comes a time in one's life when, as an honest human being, you are thrust into a situation where you are uncomfortable, morally, ethically and professionally," wrote Johnson. "I have come to that impasse in my current career. . . . Many of you out there recognize this company as the repository for the remains of baseball great

Ted Williams. When I started my employment several months ago with Alcor, I must admit I also had a curiosity about the circumstances surrounding Ted's placement at Alcor."

Johnson wrote that he was "uncomfortable, morally, ethically and professionally," with Alcor's handling of Williams, and in his criticism he concluded that his former company "did not act in good faith regarding Mr. Williams's remains and inappropriate comments were made relative to his future fate."

The public outcry following the *Sports Illustrated* piece gave renewed hope to the Ferrells. Mark Ferrell went right to the Florida state attorney's office and pressed investigators to look into the entire matter of his father-in-law's handwritten will. Frank Brothers added his support by offering an affidavit confirming the dates as both he and Carter had remembered them.

"On or around November 4 or 5," wrote Brothers, "Claudia Williams called George on our business cell phone. She accused George of not being her friend because she just now found out that her father was in the hospital, on the 4th or 5th of November." Brothers concluded, as Carter had before him, that under the circumstances Claudia could not possibly have signed such a paper on November 2.

"I kept pushing the investigator," said Ferrell, "and he finally said to me, 'Look, I've got five hundred twenty cases in five counties. Do you want me to drop everything and just do this?' They thought the signature on the paper was real, and it was real. That's not the point. The point is, all of a sudden this note comes out of nowhere, from the back of John Henry's BMW, with oil stains all over it, saying this is what Dad wants? To be frozen?

"If you look at the note real closely," said Ferrell, "you can easily tell that the eleven, for November, was written on top of a four, which would have been for April. When John Henry wrote down my father-in-law's supposed wish, he just put down any old date. What he did later was call Shands in a frenzy, trying to find out the exact date that his father was in the hospital for the pacemaker surgery. If you visualize a four, you can make it an eleven by starting at the top of both sides of the four and working down. It becomes an eleven with a line in the middle, making it look like an H which is how the eleven looked on John Henry's little paper."

By the end of the summer of 2003, investigators in Florida decided there was no case, and the matter was dropped. "They had Claudia's original affidavit," John Heer said, "and they couldn't identify a victim, and so they chose not to become involved."

What made it even easier for investigators was the fact that the signature of Ted Williams looked so real. "I believe that was his signature on that paper," said Ferrell. "But this was a common practice at the house. He'd practice signing all the time. Even after three strokes, he was constantly being asked to sign his name, and sign his name, and sign his name. Before he ever sat down to sign an expensive lithograph, you know, a six-hundred or a thousand-dollar piece of artwork, or an expensive bat, John Henry or Claudia would say, 'So, how's your signature look today, Dad?' They'd put a piece of paper in front of him, and he'd practice signing his name until it looked just right. You wouldn't want to ruin expensive memorabilia with a lousy signature."

Williams's cook in Florida, Jacques Prudome, was present on many occasions to witness his employer's struggle during long signing sessions. "I also remember when he came back from the hospital," Prudome said to Bernard Goldberg during the taping of HBO's *Real Sports*. "John Henry raised hell because they put needles in [Williams's] right arm. [John Henry said, 'It's got to be the left arm.']"

"He was afraid his dad's arm or hand would be sore and he couldn't sign," added Brothers. "He would push his dad to sign things he didn't want to sign. One was never enough. A thousand was never enough."

Nevertheless, that one autograph Williams supposedly signed, which spelled out his son's plan to eventually join his father and sister in a sub-zero state, bought John Henry the kind of time he needed to keep the Ferrells and others at bay.

Mark Ferrell would hate to see other families going through the same kind of anguish, but for now he cares only for one victim in particular, his dead father-in-law, who remains in Scottsdale, his frozen head presumably still separated from his frozen body.

"John Heer contacted the Boston Red Sox, and Major League Baseball, and neither organization did anything to help us. I am so disappointed," said Ferrell. "I even went to our governor in Florida, Jeb Bush, a longtime family friend of Ted Williams. Ted supported Jeb Bush. Ted went up to New Hampshire and fought to get George Bush 41 elected. And even when Ted was ill, he went up to New Hampshire again and fought to get George W. Bush elected. And none of them, none of the Bushes, have said a word or demanded an investigation.

"Even John McCain, the senator from Arizona, has done nothing despite pleadings from all sorts of people, not from me or my wife, but from loads of people who have written and requested that he get involved. But he has turned a deaf ear to his old buddy," said Ferrell. "A lot of people like John McCain used Ted Williams for their own political gain. And once they got what they wanted, you know, he's dead now, the hell with him. To me, that's their attitude and I think it sucks."

Heer confirmed that the Ferrells reached out to McCain and the Bush family following Williams's death, but they never received a reply from either camp. "Other influential people were contacted," said Heer, "among them former Dodgers manager Tommy Lasorda, Dom DiMaggio, and [former] Mets catcher Mike Piazza." Heer said that talks with Lasorda and DiMaggio, "while cordial, went nowhere."

"Piazza and his family looked like they were going to help," said Heer, "but they never did. Mike Piazza used to say that he learned about hitting by watching films of Ted Williams. But when it came time for Piazza to step up to the plate and help right this terrible wrong, he never even swung the bat."

Ferrell said that his father-in-law was given the Medal of Freedom award by George H. W. Bush. "Actually," he said, "had he not wanted to be cremated, Ted Williams's rightful place would have been in the ground at Arlington National Cemetery, with honors.

"The newspapers turned this into a family feud, but it was never about a family damn feud," said Ferrell. "I mean, if they want to know what a family feud is go up into Kentucky and West Virginia and check out the Hatfields and the McCoys. That's a family feud. This has just been an attempt on our part to restore some dignity to a great man who fought in two wars and gave a lot to his country and entertained us for years and years. This isn't about a feud. This was about two screwed-up kids who were never in their father's life until they were teenagers. And when they finally did come into his life, they just took over and did exactly what they wanted to do."

John Henry Williams was diagnosed with leukemia in 2003, and he died in a Los Angeles hospital on March 6, 2004. He was thirty-five years old. Four days before his death, his wife, Lisa Martin Williams, and his sister Claudia co-signed a document arranging in advance for his body to be taken to the Renaker-Klockgether Mortuary in Buena Park, California, prior to being shipped to the Alcor facility in Scottsdale.

A few weeks after John Henry died, John Heer initiated a lawsuit in Arizona in an attempt to get all documents from Alcor pertaining to Ted Williams. Acting on behalf of clients Bobby-Jo Ferrell and her cousins, Samuel Stuart Williams and John Theodore Williams, the sons of her father's brother Danny, Heer said that he filed the suit under the Arizona Anatomical Gift Act.

"This is a provision specific to Arizona," said Heer, "and it entitles any interested party to receive and inspect documents of gift. The act relates to the donating of a body, and Alcor operates under those statutes."

Two months after Heer filed his suit, Al Cassidy filed another suit in Florida claiming that Bobby-Jo had breached her settlement agreement by becoming a party to the Arizona case. "She didn't want another legal fight on her hands," said Heer, "so she dropped out of the suit."

But Ted Williams's two nephews remained, and after months of stalling, Alcor finally released all the papers to Heer in December 2004. Among the documents was an affidavit signed by Lisa Martin Williams confirming that her late husband had been reunited with his father in that "bio-stasis" state, precisely as had been prescribed in the handwritten will.

"It is my desire," she stated in court documents, "that Alcor continue to preserve and maintain any and all matters in regard to my late husband John Henry Williams, in complete confidence as the disposition of my husband's remains is an extremely private matter."

Alcor, meanwhile, was so stung by the controversy following the release of details in Verducci's *Sports Illustrated* article that it has since imposed a complete media blackout in all matters relating to the Williams family. For the record, Alcor reps would neither confirm nor deny that two of its frozen patients are named John Henry Williams and Ted Williams.

David Bloom

May 22, 1963–April 6, 2003

IT IS AN IMAGE NO TELEVISION NEWS VIEWER WILL EVER FORGET: NBC NEWS correspondent David Bloom, goggles on, his graying hair windswept, riding in the back of a refurbished tank alongside the U.S. 3rd Infantry Division and reporting on the military's massive push to Baghdad during the early days of the Iraq war.

The *Wall Street Journal* characterized Bloom as one of this war's new "Scud Studs."

Former White House press secretary Ari Fleischer added that Bloom was riding his vehicle, dubbed the "Bloom-mobile" by his NBC colleagues, "to stardom." Superstardom was probably more like it. As NBC's executive director of news David Verdi put it, "David looked like Lawrence of Arabia, and the whole world stopped to watch him."

But much of the world that stopped to watch Bloom also worried about him. He was vulnerable, breathless, out in the open, and exposed to enemy fire. It was extraordinary how many TV viewers had premonitions about Bloom and feared for his safety.

"I think he was everyone's little brother, a favorite son, that kind of thing," said former *NBC Nightly News* anchor and managing editor Tom Brokaw. "I had had some fairly stern talks with him before he went over there. I said, 'I don't want you doing anything dumb. I'm not going to be walking up to your house knocking on the door with bad news. Maybe you shouldn't be doing this.' I probably had that conversation three or four times, off the air, when he was getting ready to go on from over there. I was worried that he'd be pushed too far out in front. I was worried that he'd be a combat victim."

Bloom certainly had no such worries about himself in December 2002, when he and NBC cameraman Craig White took part in a live fire exercise that the army was conducting in Kuwait. White, a thirty-two-year NBC veteran who had earned his stripes shooting combat footage in Lebanon, El Salvador, Nicaragua, Israel, and Afghanistan, was on an island off the coast of Kenya, covering the U.S. Marines in training, when the network assigned him to rendezvous with Bloom in Kuwait.

"The live fire exercise in Kuwait was the largest military exercise that the army had conducted since the Gulf War," said White. "And basically, David Bloom was given an open book. Whatever he wanted to do to cover the war he could do. He'd been pursuing this since sometime in November with the help of Retired General Barry McCaffrey. He pretty much ran the land war during the Gulf War, and working this time as an NBC analyst he led David through the whole American military system. At first, David wasn't sure whether he wanted to cover the war from Baghdad, or whether he wanted to be with an American military unit. Taking part in the live fire exercise was an attempt on our part to make a decision regarding our coverage."

McCaffrey arranged for Bloom and White to meet Lieutenant Colonel Stephen Twitty in Kuwait. Twitty was a commander in the 2nd Brigade of the 3rd Infantry Division, and he helped the two NBC employees get through the exercise.

"It's like playing in a large sandbox," White said, describing the exercise. "We camped out with the 3ID. It was a unique situation. The United States was using Kuwait to train people for desert warfare. It was pretty much assumed that we were going to war against Iraq, and that the 3ID would probably lead the charge into Iraq. Everyone there was saying that it would probably be the last great tank battle in history."

White had worked with Bloom only a few times previously, mostly on political stories in the States. But the two men didn't become really friendly until the live fire exercise. "We hit it off very well in Kuwait," said White. "David was charming, charismatic, and I loved that he was willing to go the extra mile to learn whatever he could. Nothing was too much for him. He wanted whatever we did to be better than what anybody else did. But he was wrestling with real issues regarding our coverage. He kept asking himself, 'How do I cover this war? If I go to

Baghdad and cover it there, what happens? If I cover it from the Ministry of Information, what's the downside? What's the upside?'"

It was Stephen Twitty who helped Bloom answer his own questions. "Twitty is a rising star in the army right now," said White. "We were probably the third or fourth press crew with whom he'd been involved. He trusted us to do the right thing, and to stay safe. And we trusted that he would get us to the right places to make the kinds of pictures we needed. David said to Twitty, 'If we cover this war with the 3ID, how do we get pictures back? How do we get sound back?'

"Twitty couldn't answer those technical questions," said White, "but he did say, 'I can get you right to the front of the tank battle.' That was all David had to hear. That was something that couldn't be done during the Gulf War. Those kinds of pictures never made air back then. None of that was ever reported back to the United States. There were embedded reporters during the Gulf War, but they were always part of a pool. They traveled with the troops, but given the technology back then there was no way to get those pictures back, literally, until the war was over. And given American news appetites, it was old news by the time it came back. Think about it: There were no real heroes during the Gulf War. You ask any American to name the heroes of the first Gulf War, and only two names will ever come up: Colin Powell and Norman Schwarzkopf. All the news came from them and no one else. But this time, for this war, things promised to be different."

David Verdi's relationship with Bloom went back ten years, when the two were colleagues at WTVJ, the NBC affiliate station in Miami. "I was assistant news director, and David was a very eager, aggressive local reporter who fought his way on the air," said Verdi, who advanced to the network level before Bloom and was instrumental in helping him move up.

"Right from the very beginning he set his sights on the network," Verdi said of Bloom. "I don't want to take credit for his successes, but over the years we've identified a few hot-shot local reporters who we all felt had great potential. David was one of those guys. We'd use him on *Weekend Today*, or *Weekend Nightly*. Then maybe a shot on the *Today* show, news side, on the shorter news spots."

According to Verdi, it was Jeff Zucker, in his capacity then as *Today* show executive producer, who felt that Bloom had the goods to make it all the way on network TV. "Once these hot-shot local reporters are on the *Today* show, news side, and they succeed, *Nightly News* will pick up on them. That's how a reporter breaks into the network. That's how David Bloom broke into the network, by succeeding at every level. So if you want to say was I instrumental, I certainly conspired with Jeff Zucker and a whole host of other people, including John Brown, an NBC News vice president at the time, to move David up to the network.

"When David took the anchor job at *Weekend Today*, the first thing he did was call me," said Verdi. "He said, 'Hey buddy, I'm taking this job.' He did this with a lot of people, but I'm the one who principally assigns. If you want to work for news coverage, I run news coverage. So he called me, and he said, 'Hey buddy, I'm taking this job, but I want to stay in the mix. I want to go to the hot spots.' If a hurricane were happening, he'd want to go. The recount in Florida in 2000, he'd want to be there. He'd say, 'I want to go down, I want to go down, I want to go down. I still want to be part of news coverage. I want you to put me in the big stories.' So we did. It caused a little bit of a political problem sometimes because he was big-footing the regular coverage correspondents. But it was understood that he was the guy.

"We started planning for the war in September 2002, and as we got closer David would call me and say, 'Listen, I've got some contacts. If you send me over to Kuwait, I will square it with *Weekend Today*. Just send me over. I can meet a couple of guys on the ground. They'll get me in to see a commanding officer. I can talk my way in.' So we invested a little money and we sent him to Kuwait. He met with the commanding officer of the 3rd ID, and Craig White was in there with him."

With Twitty already on their side, Bloom soon realized that his best option was to be with the troops when the shooting started. But there were still technological issues to overcome. The newest live TV technology that anyone was talking about in late 2002 was still the videophone, a herky-jerky contraption that was first used by CNN in April 2001, when the cable network covered a downed surveillance plane in North Korea.

"It was a fairly crude operation," recalled White. "It looked like something you might see on your computer, perhaps with video conferencing, but it was not pleasing to the eye. Normal video as we know it is thirty frames per second. The videophone was maybe six frames per second. That's why it was so jerky. The technology evolved later in 2001, during Afghanistan. I was there with another NBC reporter, Ashleigh Banfield, and we used a videophone. So when I told David that we could probably use a videophone in Iraq, while we were actually moving, he was not too thrilled by that. It was already herky-jerky enough when you're stationary.

"David didn't like what it looked like or sounded like under any conditions, and I wasn't happy about it either," said White. "On the way back from the live training exercise in Kuwait, we stopped to change planes at Heathrow in London. It was a few days before Christmas. And I remember saying to David, 'I think I have an idea of how to change the paradigm of videophone.' In 1998, I did a documentary on the wreck of the *Titanic*. It was broadcast live on both *Dateline NBC* and the Discovery Channel, live from the bottom of the ocean with full quality pictures, which was a tremendous technological achievement in 1998. Jack Bennett at NBC actually came up with the idea, and it involved using a special antenna similar to what is used by the U.S. Navy and civilian cruise ships. There's a company down in Florida, Maritime Telecommunications Network, and they have an up-link that stays aimed at a satellite even while you're moving on the ground. I said to David, 'If we can get a vehicle on the battlefield, we may be able to use the MTN technology to beam back perfect pictures while we're on the move.' Well, for David that was like putting a hook on a big bass. He loved the idea. It was using off-the-shelf technologies in a way nobody had ever thought of before."

White took out a blank piece of paper in the transient lounge at Heathrow and drew a diagram for Bloom that included a list of the equipment they would need to make this kind of reporting possible. White warned Bloom that it would be an expensive proposition, maybe $1 million for just the hardware. "David looked at me," said White, "and he said, 'Don't worry about the money. I'll worry about that. If we can do this, this is what I want to do.' He took that diagram and brought it back to New York."

As soon as White got back to New York, he called his boss at NBC, Stacy Brady, to brief her on his conversations with Bloom. "I said to her," recalled White, 'Stacy, you're not going to believe this, but I think it's going to happen. Bloom is so committed. He's going to make it work. He's going to get the money out of NBC.' Stacy was skeptical, to say the least."

One of Bloom's first calls upon coming back was to Verdi. Bloom excitedly reported to his news director that the army was going to let NBC travel with the troops. Verdi recalled saying to Bloom, 'Hey, David, tell me something I don't know. Everybody is going out there with the troops.' He said to me, 'No, no, no. You don't get it. They're going to let us broadcast live from the battlefield.' To which I said, 'David, everybody's going to broadcast live from the battlefield. We have videophones. Everybody's taking satellite dishes. It's no big deal.' Bloom said, 'David, listen to what I'm saying. They're going to let us broadcast live as we're rolling through the desert while they're in combat.' I said, 'David, what are you talking about?' Then he told me about his conversations with Craig White and the system that was perfected in Florida. Bloom said, 'They can build this thing. We may have to hook up a microwave, but the 3rd Infantry Division is going to let me do it.'"

Bloom continued lobbying his way through NBC, eventually working his way up to the president of NBC News, Neal Shapiro. "Remember," said White, "we're talking about a lot of money, even for our business, on a totally untried system. Nobody had ever put this together before. It was like building a land yacht."

But Bloom went to Shapiro with the idea and got a commitment. "As soon as David told me it was a go," said White, "I started working with the engineering people. Basically, we had little more than a month to put it all together."

White and an NBC sound technician immediately left for Florida, where they were joined by an engineer from MTN. The company had built a special-purpose truck for NBC equipped with a stabilized VSAT (Very Small Aperture Terminal) antenna designed to provide mobile, in-motion live broadcast capabilities. As White and his group began conducting their initial tests on some of the local roads around MTN headquarters in Miramar, the Pentagon suddenly got wind of NBC's plans.

"Here we are, rushing to complete our work in Florida," said White, "and the Pentagon finds out about the permission we've gotten from the army. Several networks wanted their own vehicles on the battlefield, not just us. But the Pentagon had always believed that we could accomplish the embed process just by carrying along a few suitcases filled with equipment. Fox, CBS, NBC, and other networks all realized it would require something more than that, something that could work while it was moving. Therefore, we had to have our own vehicle. The army understood that, and it didn't seem to be a problem. It was the Pentagon that started railing about it. I think they saw the possible downside of live television on the move, and the possible lack of control on their part. The Pentagon loved the whole idea of the embed thing because they looked at us as witnesses who might counter any negative propaganda coming out of, say, an al-Jazeera. If, for example, a school were bombed, al-Jazeera would automatically blame the United States. With embeds, maybe American journalists would act as witnesses in the army's behalf."

According to White, it was Department of Defense spokeswoman Torie Clarke who was dead set against having nonmilitary vehicles on the battlefield. "David really pushed hard," said White, "and eventually he had a face-to-face with Torie Clarke. This is not a direct quote, but she said to him something like, 'You'll get your vehicle on the battlefield over my dead body.' This was not good news to us because of our commitment up to this point, financially and otherwise."

On their next trip back to Kuwait, Bloom and White had a lunch meeting with Major General Buford Blount III, the commander of the 3rd Brigade. After the meeting, Blount's press officer matter-of-factly asked Bloom how many vehicles he was planning to use, and how many people he would need on each vehicle. "I couldn't believe the question," said White. "He was looking at David, and from behind the press officer, over his head, I waved to David, 'Six people, two vehicles. Six people, two vehicles.' David picked up my signal, and he said, 'Six people, two vehicles.' The press officer said, 'Well, officially we can only embed two people per network. But we'll work this out.'

"David and I were ecstatic," said White. "Going back to Kuwait City across the desert that night, we realized that this might actually happen. The army was basically thumbing its nose at the Pentagon. The army had thousands and thousands of vehicles ready to move, and they must have thought, 'So what's a few more?'"

But there was still the nagging problem of Torie Clarke and her boss, Secretary of Defense Donald Rumsfeld, both of whom wanted no part of intrusive TV newsmen in their nonmilitary vehicles.

"I can only assume this," said Verdi, "but they probably felt that if they did this for us, they'd have to do it for everybody. But David kept saying to me throughout, 'I'm telling you, if we just get us there, I'll talk to those guys and we'll worm our way in. Once we're on the ground, we'll get them to do it.' But David just nailed it. He talked his way in."

Having the right vehicle was just one of the issues Bloom and White faced prior to the start of the war. They also needed to make sure they had the right camera. "Because of the distances out on the desert," said White, "we had to have a special camera, a stabilized camera, very much as you'd have on a news helicopter. Think O.J. Simpson and the low-speed chase. The fact that you could see those close-up pictures was a result of what news helicopters have come to right now, and that's very stabilized long-lens pictures that allow you to show a close-up from a great distance. A company called Wescam is one of the leaders in that technology, and they also do a lot of work for the military. I investigated which of those Wescams we'd want, and that became a whole other odyssey. The one I wanted was very small and very portable. And when we tried to get it out of the country, they wouldn't let us do it. It was designed to give us great night vision capability, and long distance. And it was small and light. But for some reason the State Department wouldn't let us get it out of the country. It became a negotiation, back and forth. It even got to the White House. David had a relationship with Ari Fleischer from his days of covering the White House for NBC. Ari tried to intervene on our behalf, and it didn't work out. Eventually, we ended up with this big old vile ball, about twenty-four inches in diameter, the kind that hangs under a helicopter."

The vehicle they ended up using, a tank tow truck, "was simply the biggest vehicle we could find out there that the 3rd Infantry Division, and Stephen Twitty, in particular, allowed us to have," said White. "That's what we ended up riding on. My place was behind the camera and David Bloom's place was out front, telling the world what it was like to be on the way to Baghdad."

But Bloom was not allowed to simply say whatever he wanted on television regarding the start of a ground war. In fact, the army had him under strict orders not to say anything remotely connected to troop movements on the ground until the announcement was made officially.

"Several days before the war," said White, "all the embedded reporters with the 3rd Infantry Division were brought into a tent with Colonel David Perkins, the commander of 3ID's 2nd Brigade. Once inside the tent we were given the entire war plan. Flat out. They said, 'This is what is going to happen over the next few weeks.' And basically, we had to sit on that. We were not allowed to share that information with our employers. We were not allowed to communicate that with anyone on the outside. And we were very faithful to that."

On Wednesday, March 19, at 10:15 P.M., East Coast time, President Bush addressed the nation, saying that coalition forces had begun "striking selected targets of military importance to undermine Saddam

Hussein's ability to wage war." The president mentioned nothing specific about possible ground attacks beyond characterizing the air strikes as the "opening stages of what will be a broad and concerted campaign."

In the early evening hours of Thursday, March 20, David Verdi was watching his many TV monitors in his office, "when up pops Walt Rodgers of CNN, on the videophone, saying that ground hostilities had started.

"We were dying," said Verdi. "Walt Rodgers was on, and even though you could barely see anything because the quality was so terrible, you could still hear the tanks. I was on the phone with David Bloom, and I said, 'David, Walt Rodgers is on.'

"And David said, 'I can't go.'

"I said, 'David, you're killing us. You have to go. Let's go.'

"He said, 'No, man, I can't do it. I made a promise. If we go now, we're going to blow the whole thing.'

"I said, 'David, Walt is saying that he's driving into battle.'

"David said, 'He's full of crap. He's ten miles, fifteen miles behind us. Walt isn't at the tip of the spear. I'm at the tip of the spear. And I can't go. Not until the president announces it. You have to monitor the president.'"

In fact, NBC News had been monitoring everything coming out of the Bush administration since early in the day. "We hit every single news conference, from any government official, with the hopes that the president, or someone, would in some way give us a signal, or say that the ground hostilities had started," said Verdi. "But nobody would say it. We asked Torie Clarke. Nothing. We asked everyone, 'Have hostilities started?' And we got no answer."

A few hours later, a reporter from the Fox News Channel, reporting live from Iraq, came on talking about the start of the ground war. And Bloom remained silent. "The Fox pictures, also with a videophone, which David had as a backup, were so bad you couldn't even tell what you were looking at," said Verdi. "But the reporter, like Walt Rodgers, was trumpeting the fact that he was coming live from the desert. And we're still dying. Then Larry King came up on CNN and he was talking to Walt Rodgers, live from the desert. And Larry King said, 'These are historic first pictures of a reporter driving into battle with U.S. troops.'

"David just happened to call in then," said Verdi. "I said, 'David, we have to go.'

"He said, 'No, I can't break the embargo.'

"I said, 'The embargo? Are you kidding? Listen to this.' And I literally held the phone up to the speaker. And he listened to Larry King interviewing Walt Rodgers. And when Larry King talked about, 'Walt, you're breaking new ground,' and all that stuff, I picked up the phone and said, 'David, do you still want to wait?'

And he said, 'Hell, no. Let's go.'"

But unfortunately for Bloom, he had to wait even longer. At the very moment that King was talking to Rodgers on CNN, Bloom was separated from his Bloom-mobile. "He was on a vehicle with a microwave dish," said Verdi, "and his signal was supposed to hit the Bloom-mobile, which was to his rear. If the system is working, the signal then hits the satellite and we're good to go. But at that moment, Bloom and White had separated so far that they couldn't make the signal happen. So even when we decided to go up, we couldn't go up. So we went up with our videophone, which was just as bad as everyone else's."

Then, in the middle of the night, East Coast time, Bloom's two vehicles got close enough for him to get a signal and show up on MSNBC. It was like a test run for what would come next, at 7 A.M., on the morning of March 21, when Bloom's report opened the *Today* show using the technology that Craig White and the MTN engineers had perfected. It was 1 P.M. in the desert. The pictures were clear and vibrant. Viewers could almost feel the Iraqi wind blowing past Bloom as he waited for his cue.

Matt Lauer, who was coanchoring the broadcast from Doha, Qatar, introduced Bloom with the following words: "While we carefully watch the technology of the U.S. military in this conflict with Iraq, we're also somewhat amazed by the reporting technology that we're putting to use. And we've been seeing some of that courtesy of David Bloom, who is literally on the move with the 3rd Infantry. And we're going to join David right now. David, good morning."

"Matt, good morning to you," replied Bloom.

"David, if you can hear me," said Lauer, "I want to ask you a little about what it was like when your division reached the Iraqi border some—some hours ago, what types of resistance you saw and what it was like to be a part of that division when you entered Iraq."

"We were with the 315 Infantry of the 3rd Infantry Division, which was the lead force going into Iraq for this huge division of 20,000 soldiers and 250 tanks, hundreds of Bradley fighting vehicles,"

Bloom began. "What they did was they first spent about a half an hour hitting two Iraqi observation posts with artillery. Each of those Iraqi observation posts . . . had about 10 to 30 Iraqis inside. Because they needed to frankly wipe out those observation posts so they could not relay a message back to Baghdad and let them know the where-abouts, the lanes that those U.S. forces were crossing in. They met only light opposition there. When we crossed the Iraqi berm about two hours or so later, all we saw was the smoking remains of those ob-servation posts.

"There had been a—a couple of Iraqi soldiers had given chase to some of the U.S. soldiers, and we're told that that threat was elimi-nated, Matt."

"David," said Lauer, "can you give me a sense as to the pace you are traveling at? We can do the math then as to how many hours you've been inside Iraq. But give me a sense also how far ahead of your supplies are you? It's crucial to stay with fuel and water supplies. Have you had to stop several times during this mission?"

"I want to say first of all, Matt, I'm hearing you only intermit-tently, so you'll have to forgive me if I don't answer the totality of your question. But we have stopped. We have not yet stopped for fuel, but we've got a fuel stop coming up. We're rolling by some of the Bradleys right now. I want to show you these as we go by. These are the—the Bradley fighting vehicles, which are what the U.S. infantry soldiers ride in. They have about nine soldiers in them. Also, you can see off to my—my right here, if my photographer Craig White pans along, you can see some of these vehicles are moving quite slowly. Some of them have broken down. This isn't much of a road, Matt, it's just a—a lane. They're calling it Route Hurricane through the southern Iraqi desert, because obviously this is a very fast-moving force by tradi-tional military standards, but it's still a long train, if you will, a long convoy, thousands of vehicles, and they can only move as fast as the slowest vehicles. Basically, the Bradleys and the tanks can move a lot faster, so the smaller fuel tankers, the 2,500-gallon fuel tankers, race ahead to fuel them, then drop back and get refueled by the 5,000-gallon tankers.

"I should tell you one other interesting thing, Matt," Bloom con-tinued. "When we first crossed in, say about two or three hours ago—now we've been in Iraq for the last roughly 12 hours or so, I don't know. It was—it was 8:00 at night that the artillery shelling began. It was 10:00

when we crossed into Iraq. And it's now 3:00 in the afternoon. So that's 17 hours, roughly, that we've been in Iraq now. But as the last few hours, we've been in what was a battle zone in the first Gulf War, what these soldiers call Gulf One as compared to Gulf Two. So we saw a lot of burnt-out Iraqi tanks, a lot of unexploded American ordnance, including cluster bombs, and these vehicles had to be very careful. Not so much the tanks and the Bradleys and the—the M-88 like we're riding on right here, which is a tank recovery vehicle, much more heavily armed, but the vehicles like the Humvees have to be much more careful. They're panning ahead here, I think Craig is, and you can see some of these children and women just waving to us as we pass along. This is obviously a—a Bedouin community out here, a community only in the largest sense of the word. But other than that we've seen no Iraqi opposition whatsoever. Matt, back to you."

"All—all right, David. Thank you very much," said Lauer, who was now back on full screen and very impressed by what he had just heard.

"What an astonishing report," he said. "David Bloom with the 3rd Infantry. They call themselves the Iron Fist. And they are literally on the front lines of this conflict. Katie, back to you in New York."

There was much cheering at NBC. It was obvious that Bloom had just hit a major home run. And this stunning new technology, which was so vastly superior to whatever CNN and Fox had put on the night before, was an even bigger hit. The network, understandably, wasted no time getting Bloom back on the air after the 7:30 break. Both Lauer and Katie Couric, who was anchoring the broadcast in New York, were blown away by Bloom's on-air accomplishment.

"It's—it's amazing the stuff we've been seeing from David Bloom, isn't it?" Lauer asked Couric from Qatar. "And what's your reaction to it?"

"I mean, it really does give you a feeling of being right there with the 3rd Infantry, and—and the technology is quite miraculous," said Couric. "And I know David Bloom himself worked very hard on finding the technology that would—enable him, Matt, to cover this story, you know, at the scene real-time with the troops. So it's really amazing."

"Yeah," Lauer said, "and it's certainly paying huge dividends." This was no understatement. Nothing on any of the other morning news shows looked anywhere as good as the images Bloom was sending back.

"We want to check in now with David," said Lauer. "He is again with the 3rd Infantry. They are rolling through the southern Iraqi desert, presumably on the way to Baghdad. David, good morning to you again."

"Hey, Matt," Bloom responded. "We've actually stopped right now. And I want to tell you one thing about this camera, just in case it starts going a little funky. This camera is meant to work as we're bumping along. It works a lot better when we're bumping along than when we're stopped, just as a way of explanation if there's a problem here. But I want my photographer Craig White to pan off here so you can just see the long train behind us. It's a lot easier since the dust has stopped now because the—the vehicles have stopped. They're doing some refueling up ahead of us, and we're all basically waiting our turn. So as they stop, they still go into those defensive positions, which means that they split off half the vehicles to the left, the other half of the vehicles to the right. And that means that if, in the unlikely event that they came under an air attack, which is highly unlikely, artillery strikes possible but still unlikely, they would be in a much more safe position. We've stopped now, but we've been rolling—we crossed into Iraq at 10:00 last night local time, it's now 3:30 in the afternoon local time. I'm a little tired. You can do the math for yourself."

Bloom went on for the next ten minutes describing the vehicles and what it took to get through the Iraqi minefields. While he spoke, White moved the camera around to show some of the burned-out Iraqi tanks along Route Hurricane. Lauer and Bloom then exchanged rumors they both had heard about small numbers of Iraqi troops surrendering.

"When I've been asked about the mood of the American troops," said Bloom, "part of the good spirits is that they've heard those reports of some Iraqi troops surrendering."

"David, I mean, you've been traveling for—as you mentioned, you've been inside Iraq 17 hours now, on the road driving hard for probably a dozen hours or so," said Lauer. "And I'm watching these troops behind you now that you're stopped, getting ready to refuel or whatever, and they're taking off the flack jacket. Give me a little bit of—of what opportunity they have had over these last 24 hours, if you will, to—to relax at all, to get some food, to get some sleep, that sort of thing?"

"To get some food, I wish I could—could reach. Hold on just a second here. Hey, guys," Bloom said, pointing beyond the camera. "Hand me the MREs. Just toss me.

"I want to show you," Bloom said to his viewers. "This is Sergeant Joe Todd, and this is Private Trinity McClain, and they're the two guys who we're riding on this vehicle with. And I know that Sergeant Todd wanted us to say hi to his wife, Rosa. And, Trinity, what's the name of your girlfriend again?"

"Yahira," answered Pvt. McClain.

"Yahira," Bloom repeated. "And Trinity wanted to say hi to his girl-friend Yahira. I'd do an interview with them, but we've got this—only this little mic set up right here, but we'll—we'll make those arrange-ments later.

"You asked about food," Bloom said to Lauer. "All we're doing is grabbing these MREs, the 'meals ready to eat,' which, frankly, are pretty good. My compliments to the military chef. I mean, basically, as you're rolling along, you could pull out and have some fresh fruit, you could have a—a granola bar, you can—you can make—if I had a—if I had a knife. You got a knife on you, Trinity? Sergeant Todd has got a knife on him. I'll cut this open, Matt, and you can see what's inside. As to sleep, because we were the lead force, Matt, we—we were able to—to stop for a few hours and get some sleep in this vehicle. But—but other than that, there's no sleep. Sergeant Todd, who's the tank commander, is mount— is manning this gun. And if Craig White can pan over here, my photog-rapher Craig White can show you the gun that Sergeant Todd normally sits at. And then Private McClain normally sits at the front of this M-88, and he drives. And he's the only driver, and Sergeant Todd is the only gunner, so they're not getting much sleep as we're rolling along. Basi-cally, what you've got, Matt, are things like this: beef stew. And you— you throw them open as you're rolling along, you've got some crackers, you've got a heating unit. Let's see what else we got here. Some assorted Charms and some cheese spread with jalapeños. And that's what we're eating as we're rolling along. Obviously, we don't get a chance to change or take a shower or anything like that. This is the first time I've taken off my sunglasses, which I hope I haven't lost here in a while be-cause once we start rolling again, the dust kicks up, and it makes it very difficult to see."

Bloom was on again during the eight o'clock hour, and then he ap-peared three hours later on a special eleven o'clock edition of the *Today* show. In fact, Bloom did quite a lot of on-air talking that day, and White was concerned that his reporter had revealed too much information about their whereabouts.

"That was a small bone of contention between David and myself," said White. "The ground rules were that we couldn't talk about specific plans, or where we were. And that's how we played it, fairly close to the vest. But later that night, as we were doing pictures with a night scope, the terrain was changing rapidly. We were now heading off to the west, climbing up into a higher area, and it was very rugged terrain. It was obvious that we weren't going to Baghdad straight away. We were going way out of the way, and anybody watching who knew anything about Iraq would have known that immediately. But David was in full swing. We were doing live shots almost continuously. And I said to David, 'We can't do this anymore. We can't do this if you're going to live up to this promise of not telling people the battle plan or where we are.' Going west was supposed to be this big secret. And from the west, we were going around to the north of Baghdad, and then the plan was to swing into Baghdad from the north. I remember, after we heard the battle plan, I said to David, 'We're screwed. They want to take away our ability to go live.' I remember thinking, 'We have better equipment than anyone else, and we may not be able to show too much of our surroundings.' Mostly we were careful not to do that, but on that first day we probably showed too much."

Surely no one at NBC in New York cared that too much was being revealed. Executives there knew only one thing: The more Bloom they had on the air the better everyone felt. His segments connected with viewers, and he was doing wonders for the ratings.

But working live for NBC in these kinds of conditions can have some major drawbacks, especially during the vicious sandstorms that swept across the Iraqi desert over the next few days. If David Bloom had been employed, say, by CBS or ABC, he'd do his live shot once and then wait until it was time to do another one. Neither CBS nor ABC has a cable outlet. NBC has two, MSNBC and CNBC. As soon as Bloom finished his spot on *Today*, he'd do one for MSNBC, then CNBC. And being a regular contributor on Don Imus's radio show, Bloom also did a few live shots for him. And he did others for Canadian TV. That's a lot of talking, with no mask on, during a sandstorm. And Bloom did all of it without any complaints.

"Could it have compromised his health? I don't know," admitted Craig White. "I've spent a lot of time in bad places. I'm a rock climber.

I've been on walls for twelve days at a time, at places like Yosemite and in caves for two or three weeks at a time. But David really hadn't done this before. We had a producer, Paul Nasser, who was with us, and he had never done anything like this before. And it was a big physical shock. These guys had never really spent much time in a tent or in a sleeping bag. Not that we got that much time. One of the big things we learned about the military is that they don't plan to let their people sleep. The whole time [going] north people were not sleeping. We'd go seventy-two hours on two hours of sleep. We were all sleep-deprived. But David in the sandstorms was playing big back in the United States."

David Verdi said that it has to be up to all reporters out in a sandstorm to regulate themselves. "If you're a correspondent and I assign you to cover a school lockout in Cincinnati, you can't say no," he said. "But a war assignment is completely voluntary. And once you're on assignment in a place like Iraq, and I tell you to go to Tikrit, you can turn around and say, 'No. Tikrit is too dangerous. We can't go.' You have that authority. David had that authority. He had the ability to regulate what he was doing and when he was doing it. Everybody who was embedded went twenty-four hours nonstop. What effect that has on your health is hard to say. I don't know if it's any more difficult talking to the camera in a sandstorm than it is talking off-camera to your friends in a sandstorm.

"I think people may have worried about David because he was so visible," said Verdi. "He was extremely photogenic. He was youthful. He had that whole look about him. We were very aware that he was becoming a popular figure. We were starting to get mail and e-mail about him. As an organization, we were absolutely aware that David was emerging as the face of the war for us. And David was aware of that, too. Absolutely."

But according to Verdi, you'd never know it from their conversations. "Here is how our conversations would go," said Verdi. "And I'm saying this without any sentimentality and without any hyperbole and without any changing of the facts. David would say, 'Hey, David. How ya doing, man?'

"To which I would say, 'How am I doing? Forget how I'm doing, David. How are you doing?'

"And he'd say, 'Oh, I'm okay. Hey, listen, you guys must really be under the gun there, right? You've been up for seventy-two hours now. How are you holding up?'

"And I would say, 'David, I'm sitting in my office eating hamburg-ers. What do you mean, how am I holding up? I want to know about you. You're in the sandstorm. You're all covered with dirt. What's go-ing on? Are you afraid? Tell me what's going on.'

"And he'd say, 'David, I'm fine. Don't worry about me. I want to know how you guys are doing.' Honest to God, that's what he would say."

But the three days of sandstorms combined with the unending noise of motion and the cramped space on the Bloom-mobile was be-ginning to take its toll. "On the morning after the first sandstorm," said White, "David looked at me, and he said, 'Man, that sucked.' It was clear in the morning, but people got lost all during the night. Sol-diers got lost in the desert. They would go out to go to the bathroom thirty to forty feet away and not be able to find their way back. I re-member trying to get my eyes open. Our eyes were just glued shut from the gunk.

"We knew we'd come back with sinus infections, at the least," said White. "And David knew his hearing would probably never be the same. Everything was so loud on that vehicle. I wore earplugs the entire time. But David didn't because he had to hear communications to and from New York.

"Then, on Wednesday, April 2, he said to me, 'I pulled a muscle on my lower leg.' He thought he did it getting off our vehicle. The last step is probably three and a half feet off the ground. So it was under-standable that he might have pulled a muscle.

"I said, 'Let's go see a medic.' And we did. David got some ibupro-fen, the pain reliever, and a wrap and some cream for his leg. Nobody made too much of it. It was a pulled muscle in a leg. You have to re-member, we were also losing weight during this time. The nighttime temperatures were cold, usually down in the thirties. And there were a lot of days and nights we spent in chemical gear, or MOPP, as the army calls it, for mission oriented protective posture. MOPP 4 is full chem gear: masks, gloves, boots, complete chem gear. It was a scary time for us. Mostly they kept us at MOPP 1, which is having the chem bottom suit on and the chem top suit on, but the mask and everything else can be strapped to your side. So between that, and the stress of being up for so many hours at a time and eating MREs that aren't exactly great, peo-ple started losing weight. Every soldier lost weight. By the time we crossed the Euphrates, which was probably sometime around April fourth, everybody was probably down twenty-five to thirty pounds. David certainly lost that kind of weight.

"And for two days we had to make do with bad water," said White. "Helicopters that were supposed to bring more bottled water to us never made it because of the sandstorms. So in addition to David having a problem with his leg, he also didn't want to drink this other water, which I think came out of the river. So that meant he was dehydrated, too."

On Saturday, April 5, Bloom's producer in Iraq, Paul Nasser, suspected that Bloom might be worse off than he was saying. NBC has a global assistance hotline that can be called at any hour for any issue, including medical problems. At Nasser's urging, Bloom called the number and was put on with a doctor. He told the doctor about the pulled muscle. The doctor said that the condition could be more serious, that it might be a good idea to have his leg looked at. But Bloom knew that seeking medical attention at that point meant he would have to leave the Bloom-mobile and essentially take a television time out from the story of his life. For someone who is used to being on TV, like Bloom, nothing is worse than suddenly having to cope with not being on TV. The doctor Bloom spoke with even mentioned the possibility of a life-threatening thrombosis, or blood clot. But Bloom would not be swayed from his mission.

"David either chose to ignore the doctor's advice, or knew that he could have it looked at within two days, once we got to Baghdad," said White. "Getting out of where we were at that point in the middle of a war was just not something that was easy to do. Not to mention the fact that here he was at the height of his career doing what he loved doing. He made that choice."

"David's decision wasn't about career," Verdi insisted. "It was about climbing Mount Everest. It was that kind of challenge. And David saw the summit. Maybe he should have turned around. You know, 'The storm's coming in. Turn around and get the hell off that mountain.' But he was ten feet from the summit."

"David was way out at the end of the pipeline at that point," added Tom Brokaw. "Getting back to anywhere was problematic at best. He was a young healthy guy. The idea that he might have a blood clot, I can picture him wanting to wait. They were on their way to Baghdad. Guys were getting shot at. I can absolutely understand his mind-set."

"I've tried to put myself in David's position," said Verdi. "It's human nature to think that you're not as bad off as they're telling you. It's human nature to think that you're a little invincible, and that you're going to get through it. It's also human nature to think, 'Hey, I came this far. I'm not letting anything stop me now.' And I believe that David believed he was perfectly okay, and that he'd get through it."

But in an e-mail to his wife, Melanie, composed and sent that same day, Bloom was not nearly as positive about his eventual outcome. The only thing he seemed sure about was the love he had for his wife, his three daughters, and God.

"It's 10 A.M. here Saturday morning," Bloom wrote, "and I've just been talking to my soundman Bob Lapp about his older brother, whom he obviously loves and admires very much, who's undergoing chemotherapy treatment for leukemia. Here Bob is—out in the middle of the desert—and the brother he cares the world for—who had been the picture of health, devoted to his wife and kids, is dying. Bob can't wait to be home to be with him, and I can't wait to be home to be with all of you. You can't begin to fathom—cannot begin to even glimpse the enormity—of the changes I have and am continuing to undergo. God takes you to the depths of your being—until you are at rock bottom—and then, if you turn to him with utter and blind faith, and resolve in your heart and mind to walk only with him and toward him, picks you up by your bootstraps and leads you home. I hope and pray that all my guys get out of this in one piece. But I tell you, Mel, I am at peace. Deeply saddened by the glimpses of death and destruction I have seen, but at peace with my God, and with you. I know only that my whole way of looking at life has turned upside down—and here I am, supposedly at the peak of professional success, and I could frankly care less. Yes, I'm proud of the good job we've all been doing, but—in the scheme of things—it matters little compared to my relationship with you, and the girls, and Jesus. There is something far beyond my level of human understanding or comprehension going on here, some forging of metal through fire.

"I shifted my book of daily devotions and prayers to the inside of my flak jacket, so that it would be close to my heart, protecting me in a way, and foremost in my thoughts," Bloom continued. "When the moment comes when Jim or John—or Christine or Nicole or Ava or you—are talking about my last days, I am determined that they will say, 'He was devoted to his wife and children and he gave every ounce of his being not for himself, but for those whom he cared about most—God and his family.' Save this note. Look at it a month from now, a year from now, 10 years from now, 20 years from now. You cannot know now—nor do I—whether you will look at it with tears, heartbreak and a sense of anguish and regret over what might have been, or whether you will say—he was and is a changed man, God did work a miracle in our lives. But I swear to you on everything that I hold dear—I am speaking the truth to you. And I will continue to speak the truth to you, and I know that you still love me. Please give the girls a big hug—squeeze 'em tight—and let them know just how much their daddy loves and cares for them. With love and devotion, Dave."

Verdi knew nothing of the e-mail that Bloom transmitted to his wife, but he talked to him on that same day. "He was absolutely soft-spoken," said Verdi. "He said, 'I feel great out here, David. This is what I came to do. It's fabulous, and everything's okay.' He said he had just talked to his wife, Melanie. He said she was fine and the kids were fine. He said, 'David, you can't believe it. It's really beautiful out here. In an odd way, it's really beautiful. I'm worried about Craig, and I'm worried about Paul, but they seem to be holding up okay. But you know, David, I've never felt more complete about what I'm doing.'

"I asked him if he was afraid of the approaching battle, and he said, 'I'm not afraid at all. Nothing's going to happen to us. Don't worry about it.' He just had this calm about him that was very odd. Everybody who talked to him had the same impression. He said he was doing what he wanted to do, and that made him feel good. And he really thought he was going to accomplish what he came to accomplish. He was really chasing a dream. This was his idea from the beginning, and there were so many obstacles that he personally overcame. And all of a sudden there he was living his dream."

The conditions on the ground in Iraq, however, were becoming a little more nightmarish. "This was getting to be a nasty war," said White. "We started seeing bodies and blown-up Iraqi tanks. You could smell the war. You could see the war. Until then, the war had looked like a video game. You'd see a flash from a tank near us, and then you'd see another tank blow up two miles out in the distance. But by April 5 we were seeing dead bodies and blood running across the street.

"We were near a bridge," remembered White, "and not too much was happening. We were stopped. We looked around and you could see destroyed Iraqi tanks. And David was able to take a nap. We had seen our first trees in a long time. David put a cot out under a tree and took a three-hour nap. Later that day, David, Colonel Stephen Twitty, and I had a nice dinner together sitting on a cot in the shade contemplating what it was going to be like to go into Baghdad in the next couple of days. We finally had some fresh water, and we ate our MREs. David downed a whole bottle of water and talked to Colonel Twitty about the days ahead. I had been in Baghdad in July 2002, and I knew there was an incredible amount of art everywhere, statues of Saddam Hussein everywhere, sculptures everywhere. We asked how the army intended to deal with all that. Would they go in as conquerors, destroying every-thing in their path? Or would they go in as liberators, and let the Iraqis deal with the art and anything else that remained? We asked, 'Have you discussed this? Has everyone been briefed?' And they hadn't discussed it, which shocked me. There was no forethought. But that's as tough as it got that night. David and I ended up talking about our families. We had a nice evening."

Bloom spent the night sleeping in the front seat of his crew's up-link truck, so he could be close to the computers and phones. Craig White slept in a sleeping bag on a cot outside. "As I got up to go to the bathroom," recalled White, "David rolled down the window, and said, 'Hey, buddy, we can leave in a couple of hours. I found out last night. Tell the guys to pack it up.'

"I said fine, and I went over to the side and did my business," said White. "When I got back, I grabbed one of the portable phones to call my wife. In Iraq, it was early Sunday morning, April 6, but it was still Saturday night in New York. I wanted to check in with my wife and let her know I was safe. And while I was on the phone, out of the corner of my eye I looked over and saw somebody on the ground. It was David. I ran over to him. I was still on the phone with my wife. It looked as though he had fainted. I said, 'David, you fainted. But you'll be okay, man. You'll be all right.' I yelled for the medic at the same time, and the medic got there within a minute or two. I told the medic that David was probably dehydrated. The medic got an IV into him, and Paul Nasser got into a Humvee with David as the medic performed CPR. I was eye to eye with David. His pupils were dilated out and fixed. I held his hand, saying, 'David you'll be all right. You'll be all right.' I immediately called NBC, and they put me through to David Verdi."

"I was in bed with my wife," said Verdi. "Generally speaking, when the phone rings at that time at night and it's work-related, it's never good news. I answered the phone. It was Craig White. He said, 'David just collapsed. They're working on him. I don't think he's breathing. This is not a good situation. I think we're going to lose him.'

"I said, 'Craig, cut the shit. What are you talking about? What happened?'

"Craig said, 'I think he's suffering from some sort of seizure because he was dehydrated. But I'm telling you, this does not look good. I don't think he's going to make it.'

"I said, 'Craig, you need to explain to me, exactly what has happened?'

"He said, 'Listen, I'm here. The medics are on him. Paul Nasser is with him. And I'm supposed to leave. And if I don't leave now, with the tanks and all the trucks, they're going to leave me behind. You need to tell me what to do.'

"I said, 'Stay with me until Nasser gets on the phone.' Then Nasser came. And I said, 'Craig, you go.' So he went off in the Bloom-mobile with the 3rd ID. Paul Nasser got on the phone. Now Paul is not a hardened, experienced guy like Craig. Paul is a freelance producer. We'd used him in the past, but he's young, and this was his first real experience.

"While I was waiting for Paul to come on the phone," said Verdi, "I called my boss, Bill Wheatley. I told him that David had collapsed, and that Craig White is saying that David's life is in jeopardy. When Paul Nasser got on, I conferenced Bill in with us.

"And Paul said, 'Here's the situation. David has collapsed, I think from some sort of seizure with dehydration. He stopped breathing and he turned purple, but they seemed to have revived him somewhat.' Paul stopped talking when a medic came up to brief him. We could hear the medic, and we could hear commotion in the background, people shouting.

"And the medic said, 'Listen, we have to transport him. We got his heart back. But if we don't get him out of here, he's going to be in serious trouble. We've called in a chopper.'

"Paul got back on the phone and he was shaken. He said, 'I'm going to hang up.'

"I said, 'Don't hang up, Paul. Stay with us.' He said okay and he moved around closer to where David was, and we could hear them working. Bill and I could hear the medics shouting, yelling medical things.

"Paul said, 'I'm going to stay with him the whole way.'

"And I said, 'Paul, do not leave his side.'

"So he committed to doing that," said Verdi. "And then he started to describe the scene. 'His heart stopped. They got it back. He turned purple. He's got some color back. His lips moved. I see his chest moving.' Maybe ten minutes passed, and we started to hear the sound of a chopper coming. Its sound almost drowned out Paul. He yelled that the chopper was there, and that he was going to get on it with David. He said, 'It's a fifteen-minute ride to the field hospital. I'll call you when we get down again.' And he hung up.

"I said to Bill, 'I think I should call Melanie.'

"Bill very wisely said, 'David, don't call Melanie yet. Let's find out where this is going.' I said okay and I told Bill that I would call him again from the car. I got out of bed, quickly got dressed and into my car. I'm a thirty-minute drive from work. I got on the highway. It was midnight. The phone rang in the car. It was Paul calling from the field hospital. I conferenced in Bill. And Paul said, 'We've just landed and David is gone.'

"I said, 'What do you mean, he's gone, Paul?'

"He said, 'David's dead. We lost him in the chopper on the way.' He described the scene to us. He said he would stay with David. They were in the middle of nowhere. But he said he would stay with David.

"When I got to the office, I called Melanie. I said, 'Melanie, this is David Verdi.' I had been talking to the spouses throughout, so I wasn't a stranger. I said, 'Melanie, I have some very serious news to tell you. And you need to tell me who's in the house with you?'

"She was very groggy," said Verdi. "She said, 'I have friends here from Washington.'

"I said, 'Do you have adult friends there?'

"She said, 'Yes. I have a couple here from Washington, with their children.'

"I said, 'Okay, where are you?'

"She said, 'What do you mean, where am I? I'm in my house.'

"I said, 'No. Where in the house are you?'

"She said, 'I'm in the bathroom because I don't want to wake up any of the children.'

"I said, 'Melanie, why don't you go get your friend, and then pick the phone up again.' So she did. I said, 'Melanie, David's gone.'

"And she didn't believe it. We went back and forth, and she said, 'I can't even process this. I don't believe it.'

"So I said, 'Why don't you let me talk to your friend.' Her friend got on the phone and I explained to her that David had died.

Tom Brokaw was in the air, on his way to Jordan, as Verdi was busily trying to figure out whom to call next. Brokaw didn't get a call, but Bloom was on his mind during the lengthy flight.

"I was on my way to meet him," said Brokaw. "On the plane I started thinking about what I might say to David when I got there. I pictured myself throwing my arm around him, and saying, 'Okay, you've gotten the 3rd Infantry this far. I'm going to take them into Baghdad.' That would have been a little kidding time with him, and he would have loved it.

"When I got off the plane in Jordan," said Brokaw, "I knew something was wrong by the look on the face of the guy who met me. The first I thing I said to him was, 'Is it Bloom?' And he said yes. You know, of all the people we had out there we were worried that something might happen to David. He was always at the tip of the spear with the 3rd Infantry, so that put him in a position to be endangered."

But David Bloom was not killed in action. He died of a pulmonary embolism, medical terminology for the blood clot that the NBC hotline doctor feared might happen. On Monday, April 7, while everyone at NBC was trying to deal with this tragic reality, David Verdi started thinking of Bloom's final video report, which had aired on Saturday, April 5.

"Those sandstorms did a very strange thing with the camera. They gave an unearthly hue to everything. Colors we had never seen before," said Verdi. "So up comes Bloom on Saturday and his hair is filled with sand. But there's an odd color to his skin and his lips. He just looked like nothing we had ever seen before. I remember thinking to myself, 'This just doesn't look right.' We all thought it was the sun and the filtering of the light. But now, looking back, I realize that there was a guy, a great guy, but a guy who had something going on in his body."

"I've been at this a long time," said Brokaw, "and we've had other well-known people die at mid-career, or during formative times in their careers. But David obviously touched people in a lot of ways. He was our go-to guy. But he also had that kind of cherubic, midwestern quality about him, that enthusiasm. And he was so damn good at what he did as a reporter. He came on the air with great energy, but also with great clarity and insights. You know, Reuven Frank [the pioneering NBC News producer who teamed Chet Huntley with David Brinkley] used to have this great phrase about television. He would say, 'Television transmits experience.' And nothing has been as effective at transmitting the experience of what it's like to be moving across a battlefield than David Bloom in his Bloom-mobile."

Warren Zevon

January 24, 1947–September 7, 2003

THE ROUTINE, USUALLY OCCURRING AROUND MIDWEEK, WOULD BEGIN IN WARREN Zevon's gray living room, on the gray couch in front of the fireplace. This thoroughly lived-in piece of furniture was such a part of Zevon's personality that he even had names for it. He called it his "couch of pain" or his "sofa of suffering." Of course, if it got really bad and he was struggling with his creative urges and couldn't figure out what kind of song to write next, that old couch might end up being referred to as a sort of "davenport of despair."

But at a certain point during almost any given week, this sober, agoraphobic, obsessive-compulsive man in his fifties, a man who at his core was beguilingly happier than the names of his couch suggested, would dress himself in various shades of gray, and head down to the underground garage in his apartment building on Kings Road in West Hollywood. He would then get into his gray Corvette, and drive over the hill to meet Jorge Calderon for an early afternoon movie, when the admission prices were at their lowest.

Zevon and Calderon had been writing songs together for years, mostly in Zevon's gray apartment, in the small loft above the living room where he kept his recording equipment. But when the creative process slowed, as it often did, the two men would traipse downstairs to sit on the couch.

· "He'd say to me, 'Jorge, are you ready to sit on the couch of pain?' because that's where we'd have to go," said Calderon, "when we were

241

painfully trying to get a third verse after writing the first two, or a third line after two great first lines."

But the matinee showings in the San Fernando Valley were never about work, or pain. These outings were just a mutual desire on the part of two old friends to sit quietly in a darkened theater and watch an awful movie.

"We did that a lot," said Calderon, "going to see movies our wives and girlfriends wouldn't want to see with us." One of those movies was *Blood Work*, directed by Clint Eastwood, in which he starred as a retired FBI profiler who is pressed back into service after undergoing a heart transplant. The movie came out in early August 2002, mostly to nothing reviews because, after all, how many times can you watch the reincarnation of Dirty Harry as another aging vet? For most people, not too many times. For Zevon and Calderon, they probably could have sat there through the coming attractions and watched it again.

But Calderon also remembered that day for another reason: Zevon was complaining again about a lack of energy and a shortness of breath, especially when he exercised.

The subject had come up a few times over the previous month. "He first mentioned it in July," said Calderon. "Then he went up to Canada to do a few outdoor shows, and he told me the same thing. He called from Canada, and he said, 'I don't know, it must be the altitude.'"

Zevon used the same excuse with his manager, Brigette Barr. "I told him that when he came back from Canada, he absolutely had to see a doctor," she said. "He said to me, 'I don't go to doctors. I don't believe in doctors. I don't want to know what he has to say.' His biggest fear was that if he went to the doctor, he would get bad news."

Because Calderon's wife, Yvonne, had been on dialysis for ten years, he was no stranger to dealing with matters of health. Calderon refused to let up on Zevon, and he pressed the issue again, after they came out of *Blood Work*.

"I said, 'Warren, you have to go see a cardiologist. You could have an obstruction in your arteries. If your blood doesn't flow normally, it would affect your pulmonary functions and make you short of breath.'"

"And he said, 'Oh, no, it's just stress. I get stressed all the time.'

"I said, 'Dude, we're in our fifties now. You can't be taking any chances.'"

Zevon went back to Calderon's house in Sherman Oaks that day, where they were met by Yvonne, who insisted that Zevon see a doctor, if for no other reason than to get a clean bill of health and ease his mind, and everyone else's.

According to Calderon, Zevon finally gave in, and said, "Okay, my cousin is a cardiologist. I'll call him."

On August 25, Zevon phoned Calderon from the waiting room of the doctor's office, and he said, "You're going to be proud of me, Jorge. Guess where I am? I'm at the cardiologist's office."

Calderon said, "Good. It's the best thing you can do. I hope everything is okay. Just let me know what he says."

Zevon said, "Okay, I'll call you later."

Hours went by until Zevon called Calderon again. When Calderon picked up the phone, his friend said, "Jorge, you don't want to hear this."

"I told him I did want to hear it," said Calderon. "That's when he told me it was lung cancer."

Lung cancer? Warren Zevon? Sure, he smoked like a chimney for most of his life, but Zevon finally wised up and threw the cigarettes away in 1997. And even more important, Zevon was a recovering alcoholic and drug addict who hadn't gotten high in nearly eighteen years. The man was living a clean if slightly chaotic life, surrounded by books, magazines, DVDs, newspapers, and recording equipment in his one-bedroom apartment. He had more money than he cared to spend, he'd been on the cover of *Rolling Stone,* and he had the respect of his peers. And now this? Lung cancer? This was not how it was supposed to all turn out. At least, that's what Calderon thought when he heard the word *cancer.* He tried to be strong for his friend on the phone, but found it almost impossible.

"I handed the phone to Yvonne," he said, "and I just sat on the floor and, like, lost it. Yvonne talked to him while I composed myself, and then I got back on and we talked for a while."

Zevon didn't get all the news that day, just that it was lung cancer and that it didn't look good. It would be a few more days before he learned the full extent of his situation. He had mesothelioma, a rare and inoperable form of lung cancer, and to make matters even more horrible, it had already spread to his liver. The doctor estimated that Zevon would probably be dead in just three months' time.

Calderon and Zevon had been friends since they first met in 1972. A native of Puerto Rico, Calderon traveled to New York to play in a band with other Puerto Rican musicians, but soon moved to Los

Angeles in the hopes of finding a better career on the West Coast. It was late one night in L.A., "probably three in the morning," Calderon estimated, when he received a phone call from his friend Crystal Brelsford. She was waking him up in the middle of the night to ask a favor. "I have to pick up my boyfriend in jail," she said to him. "Can you help me? I don't have my car, and I need to get him home."

Calderon said he'd do it, and when he arrived at the jail, Crystal's boyfriend, Warren Zevon, was still in the drunk tank. "He had a problem with drinking. That's how we met," said Calderon. "I took them back to his place, and we couldn't get in because neither of them had a key. I said, 'Don't worry. I'm Puerto Rican. I can break into anyone's house.'

"I said it as a joke," said Calderon, "but as drunk as he was, I remember him looking at me with a smile, thinking, 'I like this guy.'"

Calderon found a window, got it open, and climbed in. And in that instant, the two men became the best of friends. "It was easy for us to hang out and have a great time," said Calderon, "and that was before we even got together musically."

The musical part of their relationship began during the recording of Zevon's 1976 album, *Warren Zevon*, which Jackson Browne produced for Asylum Records. Zevon had written a song, "I'll Sleep When I'm Dead," but he felt something about the song was missing.

"He wanted me to sing the chorus with him, but he also wanted me to say some things in Spanish during certain parts of the song," said Calderon, who later went on to help Zevon complete another song, "Veracruz," which appeared on his 1978 Asylum album, *Excitable Boy.*

From there, the two struck up a writing partnership that lasted for years. "I didn't work on every album as a songwriter," said Calderon, "but he always called me, either to sing something on his record or to help him write something."

Calderon did not work on Zevon's 2002 album, *My Ride's Here,* which was recorded for Danny Goldberg's label, Artemis Records. After the album came out, Zevon realized that he had made a mistake in not using Calderon, and he vowed not to do it again.

In 2002, weeks before seeing *Blood Work* but right after one of their other terrible matinee movies in the Valley, Zevon turned to Calderon, and he said, "I want to start working on another album right now. Let's do this one together. Let's go back to what we know how to do, and let's do it at my house. Let's just write a whole bunch of songs together, on the couch of pain. I want to write a whole bunch of songs again with you."

Immediately, Calderon said he was in, and the two men hugged, sealing the deal between them. Then came Zevon's diagnosis. Calderon figured that their plans to do another album would certainly have to be scrapped. Zevon, though, had other ideas.

"I tried to tell him that now was the time for him to be with his family," Calderon said, referring to Zevon's two children, Jordan Zevon, his thirty-three-year-old son from his marriage to his first wife, Tule Livingston, and Ariel Zevon, his twenty-six-year-old daughter from his second marriage, to Crystal Brelsford, Calderon's old friend.

Calderon urged Zevon to forget about the album, especially under these new and very difficult circumstances. "I said, 'Now is the time to take care of yourself. If you want to take a trip, or spend your days lying on a beach in Mexico, go do it.'

"He said, 'Yeah, yeah, yeah,' but after about five days," Calderon said, "Warren said, 'I've thought about it, and what would bring me the best joy would be to do what I love the best, and that is writing songs.' He said, 'I want to do this album. I want to do it like we talked about. So let's do it. I trust you. You're the only one who understands what's going on.'

"I think he said that," Calderon said, "because, one, we were brothers, and two, he knew that I had dealt with my wife's illness for so long that I was really strong about those things. I had been taking care of her, and he knew I could be counted on to be there for him, too. So I said, 'Yeah, let's do it. Let's have fun with this. Let's forget about the doctors and the illness. Let's just have fun, like we used to.'

"I also told him that I would always be there for him in a good light," said Calderon. "I said I would do my grieving behind his back, because I didn't need to bring him down. He kept telling me that all these people were calling him and coming out of the woodwork from years back. Everyone was getting him on the phone and sobbing. He was getting calls from people he hadn't seen in years, people he'd met only a couple of times. And he was the kind of person who couldn't say to them, 'Look, I don't have time for this.'

"I would tell him, 'Listen, these people are hogging your time. They're worried about their own mortality.' I told him that when he wanted to hang up, he should just say, 'My doctor is about to call me.' Or, 'I have to call my doctor right now. I need a prescription.'

"He said, 'That's a good one. I'll do that.'

"I gave him that advice," said Calderon, "and then I started griev-ing behind his back."

Calderon wasn't the only person in Zevon's life who grieved in private. Susan Jaffy first met Zevon in the early 1990s at a birthday party for their dentist, Stan Golden. A few years later, Jaffy started bug-ging Golden to fix her up with Zevon, but the dentist was slow to move.

"Eventually, Warren and I ran into each other at a tanning salon, of all places. He would kill me for telling that out loud to a stranger," said Jaffy. "But subsequently, Stan did set us up, and Warren and I wound up dating for six years."

The relationship was marked by an equal number of hills and val-leys. "We went out. Then we broke up. Then we went out again. Then we broke up again," said Jaffy. "On our second date, he said he wasn't having any more children. I was thirty-six or thirty-seven, and I was sure I wanted children. So we struggled with that issue. I remember one morning waking up in bed with Warren, and I said, 'I'm thinking of getting artificially inseminated. What do you think?'

"He said, 'I think you should break up with me and find another guy.'

"We also had this other problem," she said, "and it had to do with sex. We always had sex. Every time we were together we had sex. Even when he was with someone else, and I was with someone else, we would find a way to cheat on the other people so we could have sex. It was during one of those periods when I was trying to be monoga-mous with somebody else that Warren and I stopped talking. We didn't talk all through the summer of 2002. It had just gotten to a point where I had to say, 'I can't see you, because if I do, we're going to end up having sex.'

"I was trying to have other relationships and move on," she said. "I had met a nice Jewish guy, a lawyer, and I was trying to have a real thing."

Then came the phone call from her dentist, Stan Golden, with news that had nothing to do with her teeth. "Stan called me at seven o'clock in the morning," she said, "and I knew exactly what he was going to tell me. I heard it in his voice. He said, 'Warren's dying.'

"I called Warren immediately, and naturally he didn't answer his phone," she said. "He never answered his phone. Maybe if your caller

ID was unblocked, and he was expecting your call, maybe then he'd answer it. But usually he let the answering machine take it."

Jaffy left a message and Zevon returned the call later that day. They made a plan to meet the following day at the hairdresser. Not only did they share the same dentist, they also both got their hair cut at Alex Roldan, the salon at the Bel Age Hotel in West Hollywood.

"We used different haircutters, but it was a coincidence that we both had appointments on that next day," she said. "I arrived first, and I was sobbing. I couldn't let Warren see me crying. I never cried in front of him, not one time. For one thing, he wouldn't have allowed it. He felt really guilty about making other people feel bad, and he didn't want anyone to suffer for him. He also didn't want anyone to see him in pain, so he pretended there was no pain."

There was, however, no pretending about how Jaffy and Zevon felt about each other. "He looked so handsome that day," she said. "I remember that when he walked into the salon, I was trying to act like everything was fine, which was very hard. From the salon, we went to Tower Records on Sunset to buy a DVD. He had a fetish for DVDs. He had to get all the new things that came out. I made him buy *Kissing Jessica Stein*. We went back to his place, and we watched it. He hated it, of course, but he wouldn't tell me that. He thought it was kind of cute that I liked it. And then we made love, just like always."

The energy Zevon had for sex at that point was matched only by his energy to create new music.

"Warren felt he had a lot of songs in his mind. He felt he had something to say," said Danny Goldberg, who had agreed to have his label release another Zevon album weeks before the artist received his devastating diagnosis. "Over the years, this was a guy who sometimes had a hard time writing songs. He could get blocked, and the songs would come slowly. But given the intense reality that he was facing, one of the by-products turned out to be the many ideas he had for songs. Warren knew what he wanted to do. He said his kids were both grown. He felt he was on good terms with them, and that his legacy was his art. That's what he wanted to focus on during the time he had left."

The back-and-forth writing process between Zevon and Calderon started each day over the phone. "We would talk four, five times a day," said Calderon. "He'd say, 'What do you have? Here's what I have.' We were writing songs on cell phones. He would call me when I was in the supermarket, and we'd work on lines while I shopped. That's how it went, very fast."

"He was definitely racing the clock," said his manager Brigette Barr. "He knew he wanted to get out as much as he could. There was a part of him that didn't understand why it was coming. He even said it was good timing. He said, 'If this had to happen to me, the songs couldn't be coming at a better time.' So he did feel under the gun, but the songs seemed to come without his driving it, which amazed him as much as it amazed everyone else."

But the doctor had said three months, leaving Zevon, Goldberg, and Barr to all wonder whether Zevon's last musical hurrah might wind up not as an album but as a four-song extended play, or EP, as it's referred to in the music business.

"I didn't think he'd be able to finish an album," said Goldberg. "I just opened up a budget, paid the bills, and made studio time available. I figured we would do something with whatever he recorded. I just wanted him to do whatever he could. I really cared about the guy, and I considered him a genius and a nice guy. And those two things don't always go together."

"Warren didn't believe he would have enough time to finish an entire album either," said Barr. "I kept saying, 'Just keep going. It will be whatever it is.'"

One thing Zevon didn't want it to be was a secret. "The decision to go public with Warren's illness was made for two very distinct reasons," said Barr. "Since he was going to become sicker, he was afraid that people might think he had fallen off the wagon, or that bigger drug issues were involved. He didn't want to deal with all that speculation. But Warren was also coming off a period in his career where he wasn't getting the kind of attention he so deeply wanted. He knew there was a commercial hook to his illness, and he knew it could be used to bring some attention to himself, and to the album."

Interviews were arranged with six publications: *Rolling Stone, Billboard, People, USA Today*, the *New York Times*, and the *Los Angeles Times*. "We thought we'd get the widest possible audience with just those six publications," said Barr. "Warren's outlook about it was amazing. Anytime it became difficult, he would say to me, 'Brigette, it's just showbiz. I understand it. I get it. If you need to use it, use it.'"

"He wanted to make it public like he did when he sobered up so he could get a little bit more support in what he was doing," added

Calderon. "Let's face it, the media loves a tragedy, and Warren knew his situation would help the album. But also he wanted to make it public so that other people with cancer might benefit from his experience. He didn't just want to stop his life, like Dusty Springfield, who went to her house and didn't do anything. Warren wanted to believe, and show others, that he could work right up to the end. I remember telling him to listen to Bob Marley's last concert. He sounded like an inspired man in his twenties. And right after that concert, he collapsed backstage and they took him to a hospital in Switzerland. I said to Warren, 'That's what we need to do. Just put everything into it until the lights go out.'"

They started with two songs, "Dirty Life & Times" and "She's Too Good for Me," which Zevon had recorded in his apartment prior to the diagnosis. Jaffy believes that "She's Too Good for Me" is about her.

"He did think I was too good for him," she said.

It's entirely possible, of course, that Zevon thought other women were too good for him, as well. Calderon said it was always his impression that "She's Too Good for Me" was written for another of Zevon's longtime girlfriends, Kristin Steffl.

Jaffy allowed for the possibility that Calderon might be correct. "I can safely say that Warren was the love of my life," she said. "And I certainly can assume that I was probably one of the loves of his life."

That assumption, Calderon said, is definitely accurate. The first song Zevon and Calderon wrote together following the diagnosis was "El Amor de Mi Vida," which means "The love of my life." According to Calderon, the song was written for Zevon's Puerto Rican girlfriend, Annette Aguiler, with whom he was involved for seven years.

Nevertheless, as close as Zevon was to each of these women, he actually had a much stronger relationship with yet another woman, Ryan Rayston, a writer he had known from his years in recovery. From the moment Zevon found out that his cancer was terminal, Rayston, who had survived thyroid cancer in the 1980s, became the one person in his life on whom he most depended.

"We dated briefly when we first met," said Rayston. "But we had too much in common to ever translate it into anything sexual. It was just much more fun being friends."

This commonality between Zevon and Rayston existed on many levels. "We shared a neurosis and a collective understanding of phobias and obsessive-compulsive disorder," she said. "We found pleasure in each other's OCD. Warren was fully present for his OCD. He was an obsessive hand-washer. He would call me, and say, 'Nothing is bad luck, is it?' And I'd say no. Then he'd say, 'Nothing is bad luck, is it?' He'd have to say it twice. Then he'd hang up because that was all he needed to hear. The people who knew him best knew about this. If you bought something on a bad luck day, it was thrown out. It didn't matter if it was from Gucci or Prada. It was trash. Everything had to be gray, until he went through another stage and everything had to be orange—orange pens, orange key, orange plates, orange coffee mug.

"I'd say, 'Warren, do you want anything to drink?' And he would want a Coke. So I would bring him a Coke, and he would pop it open, and say, "This one is bad luck." So I'd get him another one, and another one, until we found one that was not bad luck.

"And he didn't like going out at all," she said. "And when he did, it was an event. He was a creature of habit. We used to eat regularly at certain places—Hugo's, for example on Santa Monica Boulevard. And we always shopped at the same places. It was all part of his charm. Warren let me in where he wouldn't let other people in, because he knew I would never judge him. He knew I accepted him, completely and totally."

Rayston's level of acceptance, however, was severely tested when Zevon decided that he was going to drink and use drugs again, after almost eighteen years of continuous sobriety. A voice message Zevon left Rayston shortly after his diagnosis hinted at where he was headed: "Hey, Ryan, it's me. I don't know your cell phone number, but you know mine if you want to give me a call. So, you know, I met the pulmonary guy at Hugo's, and I found it all quite cheery. I mean, he goes along with me, you know.

"I asked him if I could get the Elvis shit now," Zevon said, a reference to the conscious-numbing painkillers that Elvis Presley was taking at the end of his life. "And he said, 'You can get anything you want.' He also said I didn't have to go to an oncologist. Umm, he's a good guy. He's a good kid. So I'm going to go meet Jordan, and go by my office, and shit like that. Call me on the cell if you want."

"When Warren found out he was going to die," said Rayston, "he said, 'Fuck it. I'm going to drink and I'm going to do drugs.' Not drug drugs, like cocaine, but the drugs that were prescribed for him, the heavy-duty painkillers."

Initially, hearing her friend talk about flinging himself off the proverbial wagon made Rayston feel very uneasy about being around him. After all, she had been sober, too, and recovering people, in general, don't like hanging out with someone who has gone back to drinking. Rayston waited weeks before confronting him.

"He was telling everyone that he had the flu, but he was really drunk," she said. "I finally asked him what he was doing, and it turned into a fight. We didn't talk for three days. Then he called me and left a message saying that he basically understood what I was saying. He didn't stop his drinking, but he tempered it a little more. He found this great amount of drugs and alcohol to carry him through a painless day, and he did that for a while.

"He felt it was none of my business," she said. "He said he was the one who was dying. This was his life, and how dare I even comment on it."

Rayston took the issue to her twelve-step sponsor. This was new territory for her, and she wanted guidance. "My sponsor said, 'Warren's been given a death sentence. You can only pray for him right now. You can't force him to do anything.' So that's what I did. I prayed for him."

As soon as the praying started, the fighting stopped, and Rayston was back to visiting Zevon on a daily basis. If he wanted certain foods, she'd go to the store and bring them to him. If he wanted company just to watch a movie, she would lie on his bed with him and watch.

"He was probably the smartest man I ever knew," said Rayston. "He was so well read, so incredibly well versed in film and production. He had an appreciation for everything in movies, from films about bulimia on Lifetime to the best of Fellini."

But Zevon was also not about to spend whatever days he had left just watching movies in his bedroom on Kings Road. There was a record to make, and pretty soon artists like Billy Bob Thornton and Dwight Yoakam were coming into the studio to record pieces for the album. Eventually other artists showed up, including Don Henley, Bruce Springsteen, Emmylou Harris, Tom Petty, Ry Cooder, Jackson Browne, Joe Walsh, and David Lindley.

"The first session we did with live musicians was for 'Numb as a Statue,' which was one of the songs we wrote in a day," said Calderon. "Then we did 'Prison Grove' at Sunset Sound. I remember that being a long day. Warren could sing, but it was apparent he was having problems with his stamina."

Stamina was a big issue when Zevon agreed to travel to New York for an October 30 appearance on *The Late Show with David Letterman*.

"I had been talking to Sheila Rogers, who has been booking *Letter-*

man for years," said Barr. "They were all devastated when they heard the news about Warren. They wanted to give him a tribute. They wanted to do whatever they could to make him happy.

"At first, we just thought it would be too much for him," she said. "We didn't think he could make a cross-country trip. But they kept saying, 'Whatever he wants.' Then it started to be, 'He can have the whole show.' Well, after numerous conversations about how it wouldn't be cheesy, and maybe it would even be beautiful, we decided to do it."

But as October 30 approached, the fear around Zevon was that he wouldn't be able to accomplish it physically. "Up until the day before," Barr said, "we had no idea if he could do a whole show, or even one song. I asked Sheila to make alternate arrangements to have another performer standing by in case Warren wasn't physically up to it."

Flying to New York was incredibly difficult for Zevon, but he managed to do it, a full two days before the show. He boarded an American Airlines flight, sat in a first class seat, and was sick the entire way to New York. "Bringing him in two days before proved the smart thing to do because it enabled him to rest for one whole day," said Barr. "We stayed at Morgans, the hotel on Madison Avenue that Warren had been staying in for years. They gave him a penthouse suite, and unfortunately he was sick in bed the whole day.

"But he pulled it off," she said. "He got into the car and went to the show, and he did it. I really didn't think he would make it, but he got the energy and strength from some place, I don't know where. But that was totally Warren, totally showbiz. It turned out to be one of the most incredible experiences of my life. I know it meant so much to Warren to be on with Letterman. It gave him the chance to joke that he was playing his own wake."

Back in Los Angeles, Jaffy was readying herself for another night with Zevon. She cooked a stew in her Brentwood kitchen and packed it in a container. She stopped at Nate 'n Al's delicatessen in Beverly Hills to pick up Zevon's favorite chicken—dark meat only. She brought marijuana and red wine.

"For all the time we were together," said Jaffy, "we never had a drug or a drink together because he was sober for so long. But now he was looking for every drug that didn't require a tourniquet. It was, like, 'Woo-hoo, I can take drugs now.' Our first glass of red wine and first joint together was like a big momentous occasion."

So was the night that Jaffy let him relive a sexual fantasy. "He was very specific with me," she said. "He wanted to relive something that happened in 1970. He wanted me wearing a sheer floral print bathrobe over my naked body. I shopped for hours looking for that robe. I was hysterical because I couldn't find it. Then I found it. He wanted the bathrobe falling over my breast, not exposing all of it, just some of it. He wanted it to look like we had just finished having sex.

According to Jaffy, it was in 1970 that a young woman from the record company came over to Zevon's apartment to show him the artwork for his first album, *Wanted Dead or Alive*. When she walked in, Zevon was with a woman who was wearing a sheer floral print bathrobe over her naked body. Thirty-two years later, Zevon was expecting another young woman from his record label to come over to show him proofs of his 2002 album, *Genius*. Jaffy was asked to play the part of the naked woman from 1970, and she gladly accepted the role.

"He wanted me to participate," she said, "and I did. It was like an act. We put on a show."

By December, there were no more shows because it was becoming much more difficult for Zevon to perform sexually. His one solution, he felt, was to take Viagra, "which he never needed, ever, not one time, by the way," said Jaffy. "But he bought jarfuls of Viagra because he was an alcoholic, so he had to have more of everything. We had sex up until we couldn't have sex anymore, and then after we couldn't have sex anymore we had oral sex, because that worked."

And then even that stopped working.

"Christmas was the last time that Warren was really accessible and going out of the house," said Barr. "He wasn't eating much by then, so we brought Christmas to him. His two children, Jordan and Ariel, were there. Tennessee State senator Steve Cohen was there. I was there with my husband, and Ryan was there. We could all see that he was struggling."

Zevon had stopped recording during the Christmas hiatus and planned on starting up again in January. But he couldn't do it. He was too weak. "The bravery he had shown, and the humorous way he looked at his illness, really took a turn," said Calderon. "He'd say, 'It's not only Christmas and New Year's. It's my last Christmas and New Year's.' He really went down, I mean, really down and depressed. Suddenly he didn't want to go anywhere. He was thinking he was going to die any day. We tried to get him back into the studio. Noah Snyder, the engineer and co-producer, tried. Brigette tried. But he never came back to the studio after Christmas."

Zevon turned fifty-six on January 24, 2003, and Jaffy said he was very, very sick that day. "He always returned my phone calls immediately, and this one he didn't return, and I was really freaked out," she said. "I called a lot of people and they told me his fever was high. And this was a man who was not a good patient when he was well. He could be a real hypochondriac when it came to the little things. He had a headache all the time, a migraine, and there would be colds and fevers. And he complained about all of these stupid things, things that in retrospect were nothing. And here he is, with a terminal disease, going through horrific pain, and you never once heard about it. It's remarkable."

Rayston said he didn't complain because he didn't fear his own death. "He didn't like the process of dying," she said. "It was not a battle he wanted to fight, but he fought it and he wasn't afraid. He had a lot of faith. He believed in God, and he actually started going to church again after September 11, after years of being away from it. He had the knowledge that life was leaving him, and he became bombarded with so many memories and images. And he wanted to talk about them. We would talk about everything—God and spirituality, his children, women in his life, books, music, Nietzsche, Schopenhauer, and, of course, death."

"He called himself a poor starving artist in life who would receive recognition only when he's gone," said Jaffy. "That's why he kept all that shit in his apartment. He kept so much crap, and he said, 'It's going to matter when I'm dead. It doesn't matter now, but it will matter later.' He even wrote an e-mail to my mother, and it said, 'This is turning out to be one of the shrewdest career moves I've ever made.' I mean, who looks at death that way?"

"He courted death his whole life," said Rayston. "He did it in his writing, and he did it in living. And in a strange, macabre way Warren felt he had to die once he announced it to everyone. Then, when it became apparent that he was living past his supposed expiration date, he kept saying, 'I feel like I'm going to let people down. I feel like I have to die.'

"And many of us would say, 'Warren, people are praying for you. People want you to live. This could even be a miracle. Maybe you were misdiagnosed.' But there was a part of him that never wanted to let anyone down," said Rayston. "Warren was a complicated person. As big as his heart was, he was also vain, and that's why he didn't want anyone but a select few people to see him after January and into the spring. He didn't want anyone seeing him not looking his best. And that included his friends. And I don't think it was just a matter of his vanity. I think he also didn't want to disappoint people, because he was always funny. He was always on. He was always the one with the brilliant comment, the fantastic retort, and when that wasn't happening anymore, and his body was changing and retaliating, he didn't want to be around anyone."

Calderon didn't think Zevon would be able to finish the album. By early March, he still had three songs to sing, and he was filled with self-doubt and getting weaker. "He said he didn't know if he could do it," said Calderon. "A new doctor came to see him, and he said that as far as Warren's cancer was concerned, all indications were that he still had some quality time left with his family. The doctor said Warren was suffering from acute depression, and he gave him some medication that kicked in a few weeks later and actually made Warren feel stronger."

That strength enabled him to finish "El Amor de Mi Vida" in his apartment. Calderon had already sung the song's Spanish chorus. All Zevon needed to do was sing the first and second verses, and he did it. "We set up these little goals for him," said Barr, "and when he completed one task, we'd quickly establish another goal."

The next song he needed to tackle was a blues song, "Rub Me Raw." It was now April, and Zevon had managed to live five months longer than his initial diagnosis. Calderon said Zevon's depression actually made it easier for him to sing "Rub Me Raw" in a more soulful way. "As bad as his depression was for him," said Calderon, "it enabled him to reach all the way down and find a deeper sentiment. I told him he needed to sing the song with attitude, and he did. You can hear it in that song. He really got into it."

But there was still one more song to record, and that was "Keep Me in Your Heart." Zevon had begun writing it eight months earlier, right after he learned about his fate from the doctor. Calderon said his heart sank when Zevon read him the lyric, "Keep me in your heart for a while / Shadows are falling and I'm running out of breath / Keep me in your heart for a while."

"I said, 'Warren, you have to finish that song. That song is yours. That's a goodbye song.' I told him to keep going," said Calderon, "but he was having all kinds of trouble emotionally.

"He wanted me to help him write it," said Calderon. "He said,

'C'mon, man. You have to help me.' I didn't want to at first because it
was so obviously his song. But then we got together and we got it
done. I did help him in the end because I'm a songwriter. That's what
I do. He needed me to help him, and I did. When it finally came time
for him to record the vocal, he was so ready. He had been practicing
and practicing, and it showed."

On the day of the recording, engineer and coproducer Noah Snyder
set up his equipment in Zevon's loft and rigged up a special micro-
phone with a long cord so that he could sing the song seated on his gray
couch in front of the living room fireplace. Zevon's daughter, Ariel,
Calderon, and Barr were all there to witness the vocal performance.

"In all the years I've known him," said Barr, "I never heard him
sing more beautifully, more heartfelt, and more easily. It came so easy
for him that day. Honestly, it was done in three takes, and it was perfect. We all just looked at each other and couldn't believe it."

Incredibly, the album was done. The only question left unanswered
was whether Zevon would live long enough to see it released.

But a new goal was established, according to Barr, and it all had to
do with Ariel, who was pregnant and expecting twins early in the
summer. Ariel's father was getting sicker and sicker, but he was around
to celebrate when his two twin grandsons, Augustus Warren Zevon-
Powell and Maximus Patrick Zevon-Powell, were born in Los Angeles
on June 12.

Jorge Calderon recalled the joy Zevon felt when Ariel and her
boyfriend, Ben Powell, brought their infant sons over to Zevon's West
Hollywood apartment. By that time, fewer and fewer people were being
allowed access to Zevon, Calderon included.

"We were talking on the phone a lot," he said. "He was definitely keeping me away. I'd ask him about coming over, and he'd
say, 'No, no, I'm not feeling too well. I can't talk too much. I run out
of breath.'

"And I'd say, 'But I want to see you, man, even if it's just for five
minutes.'

"He'd say, 'Maybe next week,' and next week would come and we'd
end up talking on the phone again. He'd say on the phone that he was
living his low-budget Elvis existence. The windows in his bedroom were
taped so the sun couldn't get in. All he wanted to do was stay in bed and
watch his DVDs. The doctor instructed that his oxygen be placed away
from the bed, just so he had to get out of the bed to get it. Not too many

people went to see him, and that was all Warren's doing. He didn't want anyone around."

Well, almost anyone. Ryan Rayston continued to remain a fixture in Zevon's life. He knew and she knew that she would be there with him until the end. "I'd go to the store. I'd bring him videos, but most of the time," she said, "we just hung around and talked. Sometimes we'd cuddle up in bed and I'd rub his feet, or his hands, which were swollen and painful. We'd watch movies and he would fall asleep. I often just stayed in another room and read."

Susan Jaffy had limited access to Zevon, far less than Rayston, but she would take every opportunity to see him, if and when he allowed it. "He was lying in bed," Jaffy recalled of one particular visit, "and he was saying, 'Susan, you gotta get me something.'

"The 'something' he was talking about was medicine to help him take a shit," said Jaffy. "I brought over mineral oil and eight different kinds of laxatives. But he was having so much trouble going because there was cancer in his stomach. He kept having me rub his stomach. There was this huge lump, and I kept saying, 'Oh, honey, you're constipated. You're backed up. That's what the lump is.' But he knew full well that it was a tumor. I didn't want to say it out loud because I knew it scared him. But the cancer was everywhere."

But there were still some miracles left for Zevon to experience in August. His grandchildren were two months old and doing fine. His son, Jordan, and daughter, Ariel, doted on him as loving children should. Calderon sent him a coffee-table book on Ernest Hemingway in Cuba, which he loved leafing through. His VH1 special, which chronicled Zevon through the making of his album, aired on Sunday, August 24, to mostly spectacular reviews. Two days later, on Tuesday, August 26, his album, *The Wind*, was released, also to great reviews.

"I brought him over his album about a week before it came out," said Barr. "He was so, so sick, but he was also so excited. He kept saying, 'We really did this. We really did this.' Over and over again he would say to me, 'Am I really going to see this VH1 special? Am I really going to see this album come out?'

"And it was like a mantra. I'd say, 'Yes, you are. Yes, you are.' I honestly believe he never thought he would see that album and hold it in his hand," she said. "It was so overwhelming for both of us. There was the album artwork, which he designed exactly the way he wanted it, and he was holding it in his hand. That was a big milestone."

There was still one more milestone, which Rayston said was as important, if not more so, than the album. "I went to see him on the day of the VH1 special," she said, "and he said to me, 'Do you notice anything different?' I said no, and he said, 'The bottles are gone. Look under the bed.'

"I looked under the bed," said Rayston, "and the bottles of alcohol were gone. He had stopped drinking. He was sober again. I think the drinking was something he had to experience. It was like falling off the wagon and reaching down and saying, 'You know what, I'm in so much discomfort—physically, emotionally, and spiritually—that I don't want to feel anything.'

"Then all of a sudden," she said, "with everything else going on in his life—his illness, the grandchildren, the VH1 special, and the album—he chose to stop drinking. His stash was gone. He was shaking and he was scared. For months he had his little concoction, a certain amount of painkillers and a certain amount of alcohol, that stabilized him and allowed him not to feel certain things. Now he was ready to feel it all. He was a little frightened, but he was ready to go. I don't mean he was ready to die. I mean he was ready to experience what was happening on the human level. As debasing and humiliating as it was, and even as compelling as it was, he was going to experience it with the same courage that he started out with."

On Wednesday, September 3, Danny Goldberg called Zevon to tell him that his album would debut on the *Billboard* magazine chart at number sixteen, with a bullet. "I had been feeling inhibited about calling him during those weeks because I didn't want him to feel that he had to talk to me. A few weeks earlier we had a very emotional conversation about the album, and the early response to it. But on September 3 I left a message for him, and he called right back. He was extremely happy about the chart position. I told him I was confident that it would be a gold album."

Rayston said that on that same day, Zevon asked her to phone his twelve-step sponsor and give him the following message: "Warren said to me, 'When I'm gone, please call him up and thank him.' He was sober," said Rayston, "and he wanted to thank his sponsor for not giving up on him. That was an incredible thing for me to hear."

On Saturday, September 6, Jaffy said that Zevon called her and left a message on her answering machine. "He said, 'I love you, and I'll talk to you soon.'

"I knew he probably wasn't going to talk to me soon," she said, "but I called him back as soon as I got the message. I left a message on his machine that I was going to meet one of my girlfriends at Borders, because Warren and I used to go to the bookstore all the time. We'd spend hours in the bookstore. I've thought about it a lot lately, and I love that I left him a message that I was going to a bookstore.

"He was the one person I always called when I felt like I was about to jump off a ledge," said Jaffy. "He was the one who talked me down. He was the one who made me feel better. I mean, he was the calm and peaceful one. I got to tell him that he was the love of my life. No one has ever loved me that much, or that way, in my life. No one has ever been as sane. I mean, people will tell you that Warren might have been insane. But he was the most brilliant person I have ever known, and probably the sanest."

Rayston was on the phone with Zevon, late at night, on September 6, when he asked her for a favor. Zevon had a favorite grocery store, Bristol Farms, on the corner of Sunset and Fairfax, which longtime area residents like Zevon still referred to by its previous name, Chalet Gourmet. "Everybody in the area always shopped there," said Rayston. "I live only six blocks away from Warren, so that was my store, too. He said to me, 'I know you won't be able to get this, and I'll probably get sick from it, but I'd really like a hot dog before I die.'

"The next morning," said Rayston, "I went to Chalet and picked up a bunch of pigs in blankets. I decided to get little ones, because I knew that a big hot dog would make him sick. I also got him some matzo ball soup. I went to his house, and when I saw him, I thought, 'Today is the day.' I just looked at him and I was positive that this was the time."

Rayston put the little pigs in blankets in Zevon's freezer, and she gave him a few spoonfuls of soup. "I then told Warren that I would be right back," she said, "because I didn't have my phonebook with me and I didn't have a lot of numbers committed to memory. But I knew I'd have to start making phone calls very soon."

When she returned ten minutes later, Zevon was sitting on the edge of his bed. It appeared to her that he had fallen out of bed, and somehow managed to right himself. "But he was disoriented," she said, "and his TV was turned up to full volume. It was like he was listening to the TV but he couldn't hear it. I was shocked. His glasses were off and he was disoriented. I was talking so loud to him. I was practically screaming. And I guess his hearing came back, and he said, 'Why are you yelling at me?' I didn't even answer him. I just lowered the volume on the TV, helped him into bed, and fluffed up his pillows. Then I got him something to drink, and some ice for his mouth. I rubbed his head and his feet and his hands. He told me he had fallen, and that he was scared, and really tired.

"I got into bed with him and held him," she said. "No one else was there. It was just the two of us. I said, 'Warren, I'm not going to leave you.'

"He said, 'That's good, Ry-Ry. Please stay.'

"I went into the other room for a few minutes," she said, "because I knew that Warren liked to fall asleep by himself. He liked knowing that someone else was in the apartment, so I went into the living room and sat on another of his gray couches, the one in front of the window.

"I was in there for just a few minutes," she said, "when I felt something. I immediately went into the other room and Warren wasn't breathing. He had a faint pulse, and I tried CPR. I remember thinking that Warren would have appreciated the position I was in. I was on top of him, straddling him, and my mouth was on top of his. I held on to him and literally felt and heard his last breath. I knew he was gone, but I just stayed there for a while and held him."

Then came the calls, to Jordan, Ariel, Calderon, Barr, and the police. "There was an amazing amount of energy in that place," said Rayston. "The police carried Warren's body from the bedroom to the living room, and they set it down on the floor. Jorge and the children were sitting there with me, and we were all looking at Warren on the floor. It was kind of tribal. We were sitting around his body and telling stories and running the gamut of emotions, from weeping to laughing to being in complete shock and denial. But we looked down at him and we all realized that this wonderful, beautiful man was finally at peace.

"He gave me the most incredible gift. That's the way I look at it," said Rayston. "He gave me a friendship that I don't know if I'll ever find with anyone else. We were like brother and sister and best friends. The only peace I have now is knowing that he's at peace and not in pain. I think about him all the time."

"For all his intellectual sarcasm, nihilism, and sardonic wit," added Goldberg, "he clearly had done a lot of inner work that allowed him to have this incredible poise, clarity, and equilibrium during the last year of his life. It's the kind of thing that I usually associate with someone like Gandhi, or a priest, or a yogi. Warren had a remarkable center to him, almost from the minute he found out about his disease to the minute he passed away. Others who spent time with him during the last year came away with the same impression. He was almost like an example of how to handle being told you are going to die. Putting aside his artistic work, I think the name Warren Zevon, for a lot of people, became a metaphor for how to go out."

John Ritter

September 17, 1948–September 11, 2003

HENRY WINKLER GOT OUT OF BED AT 6:30 A.M., ON MONDAY, SEPTEMBER 8, the day after Warren Zevon died, and proceeded to do what he'd been doing for years: Winkler fed the dogs, exercised, shaved his face, and showered, in that order. By 9 A.M., he was in his car and on his way to work. Winkler, a beloved Hollywood figure with a nice-guy reputation whose 1974 portrayal of Arthur "Fonzie" Fonzarelli on the sit-com "Happy Days" turned him into one of the biggest stars TV ever produced, never fell victim to the seductive sound of his own success. He never needed PR people to spin his image, or legal people to keep him out of jail, or even limousine drivers to get him to the set on time.

Usually, when Henry Winkler had to be somewhere, all he really had to do was depend on himself and his own innate sense of professional behavior. And that Monday morning was no exception. Winkler left his house in Brentwood and drove over the hill to the Disney studios in Burbank. But that is where the routine ended because this would be a different kind of week for Henry Winkler. He had been asked to act in someone else's sitcom, for just one episode, over a five-day work week, beginning on Monday with a table reading of that episode's script.

A table reading is a rather formal affair by sitcom standards, with the actors all sitting behind a large table and facing outward toward the show's writers, producers, production staff, and assorted representatives from both the network and the studio. Some rehearsing takes place on Monday afternoons, followed by a more rigorous rehearsal schedule and a series of run-throughs on Tuesday and Wednesday. By Thursday, the actors are dealing with the flow of the show, moving from scene to scene and making adjustments to script changes as they come in. The episode then culminates on Friday night with a live taping in front of a studio audience.

That is the way the majority of Hollywood sitcoms work, and Winkler was as familiar with that kind of schedule as anyone in the TV business. But this was a show in its second season, with the relationships between the actors and their characters already clearly defined. That ship, so to speak, had already sailed, and Henry Winkler's only responsibility was to climb aboard briefly and increase the ship's speed by a couple of knots.

Winkler was excited driving to Burbank that morning, but he was also a little apprehensive. This wasn't just any sitcom. This was 8 *Simple Rules . . . for Dating My Teenage Daughter,* starring one of Winkler's best friends in the world, John Ritter. Winkler and Ritter had been beginning and ending each other's sentences from the day they met at an ABC event in 1978, during the first season of *Three's Company,* the TV sitcom that launched Ritter's career.

"We were sitting with our backs to each other at that event," Winkler recalled. "I moved my chair and I literally bumped into him. I said, 'Excuse me,' and when I realized it was him, I told him how much I liked this particular pratfall he did, and the way he fell out of frame in the *Three's Company* promo.' It was just so obvious that he was funny and talented and had this 'it.'"

In no time at all, Ritter and his first wife, Nancy Morgan, were joining Winkler and his wife, Stacey Weitzman, and Ron Howard and his wife, Cheryl Alley, for regularly scheduled Monday night dinners at any number of trendy Los Angeles restaurants, including Ma Maison, Le Restaurant, Le Dome, and Spago. It was a weekly get-together that continued seamlessly for many years, even after Ritter married his second wife, Amy Yasbeck, in 1999.

"We called ourselves 'The Monday Marauders,'" said Winkler, "and we were all the best of friends."

Winkler and Ritter also figured out ways to act together, as they did in the dramatic TV movie *The Only Way Out.* Winkler also directed Ritter in Dolly Parton's first TV movie, *A Smoky Mountain Christmas,* and Winkler produced for Showtime the series *Dead Man's Gun,* in which Ritter costarred.

The two men made countless charitable appearances together on cerebral palsy telethons, and even found time to work side by side in Neil Simon's play *The Dinner Party*, which they performed onstage at the Mark Taper Forum in Los Angeles, the Eisenhower Theater in Washington, D.C., and finally in the fall of 2000 at the Music Box Theater on Broadway.

"We just had this incredible rapport, this incredible timing together. It was like shorthand," said Winkler. "He was one of those guys who could tell the same story hundreds of times, and each time it was as funny as the first time you heard it. I could be rehearsing something with John, and everything was fine, and then all of a sudden he would get something in his mind and he was off. He would go on this comic jag and he would shoot off this heat-seeking missile of humor, and you literally couldn't do anything but sit down and laugh and then try to get your breath back."

The producers of *8 Simple Rules* had called Winkler with an offer to play Ritter's new boss in the season's fourth episode. The first three episodes were already in the can. The plot of the fourth episode had the two men becoming immediate enemies, with Winkler's character not liking a book that Ritter's character, Paul Hennessy, had previously written. According to the script, Winkler's character would further infuriate Hennessy with tales of everything he'd written prior to being named boss. Ritter called Winkler a few days before work on the episode commenced and left a message saying how happy he was that his friend had agreed to perform a guest-starring role.

When Winkler arrived at the lot on Monday morning, he took his position at the table with the rest of the cast, including Katey Sagal, who played Ritter's wife, and their three TV children, played by Kaley Cuoco, Amy Davidson, and Martin Spanjers, and the episode's other guest star that week, actor/director Peter Bogdanovich, who had signed on to portray one of Paul Hennessy's rival sports columnists.

Bogdanovich had known Ritter for more than thirty years and had been as close a friend to him as Winkler. Bogdanovich not only directed Ritter in three movies, *Nickelodeon*, *They All Laughed*, and *Noises Off*, but Ritter also came close to landing the Timothy Bottoms role in what is arguably Bogdanovich's most revered movie, *The Last Picture Show*, starring Bottoms, Jeff Bridges, and Cybill Shepherd.

"John was the only other actor up for Tim Bottoms's part," said Bogdanovich. "John was so good when he read for *Picture Show*. He was a complete natural. He instantly did what the great stars do: He suspended disbelief. You just believed him."

When Bogdanovich was offered the small role in *8 Simple Rules,* he didn't even have to think about an answer. "I told the producers that I would do whatever John wanted me to do," said Bogdanovich. "I said, 'Just give me the date, and I'll show up,' which is what John had done for me on three pictures."

The two men spoke on the phone a few days before the table read and couldn't wait to hang out together on the set. "We also talked about doing a picture that I'd written for him, a comedy called *Squirrels to the Nuts.* John wanted to do it, and we were figuring out a way of doing it, now that he had a hit series."

Then came the Monday table read. "John was so fucking sweet," said Bogdanovich. "We hadn't seen each other in a while, and we hugged immediately when he walked in the room. He looked great. He had lost a little weight. I kept telling him to lose weight."

"I was sitting in my chair when John came in," said Winkler. "And whenever John walks into any room he brings his Johnness in with him, this energy that just fills the entire space. We hugged and got down to business."

But for Winkler getting down to business meant hanging back for a while, and making sure not to let his Henryness escape into the room too quickly. "You have to understand," he said. "John had created a family on that set. Katey, John, and the three kids really did become a family. And Peter and I are the ones who had to walk into this incredibly concentrated and well-tuned organization. Everyone was generous and patient with me because I was an interloper. I needed the time to find what was funny, so I tried things a million different ways. And they were all right there for me."

And they were equally there, of course, for Ritter, whose natural tendency was to make others around him feel better. "He was a naturally funny person," Sagal later told Larry King on CNN. "He was one of those people that, you know, he can make anything funny. If he's just having a conversation with you, he's suddenly funny."

Sagal went on to tell King that Ritter was the easiest person to be around. "And loving and kind," she added. "I mean, truly, like, a joyful person. . . . When I first met John, I thought, 'Okay, so where's the, you know, where's the dark side?'"

She never found it. "I never saw, like, a bad mood," she told King.

"I'm sure he had them. But he just had such joy for what he was doing. He was so grateful to be doing what he was doing."

And like his friend Winkler, Ritter was also smart enough not to let his own notoriety overwhelm his work, or his life away from work. Martin Spanjers told Larry King about a valuable lesson Ritter taught him when they first started working together on *8 Simple Rules.*

"One time," said Spanjers, "we were at a benefit in Chicago, and he got to speak, and he talked about being a celebrity, and he said, he compared it to being in the sun. Sometimes it feels nice to be in the sun and you get warm and cozy, but then it takes you away from what's important and isolates you, takes you away from being normal, helping people out, and that's what John was about, you know? And then he went on to say, 'When you stay out in the sun too long, you get burned, and as we all know, the sun can kill you,' is what he said."

As it happened, Ritter appeared as nervous as Winkler during that Monday table read. "He was nervous because of Henry and Peter," recalled James Widdoes, director of *8 Simple Rules* since its premiere in 2002, who has since added the title of executive producer.

"You can imagine that from my perspective as the director," he said, "I absolutely saw both sides. I could see where Henry was coming from, and I could see where John was coming from. John and I had already gone through a season together, so I knew his moves pretty well. He was vested in the show and very vested in being the patriarch of the show. These guys were his friends, and any time he had friends on he wanted them to be great. He wanted the show to be great. And he didn't want anybody new to cause the show to be out of balance. Not that we were out of balance that week, but John just felt a lot of pressure on himself."

The show's original executive producer, Flody Suarez, had a different view of Ritter as the week started. "I didn't get that he was nervous," said Suarez. "I think it was just excitement. He wanted Henry and Peter to come off well and to look good. John enjoyed other people getting the laugh. He liked to let others get the laugh, and if that translated into nervous energy, I guess I could see that. But I felt it was just excitement.

"John was incredibly up that week," Suarez recalled. "His son Jason was starting production on [the CBS drama] *Joan of Arcadia.* His other son, Tyler, was starting school and playing baseball on the East Coast. His daughter Carly had just come back from studying abroad. And his youngest child, Stella, was turning five on that Thursday. So it was her birthday week. And he had two of his close friends starring on the show. Everyone was excited that Henry and Peter were there. John was like a little boy with a new toy. He was running around introducing his friends to the cast and telling Henry and Peter how amazing the kids on the show had become. He was very proud of those kids on the show, so he talked about the kids on the show and he told everyone what was going on with his real kids. He was a very proud father."

There had been no taping of 8 Simple Rules the previous week because of the Labor Day holiday, so this was the first time the cast and crew were together since the show's last taping on August 29. Widdoes had not been around much for the start of the second season because he was off producing another show, All About the Andersons, for the WB network. Ritter, of course, was aware that his director was doing double duty, and he made sure to leave Widdoes a few "funny and good-natured" phone messages, Widdoes said, just so he could get the point across that 8 Simple Rules was a sure thing and not the kind of show one would want to abandon.

If either man felt any awkwardness about Widdoes's burgeoning career plans, it was not evident when everyone came together to begin Episode 4. "It was all smiles," said Widdoes. "Everybody was getting to know everybody else, and in Peter's case, I don't think he had ever been in a sitcom. He was clearly unfamiliar with the drill."

"I had done one guest shot on Cybill (Shepherd's mid-nineties CBS sitcom), which was filmed at an exterior location and cut into her show, and I did do a Moonlighting with Cybill and Bruce Willis," said Bogdanovich. "But it's true that I'd never done a sitcom in front of a live audience. I did visit John on the set of Three's Company during the show's first season. Cybill and I came down to see him, and they ran it twice straight through without a cut, and he was extraordinary. It was like he was doing a little one-act play, and John loved that because it connects with the theater. He was always better with an audience."

On Tuesday, September 9, Ritter called Widdoes aside to ask him how his WB show was progressing. "He and I sort of looked at each other," Widdoes said, "and John said, 'Let's just do this show for the next five years.' He knew I had been a little scattered, and what he really wanted to know was how I was holding up running back and forth between two studios. But we had been having conversations about the future, and John made it clear how much he wanted me to stick around and do 8 Simple Rules for as long as I could. I realize the irony now, but he talked about how he believed that if we could just do 8 Simple Rules for another five years, it could be our farewell to half-hour television. It was a great thought."

Widdoes and Ritter had many of these little conversations, usually in between takes or during a set-up for a particular shot. "The truth is, we were really enjoying showing up each day and doing this show together," said Widdoes. "I have always said that one of the great thrills of my professional career was how John would come running across the set in front of the audience, and run up to me, and say, 'Quick, say this line for me.' And I'd say the line and John would go running back across the stage, and he would say the line as I had told him. But he'd say it with all the wonderful spin and charm that only John Ritter could put on a line. And, of course, I was always enough of a kid to be so flattered that John would run across the stage and ask me to say a line for him because, to me, he was the best there was. We had that kind of relationship, and we were really in full bloom that week.

"And John would also check things out with me," said Widdoes. "He said to me on that Tuesday, 'Is Henry okay? Is Peter okay?'

"And I said, 'Of course. They're wonderful.' That was John's nervousness," said Widdoes. "He wanted everyone to be comfortable and great, and they were. They were terrific. Peter Bogdanovich was hysterical in that first run-through on Tuesday."

"I was playing a complete lunatic," said Bogdanovich. "My character was in love with his boat collection, and I had dialogue like, 'Don't anyone touch my ships.' I was playing it like a complete neurotic and, I thought, a little bit over the top. But they thought it was hysterical."

On that same day, Suarez told Ritter that the producers and writers on *8 Simple Rules* had been discussing the possibility of Ritter's wife, Amy, coming on the show to perform a guest-starring role. "I asked him if it was okay to ask Amy, and he just lit up," said Suarez. "We had this idea about her playing the part of an English teacher that John's daughter has bumped heads with in school. John's character would then go in and meet with the teacher, and he'd have a similar experience to that of his daughter. John and Amy would then kind of go at each other, and we all thought that would be great. John loved the idea because this was a guy who loved having the people he cared about on the show."

Suarez made a note to call executives at ABC on Wednesday to tell them of his plans to contact Yasbeck with an offer. Widdoes remembered leaving for home on Tuesday night thinking that the episode they were working on would be remembered as one of the show's funniest episodes ever.

On Wednesday morning, September 10, Widdoes sat at home reading the latest rewrite of the script, complete with the changes that had been entered from the night before. After going through it, he was satisfied that the actors would not need another formal reading. It was ready for them to start full rehearsals on their scenes.

Work was interrupted briefly Wednesday morning when an assistant brought a phone over to Widdoes and told him the caller was his doctor. Widdoes took the call, and hung up in less than a minute. But Ritter and Katey Sagal had heard the assistant telling Widdoes that the caller was his doctor, and they rushed over to their director to find out whether he was all right.

"The doctor was calling with my results from heart and lung C.A.T. scans," said Widdoes. "I had been feeling a little funny, and it turns out that I'm fine. I'm absolutely okay. But it was a couple of months before my fiftieth birthday, and I had been going to bed a lot with my heart pounding. I hadn't experienced anything like that before, and I was concerned. So I went in to see someone, and I had tests. It turned out to be just stress and anxiety, but I was fine. And that's what the doctor was telling me on the phone. But I'll never forget John's saying, 'Are you okay?'

"And I said, 'Yeah. I had this thing, and everything is fine.'"

"And I remember his response," said Widdoes. "He said, 'Oh, good. Because, you know, that can be scary.' There I was, talking to him about my heart on Wednesday, September 10."

Ritter then helped Bogdanovich with a scene involving a bag of cookies. "I had to come in with these cookies," said Bogdanovich. "And I was having trouble figuring out the business of how I should do it. At a certain point, I'm supposed to have the cookies in my hand, and then show him. So I had to pull the cookies out of the bag, and I realize that this sounds simple, but you have to walk and talk and do the business at the same time. It's not that easy, and John said, 'Here, let me show you.'

"He showed me and it was perfect. I said, 'Okay, I get it. Thank you.'

"And he said, 'Well, you've done that for me so many times.'

"He showed me exactly what the piece of business was, because he knew I'd respond to that since that was the way I worked," said Bogdanovich. "It was very helpful and very sweet, and we had a lot of laughs."

Wednesday's run-through, according to Widdoes, "was all systems go.

"It truly went well," he said. "On the writing, producing, and directing side, we all felt the episode was wonderful. You never know what's going to happen to a show in its second season. We did quite well the first year, and with this episode we felt we were hitting our stride again, and it was exciting."

"We also had some amazing comedic talents on the set that week," said Suarez. "It was fun just sitting back and watching John and his friends figure out their rhythms together. It was kind of like a comedy school for the week."

"John was in every scene, and I was only in a few scenes," said Winkler. "When I wasn't in my dressing room doing phone work producing *Hollywood Squares,* or writing my children's novels, I was sitting in a director's chair facing the set, just so I could watch John work."

During a break, Bogdanovich and Ritter were having a quick bite at the food service cart when Bogdanovich again brought up the subject of *Squirrels to the Nuts,* the movie he had wanted to make with Ritter.

"I was saying, 'Maybe we could do it with you and Cybill,' and we were talking about how we could orchestrate it," said Bogdanovich. "John then started to walk away, and I said, 'Where are you going?'

"He said, 'I'm going to the doctor.'

"I said, 'What's the matter?'

"And he said, 'There's some kind of growth on my back, and they have to take it off. No big deal.' Then he said, 'I think I'll have them save it, and then we can give it away for charity.' He made a joke out of it, and I broke up. Then we hugged, and I said, 'I'll see you tomorrow.'"

Thursday, September 11, began on the set with a moment of silence for the victims of the September 11 terrorist attacks in 2001. Ritter, who was not expected on the set until later in the afternoon, was off taping an interview with the Museum of Television & Radio.

Museum officials had been working with ABC to put together a special, *The Funniest Families of Television Comedy,* that would include tapes and films from their combined libraries with as many new interviews as could be obtained. Ritter was asked to lend his thoughts to the special because of *8 Simple Rules,* and the family life it depicted.

The network used only one of Ritter's soundbites when the special finally aired on July 19, 2004. "I think it's a very scary time for adults and children now in the twenty-first century," Ritter said on the morning of September 11, 2003. "And I think it's very, very comforting and fun to know that TV families are having a rocky road of it, but somehow are staying together and sticking together as long as the lines of communication are open."

According to Suarez, the ability to communicate was one of Ritter's most recognizable gifts. "It was incredible how John treated everyone who walked on that set," said Suarez. "He would pull me aside on occasion and he would say, 'Keep an eye on that kid. He's having a rough time.' Or, 'She's really talented. She's not getting a lot of work, and she's really struggling. Can we bring her back?' He was thrilled when we put someone from the crew in a scene, someone who really wanted to be an actor and was given an opportunity. John was extremely generous and supportive of them and made sure everything they did looked as good as it could. That was John. He was the kind of person who enjoyed helping people, in their careers and in their personal lives. He would sit with those girls on the show and gossip with them about their boyfriends and what was going on in their lives. Not in a parental way, but he was always parental about it. He had an amazing gift to communicate with people of every age."

Widdoes spent most of the morning of September 11 preshooting scenes with the show's three kids on a school set at the far end of the soundstage. Winkler remembered watching Widdoes shoot a back-porch scene with Kaley Cuoco.

"The set was totally alive," said Winkler. "The entire crew was there. Equipment was being moved around everywhere. It was all very normal."

"Once we got all the preshooting done," said Widdoes, "I went to lunch."

"I went to lunch with the kids and their parents," said Winkler. "Still, all completely normal, warm and wonderful."

At 1:00 P.M., Ritter returned to the set to film a series of promotional spots with the other regular cast members. "Basically, it was a lot of John goofing around," said Suarez. "He threw pillows in the middle of a take. He pushed Marty Spanjers off a chair. It was that kind of energy."

"The network had sent over a packet of promos for us to record," said Widdoes. "Normally, we just put the information on the tele-prompter. The cast reads it, we ship it back to ABC, and then we get on with our day.

"John was always particularly entertaining when we were shooting promos because it gave him a chance to riff," said Widdoes. "And quite often what you have to say on a promo is kind of stupid, so John was never ashamed to point that out. He would have fun doing promos. I used to constantly joke with him that his hair was not real. And John had this wonderful way of putting his scalp in his hands and moving it back and forth, so that it looked like it wasn't real. That was one of the things we were doing that afternoon, and it was really funny. All you had to do was feed him a cue, or a thought, and he was gone and five minutes later you're still laughing. And from a director's standpoint, it was so joyous to watch because all you had to do was throw a morsel at him and the morsel became a banquet."

Once the promos were finished, Widdoes began the process of "camera blocking," which consisted of setting up his four cameramen for each scene, and then locking the various shots into place by using stand-ins until the crew was ready for the actors to be called to the set.

Winkler remembered standing off to the side with Ritter, waiting for one of his scenes to start. "They had rewritten some of my lines, so I should have been memorizing what I needed to know," said Winkler. "But instead John and I got into this conversation about the charity Broadway Cares, and how we raised thirty thousand dollars right from the stage of the Music Box Theater when we were doing *The Dinner Party* in the fall of 2000.

"All the Broadway shows were raising money," said Winkler, "and I heard that people down the street in another theater were selling personal items from the stage. And I thought, 'Oh, my God, we are going to do that and we are going to win.' And so every day for fifty performances, matinees included, John and I took Polaroid pictures with any human being in the audience who was willing to pay twenty dollars a shot. We held auctions from the stage. John was the auctioneer. It was incredible. We sold props. We sold the handkerchief that I used in the play. In the end, I think, we beat Reba McEntire by seventy-five dollars. She had been selling her boots and earrings down the street in *Annie Get Your Gun.*

"We were the first straight play to win the competition, and that's what John and I were talking about at that moment," said Winkler. "It was just a fantastic part of our time on Broadway. So we were laughing, and we were proud that we remembered. And then John said he was going to get some water, and I said, 'I'm going to go memorize my lines so I don't stink up the room.'"

Widdoes recalled that he had just finished blocking a second scene when Ritter came up to him. "He said he wasn't feeling well," said Widdoes. "He said, 'I'm feeling a little sick to my stomach. Is it okay if I go upstairs to lie down for a little while?'

"I said, 'Of course. I'll just use a stand-in. You just go up and lie down and feel better, and we'll keep going.' I wound up finishing blocking the entire show without John," said Widdoes. "I just kept working on the assumption that he was lying down, and that he would be okay."

"I remember working on a scene with the other actors, and a dialogue coach was playing John," said Winkler. "We were all doing these scenes together, and they were terrific. But John wasn't there. Someone said that he might have some food poisoning, and maybe he was going home early. So we just did the scenes and didn't think anything of it."

"Everybody thought he was nauseous and had food poisoning," said Suarez. "When he asked for space and said he wasn't feeling well, I think I was surprised because up until that moment it had been such a normal day. We were going to shoot some scenes with Henry and Peter and John late that afternoon, and we were all looking forward to putting that on tape. I know I was ready to just stand back and marvel at what each of these three guys was going to do with a line, or a joke. And John was the kind of guy who would run over after a take and say, 'Did you see what he did? Did you see how Henry got the laugh on that?' It was really fascinating to watch him interact with everybody on that set, but especially with Henry and Peter, guys he respected so much."

Bogdanovich never actually saw Ritter that day. "My call was a little later that day," he said. "When I got there, John was already in his dressing room. They said he wasn't feeling well, and I didn't want to go in and bother him. I did ask what was wrong with him, and they said he was sick to his stomach. They just told me to wait in my dressing room. So I waited. I think I took a nap. I know I waited quite a long time. I was in there from about two thirty on. They kept waiting, thinking John was going to be all right. Then they dismissed us."

Winkler went home, as did Bogdanovich and the other cast members. Widdoes stayed only long enough to complete his camera blocking, and then he left. Suarez, however, remained behind. "I was being kept informed about everything going on that day," he said, "including what was happening to John."

Ritter's assistant, Susan Wilcox, knocked on his dressing room door, according to *In Touch* magazine, and found him in severe pain.

The magazine quoted Ritter repeatedly saying to Wilcox, "It must have been something I ate."

Then he "suddenly slumped over and fell to the floor," the magazine reported.

People magazine reported that Ritter was dressed only in his underwear and a T-shirt, and was "perspiring heavily, vomiting and suffering chest pains."

The magazine reported that a studio doctor who was called to Ritter's dressing room strongly advised him to go to the hospital. Providence St. Joseph Medical Center, where Ritter had been born nearly fifty-five years earlier, was just across the street.

"Ritter changed back into his clothes, got his wallet out of his black Cadillac sedan in the parking lot and was driven to the emergency room by an assistant director," *People* reported.

As he was leaving the Disney lot, *People* quoted Ritter saying to an *8 Simple Rules* crew member, "Don't worry. It's going to be fine."

"As soon as the decision was made to go take him to St. Joseph's," said Suarez, "I closed up the set and then went over to sit with him."

Ritter's wife, Amy, who was just a day away from her forty-first birthday, arrived at the hospital, as did Ritter's oldest son, Jason. Ritter's oldest daughter, Carly, a senior at Vassar, and his son, Tyler, a freshman at the University of Pennsylvania, were both back east at school. Stella, the one child John and Amy had together, was being looked after at home, on her fifth birthday.

Suarez called Widdoes, who was at his home in Beverly Hills. "I was just sitting down to dinner," Widdoes said, "when Flody called to say that the situation with John was not looking very good. Flody said he didn't think it had anything to do with John's stomach, and he said he'd stay in touch. I was still sitting at the dinner table talking to my twelve-year-old daughter about 9/11, and the two-year anniversary of the attacks, when Flody called again. That's when I decided to get into the car and go to St. Joe's."

Henry Winkler said he received a call from Suarez at approximately 9 P.M., changing the actor's Friday call time on the set from 11 A.M., to 1 P.M. "He said John was going to be late," said Winkler, "and I said okay. He said nothing beyond that."

Peter Bogdanovich turned off his phone and retired for the night. "I was exhausted," he said, "and I wanted to get some sleep for Friday because I knew I'd be taping in front of an audience. So I went to bed early and had no idea what was going on in Burbank."

In fact, what was going on in Burbank was a frantic attempt on the part of doctors to save John Ritter's life. Doctors detected a tear in Ritter's main artery, an "aortic dissection," in medical terms, and they rushed him into surgery as quickly as they could. But it was too late, and Ritter died on the operating table just after 10 P.M. What killed Lucille Ball in 1989 had now taken the life of the much younger John Ritter.

Widdoes was just getting off the freeway in Burbank when his wife called his cell phone. "Flody called the house to say John had passed away," said Widdoes, "so I knew by the time I walked into the hospital. It was so shocking, so unbelievably shocking. He was the sweetest man on earth."

Suarez also called Winkler. "Stacey and I had just finished watching the news on TV, and I was half falling asleep," said Winkler. "I picked up the phone and Flody was crying. He said, 'John is gone.'

"And I went, 'John is gone? John is gone?' It was like I couldn't compute. It was like I couldn't understand the English language any longer," said Winkler. "I just kept repeating, 'John is gone? John is gone?'

"My wife shot out of bed," said Winkler, "and she was saying, 'What? What? What are you saying?'

"And I said, 'Flody just said that John died. John passed away. Oh, my God. Oh, my God.' It was incomprehensible on every level."

Bogdanovich didn't find out until the following morning. "People had been leaving me frantic messages, saying, 'Call me, call me, call me,' all night long," he said. "I spoke to Amy and she told me what had happened, blow by blow. John had no idea that anything bad was going to happen, because he said to Amy, 'Don't tell the children. They'll just get worried.' That's the last thing he said to her."

Yasbeck was understandably still reeling when she appeared on ABC's *Primetime Thursday* just five weeks after her husband's death. Ritter was "not sick at all. . . . Nothing," she told Diane Sawyer. "Complete shock and surprise. Really healthy. Getting in, actually, great shape."

Yasbeck recounted how her daughter, Stella, reacted as she watched a tribute to her father on TV a few days after his death. "At the end [of the TV segment]," Yasbeck said, "[Stella] stood up on the bed and she put her arms up in the air, and she said, 'Drop him.'

"And I just, I said, 'What do you do?' I mean, I didn't get it at first.

"And she said, 'I'm talking to heaven. Drop him.'

"And . . . I said, 'Stella . . . I know for sure that's not going to work.'

"And she said, 'But what if we never tried, and that's what would have worked?' . . . It's like he's kind of sent us all off into the world without him," said Yasbeck.

In September 2004, one year after Ritter's death, Yasbeck and Ritter's four children filed a wrongful death and medical malpractice lawsuit against Providence Saint Joseph's Medical Center and the physicians who attended to Ritter after he was brought into the emergency room. Yasbeck's suit alleges that her husband was misdiagnosed by doctors who first believed the patient was having a heart attack, when in fact he had already suffered a tear in his major coronary artery.

"As a result of the defendants' negligence," the lawsuit states, "Mr. Ritter suffered an untimely death. . . . If proper procedures had been followed to diagnose and treat Mr. Ritter's symptoms, he would be alive and well today."

On November 12, 2004, the hospital filed an answer to the court, denying every claim made by the Ritter family. "Defendant further denies," the court document stated, "that plaintiffs have sustained damage resulting from any wrongful act or omission of defendant or any of its agents or employees."

Both sides have filed numerous motions since then, but the case is still pending. For its part, the hospital continues to maintain a "no comment" policy on the matter. And all a Ritter family spokesperson will say is that the case remains in litigation.

And like the family, Henry Winkler is sure he'll never entirely get over the loss of his friend. "It makes me so angry and sad that he's not here," said Winkler. "There are times when I think, 'Oh, my God, I've got to call John.' And I can't."

Acknowledgments

BOOKS MAY BE WRITTEN IN SOLITUDE, BUT RARELY ARE THEY PUBLISHED WITH-out a lot of collaboration and support.

The Last Days of Dead Celebrities could not possibly have made it this far without the help of many people. Chief among them is Harvey Weinstein, and I thank him for his belief in an idea and his patience in allowing that idea to become a reality.

I also can't say enough about the collective talent at Miramax, and the advice, aid, and comfort I received along the way from Jonathan Burnham, Rob Weisbach, Judy Hottensen, JillEllyn Riley, Kristin Powers, Katie Finch, Dev Chatillon, and especially Matthew Hiltzik.

I benefited greatly from the work of two tireless research assistants, Mara McGinnis and Tiffany Speaks, and the legal counsel of Allen Grubman and Peter Grant.

Then there were others who helped me secure interviews, talked to me at length behind the scenes, and otherwise pointed me in the right direction. They are Rift Fournier, Audrey Lincer, Jonathan Wolfson, Lee Solters, Gary Stromberg, Vic Garvey, Barbara Levin, Irving Azoff, George Schlatter, Liz Smith, and especially Todd Gold.

Finally, and most importantly, I thank my wife, Lois Mathias, my coauthor on *Never Forget* and my coauthor in life, and our two extra-ordinary sons, Jesse Fink and Brian Fink.